"A powerful voice."
France Culture

"Over rupture and conflict, Amin Maalouf has always
preferred epics of encounters, beginnings, and connec-
tions."
Le Point

"An alarming report on the state of the world."
Le Soir

•

Praise for Disordered World

"With his consciously nurtured multiple identity, Maalouf
is just the sort of interlocutor this period needs. He reaches
deep into unmined seams of cultural history, scything
elegantly through cliché and conventional models of
received wisdom."
Financial Times

"Should be prescribed reading in the Foreign Office and on
the foreign desk of newspapers and the BBC."
The Spectator, Books of the Year

"Stimulating and provocative."
Sunday Times

"Maalouf is perfectly placed and wonderfully qualified to
shed light on the pervasive sense that there is a cataclysmic
battle in progress between civilisations and systems of
belief. *Disordered World* is full of insight."
The Observer

Praise for Amin Maalouf

"Maalouf is a thoughtful, humane and passionate interlocutor."
New York Times Book Review

"He is one of that small handful of writers, like David Grossman and Ayaan Hirsi Ali, who are indispensable to us in our current crisis."
New York Times

"At this time of fundamentalist identity seekers, Amin's is a voice of wisdom and sanity that sings the complexity and wonder of belonging to many places. He is a fabulist raconteur; he tells vastly entertaining adventure stories that are also deeply philosophical."
ARIEL DORFMAN, author of *Feeding on Dreams: Confessions of an Unrepentant Exile*

"Amin Maalouf seems to follow Flaubert in looking at the East, but he centres the narrative differently: it's the Orient telling itself. You learn about the multiplicity of cultures, their openness and permeability; that the boundaries between religions are not as hard and fast as we've been led to believe."
AAMER HUSSEIN, author of *37 Bridges*

"Amin Maalouf, one of the Arab world's most influential writers, weaves extraordinary tales in his novels, mixing historical events, romantic love, fantasy, and imagination. Yet at the core of all these well-crafted works lies a deep element of philosophical and psychological inquiry into the nature and condition of contemporary man."
AUB (American University of Beirut)

"Maalouf writes intriguing novels of exceptional quality."
NRC Handelsblad

•

Praise for The Disoriented

"A thoughtful, philosophically rich story that probes a still-open wound."
Kirkus Reviews

"A powerful and nostalgic current of lost paradise and stolen youth."
Huffington Post

"A great, sensitive testimony on the vulnerability of the individual in an age of global migration."
STEFAN HERTMANS, author of *War and Turpentine* and *The Convert*

"There are novels which reverberate long after you've finished reading them. Amin Maalouf's *The Disoriented* is such a novel. This is a voyage between the Orient and the West, the past and the present, as only the 1993 Goncourt Prize winner knows how to write it."
Le Figaro

"Amin Maalouf gives us a perfect look at the thoughts and feelings that can lead to emigration. One can only be impressed by the magnitude and the precision of his introspection."
Le Monde des Livres

"Maalouf's new book, *The Disoriented*, marks his return to the novel with fanfare. It is a very endearing book."
Lire

"Maalouf makes a rare incursion into the twentieth century, and he evokes his native Lebanon in a state of war, a painful subject which until now he had only touched upon."
Jeune Afrique

"The great virtue of this beautiful novel is that it concedes a human element to war, that it unravels the Lebanese carpet to undo its knots and loosen its strings."
L'Express

"Amin Maalouf has an intact love of Lebanon inside him, as well as ever-enduring suffering and great nostalgia for his youth, of which he has perhaps never spoken of as well as he has in this novel."
Page des Libraires

"Full of human warmth and told in an Oriental style, this is a sensitive reflection told through touching portraits."
Notes Bibliographiques

"A great work, which explores the wounds of exile and the compromises of those who stay."
L'Amour des Livres

"What Maalouf discusses in this novel is nothing less than the conflict between the Arab and the Western worlds. A personal, honest search for the greatest challenge of current world politics."
De Volkskrant

"*The Disoriented* is the new, long-awaited novel by Amin Maalouf, and perhaps his most personal, emotional, and compelling. A novel about memory, friendship, love."
La Compagnia del Mar Rosso

"Maalouf addresses themes such as multiculturalism, friendship, and disruptive conflict in a pleasant style. *The Disoriented* is a book that enriches readers by providing insight into the memories and facts of life of people from other cultures."
Literair Nederland

"Maalouf manages to drag the reader into a beautiful story that honours friendship and loyalty as an essential part of a decent human existence. He does not judge his characters. No one is completely bad, no one is completely good, all of his characters are recognizable people who are attractive because of their flaws."
De Wereld Morgen

●

Praise for Adrift

"The writer and scholar delves back into his own history to analyze the tragic consequences of the shock prophesized by Samuel Huntington."
Le Figaro Magazine

"True change is possible: Maalouf shows us possible ways forward in magnificent prose filled with wisdom."
La Provence

"A marvelous, luminous piece of writing."
Europe 1

"Wonderful and terrifying."
La Grande Librairie – France 5

"Maalouf's Mani has the ring of life—a sad, glowing book."
Washington Post

"Has the feel of a 1950s Hollywood epic, in which men gesture boldly and deliver words that deserve to be immediately carved in stone."
New York Times Book Review

●

Praise for In the Name of Identity

"Speaks from the depth of a powerful intellect."
The Times (London)

"His observation of human nature in all its facets is wonderfully accurate."
Sunday Telegraph

"This book sets out quite simply what is required of civilisation in the third millennium."
Le Monde

"The clear, calm, cogent and persuasive voice from the Arab world that it seemed everyone in the West had been waiting for."
New York Times

"This is an important addition to contemporary literature on diversity, nationalism, race and international politics."
Publishers Weekly

"Maalouf has a novelist's ear for language and an historian's eye for detail: they have combined to create a masterpiece."
Tablet

"*Origins* is a family saga more diverse and intriguing than most—its stories illustrate the author's journey of self-discovery."
Books Quarterly

"A terrific evocation of the mindset of a genuinely interesting family, and the times and nations through which they travelled."
The Fiction Desk

•

Praise for The Rock of Tanios

"This is as colourful as a fairy tale, and brilliantly translated from the French."
The Times

"Told with the simplicity of fable but set on the cusp of the modern world, this is a wonderful tale."
The Independent

"This is a beautifully crafted story detailing the intricacies of the folklores and superstitions which dominated nineteenth-century Oriental village life."
The Observer

the disoriented

Amin Maalouf

the disoriented

Translated from the French
by Frank Wynne

WORLD EDITIONS
New York, London, Amsterdam

Published in the USA in 2020 by World Editions LLC, New York
Published in the UK in 2020 by World Editions Ltd., London

World Editions
New York/London/Amsterdam

Printed by Mullervisual/Mart. Spruijt, Amsterdam, Netherlands

The quote on p. 15 is from "The Romanesque Renaissance" by Simone Weil, in *Selected Essays, 1934–1943: Historical, Political, and Moral Writings*, translated by Richard Rees, WIPF & Stock

British Library Cataloguing-in-Publication Data
A catalogue record for this book is available on request from the British Library.

ISBN 978-1-912987-06-1

First published as *Les désorientés* in France in 2012 by Grasset & Fasquelle

This book is supported by the Institut français (Royaume-Uni) as part of the Burgess programme.

Twitter: @WorldEdBooks
Facebook: @WorldEditionsInternationalPublishing
Instagram: @WorldEdBooks
www.worldeditions.co.uk

Book Club Discussion Guides are available on our website.

Everything that is subjected to the contact of force is defiled, whatever the contact. To strike or to be struck is one and the same defilement.

Simone Weil (1909–1943)

My name encompasses all of nascent humanity, yet I belong to a humanity that is dying, Adam will write in his notebook two days before the tragedy.

I have never known why my parents chose to give me this name. In my home country, the name is rare, and no one in my family had ever borne the name before me. I remember asking my father one day, and he merely answered "He is our common ancestor!" as though this was something I might not know. I was ten years old, and I made do with this explanation. Perhaps I should have asked him, while he was still alive, whether, behind the choice, there was some goal, some dream.

I believe there was. In his mind, I was destined to belong to the cohort of founders. Today, at the age of forty-seven, I am forced to admit that my mission will not be accomplished. I will not be the first of a line, I will be the last, the very last of my family, the repository of their collected sorrows, their disappointments, and their shame. To me falls the hateful task of recognizing the faces of those I have loved, to nod my head and watch as the sheet is drawn over them.

I am the attendant to the dead, and when my turn comes, I will fall like a tree trunk, unbowed, calling out to all who care to hear: "I am right and History is wrong!"

This arrogant, absurd cry constantly echoes in my head. Indeed, it could serve as a maxim for the futile pilgrimage I have been undertaking for the past ten days.

In returning to my submerged country, I thought to save some relics of my own past and that of my people. On that score, I no longer hold out much hope. In trying to delay foundering, one runs the risk of hastening the inevitable ... That said, I do not regret having undertaken this journey. It is true that every evening I rediscover the reason why I left my native land; but every morning I also rediscover the reason why I never truly abandoned it. My great joy has been to find amid the floodwaters a few small islands of Levantine delicacy, or tranquil tenderness. And this, at least for the moment, has given me a new thirst for life, new reasons to struggle, perhaps even a quiver of hope.

And in the long term?

In the long term, all the sons and daughters of Adam and Eve are lost children.

The First Day

1

On Thursday, as he fell asleep, Adam was not thinking that the very next day he would fly back to the country of his birth, after long years of voluntary exile, to see a man he had resolved never to speak to again.

But Mourad's wife had managed to find words that were unanswerable:

"Your friend is dying. He is asking to see you."

The telephone had rung at 5:00 a.m. Adam had blindly fumbled for the receiver, pressed one of the backlit buttons, and answered, "No, honestly, I wasn't asleep," or some comparable lie.

The woman on the other end of the line had said, "I'll put him on."

He had had to hold his breath to listen to the dying man. And, even then, he had intuited rather than heard the words. The distant voice was like a rustle of fabric. Two or three times, Adam had had to say "Sure" and "I understand," though he did not understand and was not sure of anything. When the other man had fallen silent, he had ventured a cautious "Goodbye"; he had kept his ear pressed to the receiver for a few seconds in case the man's wife came back on the line; only then had he hung up.

He had turned to his partner, Dolores, who had turned on the light and sat up in bed, leaning against the wall. She gave the impression that she was weighing the pros and cons, but her mind was already made up.

"Your friend is going to die, he called you, you can't wait around, you have to go."

"My friend? What friend? We haven't spoken to each other in twenty years!"

In fact, for many years, whenever Mourad's name came up and Adam was asked whether he knew him, he invariably responded: "He's a former friend." Often, the people he was speaking to assumed he meant "an old friend." But Adam did not choose words lightly. He and Mourad had been friends, then they had ceased to be friends. From his point of view, "former friend" was, therefore, the only fitting formulation.

Usually, when he used the expression in front of her, Dolores would simply smile sympathetically. But that morning, she had not smiled.

"If I fell out with my sister tomorrow, would she suddenly be my 'former' sister? Or my brother my 'former' brother?"

"Family is different, you don't get to choose ..."

"You don't get to choose in this case either. A childhood friend is an adoptive brother. You may regret adopting him, but you cannot un-adopt him."

Adam could have launched into a long explanation about how blood ties were different by their very nature. But in doing so, he would have wandered into muddy terrain. After all, he and his partner shared no blood ties. Did this mean that, close as they had become, they might one day be strangers to each other? That, if one of them should call for the other on their deathbed, they might meet with a refusal? The very idea of evoking such a possibility would have been demeaning. He preferred to stay silent.

In any case, it was futile to argue. Sooner or later, he would have to give in. Though he might have a thousand reasons to bear a grudge against Mourad, to revoke his friendship, even—despite his companion's words—to "un-adopt" him, those thousand reasons meant nothing in the face of death. If he refused to visit his former friend on his sickbed, he would regret it to his dying day.

And so, he had called the travel agent and booked a seat on the first available flight—leaving that same day at 5:30 p.m. and arriving at 11:00 p.m. local time. He could scarcely have arrived more quickly.

2

Some people think only when they are writing. This is something that was true of Adam. Something that, to him, represented both a privilege and a weakness.

For as long as his hands were at rest, his mind wandered, incapable of mastering thoughts or fashioning arguments. For his thoughts to order themselves, he had to start writing. Thinking, for him, was a manual task.

In a sense, he had neurons in his fingertips. Fortunately for him, his fingers were versatile. They could move without qualm from pen to keyboard, from paper to monitor. For this reason, he always carried a thick soft-cover notebook in his pocket and a laptop in his teacher's briefcase. According to his surroundings and the nature of what he intended to write, he would open either one or the other.

That day, as he set off on his journey, it was the notebook. He took it out, looked for the first blank page, waited until the seatbelt sign went out, then folded down the tray table.

FRIDAY, APRIL 20

Since the plane took off, I've been trying to steel myself for the ordeal, imagining what Mourad might say to try to justify himself, and how I should respond; what I would have said under normal circumstances and what I can still say now, given his condition; how to allow him to pass away peacefully without lying excessively; how to comfort him without changing my position.

I am not sure that we should forgive the dying. It would be too easy if, at the end of every human life, the slate was wiped clean; if the cruelty and greed of some, the compassion and self-

lessness of others were uncritically written off. Does this mean that murderers and their victims, persecutors and persecuted would be equally innocent at the hour of their death? Not to me, in any case. To my mind, impunity is as pernicious as injustice; in fact, they are two sides of the same coin.

They say that in the early centuries of the Christian era, as the new religion was spreading across the Roman Empire, certain patricians conspired to delay their conversion for as long as possible. Had they not been told that, at the moment of baptism, all their sins would be washed away? So, they carried on with their lives of debauchery and were only baptized on their deathbeds.

I don't know whether such belated contrition has some merit in the eyes of religion. In my eyes, it has none. Neither that of the ancient Romans, nor that of my contemporaries.

That said, we have a duty to be decent at the hour of death. That moment of supreme change must contain a certain dignity if we wish to remain human. Regardless of the judgement we might be inclined to pass on the dying man and his actions. Yes, even in dealing with the most depraved of criminals.

Which is not the case with Mourad, I hasten to add. I could accuse Mourad of many things, some of which, to my mind, are very close to being crimes. But we should be wary of excess in our speech. A man may commit a crime without meriting the name of criminal. Much as I might rail against impunity, I do not consider that all offences are equal, irrespective of motive, gravity, or circumstances. Though circumstances cannot exculpate, they can, as lawyers say, be "mitigating" …

I do not doubt for a moment that my former friend's actions during the war years were a betrayal of the values we shared, and I hope he will not try to deny this. But was it not his loyalty that led him to betray? For love of his country, he refused to leave when war broke out; having stayed, he was forced to come to terms, to respond to events by making certain compromises *that would lead eventually to the unacceptable. If I had stayed, I might have acted as he did. From afar, it is easy to say no; there and then, one does not always have such freedom.*

In short, his principles were his undoing; my failings saved me. To protect his family, to defend what his parents had bequeathed him, he fought like a wild animal. Not I. Growing up in a family of artists, I was not instilled with the same principles. Not that physical courage, that sense of duty, nor that loyalty. After the first massacres, I left, I ran away; I ensured my hands were clean. The cowardly privilege of the upstanding deserter.

As we come in to land, my thoughts are even more confused than when we took off. Mourad now seems to me to be a minor, broken character, pitiable and lost in a tragedy that is beyond him. If I am still not inclined to forgive his faults, I am no less angry with the rest of the universe, and with myself.

So, I will go to his bedside, I will play my role as his secular confessor, I will listen to him, I will hold his hand, I will whisper words of absolution so that he can die with a clear conscience.

}

At the airport, no one was waiting. And this minor inconvenience, which Adam should have been expecting, since he had told no one he was coming, triggered a wave of sadness and a brief moment of confusion. It took a conscious effort for him to remember that this place where he had just landed was the city where he had been born, his own country.

APRIL 20 (CONT'D)

I go through customs, I hand over my passport, take it back, and walk outside, scanning the crowd like a lost child. Nobody. Nobody speaks to me, nobody is waiting for me. No one recognizes me. I have come to meet the ghost of a friend, and already I am a ghost myself.

A driver offers his services. I nod and allow him to carry my luggage to his car, a battered old Dodge parked well away from the taxi rank. It's obviously an unlicensed cab, there is no red license plate, no meter. I don't protest. Usually I find these things irritating, but tonight they make me smile. They bring to mind a familiar environment, a reflexive sense of caution. I hear myself ask the driver—in Arabic, in the local accent— how much the fare will be. Simply to avoid the indignity of being mistaken for a tourist.

As we drove, I felt tempted to phone cousins, friends. By now it was gone midnight, more or less, but I know many who would not have taken offence, who would have insisted on inviting me to come and stay with them. In the end, I didn't call anyone. I felt a sudden desire to be on my own, anonymous, almost incognito.

I feel pleased at this new sensation. Incognito in my own country, among my own people, in the city where I grew up.

My hotel room is spacious, the sheets are clean, but the street is rowdy even at this hour. There is also the heady rumbling of an air conditioner that I did not dare turn off for fear of waking up drenched in sweat. I don't think the noise will stop me getting to sleep. It's been a long day, my body will soon grow sluggish, and my mind with it.

Sitting on the bed, with no light but the glow of the bedside lamp, I cannot stop thinking of Mourad. I force myself to imagine him as he must look now. The last time we were together, he was twenty-four, I was twenty-two. In my memory, he is hale and hearty, carnivorous, booming. Since then, illness will have withered him. I picture him now in his old ancestral home, in the village, in a wheelchair, his face deathly pale, a blanket draped over his knees. But maybe he is in the hospital, lying on a metal bed, surrounded by IV drips, flickering machines, bandages; and, next to him, the chair where he will ask me to sit.

I will know tomorrow.

The Second Day

1

Mourad's wife called Adam on his cell phone in the early hours. Thinking him still in Paris, she said curtly, without preamble, without so much as a "hello":

"He couldn't wait for you."

In his hotel room, it was still dark. Adam let slip a muttered curse. Then he told his interlocutor that he had already arrived, last night, having caught the first flight to see Mourad as soon as he got her call.

But she simply repeated:

"He couldn't wait for you."

The same phrase, word for word. But the tone was different. There was no reproach this time. Grief, rages, and perhaps a flicker of gratitude to Adam. He mumbled a hackneyed phrase.

There followed a few seconds of silence on both ends of the line. After which the widow simply said "Thank you." as though politely responding to his condolences. Then she asked where he was staying.

"I'll send a car for you. You'll never get here on your own."

Adam did not protest. He was aware that he would no longer be able to get his bearings in this city with no street signs, no numbers, no pavements, where districts bore the names of buildings, and buildings the names of their owners ...

SATURDAY, APRIL 21

Tania is already in black. Mourad is lying neatly beneath sheets without a single crease, his nostrils stuffed with cotton wool. He has a whole wing to himself—two adjoining bedrooms, a living room, a balcony. The clinic is all marble and camphor. A place to die like a pedigree dog.

I stand at the foot of the bed and I do not cry. I bow my head before the remains, I close my eyes, I stand stock-still, I wait. I am supposed to meditate, but my mind is blank. Later, I will meditate, I will summon the memories of our dead friendship, later I will force myself to remember Mourad as he was. But here, in front of his remains, nothing.

As soon as I hear footsteps behind me, I give up my place. I walk over to Tania, I clasp her to me briefly. Then I go and sit in the living room. Which is not really a living room—three brown leather armchairs, three folding chairs, a coffee machine, bottles of mineral water, a television with the sound on mute— but in a clinic, it is a luxury. Already, there are four women dressed in black, and an old man who has not shaved. I don't know them. I nod by way of greeting, let myself slump into the only vacant chair. I am still not meditating; I am not thinking about anything. I simply try to adopt an appropriate air.

When I see other people arrive, like a delegation, I get to my feet, walk back past the deceased, hug Tania again and whisper: "See you later." I hurry out of the clinic as though chased by a pack of dogs.

It is only when I find myself out in the street, alone amid the passersby, calm in the tumult, that my thoughts finally turn to the man I have just abandoned on his deathbed.

Snatches of conversation come flooding back, laughter, images. Walking straight ahead, I think a thousand different things without pausing over any one of them. The blare of a taxi horn brings me back to reality. I nod, open the door, climb in, and give the name of my hotel. The driver speaks to me in English, which irritates me but makes me smile. I reply in his language, which is my mother tongue, but probably with the hint of an accent. To apologize for wounding my emigrant's pride, he starts cursing the country and its leaders, and launches into an impassioned homage to those who were intelligent enough to leave.

Adam merely nods politely. In other circumstances, he would have joined in the conversation; the subject is one close to his heart. But just now, he is eager to be alone, alone in his room, alone with his memories of the man who will not speak again.

As soon as he gets back, he stretches out on the bed and lies for a long time on his back. Then he sits up, takes his notebook, scribbles a few lines, then flips it over, as though starting a brand-new notebook from the other end.

At the top of the new blank page, where he usually writes the date, he writes *In Memoriam*, by way of epigraph, perhaps by way of prayer. Nothing more. He turns to the next page.

Mourad, my un-adopted friend.

We have been separated by death before we could be reconciled. It is partly my fault, partly his, and death is also to blame. We had only just begun to reconnect when death brutally silenced him.

But, in a sense, the reconciliation did take place. He asked to see me again and I caught the first flight, only death arrived before me. On reflection, it is perhaps better this way. Death has its own wisdom, sometimes we must trust it rather than ourselves. What could my former friend have told me? Lies, distorted truths. And I, to avoid seeming heartless to a dying man, would have pretended to believe him, to forgive him.

What worth would our belated reunion and our mutual forgiveness have had in such conditions? If I am to be honest, none. What has happened seems to me more decent, more dignified. In his final hours, Mourad felt the need to see me; I hastened to his side; he hastened to die. There is a sliver of moral elegance in this that does honour to our bygone friendship. I am satisfied with this epilogue.

Later, if there exists a life beyond the grave, we will have time to talk, man to man. And if there is only nothingness, the arguments between mere mortals will have scant importance.

On this day, the day he has died, what can I do for him? Only what decency commands: that I calmly evoke his memory, without condemning or absolving him.

He and I were not childhood friends. We grew up in the same country, in the same city, but not in the same environment. We did not meet until university—though then almost immediately, in the first days of our first year.

Early in our friendship, there was a party. There were about fifteen of us, I think, a few more boys than girls. If I had to make a list from memory, I would probably forget some. There was Mourad and me, and Tania of course, already Tania, who was not yet his wife but would be very soon; there was Albert, Naïm, Bilal, and the beautiful Sémi; Ramzi and Ramez, whom everyone called "the partners," "the inseparables," or simply "the two Ramzs" ... We had just embarked on student life with a glass in hand and a revolution in our hearts, believing we were embarking on our adult lives. The eldest of us was just about to turn twenty-three; at seventeen and a half, I was the youngest; Mourad was two years my senior.

It was October 1971, on the terrace of his house, a vast terrace from which, by day, you could see the sea, and by night, the shimmering lights of the city. I still remember how he looked that night: dazzled, overjoyed. This house belonged to him, before that it had belonged to his father, to his grandfather, to his great-grandfather, and to still more distant ancestors, since it had been built in the early eighteenth century.

My family, too, had once owned a beautiful house in the mountains. But for my family, it was a home, and an architectural statement; for his, it was a homeland. Here, Mourad had always felt a sort of completeness, that completeness of men who know that a country belongs to them.

Since the age of thirteen, I had felt like a guest everywhere. Often welcomed with open arms, sometimes merely tolerated, but never truly belonging. Different in so many ways, out of place—my name, my face, my bearing, my accent, my ties, both real or imagined. Irredeemably foreign. In my homeland, just as I would later be in exile.

At some point that evening, Mourad had raised his voice, and, still gazing into the distance, had announced:

"You are my best friends. From now on, this house is your house. For life!"

There had been a flurry of jokes and laughs, but only to hide emotion. Then Mourad had raised his glass, the ice cubes tinkling. We echoed him: "For life!" Some at the tops of their lungs, others in a whisper. Then we all drank together.

My eyes welled with tears. And even thinking about it today, I cannot stop them from welling again. With emotion, with nostalgia, with grief, with rage. That moment of fraternity was to be the most wonderful of my life; since then it has been ravaged by war. Not a house, not a memory has been left unscathed. Everything has been corrupted—friendship, love, devotion, kinship, faith as much as loyalty. And even death. Yes, today, death itself seems tarnished, warped.

I keep saying "that evening," but it is just a useful shorthand. Back when we knew each other, there were countless parties that now in my memory have merged into one. Sometimes, it seems to me that we were constantly together, like a long-haired horde of hippies, paying only fleeting visits to our respective families. This was not really the case, but rather how it seems to me now. Probably because together we were experiencing intense moments, living through major events. Some filled us with joy, some with indignation, and most of all we argued about them. God, how we loved to debate! What screaming matches! What fights! But they were noble fights. We sincerely believed that our ideas could sway the course of events.

At university, our constant quibbling and nitpicking earned us the sobriquet the "Circle of Sophists." Though intended as an insult we adopted the name out of sheer arrogance. There was even talk of founding a "fraternity" bearing the name. We discussed the possibility so interminably that it never saw light of day, a victim of our endless hairsplitting. Some among us dreamed of transforming our gang into a literary salon; others favoured a political movement that would spread through the student populace and later to the whole of society; still others nurtured the seductive idea that Balzac, after his fashion, had depicted in History of the Thirteen, *that a small group of friends devoted to a common cause, imbued with a common ambition, a handful of courageous, talented, and inextricably close-knit friends, could change the face of the world. I personally was not far from believing it. To tell the truth, even now, I still sometimes entertain that childish illusion. But where to find such a group? Search as you might, this planet is empty.*

In the end, our gang of friends did not become a fraternity, a salon, a political party, or a secret society. Our meetings remained informal, open, boozy, smoky, ostentatious. And with absolutely no hierarchy, even if we almost always met at Mourad's instigation, usually at his place, in the village, on the terrace of his ancestral home.

It was here, suspended between the mountains and the sea, that we would witness the end of the world. "Of the world"? Of our world, certainly, of our country as we had known it. I would go as far as to say: of our civilization. The Levantine civilization. A phrase that makes the ignorant smile and sets the teeth on edge of supporters of triumphant barbarism, those disciples of arrogant sects who clash in the name of the one true

God and know of no greater adversary than our subtle identities.

My friends belonged to all denominations and each made it a duty, a point of pride, to mock his own—and then, gently, those of the others. We were a sketch of the future, but the future would forever remain a sketch. Each of us allowed himself to be escorted, under guard, back into the fold of his faith. We proclaimed ourselves disciples of Voltaire, Camus, Sartre, Nietzsche, we called ourselves surrealists, we went back to being Christians, Muslims, or Jews, according to precise denominations, an extensive martyrology, and the pious hatred that goes with it.

We were young, at the dawn of our lives, and already it was dusk. War was looming. It was slithering towards us like a radioactive cloud; we could do nothing now to stop it, all we could do was flee. Some of us were reluctant to call it by its name, but it was undeniably a war, "our" war, the one that, in the history books, would carry our name. To the rest of the world, it was one more local conflict; to us, it was the Deluge. Our country with its fragile workings was taking in water, it was beginning to break down; and as the downpours continued, we would discover that it would be difficult to repair.

Henceforth, in our memories, the years would be linked to tragedies. And within our circle of friends, to successive desertions.

The first to leave was Naïm, with all his family—his father, his mother, his two sisters, his grandmother. They were not the last Jews in the country, but they were part of the tiny minority who, until then, had chosen to stay. There had been a silent haemorrhage throughout the fifties and sixties. Drop by drop, with no fuss, the community had disappeared. Some had left for Israel, by way of Paris, Istanbul, Athens, or Nicosia; others had chosen to settle in Canada, the United States, in England, or in France. Naïm and his family had opted for Brazil. But relatively late, in 1973.

His parents had made him promise to say nothing of their plans, even to his closest friends, and he had kept his word. No whispered secrets, not even a faint suggestion.

On the eve of their departure our gang got together, as we did almost every night, at Mourad's place or Tania's, in the village, to drink mulled wine. It was late January or early February. The old house was freezing. We were huddled together around a brazier in the small living room.

We talked about a thousand things, I suppose, as we did whenever we met; about people we liked or disliked, about political events, about trivial things, about a film director or a novelist who had recently died ... Obviously, I don't remember what fuelled our conversation. The one thing I do remember, because it struck me at the time and I have often thought about it since, is that at no point was there any mention of emigration, exodus, or separation. It was only the following evening, when we found out that Naïm had left, that the evening came to seem, in hindsight, like a farewell party.

And yet, there had been a curious incident. We had been talking about this and that when Tania suddenly started to cry. Nothing in what we had just said seemed to explain these tears; all of us, including her fiancé, Mourad, were bewildered. I asked her what was wrong, but she was sobbing so hard she couldn't answer. When she had calmed down, she said: "We'll never all be together again." Why? She did not know. "The feeling just suddenly occurred to me as a certainty, that's why I started crying."

To reassure her, and to break the spell, Mourad suggested we meet up the very next day, at the same time and the same place. No one raised any objections. I would not swear that everyone, without exception, said "see you tomorrow," but it was taken for granted.

We went our separate ways at dawn. I had just bought my first car, a tobacco-brown Volkswagen Beetle, and I was the one who drove Naïm home. He said nothing to me about his plans. Even when we were alone, driving through the dim, deserted streets, he said nothing.

Later, years later, he would tell me in a letter that his parents had spent that night waiting anxiously for him. They were afraid he might have decided not to leave with them, to stay with his friends, and were wondering whether to leave without him or postpone their departure to another date. When he finally arrived home, no one in the family would speak to him.

But in the end, he left with his family, forever. The first defection in our ranks.

After him, it was Bilal. A very different way of leaving: death.

When I feel the urge to curse all those who took up arms, I am reminded of Bilal, and I am tempted to make one or two exceptions.

He was a pure soul.

No one can know for certain what is lodged deep in the heart, but I knew Bilal intimately and don't think I am wrong. He was a troubled soul, but pure, yes, and without a whit of spite.

We shared a friendship, an affection, and a certain complicity; in fact, for several months he was my closest friend—a brief but intense period during which we would meet up every day; either he would call to collect me, or he would arrange to meet me in a café downtown; then we would wander the streets for hours, putting the world to rights.

We talked about Vietnam, about the guerrillas in Bolivia, the Spanish Civil War, the Long March; we talked, a little enviously, about the cursed poets, about the murdered poets, about Lorca, about Al-Mutanabbi, about Pushkin, and even about Nerval and Mayakovsky, even though they killed themselves; and we also talked about love.

One day, while we were walking, we were caught in a downpour. At first, as a game, a kind of childish bravado, we pretended not to care and carried on strolling at the same pace, shoulders straight. But within seconds we were drenched. And so we ran, all shame forgotten, and sheltered under an awning. We perched on a stone frieze. The name of a girl cropped up in our conversation—a girl we both knew. We talked about her with a complicity, baring our souls in a way that, even today, troubles me and makes my fingers tremble. Afterwards, for several long minutes, we were silent, as though waiting for our inner turmoil to calm. Then Bilal asked me:

"Adam, don't you think we were born in the wrong era, you and I?"

"When would you like to have been born?"

"A hundred years, two hundred years from now. Humanity is metamorphosing, and I'd like to see what it will become."

His boyish impatience made me feel, in spite of myself, a wise old man.

"Because you think there's a finish line where you can go and wait for the rest of us? Think again! No matter where you place yourself in the march of time, there will always be a before and after, events that are behind you and others looming on the horizon that will come towards you slowly, day by day. It is impossible to see everything in an instant. Unless you're God ..."

Hearing these words, Bilal leapt to his feet and strode out into the driving rain, howling like a madman:

"God! God! Now there's a fine occupation!"

About a week after that conversation, he vanished. He didn't call me anymore, and none of our friends had any news of him. We were all convinced that he was with his beloved.

I ran into him only once, in the university library. He had come to do some photocopying.

"We don't see you anymore," I chided him in a whisper.

He brought a finger to his lips.

"Shhh! I'm in training! If you want to be God, you have to become invisible."

We laughed together one last time.

He had come to photocopy a pamphlet or a poster. When I went over, he covered it up. I didn't insist. I suggested we go for a coffee. He made some excuse and slipped away. I would not see him alive again.

One day—late November, the 30th, maybe the 29th—I had a call from Mourad, early in the morning.

"I've got bad news. Really bad news."

The night before, in one of the suburbs of the capital, there had been an exchange of fire between two armed groups. Such incidents were increasingly common, so much so that we had ceased to take them seriously, except when there were numerous victims. In this particular incident, only one fighter had been wounded. I had heard about it on the radio and not given it a second thought. It was one headline among many.

The fighter had died of his wounds, and it was Bilal.

"Did you know he'd taken up arms?" I said.

"No," Mourad said, "He didn't tell anyone. But I can't say I'm surprised. I expect you're not either ..."

I had to admit that, for my part, I had known nothing, suspected nothing, sensed nothing. The idea that one of my close friends, a poet, an idealist, a ladies' man, might wish to join the nocturnal militia, machinegun in hand, to fire a hail of bullets at the neighbouring district—no, honestly, the thought had never crossed my mind.

Six months after the death of Bilal, our ranks would suffer another defection: mine.

2

Adam was immersed in his memories when the telephone in his hotel room began to ring. It was one of Tania's nephews calling on her behalf to ask whether he would like to say a few words at Mourad's funeral, "in the name of his childhood friends."

Since he seemed hesitant, the nephew thought it useful to give a list of the key figures who would be speaking. At every name, or almost, Adam winced. But, given the circumstances, he did not have the effrontery to refuse point blank. He was still struggling to find the words when the young man said, "It's on Wednesday at 11:00 a.m." Adam instantly clung to this banal detail as if to a lifeline, explaining that, unfortunately, it would be impossible for him stay in the country until then since he was overseeing exams with his students that very day.

A barefaced lie! he admitted that evening in his notebook. *I've been on sabbatical since February, I've got no lectures, no tutorials, and no exams until next October. But I wouldn't want to speak at Mourad's funeral for anything in the world.*

Why lie? At the time, I wouldn't have been able to explain. The request caught me off guard, so I said the first thing that came into my head.

Usually, I trust my instinct; not that it is infallible, but over the years I've noticed that I made mistakes much more often when I thought about things, when I tried to take into account all the ins and outs of a situation, or, worse, when I tried to mentally create a list, two columns weighing up the pros and cons.

As a result, these days I distinguish between two modes of thought. In the first, my mind works like a cauldron; it melts down all the factors and, unbeknownst to me, "computes" them, and delivers the results in a simple, succinct phrase. In the other, my mind is like a common kitchen knife; it applies itself to carving up reality using crude notions like "advantages" and "disadvantages," "emotional" and "rational," and only succeeds in confusing me even further.

How often have I made disastrous decisions for excellent reasons? Or, contrariwise, the best decisions with no regard for common sense!

So I came to the conclusion that it's better to make the decision first, in a split second; after which I can take the time to look deep inside myself to make sense of that decision.

As for the funeral, I didn't need much time to justify my spur-of-the-moment refusal, at least to myself; and, thereby, assuage my remorse.

Given the way that Mourad had behaved in recent years, I have no reason to add to the tributes that will be paid to him, albeit posthumously. It is one thing to politely offer condolences on the death of someone you knew; it's another thing to come all the way from Paris to speak at his funeral, surrounded by his political allies, his business partners, his patrons, and his protégés. All the eminent people my former friend probably frequented during the morass of war, I know only too well the means they used to become rich and powerful. I wouldn't want to speak before them or after them, I don't even want to shake their hands.

I left this country precisely so I would not have to shake such hands!

A few minutes later, the widow herself telephoned. To insist. Could Adam not postpone his departure until the end of the week? He reiterated his refusal, repeated the same line, clearly, a little brusquely, in order to avoid any emotional blackmail.

"Sorry! I have to go back. My students are counting on me."

There followed an awkward silence during which Tania could not find the words to persuade him and he could not find the words to make his excuses. In the end, she said, apparently resigned:

"I understand … Anyway, I'll never forget that you took the first plane to come and see him."

Her magnanimous attitude immediately rekindled Adam's burning guilt. Not enough for him to change his mind, but enough that he felt the need to make up for his absence at the funeral with some gesture of affection …

"I'm planning to write to our mutual friends to let them know what's happened. I'm sure they would want to send you their condolences. Albert, Naïm, a few others …"

"Yes, please write to them," Mourad's widow said. "It's been years since I've heard from them. I'm sure they'll be sad."

"Of course."

"It would be wonderful if we could bring all his old friends together again. Next April, maybe, for his birthday. Do you think they would come?"

"Why not?"

"We could even do it earlier. The 'fortieth day,' maybe."

In accordance with an ancient tradition preserved by various communities in the Levant, a memorial takes place forty days after a person's death. Adam felt that this would be too soon to rally his old friends. But he did not want to upset Mourad's widow.

"If that's what you would like, I can certainly suggest it."

"What about you, would you come back?"

"We have lots of time to talk about that later …"

"You're prevaricating."

"No, Tania, I'm not prevaricating, but everything can't be decided right this minute. I'll write to Mourad's friends and sound them out. Afterwards, we'll see where we stand."

"You're prevaricating," she said again. "Tomorrow, you'll fly home and the whole project will be forgotten. Your friend would have so loved ..."

The words caught in her throat.

"If you like, I'll come and see you this evening and we can talk calmly about a reunion, that way I can make a definite suggestion. How does that sound?"

For Adam, this was not simply a means of cutting short a conversation that made him uncomfortable. He genuinely wanted to see Tania again before he left. He felt that he had spent very little time with her. After all, it had been at Tania's request that he had made the journey, and he had barely spoken to her. Just that furtive visit to the hospital, that almost wordless embrace. He told himself that the least he could do was spend some time with her, especially if he intended to leave before the funeral.

"Tell me what time you're likely to be alone ... I'll come and see you."

A long silence. But for the background noise, he would have thought the call had been cut off.

When, at length, Mourad's widow replied, Adam detected a hoarse sarcasm in her voice:

"My poor Adam, you really have become an emigrant. You're asking me when I'll be alone? Alone, in this country, on a day like this? For your information, I'm in the village, in the old house, and there must be a hundred people here, maybe two hundred. Neighbours, cousins, vague acquaintances, people I've never even met. They're everywhere. In the reception rooms, in the kitchen, in the hallways, in the bedrooms, out on the big terrace, and they'll be here all night and for days to come. Alone? Did you really think I would be alone? Why don't you go, leave, don't worry, catch your flight, go home, to Paris, we'll see each other some other time, in other circumstances."

Adam could hardly reply in the same tone on the day that Tania had just lost her husband. Though infuriated by her sudden aggressiveness, all he could say was, "That's good. We'll see each other again. Look after yourself."

And then he hung up.

I didn't deserve to be attacked like that! I was trying to be kind, to be considerate. I was trying to do what she wanted. She had no excuse to attack me like that.

Maybe I was wrong to ask her if she was going to be on her own. She might have taken it as a criticism, or a sign of pity. All I meant was that I'd wait until her guests had left and go and visit her when she was with family. But what I said was just an excuse. The real reason that she's angry is because I've refused to speak at Mourad's funeral. And maybe, if we go back farther, my long quarrel with him, one I could have put an end to if I'd agreed to give a eulogy. But that's something no one can persuade me to do. Not with flattery, not by pleading, and certainly not with that kind of vicious outburst.

I've tried being reasonable but it's no good, I can't calm down. I'm furious!

What really hurt about Tania's tirade was her telling me to "go home." Alright, so maybe these days I do consider Paris to be "home," but does that really mean I can't also say I'm at home in the city where I was born? It certainly doesn't give anyone the right—friend or otherwise, grieving or otherwise— to blatantly call me a foreigner.

Since they're so desperate to be rid of me, I'm not going to leave! I'm the only one who gets to decide when I leave.

3

Truth be told, Adam had no desire to leave the country any time soon.

When he used his duties at the university as an excuse to avoid speaking at the funeral, he had felt trapped. There was nothing forcing him to catch a flight the following day, the day after, or any time soon. He was only just beginning to get his bearings again, and he did not yet feel any sense of weariness.

In a way, Tania's hostility had set him free. If she had remained polite and friendly, he would probably have had qualms about staying in the country and not attending the funeral, and would have left. Reluctantly, perhaps, but he could not have done otherwise.

Now, he was determined to stay.

A plan had formed in his mind, and he had immediately telephoned Dolores, his partner, to let her in on the secret. He intended to extend his stay in the country, but would cover his tracks.

No sooner was the decision made than he set to work. He called down to reception to ask that they make up his bill, and took the opportunity to ask how long it would take to get to the airport. He wanted to be sure that, if anyone tried to reach him, they would be told that he had already caught his flight.

For the same reason, as he left the hotel, he avoided taking any of the numerous waiting taxis. When the first driver in the queue opened the passenger door, he pretended that he had some things to buy in the local shop and walked off, wheeling his suitcase behind him.

He walked for a few minutes, rounded one corner, and

then another, before hailing a passing cab. He gave the driver the name of the village, Bertayel, and that of a hotel, the Auberge Sémiramis.

Only after the cab had left behind the urban traffic snarl and turned onto a mountain road did Adam call the manager of the hotel. Her name was indeed Sémiramis and she had been one of their circle of friends at university. He had lost contact with her in the period after he left for France. But they had been in touch since; she had twice been to Paris in recent years and had dinner at his apartment; he had introduced her to Dolores, and "the beautiful Sémiramis" had made him promise that he would come and see her when he came back to the country.

He dialled the number, and without even explaining who it was, said:

"I'm in a taxi. I'll be at your place in half an hour."

"Adam!"

It was almost a scream.

"I didn't even know you were in the country."

"I flew in yesterday. Have you got a room for me?"

"You can show up here whenever you like, even in high summer, and there will always be a room for you. That said, I'm not doing you any favours by giving you a room today, the hotel is almost empty."

"Excellent!"

"You think so? My accountant doesn't share your opinion."

She laughed, and Adam felt the need to apologize, though he laughed too.

"All I meant was that peace and quiet is exactly what I'm looking for. I didn't tell anyone I was coming, and I haven't seen anyone. Except Tania, but she thinks I'm on my way to the airport. I assume you've heard ..."

"About Mourad? Yes, of course."

"Had you seen him recently?"

"Once or twice. What about you? I know the two of you had a falling-out. Did you ever make it up?"

"Yes and no ... I'll tell you about it. Are you thinking of going to the funeral?"

"Yes, obviously. Aren't you going?"

"I don't think so."

"You're wrong. You can't shirk a funeral."

"I have my reasons. I'll explain later ... I'd rather no one knew that I was in the country. I'd like to hide out for a few days. I really need it. I don't want to see anyone except you."

"Don't worry, you won't see anyone! And no one is going to guess that you're staying at the hotel. I'll lock you in your room and keep the key."

"We don't have to go quite that far!"

Two fleeting laughs. A silence. Then, out of simple politeness, she asked:

"Dolores isn't with you?"

"She couldn't come. It was all decided at the last minute. She's working. Will you have me all the same?"

"I can't wait to see you ..."

By the time the cab turned into the tree-lined path leading to the hotel, Sémiramis was already waiting by the gate, flanked by three of her staff, an elderly caretaker, a uniformed receptionist, and a very young porter who opened the boot and took out the suitcase the moment the cab pulled up.

"Room eight," Sémiramis told him.

Adam took out his wallet to pay the fare, but the driver waved away his money and took the banknote the hotel owner had thrust through the open window.

"You've been abroad far too long, you've forgotten the

customs here," she said assertively, to forestall any protests from her guest.

Was this really how things were done in his native land? Adam was not sure. But the reasoning left him paralyzed. Every emigrant worries about making a faux pas, and those who stayed behind can easily trigger the fear of ridicule and the shame of having become a common tourist. He stuffed his wallet back in his pocket.

For the same reason, as he stepped out of the car, he hesitated about hugging his friend, as he would instinctively have done in France. With the cab driver and the staff watching, had he not better simply shake her hand? And so it was she who put her arms around him and, after a brief hug, led him to the front door, with its leaded glass canopy in the Belle Époque style.

An hour later, he and Sémiramis were sitting at a table on the top floor of the hotel, on a veranda framed on three sides by picture windows that, in the darkness, acted as mirrors, reflecting them and the glow of the candles.

They were brought a dozen small plates, a dozen more, and then ten more hot and cold mezze that would have easily fed and sated a horde of holidaymakers.

"Are you sure there's enough for the two of us?"

"It's all for you; I've already eaten," Sémiramis said without smiling.

"I was just kidding," Adam said quickly, fearing his remark had been misinterpreted.

"And I was just winding you up," his hostess said with a roguish smile, before adding, "You used to say I had a sense of humour, remember? We never needed to spell things out, you and me, a nod and a wink was enough. So don't feel you have to tell me where I'm supposed to laugh ..."

"Don't be mad at me, Sémi! It's not easy coming back

here after all these years. I feel I have to be careful, re-strained, circumspect. Maybe because I've lost my bear-ings. I'm constantly afraid of offending people's sensibil-ities. Even when I'm with old friends. I don't know whether I can still talk to them the way I used to. People change, you know."

"Well, I haven't changed, Adam. I'm not as young or as thin as I was, but inside, I haven't changed. I'm not some random woman, and you'll never be some random gentle-man. God, how I hate how time has changed us all into preposterous old people. Here I am playing hotel man-ager and you playing the eminent professor.

"But not tonight," she said, raising her champagne flute.

"Not tonight," Adam echoed, as though it were an oath.

They clinked glasses and brought them slowly to their lips. "The beautiful Sémiramis" had changed very little— even less than she admitted. Her bronzed complexion was not betrayed by any visible wrinkles, her eyes were still that deep, emerald green; perhaps she was not svelte, as she admitted, but in Adam's memories she never had been. She was taller than most women in the country, and had always been "curvaceous," not to say "buxom," which had done nothing to diminish her charms, either in the past, or now.

The waiter soundlessly padded over to the table carry-ing a bottle wrapped in a napkin. He refilled the glasses, then said to his boss:

"A little more light?"

"No, Francis, we'll be fine with just the candles."

The man nodded and returned to his station.

"I miss those times," Sémiramis went on. "More than you do, probably. I'm sure you'll say that it's a cliché, a woman of forty-eight hankering for the days when she was eighteen ... But in this country, in this part of the world, it's something else. I feel as though I'm on a road, and every time I take a step forward, the place where I was standing crumbles away. Sometimes, I even feel it crumbling beneath me, and I have to move quickly so as not to be swept away by the landslide."

The Third Day

1

When he woke, Adam wrote an entry in his notebook, dated April 22:

This Sunday morning, a single breath of air made me realize how much I have missed my mountain all these years, and how much I want to let myself be cosseted here.

Sémi, bless her, has put me in a room that overlooks the valley. I have a little table by the window; whichever way I look, I can see only Aleppo pines, I inhale the breeze that has caressed them, and I feel I would like to stay here until the end of time. Reading, writing, daydreaming, suspended by the rounded peaks and the broad expanse of the sea.

A voice in my head keeps whispering that soon I will tire of it. That tomorrow my overweening arrogance will command me to leave just as today it commands me to stay. And I will feel an urgent need to get away, just as today I feel a need to immerse myself. But I have a duty to silence my inner Cassandra.

Emerging slowly from his comfortable numbness, he begins to leaf through the notebook looking for a story he began the previous evening, before he had been interrupted by the phone calls from Tania and from her nephew and forced to flee the capital and seek refuge with Sémiramis. The last sentence read: *Six months after the death of Bilal, our ranks would suffer another defection: mine.*

He copied these words onto a new page, as though the better to pick up the thread of memory.

My friends always believed that I left on a sudden impulse. Nothing could be further from the truth. Even I gave credence to the theory for a while, so as not to have to explain myself. When I was bombarded with questions, I would say that, one night, I calmly told my grandmother, who I was living with at the time, that I intended to catch a boat to Paphos the next day, and from there I would fly to Paris. In saying this, I was not lying; I was not saying anything untrue, but I was leaving out the most important part. That the decision I announced that day had been developing for some time. I would often lock myself in my room for hours with a book, then I would set it aside, lie down on the bed, eyes wide open, and try to imagine what was going to become of our country, of this region, after years of war, mentally projecting myself towards the finish line where Bilal wanted to be so he could know "the whole story."

I was not interested in this "whole story." However much I turned it over in my mind, all I could see around me was violence and regression. In the Levantine universe that was steadily growing darker, there was no longer a place for me, and I did not want to carve one out for myself.

It was after many months of silent contemplation, cool conjecture, and waking dreams that my decision was made. One day, it burst forth, but it had been a long time maturing. And, in fact, my grandmother was neither surprised nor saddened. I was all she had in the world, but she loved me for myself, not selfishly, and she wanted to know I had a shelter, not simply a hiding place. She gave me her blessing so that I could leave with peace of mind and no regrets.

Once I landed on the island, I presented myself at the French consulate, which had requested a letter of recommendation from my own consulate in order to grant me a visa. Ah yes, things were still civilized back then! I did not have to press my thumb onto an inkpad and leave my digital signature on the register; the letter from my consul was sufficient. He had written it in his most elegant handwriting while I sipped coffee in the corner of his office; I immediately brought it to the French consul, where I was offered another cup of coffee.

Perhaps I am embellishing events, I no longer remember the details; but I remember my feelings at the time, and the aftertaste left by the episode. No bitterness. It is in the order of things to leave one's country; sometimes, it is necessitated by events; if not, one must invent a pretext. I was born, not in a country, but on a planet. Yes, of course, I realize that I was also born in a country, in a town, in a community, in a family, in a maternity unit, in a bed ... But the only important thing, for me as for every other human being, is that I was brought into the world. Into the world! To be born is to be brought into this world, not into this country or that, this house or that.

This is something that Mourad never managed to understand. He was prepared to accept that a man might leave his native land for a time while the battle rages. But, to him, to choose to carry on living, year after year, in a foreign land, in the anonymity of a vast metropolis, was not merely abandoning his mother country, it was an insult to one's ancestors, and, in a sense, a self-inflicted wound to the soul.

While I continued to closely follow everything that was happening in the country, I no longer thought about going back. I never said to myself, "I will never go back"; I said rather, "Later," "Not this summer," "Maybe next year." Deep down, I promised myself—with a flicker of pride—that I would not go back and settle there until it was once again the country I had known. I knew this was impossible, but the condition was non-negotiable. It still is.

It is my way of being loyal, and I have never wanted to adopt another.

Little by little, my friends realized that I would not come back. And a number of them wrote to me. Some to tell me I was right, the others to lecture me.

2

Adam left the table and went over to his suitcase to fetch a bulging, sky-blue folder he had brought with him from Paris. It was marked, in large black felt-tip letters, *Letters from friends*. He set it on the bed, lay down next to it, removed the elastic band, took out a pile of envelopes, and began to read.

It was not until an hour later that he got up, clutching a number of pages, in order to copy certain passages into his notebook.

In the country, rumour has it that you've left never to return ...

Excerpt of a letter from Mourad, dated July 30, 1978, which reached me in Paris thanks to the diligence of a traveller.

Every time someone mentions your name, I pretend to be angry. Which spares me having to say anything. The thing is, between me and you, I no longer know what to say. Last year, we spent all summer waiting for you; you didn't come. You were "working," apparently. I thought people in France took holidays in the summer, in August or in July. Or even in September. Not you! You were working! I shouted at our friends: "You think he's going to end up like the people over there, spending the whole year pretending to work but surreptitiously checking the holiday calendar? Oh, no, Adam hasn't changed, he'll never change! He is working like an emigrant, day and night, come rain, come shine, whatever the season ..."

But, as the proverb says, the leash on a lie is a short one. That morning, your grandmother announced to everyone that you were taking a month's leave and had rented a house in the Alps. She seemed proud, God forgive her, and she showed me the letter you had sent her. This was what made me decide to write to you at once.

I'm not trying to pressure you, but if it is true that you never want to set foot here again, at least tell me, you bastard, so I can stop making myself look stupid by defending you. If you prefer the Alps to the mountains here, at least have the guts to write and tell me.

Our mountain was being sung about in the Bible when those Alps of yours were no more than a geological accident, a common fault. The Alps first appear in history only when our ancestor Hannibal crossed them with his elephants in order to mount an assault on Rome. Which is what he should have done— headed straight for the city and occupied it, before Rome came and occupied us. But I suppose none of this interests you anymore, you probably don't even remember who Hannibal was.

A house in the Alps? Traitor! There are so many houses waiting to welcome you here. Mine, first and foremost. You should be ashamed! [...]

Tania says she sends her love. She might, but I don't. I don't know you anymore.

In the same envelope, there was a second letter. At first when I saw the pinkish, translucent sheet folded in four and recognized Tania's elegant hand, I assumed she had slipped it in without Mourad's knowledge. But I quickly realized that he had obviously agreed to allow his wife to add her voice to his. Because, to be honest, although she seemed to take a different tack, she was the one who was most bitterly critical.

My dearest Adam,
I'm sure you will recognize Mourad's letter as a gesture of affection, disguised, out of masculine reserve, as a scolding.

Do I need to tell you that you left a void in the lives of your friends that nothing and no one can fill? That your absence is all the more painful in these terrible years? If you were here in front of me, you would pretend to be surprised, but I wouldn't believe it. I have always seen your apparent modesty as the sign of good manners rather than a genuine humility. Behind that affable, courteous, timid exterior, you are the most arrogant person I know.

Don't protest! You know that it's true, and you know that I say it as a loving sister. Yes, you are the most arrogant person, and also—you will protest even more forcefully at this—the most intolerant. A friend lets you down? He's no longer your friend. The country lets you down? It's no longer your country. And since you are easily let down, you will end up with no friends, no country.

I profoundly wish that my words might have some effect on you. That they might persuade you to be more tolerant of the country, to accept it for what it is. It will always be a country of factions, of chaos, of unwarranted privilege, nepotism, and corruption. But it is also a country with a gentle way of life, a country of human warmth, of generosity. And the country of your truest friends.

Another virtue of our country is that here it is possible to create a carefree oasis. Even when every district of the city is in flames, our village, our old house, and its vast terrace are exactly as you knew them. A few friends still join us occasionally, as they did back then. Others no longer come; we will always miss them, and I like to think that they miss us a little, too.

Mourad keeps telling me that you are nothing to him now, which means exactly the opposite. He tells me that you've become a stranger, a foreigner, that, with time, you will become more so—and in this he is probably right. But I send my love to you all the same, all my love ...

I carefully preserved these letters, but I cannot remember answering them.

While it was complicated at the time to receive letters from my homeland, sending letters there was more precarious still. The postal system had ceased to function, one had to trust in a traveller to deliver it by hand. A mission that could prove dangerous. The courier sometimes had to enter battle zones; and if he did not wish to run such risks, and asked the addressee to come and pick up the letter, it was the latter who risked death.

For this reason, we did not write to those who had stayed behind. We telephoned. Or, at least, we tried. Nine times out of ten, without success, but from time to time, the call got through. And in the first few seconds, we rushed to say what was essential, because the line could go dead at any moment. So, we first asked after the health of those closest to us; we registered any urgent requests, primarily, any medications no longer available there; we briefly mentioned the letters that we had received or sent; there was talk of friends who had left or were preparing to leave. Only then, if the telephonic Fates were kind and the call was not cut off, did we allow ourselves the luxury of talking about other things.

Mourad claimed that, in one of our conversations, I responded to his reproaches by saying "I didn't leave, it was the country that left." It's possible that I said it. It was something I said a lot at the time, I liked the expression. But it was only a joke. Of course, I was the one who left. I made the decision to leave just as I might have made the decision to stay.

Which does not mean that it was my fault, if there is a fault. Every man has the right to leave, it is for his country to persuade him to stay—despite the aphorism of pompous politicians: "Ask not what your country can do for you—ask what you can do for your country." Easy to say when you're a millionaire, when you've just been elected president of the United States at the age of forty-three! But what exactly is John F. Kennedy's maxim worth when you live in a country where you cannot find a job, a doctor, a place to live, cannot get an education, cannot vote freely, express an opinion, or even walk the streets? Precious little!

Your country must first honour certain commitments to you. You must be considered a full citizen, not be subjected to oppression, discrimination, or unwarranted privations. A country and its leaders have a duty to ensure these things; otherwise, you owe them nothing. Neither a commitment to the land, nor a salute of the flag. The country where you can live with your head held high is one to which you will give everything, sacrifice everything, even your life; the country where you must live with your head bowed is one to which you give nothing. Whether it is your country of refuge or your native country. Magnanimity breeds magnanimity, indifference breeds indifference, and contempt breeds contempt. This is the charter of free individuals and, for my part, I acknowledge no other.

So, I was the one to leave, of my own free will—or almost. But I was not wrong when I told Mourad that the country, too, had left, and had gone much farther than I did. After all, in Paris, I am a five-hour flight from the city where I was born. The journey I made two days ago is one I could have made on any day in recent years: I could have decided to go back to the country in the morning and been there by nightfall. My grandmother's old apartment has long since been there for me to use, I could have moved back in and not left the following day, the following month, or even the following year.

Why did I never take the plunge? Because the country of my childhood had been transformed? No, that's not it, not at all. It is in the nature of things that the world of yesteryear should fade. It is also in the nature of things that one should feel nostalgic. But the disappearance of the past is easy to get over; it is the disappearance of the future that one cannot overcome. The country whose absence saddens and fascinates me is not the *country of my childhood, but the country I dreamed of, one that never saw the light of day.*

People constantly tell me that this is how it goes in the Levant, that things will never change, that there will always be factions, privileges, corruption, blatant nepotism, that we have no choice but to make do. When I reject this, they call me arrogant, even intolerant. Is it arrogant to hope one's country will become less antiquated, less corrupt, less violent? Is it arrogant or intolerant to refuse to be content with an approximation of democracy, a sporadic civil peace? If it is, then I confess my sinful pride and curse their virtuous resignation.

But this morning, at Sémi's place, I am rediscovering the physical pleasure of being in my native land.

I write those last words as if I needed to relearn them. My native land. My country. My homeland. I know all its failings, but during these days of rediscovery, I have no desire to remind myself that I am only passing through, that, in my pocket, I already have a return ticket. I need to believe that I am living here for an indeterminate period, that the horizon is not cluttered with dates and commitments, that I will stay here in this room, in this little mountain hotel, for as long as I need to.

I know that there will come a moment—two days, two weeks, two months from now—when, once again, I feel compelled to leave; by the behaviour of others, or by my own impatience. For the moment, I refuse to think about it. I live, I breathe, I remember.

}

Adam emptied the contents of the sky-blue folder onto the bed, surprised at all the things he had collected over the years. Not just letters, as it said on the folder, but press cuttings, passport photographs, group photos, even his first *carte de séjour*.

By what twisted logic had he filed this in a folder marked *Letters from friends?* He did not have the faintest idea; it was like discovering another Adam, one whose reasoning he could no longer understand.

I can only think that, for the emigrant I was during those years, becoming a resident of a country other than my own was not simply a bureaucratic process, it was an existential choice; and that, to me, my friends' writings were not simply opinions, but inner voices. Try as I might today, I can no longer remember my feelings at the time, or put myself in the shoes of the young émigré I was back then.

A historian is expected to know that Reason is a matter of dates. So, I simply record this fact and make no comment. Before returning to my memories.

How many times had Tania written that to me she was "a sister," "an older sister," or "a loving sister!" It was her way of expressing her affection while avoiding any ambiguity. Obviously, I'm referring to a long time ago. Since the falling-out between Mourad and me, there has been very little communication between us, and very little warmth. Especially these last few days ...

It was inevitable, but even so, I regret it. From the very first time we met—in the university canteen—she and I were bound by an intense friendship. More than a friendship?

Maybe, I don't know ... I could rack my brain and try to remember whether there was something else about the way I saw her when I was seventeen. But I don't see the point of such soul-searching. Love is not a crimson thread to be distinguished from the black, white, gold, or pink threads that might be dubbed "friendship," "desire," "passion," and Lord knows what beside. There must have been a thousand tangled feelings in the heart of the teenage boy I was back then. But I met Tania when she was with Mourad, I never imagined myself "with her," and I never felt the slightest resentment.

That said, at the time I felt a deep affection for her, one that I have never questioned, despite everything that happened with her husband. Because I believe she is innocent? Not really. We are never entirely innocent when it comes to the actions of those we love. But is that a reason to reject them? Should Tania have withdrawn from Mourad when he began to behave disgracefully? I don't believe so. She had a duty to stay with him. And yet, her loyalty to her husband made her complicit. Oh yes, the threads of conscience are as difficult to disentangle as those of emotion.

It would be simple if, on the road of life, we simply had to choose between loyalty and betrayal. More often than not, we are forced to choose between two irreconcilable loyalties; or— and it amounts to the same thing—two betrayals. There came a day when, in the throes of events, I had to make my choice, and Mourad had to make his, as did Tania. The tally of our betrayals: one exile, one malefactor, one accomplice. But that is also the tally of our loyalties.

In remaining by Mourad's side, Tania became his accomplice, but it would have been despicable if she had walked away. Such is life. Sometimes the commitments we undertake at twenty cannot be abdicated and the most honourable thing to do is to carry on. I do not condemn her, nor do I acquit her. In any case, I am not a tribunal.

*I do not judge? Yes, I judge, I spend my life judging. I am pro-
foundly irritated by people who look at you in feigned indignation and say: "Are you judging me?" Yes, of course I am judging
you, I am constantly judging you. Every creature endowed
with a conscience has a duty to judge. But the sentences I hand
down do not affect the lives of the "defendants." I confer or revoke my respect, I measure out my cordiality, I suspend my
friendship while I await further evidence, I become more distant, I become closer, I turn away, I grant a stay of execution, I
wipe the slate clean—or pretend to do so. Most of those involved
do not even realize. I do not communicate my judgements, I am
not one to point the finger, when I observe the world it incites
only an internal dialogue, a ceaseless dialogue with myself.*

As for Tania, I would have judged her much more harshly if her
first decision had been made for the wrong reasons. I mean if,
at twenty, she had fallen in love with a despicable man—won
over by his wealth, his family name, or, worse still, by his
toughness, his "macho" character. I confess that I have very
little tolerance for such things. I can easily understand how she
fell in love with the Mourad I knew when I was young. He was
a man of great warmth, his house was always open, he enjoyed
entertaining his friends and making them feel they were at
home there.

He had generosity, humour, and a keen intelligence that was
not immediately apparent. He liked to give the impression that
he was an unsophisticated mountain man, but that was a ploy.
It allowed him to say exactly what he thought without restraint. He often came out with harsh truths that, from anyone
else—from me, for example—would have seemed so brutal or
spiteful as to obliterate years of friendship. From him, people
accepted them, no one held it against him, they thought, "That's
just Mourad!" and the lapse was two-thirds forgiven.

The character he constructed for himself allowed him considerable freedom. When I say "constructed," it sounds as though I'm implying that it was the result of shrewd calculation. Yes and no. It was his natural persona, but he played it with great skill. Like great actors who use their own personality to lend weight to the character they are to play on stage.

I can understand how Tania fell under his spell, we all did, me perhaps a little more than the others.

What fascinated me about Mourad when I met him at university, was that he already seemed to have lived a lot. In our little group, there were people younger and older than he was, and yet he was a big brother to all of us, he was the one who made everyday decisions on our behalf. A leader? No, we didn't want a leader, we rejected authorities and hierarchies. But he had a certain preeminence.

He must have assumed adult responsibilities very young, and that had made him more mature. His father had died of a heart attack at forty-four when Mourad was seven years old. He was an only child, his mother was twenty-eight and she never remarried. Until then, she had lived in the shadow of her husband, and now she intended to live in the shadow of her son.

She consulted him about everything, entrusted him with every responsibility. Whether it was choosing the school he would attend, buying a car, paying the gardener, selling a plot of land, repairing a roof or a wall, she would explain the pros and cons to her son, introduce him to the people concerned, then ask him to make the decision.

He was like one of those heirs who ascend the throne as a child and are forced to behave like adults. In a sense, his mother was his regent.

When I met Mourad he was nineteen, and the respect his mother bore him could have seemed like a sign of modernity. We had just come through the sixties, and some parents attempted to be their children's friends. I quickly realized that, for Mourad's mother, this was not the case. In fact, it was the reverse—lingering archaism rather than precocious modernity. If her only child had been a girl, I suspect she would have tyrannized her. But her son, her little man, she worshipped. She did not treat him like a "friend," but like a lord, and in doing so she believed she was fulfilling the role assigned to her for all eternity.

In behaving as she did, she ensured that, from an early age, he developed a self-confidence, a pride in who he was and what he possessed, and an undeniable sense of duty—at least towards his family. Without knowing, she also contributed to his unhappiness.

Her name was Aïda. She always dressed in black, as though her husband had only just died. But she was friendly, often cheerful, and not without a sense of humour; I think she was fond of me—at least while I was her son's best friend.

Mourad told me one day that when he had a falling-out with someone, he avoided telling his mother, because she immediately turned against that person, making any reconciliation impossible. I assume she has hated me these past few years.

Is she still alive? I don't know. Probably not. If she were, I would have seen her at the hospital.

4

Sémiramis knocked on Adam's door and brought him a bowl of fruit—blood-red cherries, apricots, green plums, and a mango from Egypt. He thanked her and planted a kiss on her forehead, making no attempt to persuade her to stay.

To show that she understood his desire not to be disturbed, she simply whispered, "When you want dinner, just give me a shout!"

With a nod and a look, he agreed—then, without waiting for her to close the door behind her, he plunged back into his old papers.

In August '68, a few days after the double letter from Mourad and his wife, I received a letter from another friend, Albert, also brought to Paris by a traveller passing through, a letter that took exactly the opposite view. Ever since, I have kept them pinned together with a large paperclip. The paperclip has rusted now, leaving a sepia mark on the front of one and the back of the other.

My very dear Adam,

That lunatic Mourad has been shouting from the rooftops that he wrote to you yesterday to say "things you need to hear before you go completely deaf." I don't know what he has said to you, but I can guess, and I feel it my duty to give you a rather different opinion.

I'll begin by asking you not to bear a grudge against our mutual friend, regardless of what he wrote. You and I never hung around with him for his tact or his sophistication, did we? The few things he does know, he never quite understood properly, if you understand what I mean. We love him because he's a good guy, a gruff mountain man who says more than he thinks, and because his tirades are well-intentioned. And we also love him because of Tania ... That said, if you do decide to reply to him, don't mince your words!

Here, then, is the truth about our daily life, a truth our mutual friend will have been careful to hide from you.

I write these few lines by candlelight. We have electricity for two hours out of twenty-four, and tonight, there is no point hoping. In any case, I have no idea how I am going to send you this letter when it is finished. One of my neighbours, Khalil, is thinking of going to France for a few days, so I will entrust these pages to him; unless he changes his mind, in which case I will have to keep an eye out for someone else ...

In a normal country, you write, you stick on a stamp, you slip the envelope into a postbox. Here, a commonplace activity that happens millions of times a day all over the planet, has become unthinkable.

This is the point we have come to! What, with the postal service, the electricity, and everything else. The planes still fly intermittently, for those who are not kidnapped on their way to the airport. Buildings have become barricades, the streets are shooting ranges, skyscrapers have become reinforced concrete watchtowers. Parliament isn't a parliament anymore, the government isn't a government, the army isn't an army, religions are no longer religions; they're factions, parties, militias ...

There are people who are astounded by such an atypical country. Personally, I see nothing admirable about it, nothing amusing, and nothing that makes me proud. I stupidly dream of a country like any other. You flick a switch and, *click*, a light comes on. You turn the blue tap and cold water comes out; you turn the red tap, and there's hot water. You lift the receiver and—miracle of miracles—you hear the dial tone! My neighbours tell me that if I was more patient, if I pressed the receiver to my ear and held my breath, I would eventually hear a faint click, a sign that the line is about to work.

I will never be patient enough … It's true that my ancestors lived for centuries with no postal service, no telephone, no running water, no electricity, and that, in theory, there is nothing to stop me from doing likewise. Except that they did not have lifts, and they did not live, like I do, on the sixth floor with an amazing view of the fireworks!

In short, you were right to leave, and you are absolutely right to spend your holidays in the Alps. Obviously, your friends would love to see you again, but the only person who is really worried about you is your grandmother. And every time I call round to see her, she tells me that she is happy that you're far away, that you're safe, even if it means she doesn't get to see you anymore.

Me? I would say exactly the same thing: Stay where you are. Take care of yourself! Enjoy life! And from time to time, raise a glass to your faithful friend,

Albert

Adam slipped the letter back into the envelope and laid it on the table. It bore his name, carefully copied out, and the address where he had lived at the time.

Then he went over to the bed to fetch another envelope he had already taken out of the folder, and he laid it next to the first. The same handwriting, the same addressee, the same address. Identical, but for a single detail: the first had no stamp, the second bore a French stamp with the image of Marianne, postmarked Orly airport, where it had been posted in December 1979.

The two letters were separated by barely six months. And an entire world. Just as the first was cheerful, outraged, pugnacious, so the second was silent and resigned; it contained only a card of icy white and, in the middle, five short lines:

Albert N Kithar
left us yesterday
of his own free will.
May his friends forgive him,
and may they remember him as he was in life.

In copying into his notebook these words written and printed twenty years earlier, Adam took care to set them down in exactly the same way. He reread them, and reread them again. Then he stretched, only to pause mid-gesture, to remain like this, suspended, like a petrified bird that can no longer take wing.

Only after a long minute did he rest his elbows on the table and once again begin to write.

Holding in your hands a letter announcing that a loved one has just taken his life is one of the worst ordeals a man can endure. I had read about it in books, and I had seen it in films, but to experience it oneself is a very different thing. I remember that my hands would not stop shaking. I tried to calm them but I couldn't. I tried to call out to my girlfriend, it was Patricia at the time. She was close by, in the bathroom, but my voice could not reach her. In the end, all I could manage was a strangled cry. She had rushed in, panicked, thinking I was ill. I had simply handed her the announcement. And only when she took it from my hands did they stop trembling.

The other memory I have of that hateful episode is one of utter helplessness—not just the powerlessness one always feels when faced by the irrevocable, by absence—but an additional helplessness, linked to the events that were happening in the country.

I tried to call Tania and Mourad, then other friends, then my grandmother, without success. The calls could not get through. For hours, we took turns, Patricia and I; we carried on all day and into the late evening trying to make contact. There was simply no longer any telephone connection. At best, we heard a distant click and a humming silence, followed by the beep-beep-beep of an engaged tone; otherwise it was a voice recording of a woman who could not connect our call and asked us to kindly call again later, call later, later ...

When the line was finally reconnected, for some mysterious reason, and Tania's voice could be heard, it was past midnight.

"I hope I didn't wake you. I tried calling earlier ..."

"Don't apologize, we never go to sleep before two o'clock. I'm so glad to hear your voice., Let me put Mourad on."

The first words of her husband were intended to be sarcastic:

"Let me guess, Adam. You're calling to say you're coming back to us, is that it?"

Ordinarily, I would answer him in the same tone. But that day, I remained serious, and a little cold.

"Not just yet, Mourad ... I just wanted to know if everything is alright."

"Here, in the village, things are fine. In the city, at night, there are still some shots fired, some explosions. Minor skirmishes between this neighbourhood and that. Same as always. Nothing serious ..."

"Have you heard from Albert?"

"No, and I have no desire to."

I was steeling myself to tell him about the announcement, but hearing his reaction, I stopped myself. Clearly, he had not received the same letter I had. So I decided to let him talk before announcing the news.

"If I understand rightly, you had an argument ..."

"He was becoming unbearable! He never stopped complaining: 'My electricity has been cut off,' 'My telephone isn't working,' 'I've got no hot water,' 'I can't sleep for the explosions.' As if he was the only one in that situation, as though the war were being waged against him personally ... Every time he came to visit, he'd start whining. 'Why do we stay here?' 'How can people live in such a country?' —he was becoming tiresome. For as long as he was here with us, Tania couldn't stop crying. Things are depressing enough as they are, friends are supposed to comfort you, to distract you, not to depress you even more. The other day, I had enough, I told him I didn't want to see him here again."

"You were wrong, Mourad! You should never have done that!"

"He deserved it!"

Then I read him the text of the announcement. Three, four times he whispered, "My God! My God!" His voice was not the same. I could tell he had gone pale. I could hear Tania next to him asking what had happened. Mourad handed her the phone. I read the five fateful lines. Like him, she murmured, "My God! My God!" Then, "God forgive us."

Feeling the need to lessen the impact of the blow I had dealt them in the middle of the night, I said, though I only half believed it:

"All is not lost. When Albert sent me that message, he was still alive, and we can't be sure that he carried out his threat. It's not easy to kill yourself, it is a brutal gesture, a man might pull back at the last minute. I was calling to offer my condolences, I assumed you would have heard he was dead and you would both be devastated. The fact that you haven't heard anything is reassuring; maybe nothing has happened yet, maybe he changed his mind."

"Yes, maybe," said Tania, who did not seem to believe it any more than I did.

Mourad called me the following morning to tell me he had kicked in the door of Albert's apartment, but he wasn't there. Not alive, not dead. His neighbours had not seen him for days, and no one knew where he might be.

My grandmother had had no news either. Taking infinite precautions, I sounded her out, avoiding any reference to his disappearance, pretending that I had a message for him and that I couldn't get in touch with him to pass it on. I hoped that she would say, actually, he had just dropped by to see her. I knew that, since my departure, Albert visited her regularly. Of all my friends, he was the one who was kindest to her. Whenever she saw him show up at our door, her face lit up; if two weeks passed without him dropping by, she would ask me why we didn't see him anymore. "The boy is all alone in this world," she would sometimes say, as though to justify this maternal tenderness for a stranger.

It was true. Albert had no family. As far back as I can remember—and we knew each other as children—he had always been alone. His father had worked in Africa, his mother had been committed to a sanatorium in Switzerland; then they had died, first one, then the other: she from tuberculosis, people said; while he had been murdered. If I wanted to be meticulous, I should insert "people say" or "people said" at the end of every sentence, given that Albert never talked about his family, except in vague allusions. Even after we became close, it was not a subject I ever felt I could broach with him.

All I knew, or thought I knew, I gleaned from whisperings at school. We went through Jesuit school together. I must have met him for the first time when I was six and he was seven. Which doesn't mean that we were childhood friends. He was a boarder, I was a day pupil, and these two "tribes" rarely mixed. When class finished, we got onto a bus that took each of us back to our own houses. They, the boarders, stayed behind, together.

In a sense, Albert's case was not out of the ordinary. When a pupil was a boarder, it was usually because his parents were not around. But, obviously there is not around and "not around," and the rumours were not all the same. Not all absent mothers were rumoured to be consumptives, and not all absent fathers ended up being murdered. Bootlegger? That was the rumour that went around at school. He might have been an honest salesman, a reckless contractor, a road builder, even a civil servant in the colonial administration, but the word that cropped up in the whispered conversations was a half-Arabic, half-Turkish word—meharrebji, which means smuggler. Personally, I had no desire to embarrass Albert by asking questions. Looking back, I think it was my discretion that first brought us together, and later cemented our friendship. With me, Albert had no need to be on his guard.

What is certain is that Albert never lived with his parents, and that his father died a violent death when we were about ten or eleven and in the fifth grade.

Usually, when a pupil lost a close relative, he went home to his family for a few days. Albert didn't go anywhere. It seemed he had no family in the country. He stayed at school. He was simply excused from classes for a day or two.

A mass was celebrated in memory of his dead father. "Have a thought for your friend Albert, who has just lost his papa!" the priest said, and then exhorted the student not to allow hatred to take root in his soul, and leave to the justice of God and of men the task of punishing the guilty. This was how we found out it had been murder.

All eyes naturally turned towards the boy concerned, who was not in tears, as I had expected him to be. It's true that he had not lost his father just now, he had lost him a long time ago, if he had ever had him.

I remember the very first time my attention was drawn to him. A young, inexperienced teacher had just announced that he was organizing an excursion, and rashly told pupils to add their names to a form lying on his desk, making it clear that he could take only the first ten who signed. All our classmates rushed at once, instantly triggering a bedlam of jostling, elbowing, brawling, and shouting. I had stayed in my seat and, *from behind me, I distinctly heard someone mutter "Barbarians!" I turned around, our eyes met, and we smiled. This is the moment when our friendship was born.*

I suppose Albert must have had the same word on his lip the day he heard that his father had been murdered; and also, much later, as he stared out the window of his sixth-floor apartment, watching the "fireworks" of war.

"Barbarians!"

It was dark, that Sunday, when Sémiramis came back and knocked at Adam's door, less unobtrusively this time.

"I can bring you up a tray if you like, but I honestly think you should take a break. You've been working since dawn. You don't fancy joining me in the dining room?"

"Like yesterday?"

"Like yesterday. The same mezze, the same champagne, the same temperature. And, of course, the same hostess ..."

She accompanied the words with a captivating smile it would have been futile to resist.

Ten minutes later, they were sitting exactly where they had been the night before. The hotel owner could have added "the same waiter, the same candles."

She allowed her friend a few mouthfuls, a few sips, before saying ingenuously:

"I suppose it would be impertinent for the mistress of the house to ask her guest what work it is he finds so engrossing. You never go out, you barely talk, and if I hadn't forced you, you wouldn't even have come up to eat. What's more, you're dishevelled and you look exhausted, as though you'd just been in a fight ..."

Adam simply gave her a smile and an affectionate pat on the arm. Then he ran his fingers through his hair like a crude comb. She waited. The silence continued. After two interminable minutes, just when the "mistress," having given up hope of getting a response, was about to change the subject, her "guest" said, in a tone of feigned contrition:

"I have a flaw that is all too common among historians: I am more interested in bygone eras than in my own, and in the lives of my subjects than in my own. Ask me about the Punic Wars, the Gallic Wars, or the Barbarian Invasions and you won't get me to shut up. Ask me about the wars I've lived through, in my country, in my region, about the clashes in which I've been an eyewitness, or lost friends, or very nearly been among the victims, and you'll get no more than two or three sentences at most. Ask me about Cicero, about Attila and I'm voluble. Talk to me about my own life, those of my friends, and I'm dumbstruck."

"Why?"

"The primary reason is related to my profession, as I said. When a historian says 'my era,' what spontaneously comes to mind is not the one into which he was born, the one he did not choose, but the one to which he has decided to devote his life—in my case the Roman Era. That said, I'm not a fool, and I'm not trying to hide from the facts, as they say. There is no Herodotean oath that compels a historian to remain within his period. The truth is, I've always felt uncomfortable, pathologically uncomfortable, whenever I've wanted to talk about myself, my country, my friends, my wars. But over the past two days, since I've been here, I've been forcing myself to try and overcome this problem, or rather this debility."

"And are you?"

"Not completely. At times, I manage to marshal my

memories and recount an episode. But most of the time I get caught up in daydreams, reminiscences, regrets ..."

As though to illustrate what he had just said, he fell silent and gazed into the middle distance. For several long seconds, his friend allowed him to drift before bringing him back to earth with a second question:

"And have you been thinking about it for long?"

"My mental debility? Yes, for years now. But I lived with it, I didn't try to overcome it. I had specific projects lined up for my sabbatical. Then the ghosts of my childhood burst into my life. Out of the blue! Seventy-two hours ago, I hadn't even begun to think about making this trip. Even yesterday, when I landed ..."

Again, he fell silent, and again he stared into the distance. Clearly he was still making sense of things, but only to himself, and his friend felt as though he had not even realized he was no longer speaking.

When he came back to her, he said, stricken:

"I'm supposed to be working on the major biography of Attila that my editor has been waiting on for the past fifteen years."

It was now Sémiramis's turn to lay a protective hand on his arm.

"You look exhausted again. Don't say any more. We can talk about all of this later, later ..."

The Fourth Day

1

The moment he opened his eyes, Adam began writing again.

The bellboy who brought up his breakfast found him already at his desk, poring over his notebook. His bed was unmade; but to judge from his face, he had slept little.

MONDAY, APRIL 23

All night, names, voices, shadows, faces, have been fluttering inside my head like irritating fireflies.

In my state of semi-wakefulness, genuine memories melted into fantasies and dreams. So much so that, when I got up, my mind was muddled and my sense of judgement precarious.

I shouldn't start writing straight away, but I can't stop myself. I'm counting on strong coffee to put things into perspective.

The backdrop to his restless sleep had been the tragedy that occurred twenty years earlier, the one he had begun recounting the night before.

Reconstructing it in a faithful, coherent manner required a mammoth effort of memory and perspective. Because, if the death of his childhood friend was, as it evidently was, one of the incidents of the war in which the country was mired, Albert's fate was different to that of the unfortunates who had their throats cut by bloodthirsty militias, who were mutilated in random bombings, or were gunned down by the snipers hiding on the rooftops. Since he had clearly expressed his intention to take his own life, his action took on a very different significance—a revolt against the murderous folly.

We, his friends, were mostly concerned to find out what had become of him, whether he had actually committed suicide as his strange announcement suggested. Those of us who were still in the country, particularly Mourad and Tania, played an active role in the search. It should be said that we could no longer count on the authorities, who had lost all authority in the country; nor, obviously, on the family of the "missing person," since he had none.

Despite our efforts, every day we seemed a little more in the dark. Having failed to find him at his apartment, having questioned his neighbours without gleaning any useful information, we had no idea where he might have gone to commit his desperate act, how he might have planned to go about it, and why there was still no sign of his remains.

It happened during the Christmas holidays, and there were endless discussions between those of us who knew Albert, especially his friends from school and from university. Everyone had their own version of the incident, one that broadly reflected their personal worries and fears rather than the reality of the event. I received numerous telephone calls and many letters that I have carefully kept. Including this letter from one of our old history teachers, Father François-Xavier, who was then running a school in Mulhouse in Alsace.

My very dear Adam,

I trust that these few lines find you and those close to you in good health.

The news from your country continues to be very painful for those, like me, who have known and loved it. And this morning, I have had word of a tragedy of a different nature, the disappearance of my former pupil Albert Kithar, which, I am assured, is not related, or not directly, to political violence [...]

Back when I was teaching at the Collège, I found Albert a difficult but endearing boy. I do not think he paid much heed to the things I endeavoured to teach his classmates. I can see him still, at the back of the class, head bowed, engrossed in a book—usually a science-fiction novel, if memory serves. And yet he was not as indifferent, not as absent as he appeared. Whenever I mentioned a subject that interested him, he instantly turned his attention on me.

I remember a class in which I was discussing Benjamin Franklin. I had talked about his ideas, his role in the struggle for American independence, his time in France on the eve of the Revolution. Through all this, Albert was manifestly absent. I was constantly watching him out of the corner of my eye, as a shepherd is supposed to keep an eye on a stray sheep. At some point, I raised the subject of his discovery of electricity. Albert sits up, and his gaze, usually elusive, becomes focused and intent. I had intended to quickly pass over this aspect of Franklin's work, but, so thrilled was I to have caught Albert's attention for once, that I ended up spending several minutes giving a detailed explanation of the kite experiment and the invention of the lightning conductor. I think I remember that, in my enthusiasm, I even suggested an impromptu theory about the relationship between Franklin's experiments with electricity and his adherence to the philosophy of the Enlightenment.

I have, as you can tell, fond memories of that period which now seems so remote. Since that time, I cannot but take a profound interest in the fate of your country, and in the destiny of the promising young men I knew there.

I would be most grateful if you could keep me informed of any developments in this worrying event, which, I still dare to hope, many not end in grief [...]

Faithfully yours,

François-Xavier, W., s.j.

A week later, the truth was eventually revealed.

What happened is more or less as follows. On the afternoon of Tuesday, December 11, Albert heads off on foot to visit a former classmate who is travelling to France the following day. He gives him three envelopes, obviously containing the famous "notices"—including the one addressed to me—and asks him to post them the moment he lands at Orly airport. Although he is asked to come inside, he stays on the doorstep and quickly leaves, explaining that he wants to be home before it begins to get dark. The other does not insist. The situation in the capital is very tense. There had been a number of clashes the night before, and there was still the occasional sound of sporadic gunfire. Those few people who ventured out onto the street did not linger long.

Albert had planned to lock himself in his apartment, tidy the place a little, perhaps add a post scriptum to the farewell letter he planned to leave for the friends who would find him, swallow a massive dose of barbiturates, then lie down on his bed in a dark suit, arms by his sides. He was not worried about his safety on the streets, he was simply in a hurry to carry out the plan he had made, mentally running through the various things he intended to do.

Then, at the corner of a deserted street, a car screeches to a halt, and two young men jump out armed with guns, Albert does not even give them a glance, he simply takes a step to his left so he is walking closer to the wall. Engrossed in his thoughts, he does not realize that the militiamen want him. Not him, Albert Kithar in person, but the anonymous passerby that he was. The armed men were looking to kidnap someone—anyone—who lived in the district, and there were no other pedestrians on the streets.

His kidnappers grab him by the arms and drag him into the car, which drives off at top speed. Hoping to scare him, they warn him that if he screams, if he struggles or tries to escape, they'll put a bullet in his head.

When he responds to their threats with a howl of laughter, as though he has just heard a hilarious joke, they assume they have happened either upon a simpleton, or upon the bravest man in the country.

When they reach their hideout, they lock their prey in a garage with his hands lashed behind his back and his eyes blindfolded. Still, Albert is smiling like a fool. A brawny man comes and sits opposite him and, in a tone intended to be venomous but which sounds apologetic, he says:

"They've kidnapped my son."

The captive stops smiling. In a neutral voice he simply says:

"I hope he comes back safe and sound."

"You've got good reason to hope so," the other man says. "If my son doesn't come back, I plan on taking your life."

Albert replies that he has no interest in his own life. In saying it, he uses a common expression that means "I don't give a damn."

"What do you mean you don't give a damn? About your own life? Don't try to play the tough guy! And stop smiling like a halfwit. You'd do better to pray that my son is returned to me if you want to save your skin!"

"I don't want to save my skin," the hostage insists.

He tells his jailer to slip a hand into the inside pocket of his jacket, which contains his identity card, a "death notice" like the one he sent to me, and the most recent draft of his farewell letter, containing the passage: "By the time you find this message, I will already have done what I've decided to do ... I don't want any of you to feel responsible for my death, or for anyone to think that if they had done something earlier, they might have prevented it. I didn't make this decision yesterday. It has been too late for far too long ..."

The man takes the time to read and reread the letter, his lips moving from time to time. Then says, in disbelief:

"You were heading home ... to kill yourself, is that it?"

Albert nods.

"And we came along and stopped you?"

Albert nods again.

A brief silence. Then the man starts to laugh uncontrollably, and after a few seconds the hostage, though still bound and blindfolded, throws his head back and laughs too.

It is the jailer who first manages to recover his composure and in a tone that is curious but not hostile asks:

"Why?"

This man who, a moment earlier, was threatening to kill the hostage without a second thought now seems shaken by the idea that this well-dressed young man who seems of sound mind was preparing to take his own life.

"Why?"

Albert was never one for confidences. And certainly not for confiding in a perfect stranger. But that day, perhaps because at the point when he was kidnapped he had been mulling over the text of his farewell letter; perhaps because, having made his preparations, set the scene, and set in motion an infallible mechanism, control of his destiny had suddenly been wrenched from him, and he felt unsettled; perhaps because the person asking the question was a despondent jailer, and it would be an epilogue appropriate to the absurdity of life here on earth—he began to talk.

Oh, it was not a torrent of words, nor a confession. Indeed, Albert was incapable of using words to illuminate the murky waves that had carried him to the brink of suicide; all he told his improbable confessor were the obvious things people say in such circumstances, that life had lost all meaning, that he felt cut off from the world, that he felt suffocated by the war raging all around ... But the man would not give up. Adopting a stern voice and placing his hands on the shoulders of the hostage— though with no intention of untying his bonds or removing his blindfold—he began to lecture him, reeling off the hackneyed phrases of grief-stricken fathers.

"Think about your parents, they fed you, they watched you grow up, they dreamed of seeing you graduate, dreamed of seeing you married! Now here you are, a handsome young man, and instead of finding a pretty girlfriend, you're thinking about ending it all? What a shame! What a waste! What an abomination! When you have your whole life ahead of you!"

"My whole life ahead of me, huh?"

Albert's tone was only faintly ironic, but the theatrical flailing of his bound limbs and blindfolded head was enough for the two of them—first his kidnapper, then himself—to burst into hysterical laughter.

2

It was not uncommon at that time for the families of a kidnap victim to react by capturing one or more members assumed to belong to the opposing camp in order to use them as bargaining chips.

But this was not the most usual practice in the case of a kidnapping. Generally, if a man did not come home and it was believed that he had been kidnapped, his family would turn to some local dignitary who, in turn, would get in touch with a mediator. The mediator would seek to find out the identity of the kidnappers, their motives, their demands, and who was most likely to make them see reason; he would confirm that the hostage was alive and well treated, then set about negotiating his release. Such mediators, invariably voluntary, were generally impartial and were very effective, if not called upon too late.

From a distance, all the kidnappings could seem similar; on close inspection, to the trained eye, no two were identical. Sometimes—though this was rare—the motive was financial: a wealthy individual was abducted and the family was forced to pay a ransom. Financially motivated crimes were commonly called "sordid," a somewhat perverse epithet since it seems to suggest that the other crimes had a certain nobility. So, the massacre of innocents for political or religious reasons would not be sordid since there was no attempt to extort money? So, kidnapping a man with the intention of torturing him, murdering him, and dumping his body in the street could not be considered sordid if the motivation was simply to intimidate or to escalate violence? Surely such tacit complicity is inexcusable and degrading? Any man who abducts, tortures, and humiliates another is scum, whether he is a common criminal, a militant, an officer of the law, or a political leader.

However, the abduction of our friend Albert was not motivated by political cynicism, it seemed, nor by fanaticism, nor by money.

The man holding Albert hostage in his workshop was not a conventional kidnapper. In peacetime, it was unlikely he would ever have committed a crime; in fact, he might have been a model citizen. He was a garage mechanic who had spent his life working all hours, happy to get his hands dirty, dreaming that one day his son might get a degree in engineering. A dream that had come true three years earlier. To celebrate his graduation, he had given his high-flying son a flashy brand-new car so he could drive it across the city and proudly park it outside the offices of the company that had recruited him; the only cars he had ever owned were those he had patched up himself.

The son's beautiful car had been found abandoned one morning in December, on a street close to where Albert lived. Before the kidnappers could be identified, militiamen belonging to the mechanic's extended family staged an abduction in the neighbourhood in question, grabbing the first pedestrian they found. According to the rules of this wretched game, Albert's family and friends should have contacted a mediator to ensure that the incident ended with an exchange and both hostages could be returned to their families.

But this time, the hostage had no family, and precious few friends. Nor did those friends have any reason to be aware of what was happening. Why would they suspect a kidnapping when they had written proof that Albert had decided to take his own life?

It was not until three weeks after the disappearance of their friend that Tania and Mourad, puzzled that no remains had yet been found, got in touch with a potential mediator—a former member of parliament. They provided the man with the name and a description of their friend, and the last date on which he had been seen.

Two days later, I picked up the phone in my Paris apartment and heard the words:

"He's alive."

Mourad said it without a glimmer of joy in his voice, not at all the way I might have expected to hear such astonishing news. I did not feel that I could show any sign of relief, and so, warily, hoping simply to trigger the next sentence, I said:

"But ...?"

"But he's being held captive by a garage mechanic whose son has been kidnapped."

"For a hostage exchange?"

"That's right. Except that his son is dead."

"God in heaven!"

"Right now, the father still thinks his son might be alive. He's still hoping for an exchange."

A long silence on both ends of the line, and protracted sighs as Mourad and I imagined how the man would react if he were to learn the truth.

After a moment, I stated the obvious:

"We need our friend to be released before that."

"Negotiations are under way. We just have to hope they're concluded in time."

Again, a vast expanse of silence.

"So, how come you and I know that the son is dead if his father doesn't?"

"I assume he's heard contradictory rumours in recent days," Mourad said, "and he's clinging to the idea that his son is alive and will come back to him. I hope the mediators know what

they're doing. If not, when he does find out the truth, he'll go berserk and he'll take it out on his hostage."

"Poor Albert! He decides to kill himself, discreetly, cleanly, with no fuss and with as little pain as possible. Instead, he gets himself kidnapped and risks being tortured, mutilated, and having his body dumped on a rubbish tip. His own death has been stolen from him."

A pause. Then I went on:

"When I think that, of all our old friends, Albert was the only one who never took an interest in this war."

Mourad agreed:

"When I went into his apartment, I didn't find a single newspaper, new or old. Nothing but science-fiction books, walls and walls of them, carefully arranged in alphabetical order. And display cabinets full of music boxes. Did you know he collected them?"

"Yes, he showed them to me one day. He used to buy them in junk shops, repaint them, and repair the mechanism. He only had to see one to know the period it was made and who had made it."

"There are dozens of them. Some of them must be worth a fortune, if he wanted to sell them."

"That was never his intention. Besides, who would he have sold them to? Who but him would have thought of buying music boxes in the middle of a war?"

We laughed. Then we stopped laughing. Mourad felt guilty.

"To think I threw him out of my house! I can't stop thinking about it. It's like I pushed him over the edge. I feel so angry with myself."

"Me too, I'm angry with myself for leaving without worrying about the people who stayed behind," I said in an attempt to temper his guilt.

"If he comes through this alive, I'm going to encourage him to leave too. He has no place in this country ..."

"What about you, Mourad? Do you still think there's really a place for you there?"

"There's no place for me elsewhere," he said in a tone that put an end to the conversation.

Another silence. Then he asked:

"Wasn't it you who once said to me: 'Even if you don't take an interest in politics, politics takes an interest in you'?"

"It's not my line, I must have read it somewhere. I don't remember who wrote it ..."

When it came to quotations, I had always taken provenance very seriously. My old friend knew this and would often amuse himself by tossing me a quote so I would chase after it, like a greyhound after a rabbit: "I don't suppose you know who said ..." In those days, there were no prodigious "search engines" that could give you the answer in the blink of an eye. I had no choice but to search and search, particularly in the countless dictionaries of quotations that occupied—and still occupy— several shelves in my bookcase. I would eventually find an answer, but it was rarely conclusive. As a general rule, very few famous quotes were said by the people to whom they're attributed. Julius Caesar never said "Et tu, Brute?"; Henri IV never said "Paris is well worth a mass!"—though he obviously agreed with the sentiment; and his grandson Louis XIV never said "L'État, c'est moi!"

As to the quote Mourad had just mentioned, I quickly discovered that the original was phrased: "Be on your guard: if you do not take an interest in politics, politics takes an interest in you." There was some dispute as to the source, and it was alternately attributed to Pierre Paul Royer-Collard and Abbé Sieyès, both writing during the French Revolution.

The original phrasing is more pertinent than the version Mourad remembered. It says, "If you do not take an interest in politics," not "Even if ..." In other words, it is not simply a banal observation that politics affects everyone, even those who take no interest in it; what the writer is saying is that political machinations particularly affect those who take no interest in them.

It's absolutely true! Albert was not kidnapped despite the fact that he took no interest in this bloody war, but because he took no interest. A paradox? Only superficially.

When there was a settling of scores between two militias, two districts, two communities, militants on all sides went to ground. Those who had taken part in battles or massacres rarely ventured outside "their" zone unless there was a chance that it might be invaded, when they fled and hid out elsewhere.

Who did not feel the need to run away or to hide? Who went on crossing the demarcation lines between the zones? Who refused to leave neighbourhoods or villages when there was an invasion of "others"? Only those who had nothing to reproach themselves for, those who had taken part in no battles, no kidnapping, no massacre. And it was these innocents who ended up bearing the brunt.

Yes, it was from among the vast flock of apolitical sheep that the Minotaurs of the civil war chose their prey. The abduction of Albert was not the result of an unfortunate combination of circumstances, it was the tragicomic demonstration of a recognized paradox.

There followed painful weeks of negotiations. Thanks to Mourad's daily briefings, I managed to follow the discussion closely.

"We've reached an impasse," he told me one day. "I don't dare go any farther for fear of triggering a disaster."

Then he explained his dilemma:

"The kidnapper now knows for certain that his son is not coming back. He is still saying that he intends to execute our friend, but he hasn't done so, and I feel that the more time passes, the more difficult he will find it to kill him in cold blood. He keeps him tied up, but he hasn't tortured him and he's not starving him. Some people have suggested that I offer to pay a ransom. I haven't done it. It's possible I might at some point, but right now I don't think it's the right solution. I'm afraid the kidnapper might react badly. The mediator gave me a phone number for the poor man. I call him every two or three days and get him talking, I listen patiently, I offer sympathy and consideration. I've established a relationship of trust, one that I don't want to ruin with some blunder. But we can't take the risk of just leaving Albert indefinitely at the mercy of this man and his family. I feel as though I'm trapped between two cliffs: I can't go forward, I can't go back. How much longer can this carry on? I have no idea."

While I am racking my brain for a solution, Mourad highlights a second problem, even thornier than the first.

"And to be completely honest, there's something else that's been bothering me. I can talk to you about it because you must feel the same way. This whole kidnapping thing hasn't made me forget the attempted suicide. Given the way he is, I feel Albert's life will be at greater risk if he's released than if he stays in captivity.

"If this were anyone else, my only thought would be to get them released and bring them safely home. With Albert, I'm not so sure. I can't stop thinking about the logical consequence: we bring him home and the following day he is found dead in his bed with a new farewell letter on the table."

Exhausted by this effort of memory, Adam felt the need for a break. To rest his head and his eyes, and to marshal his thoughts.

He had been working without interruption since morning and was no longer in any fit state to write. But he was so engulfed in his memories that he was incapable of stopping. Eventually, he went and lay on the bed, promising himself he would get up in five minutes.

The sun was low, but since his room faced the sea and therefore the sunset, it was still bathed in a rosy glow that was soft yet intense. He felt the desire to let sleep creep over him, and he no longer had the strength to resist.

He was woken several hours later by a friendly hand laid gently on his shoulder, his face, his forehead. When he opened his eyes, he noticed it was night.

"Pure spirit, I am your mortal conscience," said the cheerful voice of Sémiramis.

He smiled and closed his eyes again.

"Dinner is ready," she said.

"No, thanks, I'm too tired; I think I'll just go back to sleep."

But the visitor was not moved to pity.

"No, Adam. You didn't have lunch, you've spent the whole day writing; I'm not having you get sick under my roof. You're already dressed, so just get up, give yourself a quick wash, and come downstairs."

There was clearly no point in arguing.

"Very well, my chatelaine, I shall be right there. Give me ten minutes."

If the title her dozing friend had just conferred upon her made her smile, it did nothing to lessen her determination. She went out and closed the door, but not before turning on all the lights.

3

The table had already been laid, and the dishes covered with upturned plates to stop them from getting cold.

Still not entirely awake, Adam ate little and talked even less. After several long minutes, he felt obliged to say:

"I've never been very talkative, but tonight it verges on rudeness ... I'm sorry. My only excuse is that the surroundings in which I've found myself these past two days are conducive to concentration. Even when I stop writing on the page, I'm still writing in my head."

"The silence, the mountain, the light, the sea on the horizon, the air purified by umbrella pines ..."

"... and the feeling of being the prisoner of some benevolent deity."

She laid her hand on his.

"You can't imagine how happy it makes me to hear you say that."

"That I feel like a prisoner?"

"Even that! I've done everything I can to make this an oasis of serenity and cool waters, and you've just told me I succeeded."

"Except that instead of cool water, we have champagne."

"Champagne is my idea of cool water."

The raised their glasses, touched the rims, and drained them. No sooner had they set them down than the waiter came and refilled them. Sémiramis glanced at her watch.

"You can go home, Francis, it's after midnight. I'll turn off the lights. Just leave the champagne here."

The man brought over the bottle and the ice bucket, bowed to his boss and her guest, and then disappeared.

"My first memory of you," said the hostess as soon as they were alone, "was when you offered to take me home after some evening out. Do you remember?"

"Like it was yesterday."

That evening, a group of them had had dinner in a little student restaurant near the law faculty, appropriately named Le Code Civil. After the meal, Sémiramis had asked if anyone could take her home. Adam had volunteered instantly. They had stepped out into the street. Then they had walked and walked.

"The first five minutes, I assumed we were heading to your car and I was just wondering why you'd parked so far away. It took a while before I realized you intended to walk me home."

"I had been staring at you all through the meal, I was completely captivated. And when you asked if someone would take you home, I didn't think for a second, I instantly volunteered; like those children who when they hear the words 'Who wants ...?' immediately scream 'Me!' before they even know what is on offer. In my case, I knew, and I was afraid someone would get in before me."

"At first, I was livid. Mourad had his car with him, Tania had hers, and there were probably others. They could have run me home in five minutes. It was late, my parents were expecting me, and because of you I was going to get a telling-off. But, gradually, I started to enjoy the walk. The weather was pleasantly cool, I was seeing the city in a new light, and I found your conversation amusing. Later, I found out that you didn't talk much, but that night you couldn't stop. You must have been nervous ..."

"I was mortified! I remember the feeling as though it were yesterday. When we left the restaurant, I realized that there had been a misunderstanding. You obviously assumed that I was driving you home in my car, but I didn't have one, not then. What could I do? Apologize, then run after the others to try and catch someone with wheels? I would have felt humiliated. So, I pretended that my plan had always been to walk you home."

"In Paris, it would have seemed natural, I suppose. But here, it was so weird. No one went anywhere on foot …"

"Especially at night! There were hardly any footpaths, and even long before there were armed militiamen, and roadblocks and booby-trapped cars, there were potholes in the roads bad enough to break your leg."

"I was convinced that when we reached my parents' building, in the dimly lit corner next to the stairs, you would say goodnight and you'd kiss me."

"That's exactly what I wanted to do! But I didn't have the guts. In my head there was a miserable little voice whispering: 'Don't spoil this beautiful moment by doing something inappropriate. This girl trusts you, don't take advantage. Behave like a gentleman!' All the precepts of my so-called 'good breeding' conspired to leave me paralyzed. But there was a moment when I decided to defy them. There was a gaping hole in the road and I took your hand to guide you around it. Then I 'forgot' to let go. We walked a little way hand in hand, and you were the one who let go."

"Now that, I don't remember at all!"

"I still remember it because I went over and over it in my mind. When you let go of my hand, I concluded you were trying to tell me not to go too far, too fast. You'd done it gently, tactfully, without offending me, but to me, it was a message."

"If that's what you thought, you were wrong. I don't remember all these details, but I do remember one thing: I wasn't trying to put you off. Quite the opposite; I wanted you to kiss me in the doorway, I was convinced you were going to, and I was disappointed when you didn't. That, I've never forgotten."

"Even now, I feel a twinge of regret. Can you imagine? How many years later?"

"Let's not count. And it's not just the years, but the lives, the consecutive lives …"

What the two friends did not say, though the thought had occurred to both of them, was that the opportunity to kiss had never again presented itself. Since this had occurred early in their first year at university, when they were taking the same courses and belonged to the same circle of friends, Adam should have had dozens of opportunities to walk Sémiramis home and to say goodnight on the very spot where he had failed to kiss her the first time. But that first time had been the last.

When, a few days later, the group had met up again, Sémiramis had arrived with one of their friends. Their every gesture proclaimed that they were "together." Adam could not tear his eyes away from their entwined hands. To save himself heartache, he decided right then to convince himself that she had been with this "other guy" for some time and that he had therefore been right not to try to kiss her since she could not but have rejected him. But this was not the case. The truth was that the "other guy" had had the courage to take her in his arms, whereas he had not.

Even after so many years, so many "consecutive lives," Adam still felt regret, and he felt shame. It was this which, in part as an apology to his "chatelaine," in part as a consolation for himself, led him to say:

"I've always been cripplingly shy. And although it's something I've managed to hide with age and with years of training, it's something I've never managed to get rid of. I rarely speak at historical conferences, for example. Oh, I put myself forward without much conviction, and then feel stupidly relieved when they forget to call on me. Put me in the company of a chatterbox and I can spend hours without opening my mouth. When I was young, it was even worse. I was constantly paralyzed by the fear of being humiliated, of losing face. I tried to convince myself that this lack of confidence was actually an excessive pride: if I didn't ask for anything, it was because I couldn't bear the thought of someone saying no; rather than take a risk, I found it easier not to ask."

"The same way you found it easier not to kiss me," Sémiramis concluded with a sad smile.

"Afraid so," said Adam with the same smile. "And it's something I'll regret to my dying day."

They laughed cheerfully, though without making a sound. Sémiramis divided the dregs of the champagne between their glasses and put the bottle in the ice bucket upside down.

"How about a little walk in the fresh air?" she suggested.

"That sounds reasonable. Then, I'll take you home."

"On foot, like last time?"

"Exactly … like last time," Adam echoed, thrilled to see the years, the decades, swept away.

4

Sémiramis did not live in the hotel that bore her name; at least not in the main building, but a few steps away, in a little house ringed with dense trees.

"These few metres are my protection. Without them, there would be a knock every time there was a reservation, a cancellation, or a leak. In my little house, I can read, as you can see," she said, ushering her guest inside and turning on the lights to reveal walls lined with books.

"It's not as small as all that, your little house."

"There's nothing more than what you can see. This is my library, upstairs is my bedroom, my bathroom, and a veranda."

"Where you sunbathe in summer, wearing only a fig leaf ..."

"When it comes to fantasies, I've gone one better. I had an electric service lift installed. Every morning, someone brings my breakfast and puts it in the dumbwaiter; I simply press a button and the tray appears on the veranda. It's a pleasure I never tire of."

There was a silence. They were still standing on the threshold; Adam's hostess had not suggested that he take a seat. He glanced at his watch and took a step towards the door, which was still ajar.

"If you kiss me goodnight, I promise not to cry for help."

He turned back. Sémiramis was standing with her eyes closed, her arms by her sides, her lips parted in a mischievous smile. He came back and planted a kiss on her right cheek, then her left and, after a moment of hesitation, a third more furtive kiss on her lips. Not a single part of her moved, not her arms, not her eyelids, not a single muscle in her face. Adam took a step back, prepared to leave, but seeing her still standing there motionless, he stepped towards her again, took her in his arms, and drew her gently towards him in a friendly hug. Still, she did not move. He hugged a little harder and she nestled, or allowed herself to be nestled, against him.

And there they stood, fused, body pressed against body, with no words, no apparent passion, each happy simply to inhale the other's warmth and scent. Then Sémiramis pulled away and said innocuously:

"You'll need to make sure that the door is properly closed."

This said, she stooped, slipped off her shoes, picked them up and set off up the stairs to her room without a backward glance.

As he reached the door, Adam felt the same nagging doubt he had "last time." Was he supposed to close the door from within or without? He felt confused and a little ashamed. But also amused to discover that, even at his age, he retained the same scruples, the same doubts he had as an adolescent. Would his friend be surprised to see him appear in her bedroom? Or, on the contrary, would she be disappointed and hurt if he did not appear?

Eventually, he closed the door, fastened the latch, pressed the light switch off, and headed towards the stairs, guided by the glow from above.

When he reached the boudoir of "the beautiful Sémi," he could not stop himself announcing, in a faltering voice, "I didn't leave ..." All he could hear by way of reply was the pounding of the shower.

Three minutes later, his friend reappeared, wrapped in a large white towel.

"Don't count on me to throw you out," she said.

Their eyes met, and each saw in the other a glimmer of expectation.

"Have you got another towel like that?"

"A whole pile of them. I've even left you a little hot water."

When Adam returned from the bathroom, the lights had been turned out, but the room was still bathed in a glow from outside. He unwrapped his towel and tossed it onto the shadowy form of a chair. Then he quickly slipped under the covers. Sémiramis shivered at the first contact with the cold skin of the "intruder"; but rather than move away, she pulled him to her breast so that he could share her warmth.

For a long time, they lay, pressed together, motionless, as though waiting for their bodies to be warm and dry, to become familiar with each other. Then, throwing back the covers, the man propped himself on his left elbow and slowly ran the palm of his right hand over the skin of the woman. First her shoulders, then her brow, her shoulders once again, then her hips, then her breasts, gently, patiently, painstakingly, as though carrying out a topographical survey.

As he applied himself to the task, he whispered in a low voice:

"Take the time to discover the landscape of your body. The hills, the plains, the thickets, the gorges …"

Sémiramis did not move. Eyes closed, she seemed to be focusing her full attention, her every sense, on her friend's hand as it discovered her body, redrew it, paid homage to it.

Then Adam leaned over her and pressed his lips to the places his hands had just smoothed. Brow, shoulders, breasts, but also cheeks, lips, eyelids, with no insistence, no pressures, nothing that might give the impression that this was an erotic prelude. As though, once again, he was conducting a survey. Carefully, seriously, reverently, his breath accompanied by whispered words that his friend did not quite hear, yet understood.

Then it was she who sat up and he lay motionless. She precisely repeated his every gesture, as though her skin had memorized them. First with her palm, then with her lips.

After this, she twined her limbs around him, rolling him from side to side, finding herself above him, beneath him, until she lost all sense of space. The bed, now stripped of its covers and its pillows, was a bare, white expanse on which their bodies turned in every sense, like the hands of a clock out of time.

Neither of them wanted a fleeting encounter, quickly consummated, quickly concluded. On the contrary, they wanted their night of passion to draw out, to last, to avenge themselves on time past, as though the future was but an illusion, as though the two of them had just one night, just one, this night. It was up to them to see to it that the sun rose as late as possible. Up to them to find the perfect balance between ardour and endurance.

In the middle of the night, as he caressed his lover's brow, her shoulders, the man could not help saying:

"When I kissed you, downstairs, you didn't even put your arms around me. You were so stiff, so rigid, that I wondered if it might not be better if I left."

"That's exactly what I wanted."

"You wanted me to leave?"

"No, stupid!" Sémiramis said. "But I wanted you to wonder, and I wanted you to make the decision."

"At the risk of me leaving?"

"Yes, at the risk of you leaving. I would have hated you if you'd left, and I would have been angry with myself. But I had already gone too far ..."

"Too far?"

"I had brought you to my house, in the middle of the night. I had told you that I wouldn't cry for help. I was not about to take you by the hand and drag you to my bed. The ball was in your court; it was for you to decide whether you wanted to take me in your arms, to kiss me, to climb the few steps to my room. Or whether you wanted to run away, like last time."

"Like last time," he echoed, smiling, attempting to mimic his lover's voice.

And they found themselves twined about each other again, animated by a new surge of passion.

By the time they finally dozed off, contented, exhausted, the sky was already beginning to brighten.

The night had been theirs and theirs alone, until the dawn.

The Fifth Day

1

By the time the lovers awoke, the encircling trees were already filled with a chirruping symphony of birdsong. From farther off, they could also hear the blare of car horns and the clink of cutlery from the hotel.

"The tray is probably in the service lift. Shall we have coffee, or shall we go back to sleep?"

"Coffee," muttered the man, who did not yet seem able to string together a whole sentence.

A few minutes later, he was sitting out on the veranda, wrapped in a bath towel. Wide awake and already hungry. Sémiramis had slipped on a light dress. The light was glaring and Adam had to borrow a pair of sunglasses.

"Paris is a magnificent city ..." his friend said suddenly, for no apparent reason.

He turned to her, intrigued. She continued her thought:

"... but not one where you can have your breakfast on a veranda."

Adam nodded. She went on:

"And you never get this vivid sunshine."

He nodded again. But the very mention of his adoptive city sparked in him a twinge of remorse.

"Last night, I was a coward and turned off my phone. Dolores was probably trying to call me."

A silence. Then he added, as though to himself:

"And if she couldn't get me, she probably called reception."

"No, I don't think so," Sémiramis said, taking a sip of her café au lait.

"Really? So the receptionist provides you with an itemized report of guests' communications?"

"Absolutely not, guests are free to do as they please. As

for Dolores, I know she wasn't planning to call you last night."

"And how, precisely, do you know that, my dear Miss Marple?"

"It's not a deduction, she told me herself when I phoned her yesterday."

"When you called her," Adam repeated, without the slightest hint of a question in his words.

"I called yesterday to ask if we could sleep together."

"Yeah, sure."

The man tried to force a laugh, but all that came was a snicker.

"Are you always so witty when you've just got out of bed?" Adam said, "I admire you. Personally, my sense of humour doesn't wake up until a couple of hours after I do."

"When it does wake up, let me know and I'll tell you everything ..."

"Tell me what?"

"About my conversation with Dolores."

He set down his coffee cup and studied Sémiramis's face. Her smile was impossible to interpret. He had no choice but to explicitly ask her whether she had genuinely telephoned Dolores. She nodded.

"We became friends, as you know, that time I came to dinner at your apartment. Since then, we phone each other occasionally. I'm very fond of her. I didn't want there to be any secrets between us."

He looked at her sceptically, expecting that she would burst out laughing. But, after a moment, she continued, her voice suddenly grave.

"I thought that, if I did have an affair with you, sooner or later you'd tell her, she'd end up hating me, and you'd never speak to me again. I had no desire to lose two dear friends for the sake of a night of love. So, I phoned her."

By now, the lover's face was ashen, he was breathing heavily and finding it difficult to swallow. Meanwhile, Sémiramis carried on in the same tone of voice, without turning to face him.

"Dolores already knew the story of our nocturnal stroll back when we were students. I said to her, 'I hoped Adam would kiss me that night, but he didn't. When I saw him again, I knew I wanted him to walk me home again, and this time summon up the courage to kiss me.' She laughed, and said, 'You and Adam are under the same roof and I'm five thousand kilometres away, you can do whatever you like, I can't stop you.' I said, 'That's only how things appear. This is how it feels to me: I'm in your house, standing in front of your wardrobe, and I see an outfit that I really like. Either I steal it, like a common thief, or I call and ask if you wouldn't mind lending it to me.' Dolores was silent for a minute. Then she said, 'So, how is he, my *outfit*?' I said, 'He's in good form. Though, obviously, he doesn't know I'm calling, or what I'm plotting; if you tell me to drop it, he'll never know anything about it.' Again, there was a nervous laugh and then a silence on the other end of the line. So I said, 'Let's just forget it, Dolores. It was just a passing whim. Since he's been here, I've been mollycoddling him, without you he seems lost, like a hatchling fallen from the nest that will die of starvation unless someone feeds it. It awakened a maternal feeling in me, and some old desires ... But, it's too complicated, so let's just let it drop, okay?' There was another silence, then Dolores said, 'If I do lend you my outfit, will you give it back?' I said, 'On my father's grave, I swear I'll return it in the same condition I found it.' There you go, Adam, now you know everything!"

When she had finished, Sémiramis looked at her friend

out of the corner of her eye. Would he be scandalized, amused, incredulous? Before he could utter a single word, she realized that, mostly, he was angry.

"And all this went on behind my back, as though it had nothing to do with me? You don't think you should have asked my opinion before telephoning my partner?"

"Absolutely not! If Dolores had said no, I wouldn't even have suggested showing you the house. After dinner, I'd have kissed you on both cheeks, like I did the night before, and left you to go back to your room."

"Bravo! You and she get to decide what's to be done with me, and I don't get any say."

"Not true, of course you have a say. It's not as though I forced your hand. I offered myself discreetly and then left you at the door, *literally* leaving you an honourable way out; I wanted you to be free to go, right up to the last minute. But you chose to stay with me ..."

This was unarguable. Adam laid a conciliatory hand on his friend's knee.

"That much is true. I freely decided to go up to your room, I accept that, and, if I hadn't, I would always have regretted it. But I find this conspiracy between you unsettling. 'Lend him to me and I'll give him back.' As though I'm a toy or, as you put it, an outfit."

"I just wanted to be honest. With Dolores and with you. Do you think it would have been honest for me to take advantage of the fact that her husband is staying under my roof to fulfil a desire I had back when I was a teenager? Do you think I would ever have been able to speak to her again, to hug her like a sister, if I'd allowed lies and duplicity to come between us? And what about you, would it have been honest to welcome you into my bed and then leave you to deal with the guilt on your own? Leave you to carry the burden of the night we spent together as though it were some original sin? To bring years of suspicion and deception between you and your partner? No, I'm not like that. I am a lover with the heart of a friend, it's important to me that that brief moment of intense pleasure we shared should be a flickering flame in our lives, rather than a shadow. And I expect you to appreciate that."

Adam remained silent; his hand still lay on Sémiramis's knee as though he had forgotten it. A puzzled smile played on his lips. His lover carried on:

"That said, if you're not convinced by my arguments, you can tell Dolores that I made a pass at you and you valiantly rebuffed me. I won't contradict you."

He turned to her, seeming to weigh the pros and cons, before concluding:

"I don't think she would believe me."

"No, she wouldn't believe you. In fact, if she did believe you, I'd be very annoyed."

A moment of silence passed between them. But it was not the same silence. Sémiramis was cool and mischievous; while Adam's silence seemed onerous and confused.

"Whatever you decide," she said to him, "don't feel obliged to phone Dolores right now to tell her about your night of passion. It would be in very poor taste, no sane person wants to hear something like that. What I did, I did not so you would have to say something, but so that you *wouldn't* have to say anything. She knows, you know she knows, and she knows you know she knows ... There's no need to explain, to justify, or anything else. Especially not on the phone. Later, in a few weeks, a few months, the two of you might feel the need to talk about it, in the middle of the night, with all the lights off. And each of you can tell the other why you chose to say yes to me ... I can tell you right now that the longer, more difficult explanation will be Dolores's. You, on the other hand, have the perfect excuse: me."

As she said these last words, she closed her eyes and let her dressing gown fall open. Then she proffered her lips to Adam so that he could plant the kiss that would herald their reconciliation and their belated complicity.

2

Once he was back in his room, Adam was nonetheless tempted to call his partner. Not to talk to her about the previous night, which would indeed have been in horrendously bad taste, but because he was in the habit of phoning her every morning and he had no reason not to do so that morning.

He dialled the number, not without a certain apprehension.

"You're already at the office?"

"I've just got here, I haven't even had time to sit down."

"So, you're not in a meeting ..."

"Not yet, we've got time for a chat. Just give me twenty seconds to put my things down."

She set down the phone for a moment, then picked it up again.

"Right, I'm all yours. Sémi says you've been getting a lot of work done. Maybe even a bit too much."

"It's true, I have been getting a lot done."

"On the biography?"

"No, I've put Attila to one side, I'm working on something else."

"If you're constantly working on something else, you'll never finish that biography."

"Being steeped in the atmosphere of this country again, I had other desires, you can understand that ..."

"Yes, I heard a little something to that effect ..."

She laughed, and Adam was angry with himself for using such an ambiguous phrase. He quickly explained:

"After Mourad's death, I felt a need to tell the story of my friends, of my youth, of what time has made of us."

"I understand, it's normal to feel a sense of nostalgia at

times like this. But I feel like you're losing yourself ... I know you, Adam. You'll fill hundreds of pages with stories of your friends, but it will all end up mouldering in a drawer ... Don't get me wrong, I'm not telling you not to do it. It's cathartic, and it's good for your mental health, because the death of your 'former friend' has affected you more than you care to admit. But don't kid yourself, you'll never publish it. If only because of your contemporaries ..."

"My contemporaries?"

Adam's surprise was insincere. What Dolores was saying was entirely true. He had a reputation to maintain within the community of historians, one that had taken decades to forge. He was admired for the rigour of his reasoning, his painstaking review of sources, his objective tone, his constant determination to produce something irrefutable, by even the most disputatious of his peers ... How could he reconcile the qualities that had made him a respected historian with his desire to relate the existential problems of a group of students? How would his venerable colleagues react? He could already hear them laughing ...

"You're suggesting that I give up, and go back to working on good old Attila?"

"No, that's not what I'm suggesting, honestly. Given where you are, and given the circumstances, you could hardly carry on working on a biography of a fifth-century conqueror as though nothing had happened. Write what you feel you need to write, do it honestly, think of it as a private memoir. Just remember that it's an interlude, and as soon as you're back in Paris go back to working on 'Atilla,' finish it, publish it, then you can move on to something else. In other words, allow yourself to stray a little, but not too much, and never lose sight of what is important ..."

Adam was about to say that he entirely agreed, but his partner did not give him time.

"Someone's just knocked on the office door," she said in a whisper. "They're here for the meeting."

She immediately hung up. He glanced at his watch, it was 11:30 a.m. precisely, half past nine in Paris. The time at which his partner met with her colleagues every morning.

Having been hired by a European publishing conglomerate to edit a monthly popular science magazine, Dolores had taken the risk of making it a weekly. She had had a compelling case for her decision, and her bosses had supported her and given her substantial funds. But it was clear, as much to her as to them that, if the project failed to deliver, she would bear the responsibility. Since then, she had spent most of her time working on the magazine, and even when she was not, she was constantly thinking about it and talking about it with Adam. Not that this bothered him, quite the contrary; in fact, he enjoyed playing the role of her Candide, a friendly advisor with no ulterior motive, unconnected to the magazine and the world of science.

After their telephone conversation, Adam opened his notebook and, pencil in hand, thought about the curious situation in which he had put himself.

TUESDAY, APRIL 24

I still feel worried, even though Dolores was astonishing, a perfect model of good grace and tact.

Not a word about what happened last night, and yet not a word that didn't touch on it somehow. I don't know whether each insinuation was carefully rehearsed; and maybe I saw allusions where there were none. But the message is clear: the interlude is acceptable as long as it remains an interlude.

As a code of conduct, it suits me, and I should find the fact that Dolores made it explicit reassuring. But my fears come from elsewhere—from that mundane, tyrannical notion that makes me believe I have committed a sin, one that must, inevitably, be atoned for, for reasons connected both to human nature and the laws of heaven.

My generation, the women and men who turned twenty during the 1970s, made the liberation of the body its central concern—In America, in France, and in many other countries, including mine. In hindsight, I am convinced that we were absolutely right. It is by controlling our bodies that moral tyrannies succeed in controlling our minds. It is not the only weapon they use in order to control and dominate, but, throughout the course of history, it has proved to be one of the most effective. For this reason, the freeing of the body remains, overall, a liberating act. On condition that one does not use it to justify every vulgar kind of behaviour.

What I have just experienced with Sémi has meaning, because it represents a belated revolt against my crippling teenage shyness. Therefore, our intimacy was legitimate. But it will quickly come to seem pathetic if, rather than recognizing it as a nod to our adolescence, my lover and I start treating it as a banal affair, a fumble between the sheets.

An interlude, then, my night with Sémi? Probably. She does not see things any differently. There, the word Dolores used is neither offensive nor shameful.

An interlude, too, all the things I feel the need to relate about my youth, my friends? Yes, that is probably the appropriate word. Nevertheless, it is an interlude I do not intend to bring to a close just yet. Even if the pages dedicated to the memory of my scattered friends are destined to end up in a musty drawer, to be forgotten, they still mean something to me. My life, and that of the people I have known, may not seem like much compared to that of a famous conqueror. But it is my life, and if I truly believe it deserves only to be forgotten, then I did not deserve to live.

3

When Sémi came and "kidnapped" me last night, I was in the middle of recounting the kidnapping of Albert and the fears of those attempting to get him released.

Had his abduction and his captivity been a salutary shock to our friend? Had they restored his will to live? There was no way of knowing.

"Might it not be more sensible to leave him there a little longer," Mourad wondered on the phone. "To be honest, as long as he's not being mistreated, I'm in no hurry to see him released."

I completely understood his fears. It was something that had occurred to me the moment I first heard that Albert was being held as a hostage. Was it possible that releasing him might mean delivering him to death, just as those who had abducted him had saved him? The irony of the situation was laughable, but for us, the fear was real.

While we talked, a solution began to form in my mind, one I immediately suggested to Mourad.

"If you manage to get him released, whatever you do, don't take him back home. Take him to your place in the mountains for two or three days. Then send him here to me, in Paris. After that, I'll deal with things. Do you think he'll agree?"

"He has to agree! It's the only rational solution. If he refuses, I'll kidnap him myself, I'll tie him up and ship him to you."

"Okay, I'll sign for the delivery."

I seem to remember that our conversation ended in a gale of laughter that was hardly appropriate to the tragic nature of the situation.

If Adam's notes and Tania's recollections are to be believed, this is broadly how things eventually played out. But not without a few last-minute hitches.

When he was released by his unfortunate kidnapper, Albert was left on the outskirts of his neighbourhood; Mourad and his wife, who were waiting a few minutes away, picked him up to drive him directly to their house in the village. The survivor seemed calm, as though he had never contemplated suicide, had never been held hostage. He was taciturn, but cheerful.

In the days that followed, Mourad arranged a passport from the Sûreté Générale and a visa from the French consulate, then bought Albert a one-way ticket to Paris.

Even so, there were some worrying moments. The first came on the day after his release, when the former hostage insisted on being taken back to his apartment. His friends feared that he still intended to take his life, but they could hardly say no. Mourad gave him the new keys, since the locks had had to be changed after he forced the door. Tania drove him into the city and suggested that she go upstairs with him; he firmly replied that he wanted to go up alone and she did not insist; the idea of climbing six flights of stairs was not exactly appealing, and besides, she thought, if Albert was intent on taking his own life, they could not stop him indefinitely. So she waited outside the building for three-quarters of an hour, counting the minutes and imagining the worst. But in the end, he reappeared, looking gloomy and carrying a small suitcase.

The other moment of panic occurred on the day the former hostage was due to catch his plane. Adam recounts it in his notebook.

Albert announced that, before going to the airport, he wanted to go and visit his kidnapper to say goodbye. He had promised the man, and there was no question of him reneging on his promise. Unable to dissuade him, Mourad and Tania decided to go with him.

The mechanic's house was at the far end of a cul-de-sac; the only access was via a dirt road that the previous night's rain had turned into a quagmire. The walls were the colour of concrete, as though no one had ever considered painting them. The little yard was piled with old tires.

"The man and his wife were waiting for us. They are decent people whose whole lives revolve around the garage. And, of course, around their only son, whose face is everywhere, in framed photographs, and in the missing-person posters they had printed when there was still hope. Their living room is like a shrine to the memory of the child they lost.

"Tania and I offered our condolences. Their response was polite, dignified, as befits people in mourning. Then the father, his lips quivering, whispered: 'None of this is your fault!' And, when Albert stepped forward ... You should have seen it! The man took one arm, his wife the other, and the two of them hugged him. 'You take care of yourself!' 'Promise us you won't do anything foolish.' 'Life is precious.' They started to sob. Albert burst into tears. So did Tania and I.

"When we got up to go, they started again. 'Come back and see us soon' and 'Take care of yourself.' Albert promised that he would; he swore. He was more upset than anyone—he was still crying as I drove him to the airport."

"But he did catch the plane?"

"Yes, he caught the plane, thank God. Tania and I have been waiting here at the airport for the flight to take off. Then we phoned you. It lands in Paris at about half past three."

"Perfect. I'll have a quick lunch and then go and meet him."

On the Levantine end of the line, I remember hearing a long sigh.

"We're pretty relieved to be palming him off on you. Good luck."

Remembering Mourad's words, his voice, his laugh, his determination to save Albert, the extent of our complicity, I cannot *help but think that, at this very moment, he is lying in a coffin waiting to be put in the ground. Writing down our conversation suddenly seems to me like a homage to the friend I lost.*

Would this discreet homage, made in the privacy of these pages, assuage my guilt or, on the contrary, exacerbate it to the point where I might reconsider my decision about his funeral?

No, I feel no desire to go to it. If there is to be a posthumous reconciliation between the two of us, it will not take place in public, with a microphone in front of me, but in quiet contemplation, amid the whispering of souls.

4

Having reaffirmed his decision not to attend his former friend's funeral the following day, Adam immediately picked up the thread of his story.

The "package" arrived in perfect condition. I vainly scanned his eyes and his words for the stigmata left by the kidnapping and the suicide attempt. Nothing. Albert was completely back to his old self. Or at least that is my memory of the time he spent in Paris in February 1980.

At the beginning, at the very beginning, in the first hours, I was ill at ease. I had moved him into the guest room in my apartment, I watched him constantly out of the corner of my eye and I refrained from mentioning certain things. Then, little by little, I relaxed until I was joking about everything, starting with the irony of his being kidnapped just at the moment when he was about to kill himself. From time to time, Patricia, my partner at the time, would reproach me: "Be careful, he's fragile, don't be fooled by his apparent good humour." I didn't agree with her; I felt instinctively that the best approach was to go easy on him, not to treat him like a survivor, or even like a convalescent, but like the quick-witted friend he had always been, able to laugh at anything, including his own misfortunes. I was not wrong. Two days after his arrival, I knew that the battle was won.

It was a Saturday. Both of us had woken up very early, at about 5:00 a.m., and so as not to wake my partner, we had holed up in the kitchen at the other end of the apartment. I had started making coffee, but my guest had other things in mind.

"Come on, get dressed, let's go out," he said. "For years I've been dreaming about having breakfast in a bistro in Paris. Now is my chance, let's go, my treat. And besides, there's some stuff I want to tell you."

Outside, it was cold, rainy, and still almost pitch dark. But we were so happy to be wandering around Paris together.

A brasserie caught our eye, and we took a table among the market traders and ordered a banquet—hot chocolate, pastries, jams, cheese, eggs, juice, fruit, cereal, even pancakes with maple syrup ...

"I've got a declaration to make," Albert said, "a declaration in five points ..."

His tone was solemn, almost official, though this was tempered by his sardonic smile and the half-eaten croissant in his hand.

"Firstly, what I tried to do a few weeks ago is something I will never do again, a page has been turned. I wouldn't go so far as to say that there's anything I regret. Let's just say that I don't regret the fact that things turned out the way they did. Or coming through it unscathed."

I nod several times without interrupting him. A shadow flickers across his face.

"Secondly: I am never going back. On reflection—and you might think this is stupid, but you shouldn't feel obliged to tell me—on reflection, it wasn't life that was weighing me down, I think I was just looking for a way out, I couldn't carry on living in that country, and I couldn't bring myself to leave it. I couldn't find the strength to get myself out of my apartment. I'd come to the point where I thought the best thing would be to fall asleep one last time surrounded by my furniture, my books and my music boxes and never wake up, or to wake up ... elsewhere. Fate decided otherwise, I acknowledge it, I bow before it."

There was a quiver in his voice, which he quickly hid with a cough before continuing:

"As long as I was back there, I felt incapable of leaving. Now that I'm far away, I feel completely incapable of going back. I'm like a survivor of a shipwreck. I couldn't jump when the ship started taking in water, but now that I have, it would never

occur to me to go back aboard. To me, that is another page that has been definitively turned. And not just for me, either... I don't have to tell you that the Levant we knew is lost, irredeemably."

He was right, I was hardly in a position to argue, having left my homeland before he did. But what Albert had said was too brutal, too definitive; I felt obliged to express some vague objection, while taking care not to hijack the conversation so that my friend could carry on.

"Thirdly: I'm not going to stay in France, either. I'm leaving for America. I love Paris, and I feel happy here. Thanks to the years I spent with the Jesuit fathers, nothing in France is entirely alien to me. Or to you, I imagine ... But, for what I plan to do, I need to be there, in America. I'm just hesitating between New York and California. I'll decide when I get there ..."

A silence came over him, like an internal deliberation, one that I eventually broke.

"And fourthly?"

"Fourthly, I think that, now, for the first time since I was born, I know what I want to do with my life. It's taken ... all of this."

I wait. He says nothing more. So I ask, the way we used to when we were teenagers:

"So, what is it? What do you want to do with your life?"

"I'm not going to tell you now. You'll find out when I've done it."

I thought about pressing him, but I didn't; I didn't want Albert to promise me he was going to do extraordinary things only to later feel that he was not equal to the situation. Better to let him get back on his feet calmly, with no pressure, in his own time.

Adam closed his notebook and checked his watch. Seven o'clock already, give or take a minute. He decided to call Sémiramis. She had told him she would be spending the day in the city and would call when she got back, but he wanted to call her first.

When she answered her mobile phone, he asked whether she was home yet.

"Not yet. I'm on my way. But we can talk, I'm not the one driving. Good day's work?"

"Not as good as the previous days, I was less focused ..."

"That's my fault, I led you astray."

This was probably true, but it would have been unseemly for him to say so.

"No, not at all," he protested.

But, as though he had not spoken, she added:

"You were working so well and I had to go and disturb you. You must really resent me ..."

"Oh, I do!"

He laughed and gave his lover a moment to laugh before adding:

"We shared a wonderful moment, one that we'll never forget. That's all that matters."

"Despite the regrets."

"Yes, despite the regrets."

"So, shall we have dinner together again tonight?"

"Again tonight."

"And afterwards, we go our separate ways?"

"No. Afterwards, we don't go our separate ways."

"We're having a second meeting?"

She had obviously used the word because she was not alone in the car and could not say "a second night together." Adam had no need to take similar precautions since he was alone in his room, with no one to overhear, but he decided to use the same coded language.

"No, not a second meeting, we are simply reconvening. The initial meeting was never concluded, as far as I'm aware ..."

The Sixth Day

1

In the morning, the two lovers met, as they had the previous day, on the veranda.

Adam had been the first to get up, but had waited for Sémiramis to join him so that she could press the button that brought the breakfast tray up from the ground floor.

"Today is Mourad's funeral," she remarked, preparing to nag him again about shunning the ceremony. But from the look on his face, she realized it would serve no purpose. Instead, she simply asked whether he had already written to their old friends to tell them the sad news.

"That's what I was planning to do today. While you're at the funeral, I'll write an announcement to send to our mutual acquaintances, and individual letters to two or three close friends in which I'll mention the reunion Tania would like to hold."

His lover gently laid her hand on his.

"That's good. That way you'll be participating in the funeral, from a distance."

A silence.

"And do you know who you're going to start with?"

Adam closed his eyes and nodded slightly, and in doing so, readopted the body language of the Levant, after so many years absence.

"Yes, I know."

Sémiramis was clearly waiting for him to give her a name, but he gave her only an enigmatic smile. She raised her coffee cup in a toast, as though it was already evening and they were once again drinking champagne.

"To friends in far-flung places!"

"To the survivors."

It was not a felicitous expression. His friend's eyes

misted over. She quickly recovered her composure, raised her cup again, and, with a mixture of effrontery and tenderness, said:

"To those who left!"

Back in his room, Adam threw open the window overlooking the valley. He took a long moment to breathe in the pine-scented air of the forest before sitting at his table and opening his laptop to begin the first letter.

My dearest Albert,
I am sorry to say that this email brings bad news. It's about Mourad. He died last Saturday, 'following a long illness' as people say. He was only forty-nine. His funeral takes place today.

On the last few occasions we spoke about him, we said little that was good. His death is not likely to change our opinion, I suppose; but it compels us to change our attitude.

Tania would love to hear from you. She would also like his old friends to meet up sometime soon in his memory. I feel that a ceremony with speeches in honour of the deceased would be inappropriate and embarrassing; on the other hand, I like the idea of a reunion of our old gang of friends. Think about it. We'll discuss it later ...
Warm wishes,
Adam

Having sent the email, Adam went through his electronic address book and found a number of people with whom he had been in touch in recent years, the "mutual acquaintances" he had mentioned to Sémiramis. All of them were "in emigration," to use the laconic phrase used by those who had remained in the country.

It took him some time to compose the death notice he intended to send them. He tried to find the right tone, midway between intimate whisper and official announcement. Eventually, out of sheer exhaustion, and out of laziness, he simply copied and pasted the first paragraph of his email to Albert, and the first sentence of the third paragraph—*Tania would love to hear from you*—before concluding, *I hope our next correspondence will be in less unhappy circumstances."*

He looked at his watch, it was precisely eleven o'clock, the time set for the funeral. He observed a few seconds of meditative silence; then, to avoid allowing his guilty conscience free reign, he returned to his emails to discover, to his great surprise, that Albert had already responded. Despite the fact that, in Indiana, it must be three o'clock in the morning or something of the sort.

My Dearest Adam,
Having got up because I suffer from insomnia, I just stumbled upon your email.

I am saddened by the news, and later today I will write a letter to Tania for whom I have only ever felt affection and friendship; as for Mourad, although I share your opinion on his public actions, I will never forget what he did for me during my ordeal. If he had not been able to show consideration and tact, I would not have come through it alive. If only for this reason, I think it appropriate that I pay my last respects—in thought, naturally—before his coffin. Besides, in my heart, I do not hate him; I simply regret the moral drift which, in the end, cost him much more than it did you or me.

As for the idea of reuniting the old gang, I think it is wonderful. The circumstances and the pretext don't really matter. In fact, I can't help but wonder why we never thought of doing it before … Even as I wrote those words, the answer leapt out at me. It was because of Mourad. A reunion with him had become unthinkable, a reunion without him made no sense. Following this line of reasoning, I realize that his death is the perfect pretext for us all to meet up again. Don't worry, I am not going to say that to Tania. If she needs to believe that it is Mourad's memory bringing us together, we should leave her with her illusions and her consolation.

So, yes, as far as the reunion goes, I'm in. But it can't take place in the "old country." As an American citizen, I am not supposed to travel there, as you know. Furthermore, given that my institute has ties to the Pentagon, a personal visit is not merely inadvisable, it is strictly forbidden. Sorry! If you want me to be there, the reunion will have to take place elsewhere. I think Paris would be the best place, but I'm open to other suggestions.

In terms of dates, on the other hand, I'm pretty flexible. I'm happy to fit in with whatever you decide as long as you give me a couple of weeks' advance notice.

Do it soon, I'm eager to see our friends of long ago. I've had no contact with most of them for donkey's years …

Yours faithfully,

A

Adam replied immediately, a single succinct paragraph:

Thanks for getting back to me so quickly, Albert. I understand your reservations. And since there can be no question of us meeting up without you, let's make it Paris. It suits me fine, as you can imagine. I'll talk to the others and suggest a few different dates … Regards, A

He clicked *Send*, closed his laptop, and opened his notebook at the page where he had left off the night before.

I've always known that the institute where Albert works is an important think tank linked for decades to the American military, though, until just now, he never said as much explicitly.

From someone as apolitical as he was, it is undeniably paradoxical, not to say peculiar. He ended up there by a roundabout route, but it was a logical one.

When he told me, over that gluttonous breakfast in Paris twenty years ago, that he finally knew what he planned to do with his life, he had just discovered the existence of a new field of study, one he had always dreamed about: futurology. No, not fortune telling or astrology or chiromancy, things that never interested him, nor even science fiction, which he enjoyed as a reader and even considered one day contributing to as a writer; but a recognized discipline, entrusted to "researchers who have their head in the stars and their feet firmly on the ground," as he himself described it to me.

During the early period of his time in the United States, I rarely heard from him. He sent me a letter when he arrived; I called him once on the New York number he had given; after that, silence. I carried on with my life, while he began to fashion his.

It was not until '87 that I found out what had become of him. I was reading an article about "the future of oil" in a respected magazine of international politics when I noticed, in a footnote, a complimentary reference to the "innovative work of Albert N. Kithar on the idea of the 'blind spot.'" Fortunately, the footnotes mentioned the name of the Indiana-based institute that had published his research. I quickly sent a letter to my friend care of the institute, not knowing whether it would reach him. But he must have received it quite quickly, since his reply reached me just two weeks later.

My dearest Adam,
You can't imagine my impatience as I tore open your letter, and my excitement when I discovered you had heard something about my research.

Don't get your hopes up. I didn't invent a new theory and I

haven't become a celebrity. The notion of the "blind spot" is simply a thinking tool, what in our jargon I call a "digging tool." It is no more than that, and it's not rocket science, as you'll see.

The idea first occurred to me back when we were at school. In class, we were discussing the "Declaration of the Rights of Man and of the Citizen" published during the French Revolution. Someone asked whether it included women and, if so, how come women didn't get the right to vote in France until after the Second World War? The teacher explained that, in practice, they were not included in this declaration of equality before the law, but that did not mean that they had been *deliberately* excluded. Such a view of reality, he said, was quite simply inconceivable, "invisible," to men of that era.

I found this idea intriguing, and when I became more interested in the forecasting models used in futurology, I realized it was crucial to constantly remind yourself that, in every era, there are certain things that people are unable to see. Including, of course, our own era. We can see things that our ancestors could not; but there are things they could see that we cannot anymore; and, more importantly, there are countless things that our descendants will be able to see that we cannot yet see, given that we, too, have blind spots.

To take just one example out of hundreds: pollution. Since the beginning of the industrial revolution, we were completely incapable of seeing that locating factories close to urban conurbations might pose a serious health risk; we had other concerns, other priorities. It is only in the last forty years that the issue has entered our field of vision. Another example, of the same nature, is the notion that marine resources are not infinite, that they could be exhausted, that it is necessary to conserve them. Just a few years ago such an idea was invisible, except, notably, to a tiny minority of "visionaries" whose voices went unheard by their contemporaries.

I hasten to add that I didn't invent the concept of the blind spot. Historians, psychologists, and sociologists have been talking about it for years. The contribution made by your friend Albert is specific and modest. Four years ago—the institute had not yet moved to Indianapolis—a New York state university asked me to host an introductory seminar on futurology. At the end of term, I set the students a single question, which was to be the subject of their dissertation. I formulated it thus: Every era has it blind spots, ours is no exception. There are aspects of reality that we are incapable of seeing, and it is inevitable that each of us, in a few years, will think: "How can I not have seen that?" So, I am asking that you project yourselves into the future and talk to me about a blind spot that is very difficult for us to see today, but which, in thirty years, will seem self-evident.

The responses from the students were not particularly interesting; one of the ones I remember suggested that future generations would be outraged to discover that, in our time, millions of animals were slaughtered in abattoirs and that most people found this perfectly normal—to my mind, a rather optimistic view of the future of our species ...

The fact remains that my approach appealed to some of the directors of the institute. It even became an obligatory part of interviews when recruiting researchers. "Tell me, Kim, I'm sure that, right under my nose, there is some fundamental point about the future of Asia—or Europe, or oil, or nuclear power—that I simply cannot see. Could you tell me what it is?" It is impossible to respond there and then, you have to rack your brains, to project yourself beyond what we are capable of seeing at first glance. Hence the expression "digging tool" ...

So this is how I've been entertaining myself for the past few years while everyone else thinks I'm working!

What about you, what are you up to? You didn't tell me very much about your life, your work, your plans ... Which means you now have to write me another letter.

Yours faithfully,

Albert

Since then, we've never lost touch. Back in the days of stamped envelopes, we wrote to each other at least once a year, then, with the advent of email, the frequency increased considerably. These days, it's rare for several weeks to pass without us exchanging messages. Sometimes they are brief, an article one of us has read and wants to share with the other. Accompanied by a word—yes, a single word, fascinating, or worrying, or simply regards; and signed with a single letter—A—our common initial.

I have kept a paper record of our correspondence; systematically in the case of the letters I received, less rigorously in the case of letters I sent since I didn't always make a photocopy. Keeping a back-up of emails has been more hit-and-miss. In theory, emails are saved systematically; in practice, every time one of my laptops has given up the ghost, and every time I've had to change my email address, various documents have mysteriously disappeared.

But I don't worry about that. Am I not forced, as a historian of antiquity, to work from fragments and traces? By comparison, I have an abundance of materials at my disposal for reconstructing my own past, both my personal memories and the documents I have preserved. My dilemma is elsewhere—in the mental failing that separates my private world from my public writing, as though the former could not but discredit the latter.

2

Having dutifully copied long extracts from his old friend's email into his notebook, Adam went over and lay down on the bed and once more dipped into the cache of letters from long ago, moving from one envelope to another. Ordinarily, he took great pleasure in reading the letters and was tempted to immerse himself in them and pay no heed to the time. But now a guilty conscience inevitably prevailed. No sooner did he step away from the work he was supposed to be doing than he began to reproach himself.

On this particular day, he tore himself away too quickly, all too quickly, from pleasurable indolence and went back to his computer to begin another letter he had promised he would write on this day of mourning.

My dearest Naïm,

I am writing to relate a piece of sad news: Mourad has just died of cancer. His funeral is today.

I don't know whether you kept in touch with him. Personally, I had not spoken to him for some years, as I already explained to you; but, last Wednesday, he and his wife phoned to tell me he was dying and that he wanted to see me. I flew out that same evening, but he died during the night before we had a chance to talk.

I think that Tania would love to hear from you. She also wants to organize a reunion of his old friends from university. This, in itself, is an excellent idea, regardless of the circumstances. What do you think? Would you have any suggestions as to the location and the date? I would prefer Paris, but am open to any suggestions.

Yours,

Adam

As with Albert, I made contact again with Naïm by happy accident; for several years our exchanges had been sporadic, then, thanks to email, the flow became steadier.

But in this case, it happened somewhat later, only about ten years ago, and in much the same way, except that it was not I who found him, but he who found me.

I had just published an article about Attila in a minor historical magazine that had devoted an issue to the "Barbarian invasions," one I did not expect to be read outside of France. So I was agreeably surprised when the editor of the magazine forwarded a letter bearing a Brazilian stamp. The back of the envelope bore only the initials of the sender, and the first lines gave nothing away.

Dear Professor,

I am writing first and foremost to thank you for what I learned from your article on the character of Attila. We assume that we know historical figures, we have two or three snippets of received wisdom, yet we sometimes allow ourselves to use such figures to illustrate our own opinions. Then, suddenly, we read something that makes us realize we know very little about the Hun and his era. Worse still, we discover that what little we knew was so approximate, so nebulous, that we might just as well consider it fallacious.

I was wondering, Professor, whether you have ever considered writing a biography about this figure? As a reader, I would warmly encourage you to do so. If my humble suggestion should meet with your agreement and you do decide to write such a book, I would be grateful if you could send a signed copy to the following address:

Naïm E., [...], Avenida Ipiranga, São Paulo, Brazil.

NB: No, it's not a namesake.

Obviously, I wanted to throw my arms around him, to tell him how happy I was to have found him again, to ask what he had been up to. But I restrained myself. If I was to respect the ethos of our old circle of friends, I had to reply in the same register he had adopted. Whenever one of us engaged in an elaborate charade, the trick was to remain straight-faced as long as possible, to patiently foster a sense of uncertainty, of ambiguity, and certainly not to burst out laughing at the first exchange. According to the rules, the winner was the last one to laugh.

I therefore formulated my response as follows:

Dear reader,

Your letter touched me deeply. Attila is probably one of the most misunderstood figures in history. And whenever I say at a seminar—in a spirit of provocation, I confess—that he is the grandfather of modern Europe, some of my listeners imagine that, with my being from the Levant, I am trying to insult them.

Curious that you should suggest I might write a biography! I suggested the possibility to a Parisian publisher only a week before I received your letter, and he has agreed. I already have all the necessary documentation, my outline is complete, and I should be able to write the book in a matter of months. I will make it my duty to send you a copy as soon as it is published.

An alternative solution would be to come in person and collect it from the following address:

Adam W., [...] rue du Cherche-Midi, Paris 75006.

NB: If you should visit, even if the book is not yet published, a meal will be provided, followed by Turkish coffee.

In choosing to renew our friendship in this manner, after a gap of sixteen years, we instantly reestablished a complicity we had shared back when we were at university, before the last four or five local wars, before our accursed dispersion.

Later, we rarely wrote letters to each other. When we

exchanged addresses, we also exchanged phone numbers and we would call each other occasionally. The telephone is insidious, and deceptive. It creates a false sense of proximity; it favours immediacy and superficiality; and, what is most damning for a historian like me, it leaves no paper trail.

Happily, over the past three years, Naïm and I have begun emailing. Ever since, as with Albert, we have written to each other regularly.

Once or twice he has asked how my biography of Attila is coming along. I have had to tell him that it is still at the same stage—a work in progress, which means work is at a standstill.

Was it a bad idea from the first? I don't think so. When I wrote the article Naïm referred to, I genuinely felt that I had the book at my fingertips. I felt able to recount the life of Attila from birth to death without even consulting my notes. I knew the names of his wives and the career paths of his counsellors. I shouldn't phrase it in the past tense, I haven't forgotten any of that. But the shift from a short text to a long one proved complicated.

An article requires only a few compelling ideas; a biography requires a writer to be exhaustive, to not lay himself open to criticism by specialists. For example, in an article or at a conference, it sounds impressive when I point out that Attila's principal adversary, the Roman military commander Flavius Aetius, was not a stranger to him but a childhood friend, for the simple reason that the "scourge of God" spent his adolescence not in the steppes of central Asia, but in modern-day Italy, at the imperial court; or when I claim that his reluctance to attack Rome stemmed from the fact that his dream was not to sack the city, but to be crowned Emperor there, just as, four hundred years later, another leader descended from the barbarian invasions would be: Charlemagne. But to write a biography worthy of the name, such claims have to be shored up by documentation, by compelling logic, by contemporaneous sources, which can be difficult to find a millennium and a half after the fact.

That said, I have not given up on the biography, I still plan to write it.

}

Like Albert, Naïm was quick to respond to the message informing him of Mourad's death. Since both lived in the Americas—one in the United States, the other in Brazil—they had received their emails early in the morning, before setting off for work; but it is true that, nowadays, there are few moments when we do not have a desk either in front of us or in our pockets.

Dear Adam,

Your email has plunged me into a sadness that is completely unexpected. I never thought that I would be so affected by the death of a man I have not thought about for many years now. But I suppose it is less about him than about the period his name evokes, which was one of the happiest of my life.

I still remember the last night I spent in the country—all our friends gathered in Mourad's old house, around a brazier, promising never to leave each other when in fact our paths had already parted, and events had already begun to scatter us to the four corners of the earth ...

As I write these words, I can still picture their faces, one by one. [...] And I can still see the dilemma I faced that night: should I tell you that I was leaving the following day, never to return, when I had promised my parents to say nothing about their plans? But I've already told you all this ...

I'll write to Tania today. Thank you for sending me her address. Since I left the country, I haven't been in touch with her, or with Mourad. Although there was never an argument or a falling-out as such. All contact was simply cut off, from one day to the next. People say, "life takes us on different paths." Since I can think of no better explanation, I'll go with that ...

With you, I know, things were different. You once told me that you no longer heard from them and that you did not expect to see them again, so I naturally concluded that you had fallen out. But you didn't say anything more ... Actually, now I think about it, once or twice you did mention Mourad's "machinations," without giving any further explanation. I'd like it if one day you felt you could tell me what happened, and what you hold against him. There's no rush, but I'm curious to know; you used to be inseparable! True, that was—let me count—twenty-seven years ago. God, that's depressing! But, well, we're still alive, still able to remember, still able to feel upset. [...]

Much love,

Naïm

Having read and reread the message, Adam set about replying straight away, with a certain feverishness.

Dear Naïm,

Thank you so much for getting back to me so quickly. What you said about the old house stirs so many memories for me, too. The brazier, the mulled wine, and the terrace—remember the terrace!—where we felt as though we were towering above the whole earth. And so I feel I should immediately address your perfectly legitimate question about Mourad, my attitude towards him, and the reasons for our falling out.

For so long, I've been in the habit of talking about his "machinations," about his "behaviour," about his "unforgivable faults," without taking the time to do what, as a historian, I would have done if I were dealing with a figure from Roman times, that is to say: state my accusations calmly and fairly even if, in my heart, I have already made my decision.

So I will start from the beginning, and I apologize in advance if I repeat things you already know.

For example, as I assume you know, the grand old family house that you and I still talk about with tears in our eyes, has always been the subject of various lawsuits, some dating back as far as the Ottoman Empire. Mourad's great-grandfather, his grandfather, and then his father spent nearly their whole lives in court. I won't go into details, it would be tedious and, besides, I don't have all the information. I will simply say this: over the years, and over several generations, the family acquired large tracts of land, in the village and the surrounding area; more than once they discovered after the fact that the person they had dealing with had no authority to sell and that the land actually belonged to a neighbour, or that the seller was not the sole owner, that he had brothers, sisters, cousins, sometimes many of them, all of whom had a vested interest in any transaction, and some of whom had no intention of selling. Numerous lawsuits followed ...

Of all the lawsuits that our friend inherited, one affected him more than all the others: the one that directly concerned the old mansion. I'll spare you the details and get to the crucial point, to the thing that had been making his life a misery since I first met him: one of the families in the village claimed that a wing of the house—the one where "our" terrace was located—had been built illegally on their land, and they had even succeeded in getting a judicial decision to that effect.

Do you remember the hideous hulking monstrosity on the way in to the village, Naïm? The lime-green wrought iron, the strings of garish lanterns, the boys playing football in the middle of the street who eyed us suspiciously and were slow to get out of the way to let our cars pass? That was them, those were the sworn enemies who coveted the old house.

On paper, they had the same family name as Mourad, but their clan had a nickname, "Znoud"—or "the arms"—a reference to their physical strength, I assume. Our friend liked to call them "one-arm bandits."

In fact, he treated them with profound contempt, which can only have been about class. In the village, everyone was more or less related, but Mourad's branch of the family tree considered themselves superior. I always found it shocking. Even back when our friend claimed he was left-wing and blustered about equality, he had no problem showing his disdain for his poor relations.

Actually, "poor" is probably not the right adjective. Some of the Znouds had made money, but it did not radically alter their status—because they had no contacts in the city; because the parents were not lawyers, or doctors, or engineers, or bankers; because the sons did not go to university; etc. But Mourad would never have accepted that that was the main difference between them. He justified his scorn by the fact that they married off their daughters at sixteen; that, during elections, they sold their votes to the highest bidder; and that they made their living as petty thieves.

Rereading what I've just written, I can't help but smile. Here I am snickering at the bad faith of our friend and his class consciousness, when my own description of these same people is full of prejudiced stereotypes. Since my father was an architect and my mother an interior designer, I express my contempt through aesthetics, sneering at their multicoloured house and their lime-green wrought-iron railing to disguise something that has always made me uncomfortable: the fact that, though I might claim otherwise, I too have a class consciousness. I've always had an aversion to the rich and to the poor. My social homeland is the middle ground. Neither the landowners nor the claimants. I belong to that fringe group who, afflicted neither by the myopia of the well-heeled or the blindness of the starving, can dare to cast a lucid eye on the world.

Perhaps unsettled by his own digression, Adam stopped writing and closed his eyes, so that, in his mind, he could transport himself to Mourad's village, to his funeral, to picture the coffin, the wreaths, the crowd, the cemetery, the pit in the ground, the jostling, the women dressed in black. Then he dismissed these images to call up scenes from a more distant past, on the vast terrace, or in the little drawing room, around the brazier, long ago, in another life, not dead and gone.

This brought him back to his screen, to the email he had been writing:

But let's pass over my shameful confessions and go back to the tale of our friend, and the lawsuits that constantly plagued him.

Personally, I never asked where things stood. I knew that the slightest question would have him brooding about the subject all day. And I also knew talking about it was not only redundant, it was almost cruel. Where things stood? Nowhere, obviously. As you well know, in our country, nothing is ever truly settled; things simply get more complicated, documents multiply and invariably contradict each other, folders get fatter and fatter again. Then you die, and the lawsuit is passed on to the next generation ...

Mourad was convinced that his father's heart gave out at the age of forty-four because this case was weighing on him. A burden that he, in turn, was forced to carry from childhood. And even if he'd wanted to shrug it off, he wouldn't have known how or where to start. The old house was much more than just a property to him; it represented his status, his prestige, his honour, his loyalty to his family—in short, his whole reason for existing. He couldn't just give it up. But nor could he keep it if it meant a war of attrition.

From the first, the court case was obviously the chink in his armour. And it was through this chink that misfortune and shame found a path.

It's true that, in the meantime, there had been a war. Without it, time might have trickled past with the same Ottoman slowness, and a village dispute might have remained no more than a village dispute.

Instead, from the beginning of the war, the lawsuit became entangled, if I can put it this way, with broader concerns. Mourad's adversaries armed themselves, they allied themselves to a political movement that was in the ascendant and, one day, taking advantage of the chaos raging throughout the country, they came and occupied the old house.

The leader of the clan was a young man, a twenty-five-year-old hothead with a law degree, named Chamel, if memory serves. He called himself "the Jaguar," not a reference to the animal, but to the car he had bought—or perhaps "requisitioned."

As you can easily imagine, Mourad went mad. He told anyone who would listen that he would kill the little bastard with his bare hands. As far as he was concerned, this was the end of the world. There could be no question of taking a step back, of putting things in perspective, of buying time. I talked to him on the phone several times during this period, to try to calm him down, to dissuade him from doing something stupid. A waste of time. When he saw that I was insistent, he simply said—with the pig-headedness he was sometimes capable of—that it was none of my business, that it was his house, his inheritance, his family property, and that I was nothing but an emigrant, cut off from the realities of the country. I stopped arguing. I told him I wouldn't bother him anymore.

What Mourad planned to do to take back his house, I found out—

Adam was interrupted by a call on his mobile phone. It was Sémiramis, calling from the same old house.

"The funeral is over, but there are still a lot of people here. Tania is still shaking hands with people, and I'm doing much the same. People see me standing next to her and they assume I'm one of the family. I've only just managed to slip away to call you. Right now, I'm leaning on the balustrade, in the corner of the terrace where the two of us used to sit."

"Maybe I should have gone with you, after all ..."

"Don't feel any regrets, Adam! You would never have been able to stomach the whole thing. The cortege, the ceremony, the speeches, the lies, the endless line of people waiting to offer their condolences, the burial in the noonday sun ... It was hell! I got here more than five hours ago, and I'm still not done. When I arrived, I thought, I'll kiss Tania and slip away at the first opportunity. But the minute she saw me, she grabbed my arm, and she hasn't let go since. I suppose I remind her of the happiest time in her life. The period just after she met Mourad, when our little group of friends was passionate, naïve, united. Back when we used to have dinner at Le Code Civil. When all dreams were permitted ... Obviously, she's only latched on to me because you and the others aren't here. In fact, that's why I'm calling you. You were right to avoid the funeral, but it would be good if you could make a brief appearance."

"Now?"

"No, not right now, the house is still heaving. Come around eight, eight thirty, most people will have left. Tania would be so happy to see you."

"Don't you think she'll be exhausted after such a long day?"

"Of course, she'll be exhausted, shattered. She already is. But she would still feel better for seeing you."

"I'll think about it."

"No, don't think about it. Francis, my maître d'hôtel, has a brother with a car who works for us as a chauffeur sometimes when one of our guests needs to go somewhere. I'll call him, his name is Kiwan, he'll pick you up. Shall we say eight o'clock?"

It wasn't really a question. Adam's only response was a long sigh, of surrender.

He immediately went back to his computer:

While I have been writing this long letter to you, Naïm, my friend Sémi, who is at Mourad's funeral, called me—from the terrace, yes, "our" terrace—to ask me to go and spend a little time with Tania tonight. A car is coming to pick me up.

It feels strange, telling you about the lawsuit at the very moment when I am about to set foot in the old house for the first time in a quarter of a century, when our poor friend has just been buried ... But I am leaving the sad circumstances to one side so I can carry on with my story and send it before I leave.

Exactly what Mourad planned to do to get the house back, I only learned when it was too late.

At the time, there was almost no semblance of central government in the country. In certain districts of the capital and in the mountains, we had seen the emergence of local caïds, many of whom adopted ironic *noms de guerre*; aside from the Jaguar, who I have mentioned, I remember hearing about warlords calling themselves "Rambo," "Zorro," "Killer," "Terminator," and even "Klashenn," an affectionate diminutive of Kalashnikov. There were dozens of these tinpot leaders at the time, but very few of them had any influence beyond their district, their clan, or their village. There was, however, someone of a very different calibre, a troubling individual dubbed the "High Commissioner"—you probably heard of him during his fifteen minutes of fame [...]

Such a sobriquet, inherited from the colonial period, suggested some link to a foreign power, and this man had indeed managed to make himself useful, sometimes even indispensable, to neighbouring countries that, at some point or other, had sent troops into our unfortunate country.

I'm not telling you anything when I say that, every time our territory was invaded, there were some among out compatriots who were prepared to collaborate with the invaders, clear a path for them, offer to be of service and attempt to use them against local rivals. You'll probably say that, in any shattered country, there are always traitors and collaborators. And you're right. But it seems to me that in our country, we are too ready to do a deal with the conqueror of the moment as though there were nothing reprehensible about it.

The excuse has always been "the eye cannot withstand the drill," to quote the lurid proverb. The chief preoccupation of the various communities in this country has always been survival, survival at any cost, something that has been used to excuse every shameful compromise. Having decided to leave, to seek refuge, I am not in a position to lecture those who stayed. But that does not stop me feeling outraged, and sometimes disgusted. As I assume you do ...

The fact remains that, when it came to the art of collaboration, the aforementioned "High Commissioner" was a past master. He had managed to serve three successive invaders, persuading each that he was a loyal ally, in return for power and influence.

Since your academic background is much the same as mine, you can easily guess what words come to my mind when I talk about such people ... And you will understand my fury the day I discovered that Mourad had paid a visit to our local "quisling" to ask him to take action against the people who had occupied his house.

The "High Commissioner" was delighted. Here was a man who spent his time stirring up local factions so that he could play mediator, and there was a respected local figure, the scion of one of the great mountain families, coming to him on his own initiative to ask for help in recovering his property. He said that he was happy and honoured to welcome Mourad, and promised to settle the matter swiftly. "If there's anything I can do in return ..." our friend tactlessly suggested, not knowing whether the man wanted payment for his services. The honourable rogue took offence. What? Taking money for dispensing justice? For helping a respectable citizen to recover his property? Out of the question.

According to the ancient wisdom of the Levant, if a man who does you a service does not expect money, it is because he expects to recover his costs in some other way. Mourad knew this, but the fate of his family home blinded him to the point of losing his judgement.

On the day following the meeting, a platoon from the occupying army stormed the house, firing in all directions. Taken unawares, the village militiamen surrendered almost without a fight. But the attackers were not content simply to disarm them and throw them out. They stood the Jaguar up against a wall and shot him "as an example." Then the "collaborator in chief" called Mourad and triumphantly announced that his house had been liberated, that he and his family could move back there, and that they need fear no reprisals, since his enemies had been taught a lesson they would not forget.

Our friend swore to me that it never occurred to him for a minute that anyone would be killed, and I'm prepared to give him the benefit of the doubt, even if, in asking such a person to intervene, he should have assumed there might be bloodshed. He also insisted that only later did he find out how the Jaguar had died. Initially, he assumed the Jaguar had been armed and was gunned down during the attack; this in itself would have been serious, and more than enough for the Znoud to seek revenge. But to have been shot in cold blood in front of his brothers and his cousins was a tragedy of much greater magnitude. Man-to-man combat implies a certain degree of mutual respect, even at the moment of killing; an execution, on the other hand, is intended both to kill and to humiliate.

At the Jaguar's funeral the women of the clan wore red, to

signify that they would not wear mourning until their hero had been avenged.

And so Mourad moved back into his sprawling, ancient mansion, but something in the atmosphere of the village, and something in his mind, had been permanently tainted. Much as he protested that he had not been the first to resort to violence, that he had only retaken by force what had been taken from him by force, he felt guilty, and so he was. Guilty of calling on an armed force external to the village—and, incidentally, to the country, but that was almost less serious; and responsible for the heinous execution, though he had neither ordered it nor wished it. He assured me that he had vehemently said as much to the High Commissioner, who had squarely placed the blame on a number of hotheads whom he promised to discipline. And he further committed himself to protecting Mourad and his property day and night.

This gesture of "reparation" was probably what had motivated the execution of the Jaguar, and indeed the whole operation. The aim of the local quisling had been to make our friend dependant on him for his safety, and hence keep him under his thumb. I supposed that Mourad must have realized this, but it was too late. The fury of the opposing clan was not going to be quickly appeased, and he could no longer risk falling out with his protector.

Now dependent on the High Commissioner for his safety, and even his survival, Mourad gradually came to seem more like his right-hand man, his faithful retainer. Given the circumstances I've just described, you might say that our friend had no choice. Maybe. Although in my opinion, he would have done better to choose exile over living in the country on such terms. But that's another matter ... Back when we were still talking to each other, Mourad never said: "I don't have a choice." He commended his protector, praised his intelligence, his "sincerity," assured me that he thought "exactly like us'" and insisted that I come and meet him. My offensive comments—*what do you mean "like us"? and what exactly is this "sincerity"?*—eventually exasperated him, and our communications became less frequent before stopping completely.

When, one day, it was decided to form a government of reconciliation including delegates from the major warlords, it was our friend that that High Commissioner chose to represent him. Yes, it was by this glorious route that Mourad became a minister, and remained one for many years, managing to survive from one government to the next, frequently changing his portfolio: Public Works, Health, Telecommunications, Defence …

The laws of society are not like the laws of gravity, sometimes it is possible to fall upwards rather than down. The political ascent of our friend was the direct result of the offence he had committed. Later, by force of circumstance, he would commit many more … Principles are ropes, they are moorings; break them and you are free, but like a huge helium-filled balloon that soars, soars, soars, seeming to rise towards the sky, when really it is rising towards nothingness. Our friend soared, soared, soared; he became powerful, famous, and most of all rich, outrageously rich.

Although I have lived now for decades in France, one of the last bastions of egalitarian morality, believe me, I have not developed any hostility towards the rich. A number of my friends have become rich in recent years, as you know, and it has not changed my attitude to them one way or another. But the day I found out Mourad had bought a struggling bank for several hundred million dollars, I was deeply shocked. Because I know exactly what his financial position was like before he became a minister. We were very close, he wasn't secretive, and I had a very good idea of what he owned. He wasn't poor, but it was a struggle to maintain the house, in fact he had to sell off some land to have the roof repaired because the tiles were in poor condition. By what miracle could he possibly have saved enough to buy a bank, after a few years in government? There is no need to conduct an exhaustive investigation to know that it was dirty money. That, at best, it came from bribes and backhanders. And that's the least degrading hypothesis. If you want to know what I really believe, I think that, in business and in politics, our former friend was the public face of the sinister High Commissioner, and that he took a share of the profits from his multiple schemes: extortion, pillaging, drug trafficking, money laundering—but what do I know?

Unfortunately, our compatriots are complacent, hopelessly complacent when it comes to such practices. Because that's the way things have always been, they say. In fact, they admire the cunning of those who "make it," regardless of the means they adopt. I almost think the local motto is, to paraphrase a proverb about Rome: "In a cutthroat world, do as the cutthroats do."

In our mother tongue, to say "nouveaux riches," don't we say "war wealthy?"

By extension, we should talk about "war personalities," "war politicians," and "war celebrities." Not content to simply bring out our worst instincts, war moulds them, it shapes them such that people who might have been kind and friendly if their society hadn't imploded become traffickers, looters, kidnappers, killers, butchers. He and I dreamed of a different society, a different world. I don't forgive him anything. That he was my best friend is in no way, to my mind, a mitigating circumstance. On the contrary, it is an aggravating circumstance. The crimes of a friend sully and insult you; it is your duty to judge them mercilessly.

I did not speak to Mourad again—until the night before he died.

Is it possible to obliterate years of friendship with the stroke of a pen? Yes, that is exactly what I did. With the stroke of a pen, I obliterated our years of friendship. When someone mentioned Mourad, I would coldly say, "He's a former friend." I no longer spoke to him, I barely thought about him. Until Tania called me, last Friday, to tell me that he was dying.

But I've said too much, that's enough, I'll stop now. I will not revile his memory any more on the day of his funeral. I would like to say one more thing, specifically to you, something I have often thought when thinking about our old friend: you and I were forced to leave the Levant to try and keep our hands clean. We have no reason to be ashamed, but it would be absurd to advocate exile as the sole solution to moral dilemmas. Some day or other, a solution will have to be found for those who remain— if one exists, something about which I am not entirely sure …

But it's getting late, I have to go.

Much love,

Adam

He pressed *Send*. According to his watch, it was already 8:40 p.m. He quickly put on a tie then raced down to the waiting car.

4

It was about nine thirty in the evening when Adam arrived at the home of the deceased. Sémiramis was waiting next to the open door, sitting in the midst of dozens of empty chairs. She got up, kissed him on both cheeks, thanked him for taking her advice, then took him by the arm and led him to Tania.

Mourad's widow was upstairs, in a tiny room adjoining the bedroom. She was alone, wearing a black dress, stretched out with her shoes off and her feet up on a chair. She had obviously not been forewarned about his arrival. She made to get up, but he laid a hand on her shoulder to stop her and bent down to kiss her forehead. She put her arms around him, and her tears, which had just dried, began to flow again.

When she had regained her composure, she said:

"I thought you had already gone back to France."

"I changed my mind at the last minute."

"And I suppose you also didn't intend to come here for the funeral, but you changed your mind at the last moment."

On her face, a faint smile appeared through her tears.

"Adam is always a little late," she said, turning to Sémiramis.

Then turning to her guest, eager to temper her reproach, she said:

"I'm happy that you came. And if your friend could see you here, in his house, like long ago ..."

She glanced around her, then looked up, as though Mourad might be there, hovering, invisible above their heads.

"He would so much have liked to talk to you, to explain,

to clear up the misunderstandings. He was convinced that if you came and sat with him, listened to him, you would realize that he was right. I was not so sure. You had grown so far apart ..."

She fell suddenly silent and seemed caught up in her memories. After a few seconds, she added:

"I can say this now: he suffered every day of his life because of your falling-out."

She stared intently at Adam as though to read his mind. He felt obliged to say:

"In everything that has happened to us, there is only one true culprit: war."

But Tania's eyes were insistent, probing.

"Yes, you're right, the true culprit is the war, but not everyone reacted to it in the same way. Did they?"

At this point in the conversation, Adam was still wondering whether his former friend's widow was trying to provoke him or whether she simply wanted to elicit from him the words of comfort her husband had hoped to hear before he died.

"Not everyone was in the same situation. If I had stayed ..."

"... you would have acted as he did."

This was not what Adam had planned to say. He had a more nuanced formulation in mind: "If I had stayed, I would have been faced with the same choices he was," or something of the sort. Even so, he did not correct her, hoping that this would be an end to a conversation that felt inappropriate in Mourad's house on the day of his funeral. He nodded, gave her a sad smile, and said no more.

But Tania was not prepared to give up.

"So if you had stayed in the country, you would have acted as he did. You are honest enough to admit it. But have you ever wondered what would have happened if your friend had acted as you did? If he had decided to leave too? Did you ever wonder what would have happened if your friend, and me, and Sémiramis, and all our relatives and friends had decided that the war was much too dirty and that it would be better to leave to keep our hands clean?"

She was silent for a few moments, allowing her visitor to hope that she had finished. But she began again, in the same tone.

"The issue is not what you would have done if you'd stayed. The issue is what would have become of this country if everyone had left, like you did. We would all have kept our hands clean, but in Paris, in Montreal, in Stockholm, or in San Francisco. Those who stayed got their hands dirty to preserve a country for you, so that you could one day come back, or at least visit from time to time."

Again, she was silent for a few moments, then she said, like an old refrain:

"The clever ones are the ones who left. You travel to beautiful countries, you live, you work, you have fun, you discover the world. Then you come back after the war. The old country is waiting for you. You don't have to fire a single shot or spill a single drop of blood. And you can even choose not to shake the hands that got dirty. Isn't that right, Adam? Answer me! If I'm wrong, tell me."

"Today, you are right about everything, Tania. Whatever you say, I won't argue, this is not the day and this is not the place. May God have mercy on Mourad, and on us all."

Having said this, he stood up and ostentatiously checked his watch.

"It's late and you must be tired. I'm going back to the

hotel. We'll see each other again in different circumstances."

Tania quickly got to her feet, but not to say goodbye or
to walk him out.

"You're not going to leave like that," she said, "without
sharing our meal."

She seemed so genuinely offended that Adam wondered whether he had misunderstood everything. Had
he interpreted as a verbal attack what was simply old
friends thinking aloud? He turned to Sémiramis to
check. She signalled for him to stay calm, to sit down
again, then said in an authoritative tone:

"I've sent the chauffeur away; you can ride back with
me. We'll have something to eat with Tania, then leave
her to get some rest."

He had no choice but to obey. He sat down again. Of
course, you don't storm out of a house in mourning and
slam the door, even if the widow has said something
impolite. On a day like today, it was his duty to bear it, to
put up with these outbursts brought on by exhaustion,
by grief, and by Mourad's resolve to justify himself at the
end of his life, a resolve of which Tania was now the
guardian. Besides, the conversation had taken place in
private, between three longstanding friends.

In fact, the widow's manner changed the moment they
left the little room and went into the dining room. She
took Adam's hand and introduced him to everyone as her
husband's best friend, saying that he had come specially
from Paris for the sad occasion. Adam confirmed this
with a nod—what else could he do?

There were some thirty people left. Probably extended
family, people from the villages, a few political supporters—Adam did not recognize any of the faces. When he

arrived, he had thought the house was almost deserted. There had been empty chairs lined against the walls of the reception rooms, the hallways, the terraces, hundreds of chairs on which visitors had sat during the day, and which would be used again tomorrow and the day after. But there were still people here and there, enough to fill the vast dining room where a bountiful meal had been set out, one distinguishable from a celebration only by the subdued manner of the guests, the absence of laughter, and the recurring phrase—"*Allah yerhamo!*"— whenever anyone helped themselves, and then again when they got up from the table, "Allah yerhamo!" The calling down of God's mercy upon the deceased.

Tania had sat Adam next to her, and insisted on serving him herself. The conversation was about the people who had attended the funeral and those who had not been seen but might come the following day or the day after. The visitor "from Paris" listened, not without interest, though he said nothing.

At some point, the widow leaned over and whispered in his ear:

"Excuse me for what happened earlier! The words came out of my mouth without my even thinking. Tiredness, I suppose, as you said ..."

"Don't worry. We were among friends."

"Yes, of course. If I didn't think of you like a brother, I would never have spoken to you like that."

"I know ... but don't give it another thought, get some rest, and take care of yourself, you still have difficult days ahead."

"You'll come back and see me, won't you? I'd like to talk to you again about this reunion. If we could all be together again, on the terrace, like long ago. Your friend ..."

She seemed to find it difficult to call her husband anything else. While she was speaking, Adam realized that not once since he had seen her on Saturday had she said "Mourad." Perhaps she felt that her throat would close up if she tried to pronounce his name.

"Your friend said to me one day, near the end, when his voice was barely audible: 'How beautiful life would have been if we could have carried on meeting up with our old friends on this terrace, like we did at university. If nothing had changed.' And he started to cry."

As she said these last words, the widow began to weep once more.

Her guest simply echoed:

"If nothing had changed."

5

Only on the drive back, when he was alone in the car with Sémiramis, did Adam say aloud what he had wished he could have said to his dead friend:

"Yes, Mourad, life would have been beautiful if there had been no war, if we were still twenty rather than fifty, if none of us had died, if none of us had betrayed, if none of us had emigrated, if our country was still the Pearl of the Orient, if we had not become the laughing stock of the world, its shame, its scarecrow, its scapegoat, if, if, if, if …"

The driver assented with a long sigh. Then she drove for several kilometres before saying:

"Tania is really keen on this idea of a reunion. She must have mentioned it ten times since this morning."

"She talked to me about it too, over dinner. I told her that I think it's a good idea and that I'll do my best to make it happen. I didn't try to discourage her. She obviously feels the need to hang on to the idea to ease her grief a little. But I wouldn't want to give her hopes that might be disappointed."

"You don't think it will happen? I'm sure that most of our friends would love to meet up again, if only once before we all go to join Mourad … Personally, I would love for it to happen."

"I'd love it too. And I'm sure that most of our friends feel the same way as you and me. But they're scattered to the four corners of the earth, they all have jobs, families, obligations …"

"Did you manage to make a start today?"

"Yes, I've written to Albert and Naïm, who both replied within minutes. Albert is happy to be at the reunion, but he would prefer if it took place in Paris. As an American citizen, he is not allowed to come here ..."

"That's bullshit! In summer, half the guests at the hotel are travelling on American passports. If they're originally from here, all they have to do is use their other passport."

"It's more complicated for Albert. The institute he works for has ties to the Pentagon, which means he has to respect the prohibition."

"That's just an excuse! Since he left the country, he never wanted to come back. Long before the Americans forbade anything. He suffered a traumatic experience that he can't seem to get over. So he hides behind rules and regulations. If he really wanted to come, he'd come."

"I'm prepared to believe you. But I can't force him. If he really was so traumatized by the kidnapping, why force him to relive the nightmare?"

She shrugged.

"And Naïm?"

"With him, it's the opposite."

"Meaning?"

"He immediately replied to say that he'd come. But ever since then, I've been thinking, and now I'm hesitant."

"Because he's Jewish?"

"You don't think that would put him at risk?"

"What risk? This place is a jungle! People from all over come to this country and it's been fifteen years since anyone was kidnapped! Have you felt you're in danger since you got here?"

"Me? Absolutely not."

"You're not in danger, nobody's in danger. Think about it, it's the middle of the night, we're driving along a deserted, badly lit mountain road. Are you worried someone is going to cut our throats or rob us?"

He had to admit that, no, he felt reasonably safe, more so than in most countries.

They drove for some minutes in silence. Then Sémiramis, in a calmer mood, told her passenger that there had been an incident during the funeral:

"I thought someone would mention it over dinner, but Tania didn't say anything, and everyone else decided to keep quiet for her sake. As I'm sure you know, there's a family at the entrance to the village that Mourad didn't get on with."

Adam could not help but smile.

"That's the understatement of the year, Sémi! I know the story. Mourad hated the family and they hated him. They accused him of having their son executed."

"The funeral cortege was supposed to pass in front of their house on its way to the cemetery. As it approached, women streamed out of the house, women of all ages, I counted at least eleven. I assume the mother of the man who was killed, and his widow, his sisters, his sisters-in-law, his nieces ... They were all dressed in black, but every one of them, without exception, was wearing a scarf that was bright red, blood red. As though they had spent the whole winter knitting just for this occasion.

"The funeral procession marched past. Everyone was really uncomfortable. Tania squeezed my arm so hard I've probably got bruises. There was what is appropriately called a deathly silence. These women, lined up against the wall, their silent faces expressionless, though one or two had a faint mocking smile. Their heads and their faces were covered such that all we could see were those red scarves, which the black clothes simply accentuated.

"No one in the cortege said anything. Not a word. We scarcely breathed. Unconsciously, we quickened our step.

But crossing those few metres seemed to take an age.

"After the funeral, the procession took the same route back. The women weren't there. But everyone turned to look at the place where they had stood, and again, we felt uncomfortable, this time because they had disappeared.

"Curiously, after the ceremony, no one mentioned the incident. Or, at least, not in my presence. I suppose there will have been people whispering about it, but in front of me, being a stranger in the village, no one said anything. As for Tania, she behaved as though nothing had happened. But I'm sure she'll see those women in her dreams, and not just tonight.

"I had to tell you, but please don't mention it to Tania. And if she decides to talk about it, pretend you didn't know."

Adam nodded, then asked the driver how she had interpreted the women's gesture.

"The way they went about it was sinister, but the message was clear: the man who had had their 'martyr' shot was now dead too; by wearing black, they were prepared to join Tania in her mourning, but they had not forgotten their own grief."

Deep down, Sémiramis had the feeling that the actions of the protesting women had been a warning to the widow, that it was the prologue to a new battle between the two families for possession of the house. But she had no desire to dwell on the incident.

"A little music?" she said suddenly, with a rather forced gaiety.

The question was rhetorical since, as she said the words, she was pressing a button that launched an old Iraqi lament:

She stepped out of her father's house
And walked towards a neighbour's door
She passed without a sign or wave,
Truly my love does treat me ill ...

Sémiramis began to sing along with Nazem al-Ghazali, whose voice had so often been the soundtrack to their gatherings of long ago.

After a few minutes, she turned down the volume and asked her passenger:

"Have you put together a list of all the people who should be invited to the reunion?"

"I've got a list of about a dozen names, but there are some I'm still undecided about. For example, this afternoon, I thought about Nidal ..."

"Nidal ...?" Sémiramis said, as though she did not know who he meant.

"Bilal's brother ..." Adam said, without thinking.

"The brother of Bilal," she echoed, her voice choking on the last syllable.

The moment the name passed my lips, Adam would later write in his notebook, I realized that I shouldn't have said it. My friend's face clouded over. She didn't say another word, she just hummed along absently to the Iraqi song. To her, Bilal is a wound that has not been healed by the years, the decades, and I have no excuse, because I knew. If there was one name I should not have mentioned, it was his. But I was thinking about it constantly, and sooner or later I was bound to let it slip.

Back when we were at university, the day after the night I walked Sémi home, when we almost kissed, the young man who appeared in our group, the one who dared to hold her hand, was Bilal.

For me, the incident left a wound that I've realized since being back in the country, was lasting. But it is nothing, nothing at all compared to Sémi's trauma and the brutal death of her first lover.

When our group of friends met up two or three days after the farcical walk home, and I saw this boy and this girl arrive together, arm in arm, obviously I was upset. But I felt I had no right to say anything, nor to resent them. After all, Bilal hadn't "stolen my girlfriend"; I hadn't managed to seduce her.

In my adolescent mind, I'd constructed a whole scenario around the beautiful Sémiramis. I saw myself walking with her hand in hand on the beach, barefoot. I pictured a thousand situations in which I rescued her, consoled her, amazed her. But all this was nothing more than my imagination, and, on the strength of a smile, I had convinced myself that her dreams might be like mine. It wasn't Sémi's fault, nor was it Bilal's. If anything was responsible for my failure, it was the upbringing that had turned me into a boy who was so polite, so worried about offending, about not being liked, so mired in his books and his daydreams—that timid creature.

Over time, and with practice and instruction, I would eventually overcome my deepest inhibitions, although, even today, there is still a trace of shyness. But, back then, I couldn't help but be envious of the two couples that existed within our group of friends—who were, incidentally, as dissimilar as possible. On one hand, Tania and Mourad, a sailboat on an oil slick; on the other, Sémi and Bilal, a skiff on a raging sea.

The former were present at every event, without exception; in fact, our little group clustered around them. The latter sometimes came, sometimes stayed away; one day they would leave each other in tears; the next day we would see them wrapped around each other again. You didn't need a crystal ball to know which crew would weather the storm, and which would founder on the rocks.

I always wondered whether Bilal's decision to join an armed

faction was motivated by a shift in his politics, or by his tempestuous relationship with Sémi. And I never knew whether, when he died, they were still in a relationship or whether they were estranged or had broken up. Back then, it would have been insensitive to speculate, for fear of seeming to blame the young girl for the tragedy that had occurred. And, despite the years that have elapsed since, it's clear that the subject still can't be broached without great precaution.

I had proof of that today. The moment I saw her reaction, I bit my tongue, I said nothing more about this or any other subject. I felt it was impossible for me to apologize, continue the conversation, or change the subject. All I could do was wait. And, in silence, call to mind certain memories that explained my friend's attitude.

I remembered, for example, that when Bilal died, Sémi wore mourning. For several months she wore only black, as though she were his lawful widow. Then she sunk into a profound depression.

They had been driving in silence for several long minutes, each consumed by memories of Bilal, and by regrets, when Sémiramis suddenly asked:

"Had you seen him recently?"

Adam started. He stared at her intently, as though she had gone completely insane. She quickly clarified, without a smile but with a sigh of impatience:

"I was talking about the brother."

"Nidal? No, I haven't seen him. Not for years. What about you?"

"I saw him once or twice afterwards. He's changed a lot. You wouldn't recognize him. These days he wears the beard."

"If that's the only diff—"

"I didn't say *a* beard, I said *the* beard."

"I know, Sémi. These days tens of millions of men wear *the beard*, as you call it. It can hardly be considered a novelty. Unfortunately, the spirit of the times is with Nidal, we're the ones who have become anachronisms."

"The beard," she repeated, as though she had not heard him, "and all the speechifying that goes with it ... If you invite him to the reunion, some of our friends might feel uncomfortable."

"That doesn't frighten me. Can he hold a conversation without pulling a gun?"

"Yes, as far as that goes. He's pretty polite. But the content ..."

"Reactionary?"

"More reactionary than a Taliban, and more radical than the Khmer Rouge. All in one package."

"That bad?"

"No, I'm exaggerating a bit, but not much. He is pathologically conservative—he refuses to shake hands with a woman, for example. And when he talks about America, he sounds like a Maoist from the sixties ..."

"I get the picture. But even that is the spirit of the times. I still think it wouldn't do us any harm to hear him out."

"Even if it means some of our friends might feel threatened?"

Adam thought for only a split second.

"Yes. Even if some of us feel threatened. We're all adults, we've lost our youthful illusions, why would we need to hold the reunion in an antiseptic safe space? If Bilal's brother has something coherent to say, and if he's prepared to listen to others, I'm happy to listen to him, and to answer him."

"You do what you like, you're the master of ceremonies. But don't say I didn't warn you. If the reunion is ruined, you'll only have yourself to blame ..."

"Agreed. I'll take responsibility."

They had just turned into the private road that led to the hotel. Adam assumed that Sémiramis was going to park in front of her little house, but instead she pulled up outside the main door.

Was she going to put him to the test again, to force him to clearly articulate his desire to spend a third night with her?

No. She was elsewhere, still immersed in the memories that her passenger had rashly stirred up. Adam was tempted to apologize, but decided against it, judging that it would be more tactful not to make it too explicit.

He opened the car door; then, having checked that there was no one around, he leaned over and planted a furtive kiss on her cheek. She did not react, neither rebuffing him nor leaning towards him. He did not insist. He got out of the car and let her drive off.

The Seventh Day

1

Last night, I had a dream that was both predictable and un-settling, Adam would write in his notebook under the en-try dated Thursday, April 26.

I found myself in Mourad's house, it was seething with peo-ple, as it must have been yesterday. But I simply pushed through the crowd to seek refuge in a room where my friends were waiting for me. In fact, Mourad was there, and Tania, and Sémi, as well as Bilal, who was swathed in a gilded robe, enthroned like Jupiter on Mount Olympus, his face framed by a luxuriant red beard. A woman's voice whispers into my ear, "He's changed so much." I say smugly, "He told me beforehand." Then I laughingly say to my friends, "All the people out there think we're dead!"

It goes without saying that the dream was rather more cha-otic. In setting it down, I have made sense of it, rationalized it. In a certain sense, I've reconstructed it from the fragments that I recognized—the location, the faces, the words, the colours. They all come from scenes I experienced and that are imprinted on my memory: my belated visit to the dead man's house; my conversation with Sémi on the drive back; and then that other conversation, a quarter of a century ago, with Bilal, back when we were close, shortly before he took up arms and died.

I've already talked about the long, loquacious walks we used to take, and notably the last, which, if memory serves, ended in the lashing rain, when Bilal, on the subject of God, howled, "Now there's a fine occupation!"

A little earlier in our conversation, the name of a girl had cropped up. When I mentioned it a few days ago, I simply wrote "a mutual friend." I didn't name Sémi. If I had done, I would have had to explain who she was and why we were talking about her, tell the story of our nighttime walk and my pathetic inhibitions—which at the time seemed to me like unnecessary digressions. When writing those lines about our circle of friends, I wasn't thinking about Sémi any more than the others, and I didn't expect to see her again soon. I believed I'd be catching a flight back to Paris on Monday, Wednesday at the latest, since the dying man whose last words I had come to hear had not waited for me.

Now, it seems to me that in the moment when I was setting down those episodes from my youth, something inside me changed. Two hours later, I had postponed my flight and left the capital to come and stay here, at the Auberge Sémiramis.

When writing a text, sentences follow on from each other, and those reading them don't realize that at certain moments the hand setting them down raced across the page, and at others it froze. On a printed page, or even a manuscript page, silences are erased, spaces are planed away.

I point this out precisely because, last Saturday, after having briefly alluded to our "mutual friend," I paused for a long moment. I was tempted to say more about her, to mention her by name, to explain why this conversation about her had so lasting an effect on me. Then I gave up so as not to be sidetracked from my story.

Now, I am coming back to it. The "young girl" is no longer anonymous, my recent encounter with her casts a different light on what Bilal and I discussed back then, and the context in which we came to be talking about God.

Our memory of words fades, not that of emotions. What I remember of the conversation with my dead friend is bound to be approximate, but I have no doubts about its emotional content, or its significance.

Bilal had surprised me by saying, on the subject of Sémi:

"You used to have a thing for her too … She told me."

"It's true that I found her attractive, but nothing ever happened between us."

"So, when I met her, the two of you weren't together ..."

"We were never together. Did she say otherwise?"

"No, but I'm glad to hear you confirm it. I want to be sure that I didn't steal my friend's girlfriend."

"Don't worry, there was nothing between us, she wasn't my girlfriend and you didn't 'steal' her. But why ask me about this now?"

The incident had been almost four years earlier.

"Before, you were just an acquaintance, now you're a close friend, and I wanted to make sure I hadn't hurt you unintentionally."

"No, put your mind at rest, you didn't hurt me."

"You never resented me? Never cursed me? Even when you saw us together for the first time?"

I felt uncomfortable, and he noticed this. Which simply made him more insistent.

"You don't want to talk about it ... You're wrong. It's important to talk about love. You have to dare to talk about it freely with close friends. Women talk about it among themselves; men never talk about it, or only to brag, as though their feelings of tenderness were unworthy. I'd like to live in a time where I could talk to my friends about my most recent night of passion without it seeming conceited or indecent."

With Bilal, I often found myself playing a thankless role, the purveyor of conventional wisdom, of received ideas. Though I did my best to shake it off, I invariably slipped back into the role.

That night, I had said:

"And you don't think that the emotion might lose something if people could talk about such intimate subjects with no feeling of shame?"

My friend had shrugged.

"That's the perpetual pretext that keeps us silent. In a society like ours, shame is an instrument of tyranny. Guilt and shame were devised by religions to keep us on a leash. To stop us from living. If men and women could talk openly about their relationships, their feelings, their bodies, humanity as a whole would be more fulfilled, more creative. I'm sure that it will happen someday."

This was the mid-1960s, and what Bilal was saying was in the spirit of the times. But there was an intensity, an urgency in his words. I said nothing. The extreme prudishness my friend was denouncing was so deeply rooted in me that no argument, however passionate, could dislodge it. A carapace is as protective as it is oppressive; it is impossible to shrug it off without exposing one's naked body. In fact, he was talking like someone who had been flayed alive. And when he started telling me about his first meeting with Sémi, their first words, their first kiss, the first undone button, the first embrace—it was simultaneously tender, tumultuous, and mortifying.

Strangely, I never for a moment thought that Bilal was trying to wind me up. I might have done. After all, this young man had done something I had dreamed of but had not dared to do. There was no mockery, no pride, no boastfulness in his attitude towards me. Just a longing for a deep friendship that flouted good manners and propriety.

At some point in our conversation, he said:

"I'm glad we both courted the same girl."

"Yes," I said, more to agree with him than because it was what I really thought. "It's a nice coincidence ..."

"No," he corrected me, his tone suddenly serious, "not a coincidence, a communion. As though we came from the same village and had drunk from the same spring."

We were sitting on a stone parapet at the entrance to a building, in a vaulted passageway. The rain was lashing harder, but I had ears only for my friend's words.

"Adam, don't you think we were born into the wrong time, you and me?"

"When would you like to have been born?"

"A hundred years, two hundred years from now. Humanity is metamorphosing, and I'd like to see what it will become."

I replied, "Because you think there's a finish line where you can go and wait for the rest of us? Think again! It's impossible to see everything in an instant. Unless you're God ..."

It was at this point that, standing with his arms stretched up towards the rain, he howled:

"God! God! Now there's a fine occupation!"

2

At this point in his reminiscences, Adam felt the need to phone Sémiramis. When they had parted the night before, he had felt she was angry.

"No, I was just pensive," she reassured him.

"I'm sorry. It was tactless of me."

"To talk about Bilal, you mean? Don't worry about it, it's ancient history."

This was clearly not entirely the case, since her words were followed by an awkward silence. In fact, she quickly admitted:

"No, actually, that's not true. It's a lie, Bilal will never be ancient history. I'll never feel unmoved, indifferent when someone mentions his name. But that's no reason not to talk about him. I don't want you treating me with kid gloves, I don't want you labelling me 'fragile.' The thing that would hurt me would be for a friend like you to feel he had to avoid subjects that might upset me. Even if you think I might suffer, I'm asking you not to treat me like a permanent convalescent. Promise?"

As if to demonstrate that it was duly noted, Adam said:

"There's one thing that's always nagged at me. Did you ever understand why Bilal took up arms? He was hardly passionate about politics, he loathed the war, and he had little respect for the various factions."

From the other end of the line, there came a long sigh followed by another silence, and Adam could not help but wonder whether he had been wrong to take his friend's assurances literally. However, after a moment she said:

"You're right to ask me that question. But the answer isn't a simple one ..."

"Do you want to talk about it some other time?"

"No. Are you in your room? Don't go anywhere, I'll be right up."

When she knocked at his door a few minutes later, her eyes were red and Adam felt guilty and ashamed.

"I'm sorry, Sémi! I didn't mean to ..."

With a wave, she silenced him then went and sat on a wicker chair. Without looking at him, she began:

"We loved each other very much, you know that."

"Yes, of course I know."

"Of all those who fell during the war, not one died for the same reasons as Bilal. It was literature that killed him. His heroes were Orwell, Hemingway, Malraux, the writers who fought in the Spanish Civil War. Those were his exemplars, his role models. They had taken up arms for a time so that their hearts could beat in sync with that of the century. Then, their duty done, they had gone home to write. *Homage to Catalonia, For Whom the Bell Tolls, Man's Hope*—we had read them together. I'm sure that, on the barricades, shouldering his machinegun, Bilal was not thinking about the battles to come, but about the book he was going to write.

"I was terrified. From the very beginning. But that's just one more part of the hero's image. The wife, or the mother, or the girlfriend pleading with him not to go, while he listens only to his duty ... I was a modern lover, I thought I was more sophisticated than other girls. I read the same books he did, I shared his dreams, and this meant I was entitled to say, 'This isn't nineteen-thirties Spain, where men were fighting for ideals. In our country, those taking up arms are just neighbourhood thugs. They strut around the place, they kidnap, they pillage, they traffic ...' Sometimes, he agreed with me, but sometimes he would say, 'People are always contemptuous of their own era, just as they always idealize the past. It's easy to imagine I would have been a Republican in Barcelona in 1937, or a member of the French Resistance in 1942, or a comrade of Che Guevara. But my life is happening here and now, and it is here and now that I have to choose: either I commit myself, or I stand on the sidelines.'

"He was afraid of missing out on his own era, and thereby losing the right to be a writer. He was afraid of not living intensely enough, passionately enough, and our love wasn't enough for him."

Sémiramis fell silent, and with her crumpled handkerchief, she dabbed her eyes and wiped the corners of her mouth. Adam allowed a few seconds to pass before saying:

"You've just answered another question that I always wondered about: he didn't take up arms because the two of you had quarrelled."

To his great surprise, this remark elicited a broad smile from Sémiramis.

"Our relationship was stormy, that's certainly true. We broke up, we got back together, but neither of us would ever have given up on the other ...

"It was never my fault ... Yes, I know, it's easy for me to say that when he's not here to defend himself. But I think it's something he would have readily admitted. He was always the one who started the fights, and he was the one who always made up again. Here, too, the problem stemmed from literature. From that inane myth that authors should have tempestuous relationships so they can write about their lovers. Quiet contentment blunts the edge of passion and dulls the imagination. Bullshit! A happy populace produces no history, a happy couple produces no literature. Complete rubbish. In the end, for us, there was no happy couple *and* no literature."

She caught her breath, then added:

"Our relationship was like that frenzied dance where the dancers violently pivot away from each other, spin back, and just as violently collide before pivoting away again. But at no point do they let go of each other's hands."

Another pause, a smile from a bygone age. Then she continued her story:

"He showed me the gun he had just bought, he was as proud as a little kid, he held it out so that I could take it, maybe thinking I'd be overwhelmed. I was instantly disgusted by the cold metal and the smell of gun grease and threw it onto the sofa where it bounced and almost fell on the floor; he caught it just in time and gave me an angry, contemptuous look. 'I thought you were going to start writing,' I said defiantly. He said, 'First I have to fight, then I can write.' I never saw him again. We never spoke to each other. He died four days later. Without having written anything, and without having really fought. The first mortar shell from the other district landed a few feet from him. He was sitting with his back to a wall, daydreaming, apparently. I'm pretty sure that he never even fired his gun."

"At least his hands were clean. He didn't kill anyone."

"No, no one. Apart from himself and me, he didn't kill anyone."

Sémi was visibly distressed by her memories, Adam wrote as soon as his friend had left the room. But, thinking about it, I don't regret bringing up this chapter of her past—of our mutual past, I should say, even if, for me and for the rest of our friends, the trauma was much less devastating. It was important that I gave her the opportunity to tell me, straightforwardly, that she had done everything she could to stop Bilal from courting death.

Of course, I realize that that will not take away her grief, or the inevitable feeling of guilt we all feel at the death of a loved one. But I think that making him a sort of martyr to literature, rather than the victim of a grubby skirmish, she ennobled his death, made it a little less absurd.

I was intrigued by what she said about Bilal's fascination with the Spanish Civil War. It's true that he and I often talked about it. But no more than we talked about Vietnam, Chile, or the Long March. I didn't realize that he was so obsessed with it, nor that he dreamed of being another Hemingway. When he and I discussed the Spanish Civil War during our walks together, we more often talked about García Lorca, who was one of its first victims, though he never took up arms.

That said, the last conversation between Sémi and her beloved was not unlike a lot of the discussions our group was having at that time, all of which revolved around the same subject: Was the fighting in our country merely a clash between tribes or clans—not to say between gangs of thugs—or was there some greater merit to these clashes, some moral dimension? In other words, was it worth getting involved, at the risk of losing one's life?

At that point in our lives, we all believed that the Spanish Civil War, despite the atrocities committed, was the archetypal conflict with a genuine cause, an ethical dimension, and hence one worthy of dying for. Now, as a historian approaching fifty, I have some doubts about this. At the time, I had none, and nor did my friends. The only other struggle that, to our eyes, had been worthy of dying for was the anti-Nazi resistance—whether that be French, Italian, Soviet, or German. At the tops of our lungs we sang "Bella ciao" and Aragon's "L'Affiche rouge," we all wanted to be Stauffenberg or, better yet, Missak Manouchian, the Armenian carpenter from Jounieh who had gone on to lead a faction of the French Resistance.

Our misfortune, our tragedy, was that we felt the battles we could fight in our time, in our country, lacked the same purity, the same nobility.

Not that I think we would all have been prepared to lay down our lives for a good cause, even at the age of eighteen. But it was an issue that was never far from our thoughts, or our discussions. Were we going to spend our whole lives, or at the very least our youth, without the opportunity to throw ourselves headlong into a struggle worthy of the name? And was there a just cause, one championed by men who were pure of heart, or at least trustworthy? Personally, I doubted it.

I feel certain that Bilal had the same doubts I did. Even if there came a day when, out of sheer impatience, he decided to silence them. He was mistaken, but I respect his decision, and whenever I think of him, I will never cease to say, "He was a pure soul."

}

Having written these last words for the second, or perhaps the third, time, Adam closed his notebook and opened his laptop in order to write an email on a very different subject concerning the immediate future, one also inspired by his conversation with Sémiramis the previous evening.

Dear Naïm,

Here I am writing to you again, as if my last email wasn't long enough! But you'll understand why I needed to get back to you so soon.

Last night, I ended up going to Mourad's village, as I told you, to offer my condolences to Tania. Unsurprisingly, she was sad, exhausted, at the end of her tether, and particularly upset—as her husband must have been at the end of his life—by the distance of so many friends. She talked to me again about the reunion we have been planning. She spoke about it so enthusiastically that I almost told her you had already agreed to come, and that you even wanted us to meet at the old house. But I bit my tongue, I didn't say anything, I didn't want to raise a hope that might be disappointed. I first wanted to make sure that the reunion is definitely going to happen.

Until now, I've only written to one person besides you—Albert, who reminded me that our country is still on the list of those American citizens are barred from visiting—a veto he is obliged to respect given his job. He is more than happy for us to meet up, but elsewhere, in Paris for example.

You immediately agreed unreservedly, both in principal and in terms of location, something Tania would have been thrilled to hear. Nonetheless, I wanted to make sure that you have thought about the implications—especially in terms of security. It was to clarify this point that I'm emailing again.

According to Sémi—did I tell you I'm staying at her place, the sublime Auberge Sémiramis?—I'm worrying about nothing, as is Albert. She says American citizens originally from here routinely get around the ban, and they're not worried, either while they're here or when they go back to the USA. As for you, she thinks you would be running no risk whatsoever.

Maybe she's right. I'd like to believe her ... It's perfectly possible that neither Albert's passport nor your religion poses any problem. But I prefer to make you aware of my concerns so that you can get more information, think about it, and make you decision in full possession of the facts. [...]

Forty minutes later, from Brazil—where it was not yet 6:00 a.m.—this reply from Naïm:

Dear Adam,

I understand your concerns, but they don't seem to me to be remotely justified. I'm running no risk, none whatsoever. I'll travel on my Brazilian passport, I'll blend into the crowd of emigrants who have come back to breathe the air of their homeland, no one need know anything about my religion.

My only problem is my mother. She has just turned eighty-six, and she'd have a heart attack if I told her where I was going. So I'll have to lie. I'll tell her I'm going to Greece, and she'll make me promise to wear a hat so I don't get sunstroke ...

No, honestly, I don't see why I should deny myself the trip. I've been waiting for an opportunity like this for years, so I'm not about to pass it up. An opportunity to see friends, of course, but also to see the city, the old family house—if it's still standing—and the one we had up in the mountain, where we spent every summer, and where I used to bring my girlfriends when I needed somewhere private. These days, my daughter's boyfriend—a student at the University of Rio—spends every weekend with us, in São Paulo; he sleeps here and in the morning we all have breakfast together. It's such an ordinary thing these days that even my mother finds it perfectly normal, perfectly acceptable, as though this is the way things have always been—the same woman who would have torn a strip off my sister if she had so much as whispered in a young man's ear. We boys were never as closely watched, but we constantly had to come up with clever ruses, as you remember, constantly hiding, and that house up on the mountain was my private sanctuary.

It would be such a joy to visit the places I used to know, even if they're scarcely recognizable now; and also, more generally, to see the country that I left reluctantly, promising myself that I'd visit regularly, though as it has turned out I haven't set foot there since.

At first, it was because of the war, the urban violence, the snipers, the fear of kidnappings; and when there were lulls in the fighting, I was the one who was too busy. The more time passed, the more my fears grew, and I could no longer see myself arriving at the airport, getting into a taxi, venturing into the various neighbourhoods. There came a point when I told myself that I had to stop thinking about it, to turn the page, and that, besides, almost all the people who had been dearest to me had left, either for other countries, or for the next world.

But still, I felt the urge. So, when you suggested a reunion of our friends from back then, I knew that this was the perfect opportunity to break this long absence. Which is why I've replied so quickly and so enthusiastically—as you have noticed.

So, as far as I'm concerned, the decision is made. And since I can more or less make my own work schedule, I'll leave you to choose the date, but I hope it will be soon. I have to travel to Europe quite soon, and I could combine the two trips ...

As for Albert, I'd love to see him again, but I'd advise you not to pressure him. It's true that, if he wants to, he can get around the ban, which mostly exists so that American authorities can waive responsibility if anything goes wrong. But it is up to him to assess the risks. Pass on the various opinions, don't argue for or against, and leave him to think about it. He might just change his mind. [...]

To avoid "pressuring" or embarrassing his American friend, Adam wrote the following email:

Dear Albert,

I've just written to Naïm to say ... more or less the reverse of what I'm about to say to you.

When I first told him, a couple of days ago, about the reunion that Tania is so keen to have, and I am trying to organize, he immediately suggested that we meet up, as we used to, in "the old house." I wrote back to him to ask whether he had considered the risk he might be running, and he has just replied to say that, in his opinion, any risks are negligible, and to reaffirm that he still wants to come back and visit the country.

So, now I'm writing to ask you the opposite. You said you'd prefer the reunion to take place in Paris, and I'd like to ask you to give it some more thought. Is your decision final? Is there no way of getting around the problem of the ban?

Let me just say that, obviously, I will completely understand whatever you decide.

4

Adam was still rereading the email when Sémiramis knocked on his door. He ushered her in and read the text aloud. She did not think it sufficiently firm; she would have preferred him to say explicitly that there was no risk. Adam hesitated for a moment, but eventually sent the message as written, having made some minor change for the sake of form. Then he closed his laptop and said to his visitor:

"I'm listening."

"I don't suppose you're planning to have lunch?"

He checked his watch. It was 12:15 p.m.

"No, it's too early, and I'm not remotely hungry. I'll just carry on working ..."

"In that case, I'll send up a couple of things you can nibble on while you carry on writing."

But Sémiramis had come for a different reason. She went on:

"Later this afternoon, I have plans for you. A visit. I know that you don't want to see anyone, but I think you might make an exception for Brother Basil."

Adam was on the point of asking her who this individual was, when, alerted by her mischievous smile, he changed his mind.

"Ramzi!"

"The very same."

"I knew that when he took holy orders, he adopted a pseudonym ... No, that's not the right word. What do we say, actually? I've forgotten ..."

"Not pseudonym, not alias, not nom de guerre. We simply say 'religious name.' Ramzi, comma, religious name Brother Basil."

"Of course. My mind is all over the place ... So you tracked him down?"

"I've always known where he was."

"Have you already visited him?"

"No, I didn't dare. A shameless sinner showing up among a group of monks ... I figured I might not exactly be welcomed with open arms ..."

"So, you haven't seen him since the ... change. So what makes you think that he will see us now?"

"Nothing. I've no idea whether he will. But I think if the two of us show up and knock on his door, he'll let us in."

"Is it far?"

"About two hours, maybe a little less. An hour-and-a-half drive and then a twenty-minute walk."

Adam was visibly hesitant. Sémiramis once again let out a girlish laugh.

"Trust me. I have a feeling everything will be fine."

But her friend was not convinced.

"You don't just show up to visit a friend who's decided to withdraw from the world. You have to prepare, so as not to make a blunder. I'd like to talk to someone first ..."

"To Ramez, I assume ..."

She smiled; he smiled, too. This was indeed the friend of whom he was thinking. During their time at university, Ramez and Ramzi were inseparable. And, although both belonged to the "Circle of Sophists," they formed a group within a group. They were engineering students, whereas the others were studying literature, history, or sociology; and they had been educated in English, whereas the others had attended French schools.

After earning their degrees, "the two Ramzs" jointly founded an engineering company that bore both their names.

"It remains to be seen whether the monk and the

engineer are still on good terms," Sémiramis remarked, clearly sceptical.

"Even if they're not, Ramez can still offer valuable insights. Why his friend decided to retreat from the world, what state of mind he's in, whether he receives visitors, whether he might feel threatened if we suddenly appear and knock on the door of the monastery ... These are things only Ramez can tell us. Are you still in touch with him?"

"No, but I know that these days he lives in Amman."

"So, you don't have a phone number for him?"

"I can find someone who has. Give me ten minutes."

As soon as Sémiramis left the room, I went and fetched the folder marked Letters from friends *to dig out an old letter, one of the very first that I received after arriving in Paris; written in English, it was peppered with words in Arabic and little doodles in the margins.*

Dear Adam,
We have decided to write this letter together, Ramez and I ...

I couldn't help but smile as I copied out this line, just as I smiled when I first read it a quarter of a century ago. Although the news from my friends was depressing.

We have taken a lease on offices on the top floor of a magnificent modern building with huge picture windows overlooking the sea. We took possession at the beginning of last month, and the furniture was delivered the following week. We had planned to have a small launch party on the evening of Saturday 12th. In the early afternoon, a gun battle broke out in the surrounding district. All the streets were cordoned off, and the guests could not get to the building. We had brought huge platters of canapés and pastries, and every kind of drink you can imagine. We had hired two waiters, but they couldn't get here either.

At about seven o'clock, the battle intensified, shells exploded close by, shattering the office windows. We had no choice but to shelter in the basement until the madness died down. And it was there, in the shelter, that we spent the night, surrounded by people from neighbouring offices who had been supposed to come to the launch. We had felt it was only good manners to invite them, but no one had thought it wise to venture up to the eighth floor, the most vulnerable in the whole building.

In the morning, we went back up to our new offices—taking the stairs, obviously, since the electricity had been cut off. The place was a complete ruin. Everything was strewn with shrapnel and shards of glass. The false ceiling had collapsed and fallen on the trays of pastries, and the carpet was completely soaked with beer and soft drinks. We were speechless. We slumped into a couple of armchairs in what was supposed to be our meeting room and we cried and cried. Then we passed out from despair, frustration, and sheer exhaustion, since during our night down in the shelter, we had only pretended to sleep.

We were woken by fresh gunfire, when the factions started up again at dawn. I was the first to open my eyes; Ramez was still in his armchair. His eyes were still closed, but before long, he opened them. We stared at each other, without moving from our chairs. Then we both burst out laughing. It wasn't a giggle, but a fit of hysterics we could do nothing to stop.

When we finally regained our composure, I said, "So, what do we do now?" Without taking a second to think, Ramez instantly replied, "Now, we emigrate!" "What about the offices?" "We are going to leave this office in precisely sixty seconds and never set foot in it again. We'll move to London." Personally, I would have been happier with Paris, but my associate's French is so terrible, it would have been cruel to force him to live and work in the language. Mine isn't particularly good, but it's good enough and would have improved with time. Ramez's French is beyond hope.

So, I'm writing to tell you that we'll soon be almost neighbours—next month, in theory, but by January at the latest. I plan to visit Paris anytime there's an exhibition I find interesting—which is likely to be quite often, and I would love to see you. And you should come and visit us in London …

Your friend who has not forgotten you,

Ramzi

Appended to the letter were a few lines in a different hand.

Take care of yourself, and don't believe what my associate has told you. My French is absolutely perfect; if I don't use it, it's only so I don't wear it out.

Your other brother who has not forgotten you,

Ramez

I don't remember how Ramzi and Ramez came to be part of our group of friends. But as far back as I can remember, there they were, side by side, always together. We always addressed them in the singular, as though they were one person. They were an endless source of silly jokes. "Ramez tripped on a stone, Ramzi fell over"; "Ramzi has just downed three beers, Ramez is pie-eyed" … It seems like every time we met up, there had to be some reference to this "twinship," it was a sort of ritual, and they were always the first to laugh.

In fact, they did everything to perpetuate the myth. For example, one day, while still in their first year studying engineering, they announced that they had decided to become associates. The sort of promise teenagers make. But they kept it. And after their first office was destroyed, they opened another one. Not in London, but in Jeddah in Saudi Arabia. Because, just as they were packing to move to England, they were offered a job, a vast project that would take three and a half years' work and would make them rich. They did eventually open an office in London, but it was simply a branch office, like those they had in Lagos, Amman, Dubai, and Kuala Lumpur.

As soon as Sémiramis tracked down Ramez's phone number, Adam called him. A woman's voice answered: no, he had not dialled a wrong number, this was Ramez's "cell phone," and she was his assistant. Her boss had given it to her because he was at the hospital, visiting a cousin who had just had an operation. Adam introduced himself, and the assistant, Lina, said she was delighted to speak to him; her boss had often talked about him.

At first, she assumed that he was phoning from Paris. When she realized where he actually was, she almost yelped. By happy coincidence, Ramez was there today, too.

"I'm sure he wouldn't want to leave without seeing you. He had planned to fly back to Amman at about 3:00 p.m., but I'm sure he'll postpone. I hope you haven't had lunch yet."

"No, not yet."

"If you're free, I'll send a car right now, that way you'll be able to spend some time together."

Adam was taken aback.

"Are you sure? Don't you want to check with him first?"

"There's no need. I'm sure he'll be delighted; he'll be grateful to me for organizing a surprise lunch. Just give me the address where you're staying and I'll take care of the rest."

5

A metallic silver Mercedes arrived to transport Adam to the coast, to a historic Ottoman house that had been converted into an Italian restaurant and christened *Nessun Dorma*. The car door was opened by a courteous footman who guided him to the second floor without troubling to ask with whom he was dining.

When he saw his friend appear, Ramez got to his feet and gave him a fond hug before saying, in English:

"Let's skip the part where we're supposed to say 'You haven't changed at all!'"

Adam answered in the same language:

"You've got a point, no point lying to each other straightaway."

Laughing, they sat down at a circular table on which was set a large platter of crudités, and began by observing a short silence. Although both of them had changed, it was in very different ways. Adam was beginning to go grey but he had stayed slim; someone would easily pick out his younger self in a group photograph. Ramez had put on weight, and had grown the sort of thick, broad, elegantly bushy moustache once favoured by British colonels. Curiously, this was still black, while his hair was a pale grey. If his friend had met him in the street, he would have been hard-pressed to recognize him.

"Your assistant is very charming, and amazingly efficient."

"Lina is brilliant, I'm lucky to have her."

"An hour ago, I was wondering how I could track you down so we could have a brief chat, and now here we are having lunch together. It's almost a miracle."

"You can't imagine how happy I am to see you again.

Though I suppose it's really poor Mourad who has brought us together again. I flew in this morning to offer my condolences. I had a meeting in Athens yesterday, so I couldn't attend the funeral. I'm told there were thousands of people there."

"I didn't attend the funeral either, despite the fact that that was sort of why I came ..."

He briefly explained his falling-out with Mourad, the phone call he had received from the dying man's wife at dawn on Friday, his decision to make the trip so as not to upset his former friend. Lastly, his reluctance to attend the funeral ... Ramez reassured him:

"You did the most important thing. When he phoned you, you put aside your differences to come and be with him. And you went to visit Tania after the funeral. You have no reason to feel guilty."

He said nothing for a moment, then went on, this time in Arabic:

"I've followed Mourad's career a little, and I can understand why you cut ties with him. I responded somewhat differently, given that, in my profession, I'm constantly forced to deal with people whose wealth is the result of ill-gotten gains; but I felt the same about him as you did. Even though the position he adopted during the war was one he shared with many, many people, it was hard to accept from one of us. Every time I heard Mourad described as a corrupt politician, or the right-hand man to a thug, I felt ashamed, I felt personally humiliated.

"That said, I still believe that, deep down, our friend was an honest man, and that's the tragedy. Scumbags who behave like scumbags are completely at peace with themselves; honest people who, by dint of circumstances, act like scumbags are eaten up by guilt. I'm convinced that the cancer that killed Mourad was the result of his guilt, his shame, and his remorse.

"But I shouldn't be talking like this, when the man has only just been buried ... God have mercy on him, Allah yerhamo! Let's change the subject."

The table was ringed by a screen of tall, leafy plants, mostly bamboo, creating a sense of intimacy that favoured confidences. Here and there in the vast room were towering palm trees. The maître d'hôtel was standing next to one. Ramez beckoned him over.

"To start, can we have two larges plates of antipasti, no ham on mine. As for a main course—have you decided, Adam?"

"I'm tempted by the red mullet on a bed of risotto."

"An excellent choice. I'll have the same. White wine to wash it down?"

"Not for me, thanks, I don't drink at lunchtime."

"In theory, I agree with you, it's best not to drink at lunch. But this is a special occasion, so the least we can do is have a house prosecco to celebrate our reunion."

The maître d'hôtel nodded and went off to put in the order. The two friends immediately returned to their conversation, their reminiscences, punctuated by the occasional laugh—Ramez had a particularly booming laugh. Until at some point, in the course of conversation, Adam mentioned Ramzi.

The effect was instantaneous. Ramez's face clouded over, his voice faltered. The man who a moment earlier had been so loquacious was suddenly groping for words.

Adam watched him for a moment, then set down his fork and asked:

"Do you know why he went away?"

Several seconds ticked away.

"Do I know why he went away?"

His eyes closed, Ramez repeated the question as though to himself.

"When a man decides to retreat from the world, it's like committing suicide without the physical violence. There are obvious reasons, and others that are obscure, even to those closest to him, and of which even he may not be entirely conscious."

He fell silent, perhaps hoping that Adam would make do with this tortuous response. But his friend continued to stare at him. So he went on:

"If I had to sum it up in a sentence, I would say that, deep down, he had a feeling that everything he did, everything he had dedicated his life to, was useless, futile.

"Sometimes, in the middle of a conversation, he would suddenly pause and say to me, 'Why are we doing all this?' The first time, we had just been awarded a major contract to build a palace. There we were, poring over the blueprints, and he asked, 'Why does this man need another two-thousand-square-metre palace? He already has three, to my knowledge.' He was smiling, and I smiled too and said, 'I agree with you, but he's a client, he has more money than he knows what to do with. He's going to squander it one way or another, and I'd prefer he spent it on us.' He said, 'Maybe you're right,' and that was the end of that. But over time, he made remarks like this more and more often."

Ramez paused, as though collecting his thoughts, then went on:

"Our friend couldn't stop wondering about the purpose of the projects we were commissioned to build. A company like ours, with branches in more than twenty countries, is contracted to build a thousand different things: a seaport, an airport terminal, a shopping mall, a tourist centre, a museum, a prison, a military base, a palace, a university, and so on. Not all the projects have the same value or the same ethical implications, but it's not our place to judge, is it? I'm no cynic, and I share the same values as Ramzi, but I feel it's not our role. The prison you built for a tyrant might be used to incarcerate his opponents today, but tomorrow it might be the tyrant and his cronies who are locked up there. You can't simply refuse on principle to ever build a prison. There are prisons in every country in the world, everything depends on how they are used. Our role, as a construction company, is to try to make prisons a little more humane—that's all we can do. When you have 1,837 employees, each of them with families, and you have to find the means to pay them every month, you can't afford to play at being a righter of wrongs. Don't you agree?"

Little remained of the good humour with which Ramez had greeted Adam's arrival. He now seemed beleaguered by the thousand thoughts clashing inside his head. He took several sips of prosecco, too quickly. Then he continued:

"What I've just said is only one aspect of it. Then there were the wives, our wives.

"It starts like a fairy tale. One day, I meet a girl, Dunia, and fall head over heels in love. I immediately introduce her to Ramzi. She finds him intelligent, funny, sophisticated; for his part, after their first meeting, he took me aside and whispered, 'Take her by the hand and never let her go.'

"Four months later, Ramzi comes and tells me that he, too, has met his soulmate. By troubling coincidence, her name is also Dunia. As though fate were giving us an emphatic nudge. Can you imagine? Ramzi and I have almost the same name, we've been inseparable since our first day at university, we spend our days together and our nights together, and now here we are, falling for two girls with the same name.

"So, he introduces her to Dunia and me. She is quite pretty, she seems friendly, he is visibly in love with her, and we decide to get married on the same day. It couldn't be a single ceremony, because my Dunia and I were being married by the *cheikh*, whereas he and his Dunia were to be married in church—by the bishop of the mountain—who was his uncle on his mother's side. But we decided to have a single reception. You were already in France by then, but a number of our friends came, including Tania and Mourad, Albert, and Sémiramis.

"Unfortunately, the only thing our wives had in common was their name. Mine immediately understood how important Ramzi was to me; from the day of the wedding, his wife was jealous of our friendship. When I was worried about something, the first thing my Dunia would say was 'What does Ramzi think?' and she encouraged me to take his advice. She constantly reminded me that he was a true friend and that I was lucky to have a partner who was so honest, intelligent, and devoted. To listen to her, he didn't have a single fault. I was the one who should have been jealous, hearing my wife talking about another man like that, don't you think?

"But it was the other way round, Ramzi's wife was constantly telling him not to trust me, to distance himself from me. If I so much as called him and we spent a couple of minutes on the phone and she heard him laughing at something I had said, either she would make a scene, or she would find some other excuse. It was ridiculous, and it was pathological. She wanted him to take a closer look at the accounts. She was convinced that I wasn't giving him his full share of the profits."

"And Ramzi ended up believing her?"

"Not for a second! In the beginning, he didn't even mention it to me, he felt sad about it, and ashamed. Then, one day, there was a trivial incident—I don't need to go into detail—but one that made my wife and I realize how much this woman despised us. The following day, Ramzi came into my office, he apologized, and he talked to me about her outbursts. To justify his wife's behaviour, he talked about her family history, a father who had been swindled by his own brothers, an uncle who had robbed his own nieces of their inheritance; in short, a series of betrayals that had made his wife pathologically suspicious. Ramzi said he was certain that, in time, she would grow more trusting and her attitude would change. I said, 'Of course she will.' But I didn't believe it, and neither did he, I suspect."

"He must have found it very painful."

"Excruciating. For me, it was simply a minor inconvenience; for him it was a constant torment. One day, with tears in his eyes, he told me that getting married was the worst decision he had ever made. He was angry with himself for not realizing her faults in time. The similarity of our wives' first names had seemed to him to be a sign from Heaven, but it was a trap set by Hell.

"I tried to console him, I told him that, when it came to marriage, there was no such thing as foresight, that it was a lottery, you don't know whether you've got the right ticket until afterwards. And I wasn't just saying that to console him, I genuinely believe it. In traditional cultures, where men and women spend little time together before the wedding, when they can't even talk in private before being pledged to each other for life, marriage is like one of those fortune cookies you get in Chinese restaurants. You pick one at random, break it open, smooth out the strip of paper, and only then does it tell you your fortune.

"In more developed cultures, men and women spend

time together. In theory, they have the opportunity to size each other up. But in practice, they're just as likely to make mistakes. Because marriage is a disastrous institution.

"I'm hardly in a position to say so, since I've spent the past quarter century with a woman I love and who loves me. But I still believe marriage is a disastrous institution. Before the wedding, all men are attentive, considerate, they treat the object of their affections like a princess, until the day she becomes 'their' wife; after that, they quickly become tyrants, they treat their wives like servants, they change completely and society encourages them. Before the wedding is all fun and games; afterwards, things are serious, and sordid, and sad.

"Women are little better. When they want to get married, they're all sweetness and light. Gentle, obliging, easy-going—everything to reassure their suitor. Until he marries them. Only then do they reveal their true nature that they've been doing everything to suppress.

"To their credit, I'd say that with women the transformation is not as brutal or as systematic as it is with men. The lover and the husband are two different species, like a dog and a wolf. Before marriage, we're all dogs to some extent, and afterwards, we're all wolves; to different degrees, granted, but it is a transformation that is difficult to avoid. In certain cultures, it is as inevitable as the progression from adolescence to adulthood.

"With women, it's less clear-cut. Many of them don't change very much, either because they are genuinely loving, or because they're not very good actresses and end up revealing their true nature before the man proposes. Ramzi's wife didn't fall into that category. She managed to hide her true character until after the wedding; she came across as gentle and attentive, she treated me like a brother and my Dunia like a sister. Then, overnight, she couldn't hold it in anymore, she started spitting her poison. By the time Ramzi realized, it was too late."

"He could have divorced her."

"He should have done, it's certainly what I would have done if I'd made the same mistake. But, aside from the fact that divorce, for Christians like you, is much more complicated than it is for us, Ramzi is opposed to it in principle. We discussed the possibility of it more than once ... He preferred to cling to the notion that his wife would change. He kept telling me that she needed to feel safe, to feel secure, and that it was his duty to create an environment that would help her get better.

"Then the children were born, two boys and a girl. The birth of a child is supposed to be joyful, and Ramzi tried to convince himself that he was happy. And he clung to the idea that motherhood would bring out all the love and tenderness he had seen in his wife when they first met. I didn't contradict him—what would have been the point? But by then, all I expected from her was slap in the face or a stab in the back.

"And I wasn't wrong. She went on undermining him. She fed the children the same lies that her husband refused to listen to. 'Your father is a gullible fool who lets himself be manipulated by his partner.' The slow drip of poison, day after day, year after year, gradually had its effect, I noticed it every time our two families met up. Ramzi was as affectionate as ever, his wife put on an act, but the children didn't know how to pretend. I could tell from the way they behaved what she had been telling them about me. When I tried to hug them, they flinched. Not just when they were ten, when they were four. It was sad and it was absurd.

"But the most serious issue was the lies this woman managed to plant in their minds about the business their father and I had founded. We had built up an empire, one that our children would inherit. But she spent so much time telling them that their father was being manipulated, exploited, robbed, that they grew up with a burning hatred for everything we did. As a result, not one of them wanted to study engineering or architecture, not one of them wanted to work with us.

"None of this was helped by the fact that their mother fell seriously ill. A particularly aggressive cancer that, within a year and a half, would be the death of her. The pain made her more venomous, more spiteful. Though Ramzi cared for her selflessly, she never stopped railing against him, claiming that he had always favoured the business and his partnership with me at the expense of his wife and his children.

"Since she was gravely ill, and in agonizing pain, her husband didn't contradict her. To appease her, he promised to focus less on the business and devote more time to his family. The children—who, by then, were thirteen, sixteen, and seventeen—heard all this; they saw their mother as a martyr and their father as a cold-hearted monster.

"Then the poor thing died. She was only forty or forty-one. The children channelled all their grief into a bitter hatred of their father, as though this was a natural expression of their loyalty to their mother's memory. All three of them left home. They're in America now: the girl in New Jersey, one of the boys is in North Carolina, I don't know where the other is. They haven't had any contact with their father for years. I don't think they even gave him their contact details.

"You wanted to know why Ramzi withdrew from the

world? That's my explanation. It's also possible that he had a Damascene conversion, but the tragedy that was his family was more than enough reason for a man to want to go and hole up in a monastery."

"Has he been there long?"

"The last time he came to the office was February of last year."

"So, fourteen months."

"To me, it might as well be fourteen years."

"Have you seen him since then?"

"Just once. It was ..."

Ramez suddenly stopped and looked at his watch.

"Half past three! I didn't notice the time passing. I can be pretty long-winded when it comes to him."

"What time is your flight?"

"Whenever we decide. It's my plane, and the crew is on standby, they're just waiting for my call."

Suddenly, his face broke into a broad smile.

"I've just had a brilliant idea. You're coming to Amman with me."

"Thanks for the invitation, but it's not possible."

"Let's not play at being overworked businessmen, Adam. We're back together for the first time in twenty years, we're talking to each other as if we'd never been apart. It is a glorious opportunity, why let it slip through our fingers? I'm sure you've got a thousand things you want to say, and so have I. Why can't we be the way we were back then? We never arranged to meet up, we never had to check our diaries. You'd pull up under my balcony and beep your horn, I'd come downstairs and we'd head off to a café, or to the cinema, or to Mourad's house ... For once, let's just forget propriety, forget how old we are. Let's do what we used to do. We're having lunch and, at the end of the meal, I say, 'Why don't you come back to my place for the evening, I'll introduce you to my wife, and I'll drop you back here tomorrow.' I get up, you get up, and we head off. Have you got your passport?"

"I always keep it in my pocket. Force of habit."

"Have you any medication you need to take tonight?"

Adam checked. He had them with him.

"Perfect, everything else is irrelevant," Ramez said. "We can go."

"But I don't have a spare shirt, or my toilet bag."

"Don't worry about that, I'll sort it out. Let's go."

At this, he laid his hands on the table and hoisted himself to his feet, and three seconds later, Adam did likewise.

6

From a distance, Ramez's private jet could pass for a commercial plane. The silver-grey Mercedes drove through the various checkpoints and pulled up at the foot of the airstairs. The jet's body was emblazoned with the company logo, twin crescent moons which were actually a stylized version of the initials of the founders of Ramzi Ramez Works, one of the largest public construction companies in the region.

Inside, but for the windows, it was easy to forget that this was an aeroplane. There was an office, a bedroom, and a living room that could be effortlessly converted into a dining room. Any eventual passengers were seated in one of twenty comfortable seats in a section that on a commercial plane would have had sixty.

As soon as the two friends were settled, a Sûreté officer came aboard, checked their passports with a quick nod, and wished them a pleasant flight. Once he had disembarked, the doors were closed, the air steward came to check that their seatbelts were secured, then, at a nod from his boss, he brought them two Turkish coffees and an assortment of oriental pastries.

"Sugar with your coffee?"

Adam glanced at the plate of pastries before answering:

"No, thanks, no sugar."

The two men exchanged a guilty grin, then each selected a sweetmeat and settled back in his chair to savour it.

"No sugar ..." Ramez said, laughing good-naturedly.

When he had finished the last mouthful, Adam said to his friend:

"What does it feel like to be rich?"

"You're not exactly poor, from what I've heard."

"No, I'm not poor. But my monthly salary would be just enough to buy a return ticket from Paris to Amman in cattle class. Don't get me wrong, I'm not complaining, I have no financial worries and I don't want for anything. But given the vocation I've chosen, I'm never going to be rich."

Up to this point, Ramez had simply smiled, perhaps with a little embarrassment. Now, his face clouded over. He began by repeating his friend's question, but as a statement:

"What does it feel like to be rich ... The day I realized that the company was on a sure footing, that it was earning more and more money and that I was a rich man, I felt ..."

He seemed to hesitate over his words.

"I felt as though I had recovered half my dignity."

The phrase was cryptic and unexpected. Adam was about to ask him to clarify, but noticed that his friend suddenly seemed very agitated and gave him a moment to regain his composure.

Ramez took a sip of his coffee before continuing.

"For years now, I've been waking up with two conflicting feelings, joy and sadness. Joy, because I have made a success of my profession, I've earned a lot of money, I have a beautiful house and a contented family life. But sadness, too, because my people are in the depths of despair. Those who speak the language I speak, those who profess the same religion, are everywhere derided and often despised. Since birth, I have belonged to a vanquished civilization, and since I am not prepared to renounce it, I must live with that mark on my forehead."

Silence. Still Adam said nothing; his friend went further:

"I'm not simply talking about solidarity with my own people, about empathy. I, too, feel humiliated, personally humiliated.

"When I travel to Europe, people treat me with respect—as they do anyone who is rich. They smile at me, they open doors for me with a little bow, they are happy to sell me anything I care to buy. But deep down, they despise me and look down on me. To them, I'm nothing but a rich barbarian. Even when I'm wearing the finest Italian suit, to them, I'm a beggar. Why? Because I belong to a vanquished people, a vanquished civilization. I feel it less intensely in Asia, in Africa, in Latin America, because they have been just as oppressed by history. But in Europe, I feel it keenly, don't you?"

Adam was caught completely unawares.

"Maybe, sometimes," he said without truly committing himself.

"In Paris, when you speak Arabic in public, don't you spontaneously lower your voice?"

"Probably."

"Think about the other foreigners! The Italians, the Spanish, the Russians, not to mention the British and the Americans. They're not worried about being met with a hostile or a disapproving glare. Maybe I'm imagining it. But it's how I feel. And even if I were the richest man in the world, it wouldn't change anything."

Another long silence. Ramez gazed through the window at the clouds. Adam studied them too. The steward appeared and, at a nod from his boss, cleared away the pastries and came back some seconds later with a bowl of fruit.

"Have you ever had white apricots?" Ramez asked with a note of pride.

He chose a perfect, ripe fruit of a yellow so pale it did

indeed look white. He handed it to Adam, who closed his eyes and slowly bit into it.

"Delicious! I've never eaten one before."

"The harvest is so small that they've never been commercialized. I have them shipped in specially from a little village near Damascus."

"I didn't know that such an exquisite flavour even existed!"

"I'm glad you like it. It's my favourite fruit. Ramzi used to love them too. Every year, I'd send him two crates. Now, I'll send them to you."

The two men reverently ate another luscious fruit. Then another. But their pleasure was now tainted by the memory of their lost friend.

After a long moment, Adam said simply:

"So, you went to see him ..."

Ramez heaved a sigh and nodded several times.

"Yes, I went to see him. I was convinced that if I made a solid case, I could persuade him to come back. Our friendship—unlike so many others—was never based on silence, lies, or turning a blind eye. We had always talked a lot, argued a lot, always respected each other's opinions. I thought that day it would be the same. That he would tell me about his worries, that I would comfort him, reassure him, and that, in the end, I'd have the date when he planned to come back, or at least a promise.

"But I quickly realized I was mistaken. When I saw him wearing a monk's habit, I was completely at a loss. What arguments could I come up with, me, a Muslim engineer, that might persuade a Christian monk to return to civilian life? I know nothing about theology, and I thought it would be ridiculous to talk about problems with the company. Or about anything else. My mind went blank, like an actor who has suddenly forgotten his lines. So, I launched into polite platitudes. 'Are you well, Ramzi?' 'Yes, thank you, I'm well.' 'There's nothing you need?' 'No, I have everything I want.' 'Are they treating you well?' 'I'm not in prison, Ramez, I'm in a monastery of my own free will.' I apologized. It's true, I felt as though I was in a prison visiting room. I tried to change tack. 'What I meant was, is the life you're leading here with the monks what you hoped it would be?' He said, 'Yes. I wanted a simple life, one where I could take the time to meditate, to pray, to reflect. And that's exactly what I've found.' I asked if he wanted me to fill him in on what had been happening with the company, he said no. I asked if he wanted news of his children, he said no. I asked if it bothered him that I had come to visit, he said no, but only after a few seconds' hesitation. At that point, I realized that I wasn't welcome. I stood up. He stood up. I shook hands with him, like he was a stranger. He told me he would pray for me.

"I went out, walked as far as my car, got into the back seat and cried like I haven't cried since my father died. My chauffeur was staring at me in the rearview mirror, but I didn't care what he thought. I didn't hold back, I let my tears flow. Ramzi was more than a brother to me, and now, suddenly, inexplicably, he had become a stranger. That's the sad story of 'the inseparables.'"

"So, you'd advise me against visiting him?"

"No, absolutely not. It's important to keep in touch. With me, he was on his guard, he was worried that I'd pressure him to go back to his old life. And besides, it was just after his ... his transformation. It was too soon; I would have done better to wait. A year has passed since then, he might be happy to see an old friend."

"I'll try and see him in the next couple of days. Actually, I've got a plan I'm working on. In fact, I was about to mention it before our conversation drifted off. I'm trying to get all our old friends together again for a reunion."

Ramez almost leapt out of his seat.

"That is a brilliant idea! I've wanted to do something like that for years. I loved the evenings we used to spend together. I remember the conversation, the laughter. I never really got over seeing the group disperse. Nothing in the world can replace the warmth of a group of friends. Not work, not money, not family. Nothing can replace those moments when friends get together, share their thoughts, their dreams, their food. At least, I feel I need it. Maybe I'm hopelessly nostalgic, a frustrated teenager who's never really adapted to the adult world, but that's how I feel. That was what Ramzi and I were looking for, a childhood friendship that could carry on for the rest of our lives, that could be as much a part of our professional lives as our private lives. And, for years, that's what we had, and it was amazing. And then we lost it ..."

His face began to cloud over once again.

"Needless to say, you can count me in. Just give me the date and the location of the reunion, and I'll be there. Even if I'm half way around the world, I'll be there. On the other hand, if you're hoping to persuade Ramzi to leave the monastery and join us, you're in for a disappointment. Unless he has changed completely in the past few months."

"Based on what you've just told me, I think it's a lost cause. But I'll go and visit him anyway. And I will invite him to come; we'll see how he responds."

"Who else were you planning to invite?"

"I've already written to Albert, who's based in America, and to Naïm who's in Brazil. Then there's you and me, obviously, and Tania and Sémi. Apart from Ramzi, I was thinking of inviting Bilal's brother, Nidal."

Adam watched for a reaction from his friend, but Ramez simply gave an ambiguous nod.

"Do you think it's a good idea to invite Nidal?"

Ramez seemed to hesitate, and then said with a smile of resignation:

"Yes, why not. Invite him."

"You don't exactly seem enthusiastic."

"Enthusiastic, no. But I'm not against the idea."

He thought for a moment.

"I'll tell you what I really feel. Sooner or later radical militants like Nidal become the oppressors. But right now, they're the ones being oppressed in our countries, and in the West, they're demonized. Do you defend someone who is being oppressed knowing full well that, someday soon, he will behave like a tyrant? It's a dilemma I don't have an answer to ... So, if you were planning to invite him, go ahead, why not?"

He shrugged and paused for a moment.

"Who else were you thinking about?"

"I'd like our friends to bring their wives. They'll probably get bored listening to our stories, but it will forge a closer bond. I certainly hope that your wife can come."

"I'll let you invite her when we get to Amman. I'm sure she'll be thrilled."

"I'm less sure that my partner, Dolores, will be able to join us. She works all the hours that God sends."

"Is she French?"

"No, Argentine. But she's been living in France for twenty years."

"I assume Naïm married a Brazilian?"

"No idea. I know he's married, and that he has kids of university age. But I don't know anything about his wife. If he's ever mentioned her name, I can't remember it."

"Do you realize what you've just said? You and Naïm,

you used to be like brothers, and now you don't even know the name of his wife. Any more than you knew my wife's name or I knew yours' this morning. Things like that make me sad, it makes me sick. I feel as though we've all betrayed each other."

"You're right. But we have the war and the fact that we're scattered here and there as an excuse."

"It's always possible to come up with an excuse. But if we valued our friendships at all, we would have found some way to meet up once or twice in the space of twenty-five years. I'm not blaming the others, I'm mostly blaming myself. I spend my life criss-crossing the world, I could easily have stuck pins in a world map marking the cities where my friends live so I could visit when I was passing through. Actually, I'm going to do just that. It's never too late. You're in Paris, Naïm is in Brazil—São Paulo or Rio?"

"São Paulo."

"And Albert?"

"He's in Indianapolis working for a think tank."

"Now you mention it, I remember someone telling me that. He's pretty influential, apparently."

"Possibly. I certainly know he's well respected in academia."

"I'm not surprised. Even back in university, he was a thoughtful, intelligent, imaginative guy. Most people didn't notice, because he was taciturn and withdrawn. He had to go to the United States to blossom. Are you in touch with him?"

"Yes, we email each other from time to time. It's true, he often comes out with things that are surprising and intelligent. On the other hand, I know nothing about his private life. I don't even know whether he's got a wife, or children."

"I doubt it."

"Why do you say that?"

"One day, the three of us were hanging out, Albert, Ramzi, and me. As usual, he wasn't saying much, with his pointy little nose and his sardonic smile. We were chatting about some girl. I thought she was sexy and Ramzi thought she was stuck-up. Or maybe it was the other way round. Typical teenage-boy talk. Suddenly Albert said, 'Lots of people think that you two are a couple, but no one even suspects me. Funny, isn't it?' It took us a couple of seconds to realize that our friend had just confided his most private secret. We gave each other a knowing smile. Then Albert said, in French, 'Don't go telling the barbarians!' We reassured him with a nod.

"When Ramzi and I were alone, we promised not to mention it to anyone, 'barbarian' or otherwise. You're the first person I've ever told. I know you've never had any prejudices about things like that, and even if you had, you'd have long since lost them in the years you've been living in Europe. And, I assume that, after living for so many years in America, he probably doesn't hide it anymore. Even so, I wouldn't bring up the subject, let him decide whether to talk about it or not."

"Strange that he never confided in me," said Adam, perhaps surprised, but definitely annoyed. "Do you think he included me among the 'barbarians'?"

"No, of course not, he was very fond of you, you were probably his closest friend. I think he didn't tell his secret to anyone, and that time with Ramzi and me, it just slipped out. Once he'd said it, he couldn't take it back, so he pretended to be cool about it. He smiled, but it was a forced smile. He was probably kicking himself for blurting it out. But he had no reason to worry. We never betrayed him; actually, after that the three of us were closer."

Adam looked out the window of the plane. There was nothing to be seen now but darkness. The remains of the day. He checked his watch.

"Nearly eight o'clock."

"We'll be landing in Amman in about half an hour. A small whisky?"

"No, thanks. I'd prefer another coffee."

The steward approached, took the order, and returned with a steaming cup, a glass filled with ice, and a bottle of whisky with a distinctly peaty aroma.

"So there'll be about ten of us at the reunion," said Ramez, who was clearly excited by the plan. "So, what's it to be? A banquet? A ceremony? A seminar?"

"I haven't given that part much thought. Up to now, I've simply suggested meeting up to see whether our friends were really keen, whether it would mean something to them after all these years. So far, the reactions have been positive, but there's a lot left to decide."

"You can't bring people from the four corners of the earth just for a reunion dinner and a coffee with no sugar. There has to be something more."

"You're right, but what? To be honest, I'm not much of an organizer."

"It's not your job to organize, Adam. You're a university professor, an intellectual, your job is to think, and to help us to think too. Forget about logistics! Forget about Mourad's death! Forget about the reunion ..."

"But the reunion is the whole purpose of the plan."

"Forget the whole purpose! When starting a plan, you always need a pretext, but it's important not to get too attached to it, otherwise you forget the essential."

"And what is the essential, according to you?"

"The essential, is that we've just come to the end of a terrible century, a new century has begun, one that looks like it might be more terrible still, and I can't help but wonder what fate has in store for us."

"And you think our old friends will be able to tell you?"

"Maybe, maybe not, but I need to talk about it to someone. Preferably, with people I'm close to, people with empathy and a certain ability to think. That's what I most loved about our circle of friends at university. Not so much the political ideas. We all claimed to be Marxists back then, because that was the zeitgeist. But, to be honest, I've never really understood dialectical materialism, the class struggle, or democratic centralism. I parroted things from books I'd read, or that I'd heard from people who had read them. If I claimed to be left-wing, it was only because I wasn't indifferent to the plight of the poor and the oppressed. Nothing more. And the reason I liked hanging out with our group is because they were interested in the whole wide world, not just their own little lives. They talked about Vietnam and China, about Greece and Indonesia. They had a passion for literature, for music, for philosophy and ideas. At the time, we might have believed that most people shared our concerns, but that kind of circle of friends was rare when we were young, and it's even rarer these days. I've been going to business meetings and social gatherings for more than twenty years. Most men go through life from cradle to grave without taking the time to wonder where the world is headed, or what the future will be.

"What I'm saying to you now is almost word for word what Ramzi said to me one day. At the time, I agreed with him, having no idea of the decision he was contemplating. Personally, I would never willingly retreat from the world, I am more fascinated than terrified by change. But on one point at least I completely agree with him: it's sometimes necessary to rise above the mundane and consider fundamental questions. I'm not expecting our friends to communicate some eternal truth, but I want to listen to them talking about their lives, thinking aloud, telling me their hopes and fears. We are on a cusp between two centuries, between two millennia. 2001! I realize that the numbering of years is simply a human construct, but such a symbolic year is a good time to pause and meditate. Don't you think?"

Adam's face broke into a broad smile. His friend shot him a suspicious look.

"What's so funny about what I've just said?"

"Since this morning, I've been wondering what the hell I could say to Ramzi when I go to visit. And you've just given me the answer. I'll give him precisely the same speech I've just heard you give. If I invite him to a reunion dinner for friends, I know he won't come. But if I invite him to a meditation retreat ..."

It was Ramez's turn to smile.

"You can always try, though I'm still sceptical."

"Well, it's the only card I can play ..."

"If you manage to convince him, I'll give you a plane just like this one."

"No, thanks. I wouldn't know what to do with it."

"A car, then ..."

"That sounds more reasonable ..."

"Any particular make?"

"No, Ramez, I was just joking, I don't need a jet or a car. In Paris, I go everywhere on foot, or by metro, taxi, or bus. Sometimes even by bike. On the other hand ..."

"Go on, tell me."

"On the other hand, if you were to send me two crates of white apricots every year ..."

"I've already promised."

"And if you were to add a crate of Egyptian mangoes,

the long, thin ones with rust-coloured flesh they call *hindi* ..."

"Done!"

"... a crate of sugar apples, and one of *moghrabi* oranges."

"And dates, I assume."

"No, these days I can get dates in Paris."

"Not like the ones I'm going to send."

There were still two apricots on the plate. Each of the friends took one and savoured it slowly.

7

The plane touched down smoothly in Amman. An all-terrain vehicle arrived at the foot of the steps to whisk the businessman and his guest towards one of the twenty hills that ringed the site of ancient Philadelphia.

As Adam must have expected, the Ramez residence was an opulent three-storey building of white stone set among lush gardens that sharply contrasted with the arid terrain all around. The gate swung open as the car approached, there was no need even to slow down.

As the two friends stepped down, a swarm of security men, gardeners, and servants clustered around them, holding open doors and offering deferential greetings.

A moment later, Ramez's wife, Dunia, came to greet them wearing a long grey housedress embroidered with yellow threads.

As soon as she had greeted her guest and kissed her husband, she asked, a little worriedly:

"Is Lina not with you?"

"No, she stayed behind, she had a dinner. When I fly our friend back, I'll bring her home with me."

Dunia turned to Adam.

"In our family, we take a plane the way other people take a car. You'd think we were in Texas!"

But what had struck the guest was something different.

"So you're saying that the charming young woman on the telephone who introduced herself as your assistant is actually the daughter of Ramez, well of both of you."

Both parents smiled.

"That's how she is," Dunia said. "When she's working, she never says she's his daughter."

"And so as not to give the game away, I simply say Lina."

"And then you say she's brilliant and you're lucky to have her."

"As her employer, that's my considered opinion," Ramez said, visibly happy to have the opportunity to talk about her.

"And an entirely objective opinion it is too," his friend teased.

"Lina is the love of his life," Dunia said in a tender voice.

"Whoever marries her had better treat her like a queen. Otherwise ..."

The threat hung in the air.

Adam was escorted by his hosts to what they called "his room," and which was actually a lavish apartment with a bathroom and Jacuzzi, a living room bigger than the one he had in Paris, a liberally stocked bar, a television, a computer, and a balcony overlooking the glowing city.

Laid out on the bed, still in their packaging, were a pair of pyjamas, three shirts, three pairs of socks, underwear, and an embroidered bathrobe with matching slippers.

"I think I'll just stay here," Adam said by way of thanks. "I don't suppose there's a job going at the University of Jordan?"

"It could be arranged," Ramez said with a booming laugh, "the provost is a close friend. We'll be waiting for you downstairs when you fancy dinner. But take your time, we usually eat late. Call your wife to tell her where you are. Oh, and call the hotel so they're not expecting you back tonight."

"Sound advice," Dunia said, "I wish Ramez would call me from time to time to let me know whether he's in Singapore, Dubai, or Kuala Lumpur."

Her husband took her arm, partly by way of apology, partly to interrupt.

"What difference would it make? After a certain number of trips, you don't know which city you're in; conference rooms all look the same, as do hotel rooms."

"Come on, let's let Adam get some rest."

The Eighth Day

1

When Adam opened his eyes, the room was in darkness. He picked up his wristwatch from the nightstand. It read 6:15 a.m. He raised the blinds and the sun hit him full in the face.

He was still wearing the dressing gown. The box containing the new pyjamas was no longer on the bed; someone had moved it to the table, together with the shirts and the other packaged clothes.

It seemed he had not moved all night. Though he had been supposed to join his friends downstairs for dinner. They had probably come to fetch him and, finding him sound asleep, had decided not to wake him.

He took another shower, shaved, and patted his face with eau de cologne, then he dressed and left the suite of rooms. A young woman wearing a white apron was waiting outside the door to lead him to the sun-soaked veranda where his friends were taking breakfast.

"Just as well we didn't wait for you before having dinner," Ramez said good-naturedly.

Adam apologized profusely while Dunia defended him against his friend's teasing.

"That's no way to greet a guest first thing in the morning. You'd do better to ask if he slept well."

"I don't need to ask, I saw it with my own eyes," her husband said, still chuckling. "He was snoring like a diesel engine."

"What a terrible oaf I married, don't you agree?"

She laughed and her husband laughed with her. Adam added his two cents:

"If you'd asked my advice, I could have warned you. He had a dreadful upbringing. It's much too late now. I'm afraid you were unlucky."

Ramez seemed delighted to be attacked in this manner.

"That's how it used to be, in the group. We were forever calling each other illiterate, brainless morons. But it was just a private joke. We genuinely liked each other, we respected each other. Didn't we?"

Adam nodded. Then the young woman in the apron who had brought him downstairs reappeared with a steaming cafetière and served them each in turn. As soon as she had gone, Ramez said to his wife:

"On the flight over, we talked about Ramzi. Adam is planning to go see him."

Since Adam had arrived the previous night, he had only ever seen Dunia smile. A gentle, natural, artless smile. But at the mention of their lost friend, the smile instantly faded.

"We still haven't got over his departure. His 'desertion,' I should probably say. There's something disturbing about a man abruptly deciding to leave his work, his home, his friends, to hole up with a bunch of strangers in a cabin in the mountains.

"He was like a brother to Ramez—and to me, too, for that matter. When he left, we were both stunned. You have a friend, you see him every day, you trust him with your secrets, you feel you know him as well as you do yourself, and one day you discover you didn't know him at all. You discover that there was someone else within, someone you never expected. Ramez still tries to make excuses for him, but I feel bitter about it. A man has no right to just leave like that, on a whim."

"I'm sure it wasn't on a whim," Ramez said thoughtfully.

"If it wasn't a whim, it's worse. It means that he agonized over his decision in secret without ever talking to us. It means there must have been a dozen times when he sat at this table where we're sitting this morning, and while we opened our hearts to him, he was already contemplating his decision to leave and never see us again.

"I'm supposed to forgive him because he was overcome by faith. What sort of faith tells a man to leave his closest friends, his only true friends, in order to find God? Does that mean that God is up there, in the mountain, but not here, in the city? That God is in the monastery, but not on building sites or in offices? To believe in God is to believe that he is everywhere!

"I'm sorry, Adam. It's not religion that I'm criticizing. I don't know what you believe, and I wouldn't want to offend you."

"Speak your mind, Dunia," the guest said. "With me, you're welcome to criticize every religion in the world. Mine and all the others. Don't imagine for a moment that I'll be offended."

"In any event, I'm not criticizing your coreligionists, mine are much worse. When they take to the mountains, it's not just to pray and meditate ... What I find frustrating is the way that these days people drag religion into everything, and use it to justify everything. I dress the way I do because of my faith. I eat this or that because of my faith. A man can leave his friends and feel no need to explain because his faith is calling to him. They dress it up every which way, they claim to be serving their faith when in fact they're using religion to serve their ambitions, or their manias.

"Of course, religion is important, but no more so than family, than friendship, certainly no more so than loyalty. More and more people are using religion to replace morality. They talk about what is admissible and inadmissible, what is pure and impure, always citing chapter and verse. I'd rather they worried about what is honest and what is decent. Because they have religion, they think they're exempt from having morals.

"I come from a devout religious family. My great-grandfather was Shaykh al-Islām to the sultans of the Ottoman Empire. At home, we always fasted during Ramadan. It was normal, it went without saying, we didn't make a fuss about it. These days, it's not enough to fast, you have to let the whole world know you're fasting and keep a wary eye on those who are not fasting.

"One of these days, people will get fed up of the intrusiveness of religion and reject everything, the good with the bad ..."

Dunia had become feverishly impassioned. Ramez laid his hand on hers.

"Calm down, darling. Religion didn't force Ramzi to withdraw from the world. The monks didn't come and kidnap him. He had a crisis of faith, and perhaps it was our role, as his friends, to notice, and to foresee the consequences."

"No, Ramez! Stop blaming yourself! Stop feeling guilty! You couldn't be expected to guess what was going on in Ramzi's mind. You were his best friend; it was his responsibility to confide in you so that you could discuss it. You and I have no reason to reproach ourselves. And you're right, it's not the monks' fault. If someone behaved badly, it was Ramzi. And that woman ... I won't speak ill of the dead, but if she were still alive, I'd have a few choice things to say about her."

She paused, as though groping for words, or trying to regain her composure, or perhaps to recall a particular scene. The two men simply waited in silence.

"When people come to our house," she went on, "I always look at their eyes. I try to read their thoughts. Most are probably thinking they would love to have a house like ours. But they don't all think it in the same way. Some look at it with wonder, others with envy. Some of our guests are richer than we are, most are much less wealthy and some are poor. But their wonder or their envy has nothing to do with whether they are rich or poor. It is about their outlook on life. Harun al-Rashid was a caliph, his empire stretched from North Africa to India, but he envied the great wealth of his vizier, Ja'far, and set about ruining him and stripping him of his riches. There are those who rejoice in others' fortunes, even if they share in them only briefly, partially from without. And there are those who feel threatened by the happiness of others.

"When you got here, Adam, you probably thought, 'My friend Ramez has made his fortune, he's built a beautiful house, his wife is friendly, it will be nice to spend some time in their company.' But whenever Ramzi's wife came to our house, I could see the envy in her eyes, in her pinched lips. If there was some new piece of furniture, she would spot it immediately. If I bought a new rug, Ramez could walk across it fifty times without seeing it. I'd have to say 'Look!' to get him to notice it. Whenever that woman visited, she would spot something new the moment she came in, and I could see her working out how much I'd paid for it.

"When we first moved in here we had pipes burst on three separate occasions, and one day I said to Ramzi's wife that I was afraid we'd wake up one morning with the whole house flooded, water streaming down the walls, soaking the furniture, the rugs, the drapes … I looked at her, and what I saw on her face was a look of pure, uncontrollable joy, as though I'd just told her about some wonderful event.

"I remember, that day, I felt afraid of her, and I remember

thinking, 'She'll cast a spell on my husband.' I'm not usually superstitious, but after seeing her reaction I was afraid, especially when Ramez took the plane somewhere. In fact, I told him never to mention the plane in front of her."

With a nod and a smile Ramez confirmed this, shrugging his shoulders and raising his eyebrows to make it clear he didn't believe in the evil eye. Oblivious to his reaction, Dunia carried on:

"Ramez and Ramzi made their fortunes together, neither is a penny richer than the other. But Ramzi's wealth is less ostentatious, he always was discreet and restrained. In itself that's a virtue. But for his wife, it felt like a punishment. Ramez was always more extravagant, more demonstrative, more of a show-off ..."

Her husband's eyes grew wide.

"A show-off? Me?"

With maternal tenderness, Dunia ran her fingers through her husband's hair.

"Yes, my darling, you like to show off your house, your private jet, your Mercedes."

"Can you imagine what people would say if a man as rich as I am dressed like a beggar and drove around in an old banger?"

"I'm not criticizing you, darling, I love you just the way you are, if I'd married a miser, I would have been miserable. But it's a simple fact that you never hid your wealth, while your partner preferred people to think 'He's rich, but it hasn't changed him a bit.' Correct me if I'm wrong."

"What Dunia says is absolutely true," her husband admitted. "Ramzi was happy for people to say that he'd worked hard to become a success, but he was wary when people called him rich. He was almost ashamed of his wealth. That's probably why his wife behaved the way she did. I'm sure she wanted to spend the money, but that he stopped her."

"Deep down, the boys we all called 'the inseparables' were very different from each other," Adam said softly, as though to himself. "You both became rich, but the lessons you each drew from that were very different. You felt as though Heaven was rewarding you; he felt as though Heaven was putting him to the test."

His host nodded vigorously.

"Good point! That's exactly what Ramzi thought. In fact, he used to say that God had given oilfields to the Arabs, not to reward them, but to test them, perhaps even to punish them. And on that score, I have to say I think he was right. Oil is a curse."

"But it's thanks to petrodollars that the two of you got rich."

"Yes, that's true. For Ramzi and me, it was a blessing, but for most Arabs, oil has been a curse. And not just for the Arabs. Can you think of a single country that oil has made happier? Just think about it for a minute. In every country, oil money has triggered civil wars and bloody upheaval, it has favoured leaders who are impulsive megalomaniacs."

"Why do you think that is?"

"Because, overnight, people suddenly had lots of money, without having to work to earn it. The upshot has been a culture of idleness. Why wear yourself out if you can pay someone else to work their fingers to the bone for you? It creates entire populations of indolent people with private means who are attended by whole populations of servants, not to say slaves. Do you really think that is the stuff of nation-building?"

"Have you ever felt like a slave?" Dunia said, slightly offended.

"Yes, every time I'm in the presence of an emir, I feel a little like a slave. A highly paid, well-fed slave, but a slave nonetheless."

He trailed off, trying to call up specific examples, then continued:

"The man who founded OPEC, a Venezuelan, said that hydrocarbons were the 'devil's excrement' ... He was right. I'm sure that those who write the histories a hundred years from now will say oil enriched the Arabs the better to destroy them."

In the garden, the birds had begun to sing. Hosts and guest fell silent so that they could listen and soak up some of their serenity, their apparent joy.

Then Ramez said to his friend:

"Tell Dunia about the reunion you're thinking of organizing."

Adam explained the origins of the plan. He listed the people he was considering inviting and said a few words about each. Then he spoke briefly about the circle of friends at university, their arguments, their ideals, their vain promises to always keep in touch. Then he added:

"On the flight over, I was telling Ramez that I'd like our partners to join us, but that I was worried they'd be bored listening to the stories of old comrades in arms. But after our conversation this morning, I'm convinced that there are at least two additional people who have to be there: my partner, Dolores, and you, Dunia, if you'd like to come."

"It would be a pleasure. Ramez has talked to me a lot about the period of his life before I knew him, and I'd love to hear your stories, I wouldn't be bored at all. When is it?"

"The date hasn't been set yet. I was thinking ..."

"It doesn't matter, I'm a meek, submissive oriental wife,

I make no engagements without my husband. If he's free that day, I'll be free too."

The aforesaid husband rolled his eyes to heaven, then kissed Dunia's hand and said:

"Before I forget, Sémiramis phoned last night. She was worried when you didn't come back to the hotel, and when I told her you'd come to Amman with me, she said a few choice words I won't repeat."

"It's my fault," Adam said. "I meant to call her but then I dozed off. She must be furious …"

"You'll find out when you get back to the hotel. Personally, I think you'd be better off staying in Amman, I can grant you asylum."

His guest smiled.

"No, I must go and face the punishment I so richly deserve. What time do you think we could set off?"

"I told the crew to be ready to take off at about 11:00 a.m. Does that suit?"

Adam checked his watch. It was eight thirty.

"Perfect. We have more than enough time to get ready."

"My meek, submissive spouse has decided to take me to see her mother. We'll be spending the day up in the mountains with her, then we'll come back to Amman in the evening and bring our daughter back with us."

2

Back at the Auberge Sémiramis, Adam crept quietly up to his room. But no sooner had he opened the door than the phone rang. His "chatelaine" had clearly asked to be advised the moment he arrived. But there were no reproaches, no reprimands. She simply wanted to let him know that she would be out all day, and would call when she got back so they could have dinner together.

He began taking a few notes about the conversations he had had with Ramez and his wife, especially what they had said about Ramzi, which might prove useful when he went to visit the monastery. Then he opened his laptop to check his email. He had received a long message in his absence.

Dearest Adam,

Reading your last email, and rereading the one I sent you, I realize there's been a small misunderstanding, one I'd like to clear up.

I did say that I had left the country "reluctantly," and you inferred that I was forced to by my parents. I owe it to the memory of my father to set the record straight: he didn't force me, he persuaded me, during a long "man-to-man" conversation that I will never forget.

We had had a number of heated discussions in the weeks leading up to it. Every time he mentioned leaving, I'd make my displeasure very clear, he'd tell me off, I'd become touchy, voices would be raised and my mother would start crying. The atmosphere at home was unbearable for everyone. One day, he summoned me to the little room that served as his office. He asked me to sit down, he closed the door, then—and this was unusual—he took a pack of Yenindji from his pocket and offered me one. It was the moral equivalent of a peace pipe. He lit my cigarette, then his, and pushed the ashtray so that it was between the two of us.

I remember the scene as if it happened last week, when in fact it's been more than twenty-five years! It wasn't a big room, I'm sure you remember; there was just room for the two armchairs where we were sitting. The walls were lined with books in various languages, there was a wooden escritoire inlaid with mother-of-pearl with numerous little drawers. The only light came from the window overlooking the building's communal gardens. It was cold that day, but my father had left it half-open because of the smoke.

I remember the words he used to begin his appeal: "When I was your age, I, too, had worthy friends, honest, educated, talented young men from every community, each of them with noble ambitions. They were more important to me than my family. Together, we dreamed of a country whose citizens would no longer be primarily defined by the religious affiliation. We wanted to shake up people's attitudes, change old habits."

One of their main concerns, he said, was names. Why did Christians, Muslims, and Jews necessarily have to have Christian, Muslim, and Jewish first names? Why was it necessary for people's first names to be the battle flag of their religions? Instead of naming Christians "Michel" or "Georges" and Muslims "Mahmoud" or "Abdurrahman," and Jews "Solomon" and "Moses," why not give children neutral names—Sélim, Fouad, Amin, Sami, Ramzi, or Naïm.

"That's where your name comes from," my father explained. "A lot of my friends had serious arguments with their families about it. Some gave in; I stood my ground. Your grandfather wanted me to name you Ezra, after him. To justify myself, I explained that for centuries, Jews had been forced to wear distinctive clothes so that *goyim* could recognize them at a glance, so they could avoid us, or be on their guard; names, I argued, played a similar role. I'm not sure I really convinced him, but he let me do as I saw fit.

"The reason I'm telling you all this is to show you that, when I was young, I had the same ideals you have, the same dreams of peaceful coexistence between communities, so it is reluctantly and with a heavy heart that I and my family are leaving the country where my ancestors have lived for five hundred years. But it has already become impossible for us to go on living here, and everything I see tells me it will be worse tomorrow.

"Don't delude yourself, very soon there will be no Jewish communities left in the Arab world. None. The Jewish communities in Cairo and Alexandria, in Baghdad, Algiers, and Tripoli are already dying out ... And now ours is too. Soon, there will no longer be even ten men in the city to pray together. It is a deeply sad, profoundly depressing shift, but there is nothing we can do about it, Naïm, not you, not me.

"What is to blame? The foundation of the state of Israel? I know that's what you think, you and your friends. And it is partly true. But only partly. Because discrimination and bigotry of all sorts have existed for centuries, since long before the founding of the state of Israel, long before there existed a territory dispute between Jews and Arabs. Has there been a single moment in the history of the Arab world when Jews were treated as full citizens?

"No more than anywhere else, you might say. And that's true. In Europe things were worse, a thousand times worse. I know that. It took the full horror of Nazi atrocities for attitudes to begin to change, for antisemitism to begin to be considered a degrading practice, a shameful sickness.

"I believe this change in attitudes might have spread to the Arab world. If the Nazi horrors had not immediately been followed by the conflict over Palestine, might the lot of Jews in Arab countries have got better rather than worse? I think so, in fact I'm sure of it. But that is not what happened. The opposite happened. Elsewhere, the situation for Jews has improved, it is only here that it has got worse. Elsewhere, pogroms have been consigned to the ashcan of history; here they have begun again. Elsewhere, *The Protocols of the Elders of Zion* has vanished from the shelves of respectable libraries, while here copies are churned out by the thousand.

"The other day, when we were talking about the Six-Day War, you compared the Israeli air attack on Arabic military airfields to the Japanese attack on Pearl Harbour. I find the comparison extreme, but there is a sliver of truth to it—if not in the historical facts, then in the perception of those facts. It's true that many of our compatriots now see us as citizens of an enemy power, a little like the Japanese-Americans interned in concentration camps after Pearl Harbour, who were not released until after V-J day. What would have happened if Japan had won the war, if it had held on to its conquered territories in Asia and the Pacific—China, Korea, the Philippines, Singapore, and the rest—if it had forced the United States to accept a humiliating armistice, to give up Hawaii and pay heavy reparations?

"From that point of view you might say that the Six-Day War was like a brilliantly successful Pearl Harbour. While the Israelis gloat, the Arabs are seething with rage, and we become their scapegoats. To attack defenceless civilians is despicable, but it is futile to expect a humiliated mob to be magnanimous and chivalrous. We are marked out as enemies, and we will be treated as such, even you, Naïm, regardless of your opinions. That's what it has come to. Whether we like it or not, there is no way out."

This is the first time I've set down what my father said. Thanks to you, Adam. Thanks to the questions you asked and the memories you rekindled. And thanks to the detailed explanation you gave me about Mourad's activities. As I read it, it occurred to me that the history of our families and our group of friends, of our illusions and our failings is worth recounting, because it is part of the history of our time, of its illusions, and also of its failings.

But to come back to that twilight conversation with my father on the eve of our departure, our little exodus—my mother prefers to say our "leave-taking." Actually, it was not really a conversation, it was an appeal, as I said at the beginning of this email, an appeal he had spent a long time preparing, not only to persuade me, but first and foremost to persuade himself so that he could make his decision.

I let him talk. He seemed so emotional, so sincere, so respectful of my ideas that I did not want to argue with him. It's true that, despite the bitter arguments we had in those days, I admired him, I loved him deeply, and I never doubted his moral integrity or his intellectual acuity for an instant.

Nor was I the only one who admired him. The whole community listened to his opinions with respect and looked to him for guidance. This is why we were one of the last families to leave the country. My father knew that if he were to leave, it would send a signal, and this was not something he was prepared to do lightly. For as long as there was some hope, he wanted to explore it.

At some point in the conversation I asked whether we would have been condemned to exile even if Israel had lost the war. He laid a consoling hand on my arm. "Don't think about it, Naïm, there's no point, there is no solution, I have gone over it a thousand times in my mind. Our fate was sealed long ago, long before you were born, even before I was born. If Israel had lost the last war, things would have been worse, we would have been persecuted and despised.

"In any case, you will never hear me wish for Israel's defeat, which would mean its destruction. For our little community, the founding of the State has proved disastrous; for the Jewish people as a whole, it is a dangerous enterprise; everyone has the right to their opinion—favourable or otherwise—but we can't talk about it as though it were some vague project by Monsieur Herzl. Israel is now a reality, a venture that we are all caught up in, whether or not we approve. It's as if you took my money,

Naïm, took every last *piastre* this family has, and bet it on a horse; I'd call you every name under the sun, I'd tell you you'd bankrupted us, I might even curse the day you were born. But would I pray for your horse to lose the race? No, of course not. Despite everything, I'd pray for your horse to win.

"If Israel were to lose the next war, it would be a cataclysmic tragedy for all Jews. We have suffered enough tragedy as it is, don't you think?"

At this point in the conversation, I asked him whether, in his opinion, our family's ultimate destination was Israel. He took a few seconds to answer: "No, it's Brazil." There was a quiver in his voice that made me think his decision was not set in stone. But it was, and he held to it for the rest of his life. He visited Israel many times, but he never considered settling there. My mother felt otherwise. Two of her sisters lived in Tel Aviv, and she would have liked to be close to them. But she is old-fashioned, a wife who does not question her husband's decisions. When she had doubts, she kept them to herself. In any case, her doubts were based on emotional ties that could not compete with my father's solidly constructed arguments. Whenever she heard him criticizing Israel, she was unhappy, but she expressed it in sighs or tried to change the subject rather than contradict him.

One day, years after we left, Colette, one of my mother's sisters, came to visit us in São Paulo. She was a plump, intelligent, funny woman, and my father was very fond of her. As a result, she felt entitled to tease him at the dinner table. "So, tell me Moïse, when are you going to pack up and bring your little family to Israel so we can all live next door to one other?" My father simply smiled. So, my aunt upped the ante: "Brazil is all very well, but Israel is our home, don't you agree?" My father didn't answer, and did not say another word during dinner. My mother quickly changed the subject, all the while watching her husband out of the corner of her eye, since she knew what he was like. However much he was goaded, or even provoked, he never reacted impulsively. Whatever the circumstances, he took his time, he considered things, weighed them up.

After dinner, we went out and sat on the veranda. It was as coffee was being served that my father finally decided to respond to my aunt. He didn't look at her, but stared into his coffee cup as though it was a teleprompter, and said, "We have the right to refer to Palestine as 'Eretz Yisrael,' and we have as much right to live there as anyone, perhaps a little more. But nothing gives us the right to say to Arabs: 'Go on, get out, this land is ours and has always been, you have no business being here!' That, to me, is intolerable, regardless of how we interpret the scriptures and regardless of the sufferings we have endured."

He paused and sipped his coffee, then added in a solemn tone, "On the other hand, it's true that if we had shown up timidly, apologizing for the intrusion and asking the Arabs whether they minded making a little room for us, we would have had nothing, we would have been driven out."

He paused again for a few seconds, then, for the first time, he looked into the eyes of his favourite sister-in-law. "There is no satisfactory answer to such a question, Colette. How can one cease to be a lamb without becoming a wolf? I am not convinced by the path that the Israelis have taken, but I have no alternative to suggest. So I keep my distance, I hold my tongue, and I pray."

He fell silent, as though he were praying. Then, he added in a more cheerful tone, "People here say *Deus é brasileiro!* When I first came here, I used to smile, but now I think they may be right, even if they don't believe it themselves. When the Almighty looks down on the world, which country makes Him most proud of His creation and His creatures? Which country makes Him feel glorified and which makes Him feel insulted? I believe that this country, Brazil, is the one He surveys with joy, with pride, and it is our country, over in the Levant, that He surveys with sorrow and anger. Yes, I think my new compatriots are right, *Deus é brasileiro*. This is the holy land, this is the promised land,

and humble Moses that I am, I do not regret leading his people here."

Forgive me, Adam, for responding at such length to your short phrase. But I had to do it. To honour the memory of my father, and also to set out my own ideas. Because his words as I have just recounted them to you from memory essentially encapsulate how I feel now. He handed down his vision to me just as he handed down his old books, and I feel as though I am heir to an antiquated wisdom for which our contemporaries no longer have any use. We live in an age of bad faith and entrenched positions. Whether Jew or Arab, we have been left with a choice between hating the other or hating oneself. And if, like me, you had the misfortune to be born both Arab and Jew, you quite simply don't exist, you don't even have the right to have existed; you are simply a misunderstanding, a mix-up, a mistake, a false rumour that history has already refuted. And whatever you do, don't ever dare remind either side that it was in Arabic that Maimonides wrote *Guide for the Perplexed*!

Do you think that among our circle of friends—or what remains of it—it is still possible to calmly talk about such things? Could a Jew like me explain the finer points of his opinion without instantly proclaiming himself anti-Israeli or anti-Zionist?

I ask you, and I ask myself these questions, but I'm not setting them as a condition for coming to the reunion. I would love to see the country again, to see my friends, and if it is impossible to discuss such things calmly, then I won't discuss them. I would never stoop to saying something I didn't believe, but I can easily refrain from saying everything I believe. I'll see the country, I'll gorge myself on wonderful food, I'll talk about my childhood memories and avoid contentious subjects.

Yours faithfully,

Naïm

}

As soon as he had read the long email from his friend and before thinking about how he might reply, Adam opened his notebook to set down some memories.

I never knew Naïm's father well, I would say hello and exchange polite pleasantries, but I never had a conversation with him. As I remember, he was tall with tortoiseshell glasses and dark, close-cropped hair. I remember he used to wear brown and white two-tone shoes that must have been fashionable at the time. My lasting impression of him is as a strict man, maybe because his son always spoke in a whisper when he knew he was at home.

I have a clear memory of the little study where they had that long conversation. Thinking about it, he cannot have been all that strict, since Naïm had no qualms about taking me into his study. We used to play chess there sometimes, sitting in the huge armchairs. We were completely surrounded by books in various languages, some of which looked very old. But I only ever saw the spines, I never opened any of them.

He closed his notebook, reread the email from beginning to end, then set about replying.

Dearest Naïm,

Thank you for taking the time to recount that episode in your life. I was very moved to read it, and as I did, I felt a mixture of sadness and pride.

The pride has to do with my friends. Or most of them, at least. Since I came back to the country in the circumstances I've already explained, I've been doing my best to track them down, to rediscover them, often after many years of silence, and I realize that we were the bearers of noble dreams. If I had had any doubts about it, the email you just sent would have been enough to dispel them.

The sadness has to do with what we have become. How to explain the fact that we had so little impact on events in our country, to say nothing of those of the world? How to explain the fact that we now find ourselves among the losers, the vanquished? Because we are scattered across the globe? Because the voice of wisdom that was ours has become all but inaudible?

But I'd like to get back to your beautiful letter and the serious theme it addresses so sincerely.

The conflict that so changed our lives was not a regional feud like so many others, it was not simply a clash between two "neighbouring tribes" ill-used by history. It was infinitely greater than that. It is this conflict, more than any other, that has prevented the Arab world from improving, that has prevented the West and Islam from being reconciled, that has dragged humanity back into ethnic tension, religious fundamentalism, and towards what people these days call "the clash of civilizations." Yes, Naïm, I am convinced that the conflict that ruined your life and mine is now the painful heart of a tragedy that extends far beyond our generation, far beyond our native land and our region. I am weighing my words carefully when I say that it is because of this conflict that humanity has entered a period of regression rather than progress.

Am I falling into the all-too-common trap of according too much importance to those things that affect us most deeply? Do you remember how we used to mock the people who, every time there was a clash between two villages in the mountain, would start speculating about what the Americans would do, what the French would say, how the Russians would react, as though the rest of the world had nothing better to do? As a historian, with a keen sense of the relative nature of things, I have always refrained from saying—or even thinking—that the conflict in the Middle East managed to deflect the march of humanity towards a different destination.

But, in trying so hard to avoid making one ludicrous mistake, we risk falling into the trap of oversimplification, so brilliantly summed up by our proverb *"Ma sar chi, ma sar metlo."* It's one I frequently teach my students, translating it in my own manner as "Everything that happens inevitably resembles something that has already happened." Then I vehemently refute it, since the realities of today are never those of yesterday, and similarities can be more deceptive than instructive.

In this case, it is safe to say that, in the history of the Jewish people spanning three or four millennia, the 1940s, which witnessed their attempted extermination, the defeat of Nazism, and the founding of the State of Israel, is the most dramatic and the most significant decade of all.

Your father told you as much, and I believe it as firmly as he did: at the time that you and I were born, a cataclysm had just occurred that would have both regional and global consequences, that would inevitably shatter our lives, and about which there was absolutely nothing that we could do.

In an ideal world, things might have happened differently. The Jews would have come to Palestine explaining that their ancestors had lived there two thousand years earlier, that they had been driven out by the Roman emperor Titus, and that they had now decided to return; and the Arabs who lived there would have said, "Of course, come in, you're welcome here. We'll give you half the country and we'll live in the other half."

In the real world, things were never going to happen like that. When the Arabs realized that Jewish immigration was not limited to a handful of refugees, but was an organized mission to appropriate the country, they reacted as any populace would: by taking up arms to prevent it. But they were beaten. Every time there was a clash, they were beaten. I can't begin to count the number of defeats they have suffered. But what is certain is that this series of catastrophes gradually destabilized the Arab world, and then the whole of the Muslim world. Destabilized both in the political and in the clinical sense. No one comes through a series of public humiliations unscathed. Every Arab bears the mark of a profound trauma, and I include myself in this. But this Arabic trauma, seen from the far shore, the European shore, the shore I have adopted, elicits only incomprehension and suspicion.

In the "appeal" that you recounted, your father put his finger on a crucial truth: after the Second World War, the West discovered the horrors of the camps, the horrors of antisemitism; meanwhile, to Arab eyes, the Jews did not look like brutalized, emaciated, unarmed civilians, they looked like an invading army, well equipped, well organized, and ruthlessly efficient.

And in the succeeding decades, this difference in perception merely became more pronounced. In the West, acknowledging the monstrous nature of the massacre perpetrated by the Nazis became a decisive element in the contemporary moral conscience, and this translated into material and moral support for the state in which the persecuted Jewish populations found refuge. Meanwhile, in the Arab world, where Israel won a series of victories, against the Egyptians, the Syrians, the Jordanians, the Lebanese, the Palestinians, the Iraqis, and even against the assembled Arab nations, people did not see things in the same light.

The result, and this is what I was coming to, is that the conflict with Israel disengaged Arabs from the conscience of the world, or at least the conscience of the West, which almost amounts to the same thing.

I recently read this passage by an Israeli ambassador about his career during the 1950s and '60s: "Our mission was delicate, because we had to simultaneously persuade the Arabs that Israel was invincible, and persuade the West that Israel was on the point of death." In hindsight, it has to be said that in this contradictory mission, the diplomat and his colleagues were spectacularly successful. So it should hardly be surprising that the Western and the Arabic worlds do not see the state of Israel or the Jewish people in the same light.

But, obviously, the work of diplomats alone does not explain this difference in perception. Objectively there are two separate, parallel tragedies. Most people, however, both Jewish and Arabs, acknowledge only one. How can one explain to the Jews, who throughout history have suffered persecution and humiliation and, in the mid-twentieth century, were the victims of attempted extermination, that they should be more attentive to the sufferings of others? How can one tell the Arabs, who are now enduring the darkest and most humiliating period of their history, who have suffered defeat upon defeat at the hands of Israel and its allies, who feel despised and scorned throughout the world, that they should be mindful of the tragedy of the Jewish people?

Those, like you and me, who are profoundly sensitive to these two "rival tragedies" are few in number. And, of all the Jews and all the Arabs, they are—we are—the most miserable, the most distraught. There are times when I genuinely envy those from either camp, who can say without scruples: *Let my people triumph, let the others go to hell!*

But I'll stop there. We'll soon have opportunity enough to share our misfortunes. Especially at the reunion that I am trying to organize.

On that subject, things are beginning to take shape. I've just spent twenty-four hours with our old friend Ramez. We had lunch together and afterwards he flew me in his private jet—oh, yes—to Amman, and you can just imagine the kind of "hovel" he lives in ... I'll tell you more about the visit either by email, or in person. Right now, I just wanted to say that he was very excited when I mentioned the possibility of our old friends meeting up again. We can count on him being there, together with his wife,

Dunia, who to my mind will fit into the group as though she were always part of it.

On the other hand, the other Ramz is unlikely to come. I don't know whether you know, but Ramzi has withdrawn from the world to become a monk. It happened a little more than a year ago. He and Ramez had built up a veritable empire, he had made a fortune, and then one day, he decided to give it all up to go and live as an ascetic in a monastery in the mountains. These days he's called "Brother Basil." I don't know whether to admire him or pity him. The cynics talk about depression, and maybe they're right. But there are too many cynics in this world—and far too many in this country; personally, I prefer to think that our friend faced up to genuine spiritual and ethical questions.

His "alter ego" has not gotten over it; the mere mention of Ramzi's name brings tears to his eyes. Ramez has visited him just once, and was given short shrift.

I'm planning to try and visit anyway. To talk to Ramzi about the planned reunion. I doubt he'll want to join us. But if he's prepared to see me and explain his reasons, I can at least tell our friends what he said. In that way, he won't be completely absent ...

It was at this point in his writing that Sémiramis called to tell him the hotel restaurant would be closed that night for a private party, and she had asked for some food to be sent up to her house. She was calling from her little terrace, the table was laid, and she invited him to join her.

"I was just writing an email to Naïm."

"You can finish it later. I'm waiting for you. I've opened the champagne. If you don't come soon, it will lose its fizz ..."

"Hang on to the fizz, Sémi, I'll just finish this email and send it and I'll join you. It won't take more than five minutes."

He returned to his screen.

The beautiful Sémiramis is pressuring me. And this letter is already too long, but there are two more things I wanted to say.

First, I'm delighted that you want to see the country again after all these years and I can't wait to go with you when you visit your old houses, the one in the city and the one up in the mountain—a hotbed of depravity, from what you've said. Since the statute of limitations is long past, I'm expecting a detailed confession.

Secondly, at this point it would be useful, in fact urgent, to start thinking about specific dates for this reunion. What do you think about the last week of May or the first week of June? Today is April 27, Mourad died on the night of April 20-21, the "fortieth night" falls on May 31, so I'd suggest we meet around that time, ideally for a long weekend …

If that works for you, let me know and I'll get in touch with the others tomorrow. I don't yet know exactly how many of us will be there. Albert hasn't replied to my last email yet, but I'm hopeful. Obviously, Tania and Sémi will be there, Ramez and his wife, probably Nidal, the brother of poor Bilal, and you and me … Actually, are you planning on bringing someone—the "default option," as software designers call it—or coming on your own? I'm going to try and persuade my partner, Dolores, to come; I hope she'll agree to step away from her magazine, even if it's just for forty-eight hours …

I have to go now. Much love,

Adam

He pressed *Send* and rushed to join Sémiramis in her little house.

She had left the front door open.

The Ninth Day

1

Adam returned to his room early the next morning, his mind comfortably numb, his eyes still a little heavy with sleep. He would have liked to relax, perhaps even doze in the warm breeze. But, out of habit rather than necessity, he sat down in front of his computer and pressed the power button.

Among his emails, there was one he had been impatiently waiting for and immediately opened. Signed "Dolores," it had been sent at about three o'clock in the morning.

My love,
I'm having trouble getting to sleep tonight and the loneliness is weighing on me. You have hardly been gone a week, but in the anguish of our empty apartment, I suddenly felt as though you had left months ago, and forever.

This isn't the first time one of us has gone abroad without the other. But this separation seems different. You feel very far away. Not just far from Paris, from our home, our bedroom. You feel far from our shared world. I feel as though you have gone back to a previous world, one that I never knew and in which I have no place. The sheets on our bed seem suddenly cold, and the blanket is not enough to keep me warm. I need to rest my head on your shoulder, but you shoulder isn't here.

It was clear that you were dreading this trip. If someone doesn't visit his native land for a quarter of a century, it is not because he can't make time. Plainly, you were worried about what feelings might be stirred up by seeing the places and the people of your former life. I could feel your anxiety last Friday, after the early morning phone call from your friend, but I still urged you to go.

For two reasons. The first, I told you at the time, being that when a friend, or even a "former friend," asks for you on his deathbed, you have no right to hesitate. The second reason I did not mention, but it has been on my mind for a long time, perhaps since we first met at Pancho's birthday party eight years ago and had that long conversation. When you confessed you hadn't once set foot in your native land since you left, I found the idea strange and unhealthy. Especially as you'd made it clear that you were at no risk if you went back, you were not likely to be killed or arrested, it was simply a "position" you had adopted, because your country had let you down. I felt that your position was unhealthy, perhaps even slightly pathological and I promised myself I would "cure" you. More than once, I suggested we go there on holiday, so you could show me where you had lived, but every time you shied away, you suggested we go elsewhere and I didn't want to insist—even though I was more certain than ever that there was something wrong.

Then you had that phone call at dawn. Suddenly, you had a valid reason to make the trip; in fact, given the circumstances, it was a moral obligation. Besides, you were on a sabbatical and your work on the biography of Attila had ground to a halt. If you were ever going to take the plunge, it was now, so I thought it best to push you.

Now, I regret it. I have the feeling that I've lost you. It's as though I played at being the sorcerer's apprentice, and I could kick myself. I wanted you to shake off this phobia, to have a healthy attitude not only towards the country you were born in, but towards your own past. But now it feels as though you are drifting towards another world, and that I will soon be no more than a distant voice, a fleeting image. Perhaps even a figure from the past from another of your former lives.

Then there was the incident with Sémiramis ... I promised her that I would never reproach you, and I'll keep my word. Because I am as responsible as the two of you for what happened. When

I got that strange phone call, that strange request, I could have said no. I never in my life imagined that a woman would ask me to "lend" her my partner for the night. It was preposterous, it went against nature. Or at least against everything that, until that moment, I believed was common sense. But I chose to say yes. It was a free choice, and that's why I want to say again that I will never reproach you for straying, either directly or by veiled allusions.

Why did I say yes? Firstly, because Sémi could just as easily not have asked me, she could have seduced you without my knowledge, and the fact that she included me in her decision made me feel as though I was not being entirely sidelined; besides, since the two of you were under the same roof and I was thousands of kilometres away, I figured playing the game would be the lesser of two evils; that way the indiscretion would occur with my blessing rather than against my will.

The second reason is that I wanted to prove myself worthy of your past life, of the youth to which you're still so attached. I never experienced the sixties or the seventies, when so many taboos about sexuality disappeared. I don't idealize that period, but I know that it means something to you and I wanted to show you that although I came into your life much later, I was prepared to take part in that risky game. Rather than seeming like a prude, I wanted to be your ally, your partner.

The third reason is linked to what I said at the beginning. I felt that, in a sense, you needed to exorcise your relationship with your native country, to finally come to terms with your unwarranted phobias and your nostalgia, and reliving this episode with Sémi twenty-five years later seemed to me to be therapeutic.

All the reasons I've just listed now seem pathetic and ridiculous. Tonight, I feel a little ashamed, a little cold, a little scared. I am happier with you than I have ever been in my life. And although I devote a lot of time to my career—a little too much time in recent months, I admit—it's our relationship, our love, that provides me with the energy I need. If you were to stop loving me, I would not have the strength to get out of bed in the morning. I need your eyes on me, admiring and caressing; I need your advice to support and reassure me; and I need your shoulder to rest my head on at night.

I'm not writing this to try and ruin the rest of your trip. I'm not asking you to come home right now, I'm not on the edge of the abyss. I just feel very sad and a little insecure tonight. Reassure me! Tell me that everything that's happened since you left has not changed your love for me, or your desire to come back to your little nest in Paris. If need be, I'm prepared to allow you to lie to me a little ...

Adam was tempted to phone her straightaway in order to reassure her. But in Paris, it was not yet 7:00 a.m. He decided it was better to write.

Dolores my love,
I don't need to lie to find the words to reassure you. You are not someone who needs lies, and that's why I've loved you from the moment we first met. I loved you, I love you, and I will never stop loving you. You are not my latest partner, you are the woman I have been searching for, desperately searching for, the one I was lucky enough and privileged enough to finally meet.

It is rare to find such integrity in someone without a trace of prudishness. And this strange "pact" you made with Sémi is a powerful example of what I have just said. It took daring to make such a decision. You went against the prevailing "popular" wisdom of our time, and I want you to know that I will never make you regret your daring.

What you have said about your reasons more or less corresponds to my own feelings, and if there was something childish in my actions, yours were noble and generous, you have no reason to be ashamed. I say "childish" because the theories that so appealed to us in the sixties about couples being "open" to every experience were a recipe for disaster. I was just a kid, I was a sponge soaking up the latest fads imported from France or from universities in the United States, especially those that pandered to my adolescent fantasies.

I got over them later, as many people did. But there is something that I haven't gone back on. Although I think the idea of a couple being open to every passing whim is childish, I have little respect for couples whose relationships are musty, and I have nothing but contempt for the old-fashioned couples where the woman is submissive to the man, or the man henpecked by the woman, or both. If I had to set forth my beliefs on the subject, I'd say: complicity, tenderness, and the right to make mistakes.

On each of these three criteria, our relationship seems exemplary, and what has just happened only serves to confirm my faith in its worth, its beauty, its durability.

I love you, my beautiful Argentine, and I gently enfold you in my arms so that your heart can be at peace. [...]

He signed the email "Mito," the nickname Dolores had given him, an abbreviation of Adamito, "little Adam."

2

Only after he had reassured his worried partner did Adam take the trouble to open the other email he had received during the night, this one from Albert.

Unlike their previous exchanges, this one was in English, which added a little to the intrigue. It was hardly surprising that his friend, having lived in the United States for more than twenty years, might feel more comfortable using the language of his adoptive country. All the same, there was something unusual and even unsettling about it.

Dear Adam,

I'm writing to you with good news and bad news. The bad news is that my adoptive mother is gravely ill and it looks as though she might not have much time left, which, as you can imagine, has upset me deeply. So I have to go and visit her, in the old country, if only to kiss her one last time.

The good news is that this will give me the opportunity to see you, and other friends from my childhood.

Since I have no wish to put the institute I work for in an awkward situation, I've decided to do everything according to the rules and request an exceptional license to travel so that my family obligations do not force me to contravene the directives I must comply with, as a researcher and as a citizen.

Obviously, I'll let you know my plans as soon as I have the exact dates of my visit.

Yours sincerely,

Albert N. Kithar

Why had he signed his full name rather than his first name, or simply his initial as he usually did? And who was this "adoptive mother" of whom Adam had never heard, despite knowing Albert since they were children? It was true that Albert had never been very forthcoming about his family, but even so!

He reread the email a second and then a third time. Eventually the penny dropped. If his friend in America had written to him in English, in this tone, it was clearly because the email was going to be read by others. In a sense, it was a double-sided email, containing both an official message and a coded message. What Albert was trying to tell him was that he had decided to come, and that he had found the perfect pretext for getting around the government ban.

Why resort to such subterfuge in a free country like the United States? Adam had no idea. But it was something he would be able to ask his friend in person, since he had obviously decided to come. And soon, too, given that his ghostly "adoptive mother" could not hold out for very long. This was the joyous news contained in the message, the rest was merely camouflage.

Nonetheless, Adam needed to reply in the same language, and with the same ambiguity.

Dear Albert,

I am very saddened to hear that your adoptive mother is so ill. I hope that she makes a full recovery.

I hope that when you come to visit her, we will have the opportunity to see each other. We have so many childhood memories to talk about.

I will wait to hear from you when you know the dates of your visit.

All the best,

Adam

With a satisfied smile, he pressed *Send*. He had found it impossible to imagine a reunion without Albert, the most intelligent, the most caustic, the most brilliant of them all. And the most morose, though this had rarely been in evidence since he settled in the United States.

Now, everything was set for a memorable reunion. Adam stretched himself out like a contented cat and then went and lay down on the bed, ready to doze off.

His third night with Sémiramis had been as delectable as the first two, but he had only slept in fits and starts. Between their conversations they made love, and between lovemaking they chatted, and so on until dawn.

He made the effort to sit up, and reach for the notebook that lay on the nightstand, in which he wanted to confide his thoughts.

SATURDAY, APRIL 28

Will Sémi and I have a fourth night of passion? Probably not. The "authorization" given by Dolores allowed us a period of grace without the nagging irritant of guilt. But since the email I've just received, things can't carry on as before.

True, Dolores has not explicitly asked me to put an end to the affair, but what she wants is implicit, and I can't ignore it without feeling that I've betrayed her. Dolores has been so graceful about all this. I would be unworthy of her love if I were less noble than she.

So, is that the end of it? Should I brusquely "turn the page" and push Sémi out of the love zone? If she were to suddenly open the door and come and lie down next to me, should I push her away or tenderly take her in my arms?

Having recorded his dilemmas without quite knowing how to resolve them, Adam closed his notebook, set down his pen, and fell asleep.

When he woke, another email was waiting on his computer. This time from Brazil.

Dearest Adam,

I have a lot to say to you about the conflict in the Levant that marked us both and that is clearly not about to end any time soon. If we agree on the essentials, there are also a number of differences. But, paradoxically, these differences are what bring us closer together.

You deplore the fact that your people are disconnected from the conscience of the world, or at least of the West. I deplore the fact that, these days, my people are disconnected from what was, for centuries, their most historic, their most emblematic, their irreplaceable role: that of the leaven of global humanism. This was our universal mission, the mission that earned us the hatred of fanatics, of regional chauvinists, of all narrow-minded people. I can understand our desire to become "a nation among nations," with its own sense of belonging. But in the process of this mutation, something essential is being lost. It is not possible to be fiercely nationalist and resolutely universalist.

I suppose we'll have the opportunity to discuss this at greater length and in greater depth. But, for the moment—it is precisely 5:20 a.m. here, and I haven't had my first cup of coffee—I don't feel able to argue coherently. The reason I'm writing to you at dawn is to respond to your suggestion about dates for the reunion. On that subject, I have a little problem ... but also, maybe, a solution.

I have to fly to Milan for a week on May 8, and the ideal solution would have been for me to make my "pilgrimage" in mid-May. Which might have coincided with the dates you've suggested. Unfortunately, that's not possible, because just after Milan, I have to go to Mexico for an important conference.

The only possibility I can think of is if I make a detour via the old country before going to Italy. That would mean sometime in the next few days. Will you still be there? And do you think our other friends could be there, so we could all meet up?

I realize this is all very rushed, and I'll completely understand if you and the others have plans in the near future. But, as far as I'm concerned, if I don't come right now, I'll have to postpone the visit for several months. In fact, I have the feeling that if I don't seize the opportunity right now, there might not be another for a long time …

So, that's why I'm writing at this ungodly hour … Think about it, talk to our friends, and let me know as soon as you can.

Much love,

Naïm

Adam hastily replied, without troubling to think about it or to consult anyone.

I've got just one word to say to you, Naïm: COME! Don't hesitate. You've got an opportunity, don't let it slip through your fingers. Come! God knows when we'll get another chance to meet up.

Personally, I'm not planning to go back to Paris anytime soon. I'll come and meet you at the airport, probably with Sémi, who'll propose that you stay at the auberge that bears her name, which is "out of this world." I suggest you accept. We'll have adjoining rooms, and we can talk until dawn.

I look forward to hearing from you very soon. Correction: I look forward to you sending me your flight number and your arrival time.

Just to be sure, he immediately called Sémiramis on her mobile phone.

"Naïm has just told me he is going to come soon, possibly next week. I've suggested that he take a room here."

"You did wisely, it's an excellent hotel."

"I even promised he could have the room adjoining mine."

"No problem, it's still low season. The regulars won't arrive before June. Until then, as you've seen, the place is more or less deserted. And don't say you're glad!"

"No, I've learned my lesson, your accountant is tearing his hair out, etcetera, etcetera."

"And he's warned that he might soon have to file for bankruptcy. Not this year, though, not yet."

"On a different subject, Albert has diplomatically let me know that he's found a way to get around the US government directives. But best not to say anything until he's here with us."

"It's all good news today."

Then, lowering her voice, she added.

"It seems as though last night brought us good luck."

"We did what we had to so that fortune might smile on us."

When he set down this conversation in his notebook a little later, Adam would comment:

I said it joyfully, and I immediately felt a pang of shame. Because the early hours had brought me other news that I had been careful not to disclose to the woman with whom I had spent the night. Obviously, I'll have to let her know before long that our intimate "parenthesis" must come to an end. But I'm in no hurry to do so. Difficult things must be dealt with when they arise, but there's no sense rushing to do them.

I shall do as the wisest of the Romans did long ago: I shall play for time.

]

It was that Saturday, in the early afternoon, that Adam went to the monastery to which his old friend Ramzi had withdrawn to become Brother Basil.

"Since the plans for this reunion of yours are starting to take shape, I think it might be the right time to go," Sémiramis had suggested.

"You're right. Even if Ramez and his wife don't hold out much hope ..."

"If you go with unrealistic expectations, you're bound to be disappointed. Tell him you wanted to visit and hear him out, to try and understand his motivation, to see an old friend again. If only for that, it's worth it, surely?"

It took more than an hour and a half for them to reach Al-Maghawer, Les Grottes, the village where the monastery of the same name was located. To reach the monastery, they had to take a steep, narrow path with crude steps cut into the cliff face that could only be navigated on foot, or on a donkey.

It was not until she stopped the car in the shade of an oak tree that Sémiramis told her passenger:

"I've been thinking while we were driving, I'm not going to go up to the monastery. You'll feel more comfortable on your own."

Adam protested only feebly. He, too, had been thinking, and he had reached the same conclusion. He did not yet know what he planned to say to Brother Basil, every word would have to be carefully weighed, and the presence of a third party might make the situation more difficult to manage.

"What will you do in the meantime?"

"I have some good friends in the village, they'll be delighted to see me."

He was not sure that she was telling the truth, but it suited him to take her at her word.

Donning an old straw hat he had borrowed from the hotel, he set off up the stone path.

Adam would later write a detailed account of his visit.

The monastery where Ramzi has chosen to live is clearly very old, and much of it is still in ruins. But one wing has been remarkably restored using weathered, slightly irregular stones that don't offend the eye or clash with the surrounding landscape.

I knock, and the door is opened by an African monk, a giant of a man with a grey beard who speaks Arabic with a heavy accent. Probably an Ethiopian from the high plains of Abyssinia. I ask for Brother Basil. The monk nods, then steps aside and ushers me into a small room furnished only with a bare table, a battered leather armchair, and four wicker chairs. On the wall, a wooden crucifix of modest dimensions.

This is clearly the visiting room that Ramez mentioned. To my eyes, the place is more reminiscent of a school than a prison.

I am about to sit down when my friend arrives. I am surprised by his appearance, but not in the way I had expected. The last time I saw him was in Paris, in a gourmet restaurant; he had just negotiated a major contract and was still wearing the dark suit he favoured for such meetings. I had assumed that this time he would be in a monk's habit, with a rope by way of a belt and a pair of sandals. But this was not the case. If he had left behind his business suits, he had not adopted what I imagined as a monk's habit. Simply a pale ivory soutane, and a bald patch like a tonsure that he no longer attempted to hide, as he used to, with a comb-over.

He seems happy to see me. Even so, I ask him not to be annoyed with me for showing up unannounced. I tell him I am only passing through, that I will be in the country only briefly, and for the first time in many years.

He gestures me to sit down, and takes a chair on the other side of the table, then, having stared mischievously at me for a moment, he says:

"You haven't changed."

I can hardly say the same thing to him, so I say:

"You look like you've got a new lease of life."

This is genuinely my impression, and it visibly pleases him. Not so much out of ordinary vanity, but because there is something implicit in the compliment. What makes him seem so rejuvenated is his serenity, and a certain nonchalance. He may be carrying the weight of the world on his shoulders, but he has shrugged off his family and his professional worries and, if I can express myself in venal terms, he has not been short-changed.

"This place is an oasis," I say, for want of a less hackneyed image.

"No, quite the opposite," my friend calmly corrects me, as though he has already considered the comparison. "The world is an oasis, and here we are in the vast immensity that surrounds it. In an oasis, people spend their time loading and unloading caravans. Seen from here, the caravans are no more than silhouettes on the horizon. Nothing is more beautiful than a caravan seen from a distance. But when you come closer, it is noisy, dirty, the camel drivers are quarrelsome, and the animals mistreated."

I am not sure whether this in an allegory or an actual memory, given that when Ramzi worked in the Arabian Peninsula, he doubtless had occasion to travel in a caravan. So I simply smile and nod and do not say a word.

He falls silent for a moment, then continues, in a less florid style.

"In the early years of my life, I dreamed of building the world, and when all's said and done, I didn't build very much. I promised myself I would build universities, hospitals, research laboratories, state-of-the-art factories, decent housing for ordinary people, and I spent my life building palaces, prisons, military bases, shopping malls for feverish consumers, unliveable skyscrapers, and artificial islands for deranged billionaires."

"There was nothing you could do. That's the nature of oil money. You had no control over how it was spent."

"That's true, people squander their money as they choose. But that doesn't mean you have to go along with their crazy ideas, you should have the courage to say no. No, your Highness, I will not build you an eighth palace, you already have seven that you barely use. No, gentlemen, I will not build you a sixty-storey tower in which every floor rotates independently; in a year, the machinery will be clogged with fine sand, the cogs will seize up, and all you will be left with is a twisted shell that will rot and rust for the next four centuries."

If at first the righteous indignation of the monk-cum-civil-engineer is accompanied by a smile, this quickly turns to a pained rictus.

"I spent my whole life building, and when I look back, there is not a single thing I am proud of."

I am about to say that he is being too hard on himself, to remind him that, in the Gulf States, he had built a high-tech hospital, a remarkable museum of archaeology—which I visited with my students three years ago—and a university campus often described as a model of the genre. But it is futile to respond to existential angst with a catalogue of achievements. I decide to say nothing, to ask nothing, even when he falls silent. By respecting his silences as much as his words, I allow him to follow his own thought processes, believing that in the end he will answer my unspoken questions. Particularly the most obvious question: why did he become a monk?

"What changed in me was not my religious convictions," he says at length, "but the conclusions that I drew from them. As a child, I was taught: 'Thou shalt not steal,' and it's true that I never pinched anything, never dipped my hand in the till, never doctored my invoices, never took something that did not belong to me. In theory, I should have a clear conscience. But to be content with such a literal observance of the commandment now seems to me absurd and cowardly.

"If leaders wrongfully appropriate the wealth of their country, and give you a small part of that fortune to build them a palace, are you not complicit in an act of pillage? If you build a prison where innocent people will be incarcerated, where some will be tortured to death, are you not breaking the commandment 'Thou shalt not kill'?

"I could go through each of the ten commandments and, if I am less than honest, I could be at peace with myself knowing that I have always observed them. But if I am honest, I have to admit that I respect them only ostensibly, superficially, just enough to 'clear my name' in the eyes of the Creator. The world is full of pitiful people who believe that God can be duped, that it is enough not to kill, not to steal, to keep their hands clean."

For a brief moment, I thought that Ramzi's criticism was directed at me. Given that I have boasted of how I left my war-torn country in time, and—specifically—managed to keep my hands clean, his words prompted in me a little more humility and a little less complacency. But I don't think this was his intention, I think he was referring to his own previous actions. In fact, he immediately added:

"I suppose that, seen from the outside, people assume I'm having some existential crisis triggered by age, exhaustion, and private tragedy. I see things very differently. I think it was logic that persuaded me to come and live here. Though it's true that my decision was made easier by my circumstances. My wife had just died, my children were grown up and lived far *away. Men are often connected to the everyday by invisible threads. In my life, some of those threads had snapped. I didn't have many ties, I could cut loose, and I did ..."*

Without worrying too much about whether this is the right moment, I decide to mention his former partner.

"I've just seen Ramez and his wife. They talked about you."

I say nothing more. There is a silence. Gazing up at the skylight above our heads, Ramzi seems on the brink of tears. I am tempted to change the subject, but I stop myself, preferring to wait until he has calmed down.

After a long moment, he says gravely:

"I was very unfair to ..."

Abruptly he trails off. He obviously has a lump in his throat. He pauses, as though to catch his breath. But when, some seconds later, he speaks again, it is to say:

"A wisp of cloud has mellowed the sun. What do you say we take a walk outside?"

As one, we get to our feet and I follow him out of the building and along the stony path. He is right, the sun is no longer blinding, so I carry my straw hat.

After a few minutes, we come to a tall tree, a walnut tree. My friend sits down on a flat stone and gestures to another, even flatter, and I in turn sit down.

To rekindle the conversation, but without mentioning Ramez's name again, I say:

"He seems lost without you."

Brother Basil gives me a long smile and then says, in a more composed tone:

"As far as our work together goes, I'm not worried, and I feel no regrets. He was used to having me in the office, he'll get used to me not being there. But I owed it to him to explain my decision. The problem is that, when the moment came, I had no desire to argue about anything. I didn't feel able to explain my inner turmoil to someone on the outside, not even my best friend. He came to visit one day ..."

"He said."

"I didn't welcome him like the brother he has always been to me. It was much too soon, I had only just moved into the monastery and he clearly hoped to bring me back with him. I had to defend myself, so I behaved coldly. There are times when a person needs to be completely alone with their private struggles, when the slightest intervention feels like an act of aggression. I had no choice but to push him away. I tried to do it as gently as possible, but I'm sure I hurt him. I know he will have suffered because of it, and I did too. Are you likely to see him again soon?"

"Yes. We've planned to meet up again in the coming weeks."

"Well, tell him ... Tell him what I've just told you. Tell him I'd like to see him again, that he is welcome here. Alone, or with his wife."

"They'll be happy to hear it, they've never really got over you leaving, and they'll be comforted to know that you still think of them as friends."

For a long moment, we sit in silence, he and I. Then he gets to his feet and gestures for me to follow. We set off down a stony path that seems to be an extension of the one I had taken to reach the monastery, which is now below us as we climb higher. I start to get out of breath while my friend, despite being chubby, carries on bounding from rock to rock like a young goat.

Our path leads us to a sort of cavity carved into the cliff face.

"Come and look at this. Follow me."

It is a low door, he has to stoop to go inside. I follow behind. Inside, it is murky, but gradually our eyes adjust to the darkness. Then Ramez opens the wooden shutter blocking the window. The cave is illuminated.

And I stand there, wide-eyed, gaping, a lump in my throat. The walls are painted with frescos depicting various people, *their heads ringed with circular or oval haloes. Their hands are clearly visible, meticulously drawn, stretching out in front of them as though to accept an offering, their eyes are accentuated as though with kohl, their bearded faces are sad. There are animals, too, their heads ringed with saintly light, notably a lion and an eagle representing the evangelists.*

"There are seven other rooms like this, but they are in poor condition. Humidity, vandalism, ignorance, neglect. And simply the passing centuries. This one probably dates from the thirteenth century. Astonishing, isn't it? And to think that most people don't even know that this place exists."

"To my shame, I'm one of them. At least I was until this afternoon."

"As was I, until three or four years ago. One day, the bishop of the mountain asked me to come with him to visit a ruined monastery and advise him what to do to prevent it from completely crumbling into ruins. I came, I wandered around, and when I saw these caves, I decided to stay. I won't say that this was the only reason for my decision, but it was the trigger. I was shaken by this mixture of beauty, piety, and fragility. I told the bishop that I would personally oversee the restoration, that I would pay for the work myself, and that I would be happy to have a little cell here where I could sleep from time to time while the restoration was in progress. That's how it began. I buttressed the old walls, did some renovation work, closed up the caves to protect them from vandalism and weather. Can you believe that some visitors carved their names into the murals with penknives? Look here. And here. and here."

There were names, carved hearts, and also crude, gratuitous, hateful slashes.

As we leave the cave, Ramzi locks the door, slips the keys into the deep pocket of his soutane, then leads me along a path to a plateau, a sort of barren esplanade where the ground is laid with a curious pattern of alternating black and white flagstones arranged in geometric patterns. Father Basil tells me it is a meditation labyrinth, one he made with his own hands last summer. He asks me whether, since I live in France, I have seen the ones in the Amiens or Chartres cathedrals. I confess my ignorance. So he explains the purpose of the labyrinth is to occupy the intellect with a practical task, that of following the path, so that the mind, thus freed, can drift to other spheres.

"The next time you come to visit, you'll stay at the monastery, and in the early hours, you'll come up here with me, you'll follow the path, moving slowly along the black flagstones, and you'll feel the effect."

With a certain solemnity, I say:

"I accept your invitation. I'll come back."

I glance at my watch.

"It's already five thirty. It's time for me to get going."

We walk down to the door of the monastery.

"I look forward to your next visit, you'll eat with us and stay here overnight."

"Yes, I will. I promise."

I make to shake his hand, but he pulls me to him and, for a long moment, he hugs me hard.

4

When he walked down from the monastery, straw hat in hand, Adam found Sémiramis exactly where he had left her, sitting in the car beneath the same oak tree, and felt guilt for abandoning her for more than two hours. At first she pretended that she had gone to visit her friends and had only just got back. This was a lie, as she eventually admitted. Her passenger apologized profusely.

"If you want me to forgive you," she cut him short, "tell me everything. From the first minute to the last."

This he did straightaway, making sure he did not forget or conceal anything.

His account was so animated, so enthusiastic, so emotional, especially when he described the ancient cave chapels, that his friend seemed worried.

"Please tell me you're not thinking of becoming a monk too!"

"I wouldn't say it was unthinkable in my case, but no, I don't plan to. I have a job I love, students who are waiting for me, a woman who loves me ..."

"A mistress," Sémiramis added neutrally as though simply adding to the list.

"That had completely slipped my mind."

"Bastard," she said gently, as though stroking a cat.

"But you don't need to worry, Ramzi didn't try to convert me."

"But he did suggest you come and spend some time at the monastery."

"Just one night, so that I can wake up in these surroundings ..."

"If I were you, I'd be careful. Men are a lot more vulnerable than they think. Especially at your age ..."

"Vulnerable? Yes, maybe. I do succumb to certain temptations. But not all of them."

She slapped his thigh, and he furtively stroked the hand that had slapped him.

"I know Ramzi, he's not the type to proselytize. His faith is decent and—how can I put it?—gracious. He has always been a courteous, considerate man, and his faith is like him. When I arrived, I was worried it might be the opposite, that he might be too reserved, too caught up in his mediation, too distant, the way he was with Ramez. So, actually, I was pleasantly surprised. Given that he decided to withdraw from the world, I was surprised that I felt closer to him than before, he was more attentive, more thoughtful, more direct.

"Religion has never been my cup of tea, but I have to confess that I admire and respect the man he has become. I even feel comforted to know that I have a friend in a monastery. And I will come back to visit him, as I promised. I'll spend the night in a cell like his, and in the morning, I'll go with him up to his 'labyrinth' to meditate as I walk."

On the drive back, the overcast landscape had lost all appeal. The journey seemed interminable. On several occasions, Adam almost dozed off, but he fought off sleep, fearing that the driver would doze off too and the car would end up at the bottom of a ravine.

At some point, they started singing. Sémiramis had always had a powerful, melodious voice, which enchanted her friends back when they were students, and she had a vast repertoire. She moved easily from Egyptian to Iraqi Arabic, from English to Greek, from French to Creole to Italian. She also knew Russian, Turkish, Syrian, and Basque songs, and a number of Hebrew hymns that echoed with the word *Yeroushalaim*. Adam did his best to accompany, humming along softly and singing more loudly when he remembered a chorus. His singing was not out of tune, but his voice was not easy on the ear. He knew this and so, that evening, for most of the songs, he simply tapped out the rhythm with his fingers. Had he not been worried that they might miss their turnoff, he would probably have stayed silent, his eyes closed, allowing himself to be lulled by his friend's voice.

At some point, he said:

"Did you never thinking about being a professional singer?"

"I considered it," she said with no false modesty.

"And?"

She sighed.

"And my father said: 'I won't have a daughter of mine wriggling her hips in some Cairo cabaret.'"

"And that was that?"

"That was that. My father had spent his youth in cabarets in Cairo. Apparently, every night, he would get drunk, sing at the top of his voice, buy champagne for everyone, and climb up on the tables. To my grandparents' horror, he even fell in love with a belly dancer. Not that he ever told me, obviously. All parents are supposed to have led exemplary childhoods, aren't they? But other members of the family told me. It was only after his own father died that he settled down, took over the family business, and got married. He had three children and vowed he would not let any of them—especially not me, his daughter—lead a dissolute life."

"I only just remembered that you were born in Cairo. I knew, obviously, but it had slipped my mind. Probably because you don't have an accent. Or, rather, you do—if I listen closely, I can just make out an Egyptian accent when you speak French. But not when you speak Arabic."

"I don't have an accent when I speak Arabic. In our family, we rarely spoke the language, though my father was from Byblos and my mother from Damascus. They spoke only French—to each other, to their brothers and sisters, to their friends, it was always French, like Russian aristocrats in a nineteenth-century novel. They only spoke Arabic to their driver, their cook, and their doorman. In the circles they moved in, it was commonplace. Worse still, when they talked about the locals, they said 'the Arabs,' as though they themselves were British or Greek."

"But when your father went to cabarets as a young man, got drunk and climbed on tables, I assume he didn't sing in French or English or Greek ..."

"No, you're right, he sang in Arabic. And when he took his dancer, whose name was Noureleyn, in his arms I'm sure it was in Arabic that he whispered sweet nothings. You do, too, actually."

Adam looked at her, intrigued.

"Yes, you too," she said, "you can only whisper in Arabic. We spent the whole evening speaking French, but when we went to bed ..."

"Probably. I don't really notice. But now you mention it, it's true that all my terms of affection come from Arabic."

"Even when you're with someone who doesn't speak the language?"

"The problem did arise when I first met Dolores. She would sometimes criticize me for being silent when we made love. I explained that affectionate terms occurred to me spontaneously in Arabic, and I didn't want to say anything since she didn't know the language. She thought about it and said 'I want you to whisper them in my ear as though I understood.' And I did. Then she wanted to whisper them too. At first, she learned what she had heard, speaking to me as though I were a woman. And her accent was laughable. But little by little I taught her the right words and the correct pronunciation. Now we make love in Arabic, which creates a singular complicity between us."

Sémiramis gave a little laugh and Adam felt a sudden panicked twinge of regret.

"I should never have told you that. She wouldn't care about the rest, but for me to tell you what we whisper to each other in bed is a betrayal."

"Don't worry, I won't mention it."

"That's not enough. You have to make me a solemn promise."

"I swear on my father's grave that I will never reveal a word of what you've just said. Not to Dolores or to anyone else. Will that do?"

"It'll do. I'm sorry for insisting, but I'm angry with myself for talking about such intimate things. It's not something I usually do."

"Relax, Adam, it's me, Sémi, your friend, your loyal friend, you're allowed to let your guard down for a few seconds. I tell you my secrets, you tell me yours, neither of us need suffer, it will simply bring us a little closer together."

She gently laid a hand on the leg of her passenger, who was thoughtful for a moment before asking:

"How old were you when you left Egypt?"

"Barely a year old. It was just after Nasser's coup d'état. My father had done something foolish, and he didn't dare stay in Cairo."

"Something foolish?"

"Very foolish, yes."

She smiled and said no more, Adam allowed her to collect her thoughts.

"Obviously, I don't remember any of this, but I was told

the story so often that I feel as though I lived it.

"Back when my father was a student, in the 1940s, there was a lot of political excitement. He never personally belonged to a political party, but among his university friends, there were communists, Islamists, monarchists, nationalists. He used to tell me that some days, you'd see dozens of students show up dressed in yellow, or in green, trying to march in step, shouting slogans—and you knew a new political party had just been founded. Most of these groups were more ridiculous than frightening, and they usually disappeared within a few months.

"The Ikhwan—the Muslim Brotherhood—was much more serious. Thousands of young men joined them, and when the Free Officers led the coup d'état in 1952, everyone assumed that Nasser, Sadat, and their cohorts were members of the Muslim Brotherhood in uniform. According to my father, some of them were; but once they had seized power, they distanced themselves from the movement, in fact they did their best to temper its influence in the country. To such an extent that in '54, the year I was born, disillusioned Islamic militants fired shots at Nasser while he was giving a speech. They missed, but not by much, and the incident was followed by a brutal crackdown. Thousands of militants were arrested, and many of the leaders were summarily executed.

"One of the conspirators, a nineteen-year-old named Abdessalam, was the younger brother of one my father's closest friends. After the attempted assassination, he had managed to flee; the police and the army were hunting him, and there was no doubt that, if he was caught, he would be lynched there and then. So my father decided to hide him in our house."

"You're not telling me he hid the man who tried to assassinate Nasser?"

"Very foolish, wouldn't you say?"

"That's a little more than foolish ... It's sheer lunacy! What can possibly have been going through the head of a nice middle-class Catholic man for him to risk his own and his family's lives by hiding not only a killer, but, worse, an Islamist?"

"That was precisely his logic—he assumed the authorities would never think to look for Abdessalam in the house of a nice bourgeois Christian family. And he was right, they searched the mosques and the working-class districts with a fine-tooth comb, but it never occurred to them to search our house."

"But why did he do it? Was he sympathetic to the Brotherhood?"

"Absolutely not. He cordially despised them before this happened, and went on despising them for the rest of his life. If he sheltered Abdessalam, it was because he was nineteen and shaking with fear, and his best friend had begged him to do so."

"And your mother agreed to this?"

"My father never asked her. His friend showed up one night with his kid brother, who had shaved off his beard to avoid capture and now looked like a prepubescent boy, though with eyes like a hunted animal. We lived on the ground floor and, in the back garden, my father had a studio where he painted in his spare time. He was really good, actually, I'm sure if he'd been born in Europe he would have been an artist. Anyway, the young man hid out in this studio and never set foot outside. My father secretly brought him food. This went on for several weeks, and no one in the family noticed anything. Not even my mother, who never went into her husband's studio.

"When things had calmed down and the authorities

gave up hope of finding him, the fugitive left. My father later found out that he left Egypt for West Germany, which was where most of the exiled Muslim Brotherhood settled at the time.

"My parents were never questioned, but my father was uneasy. He was convinced that someday or other, the story would leak out and the authorities would make him pay for providing succour to the enemy. So he sold the house, the business, everything he owned, he took his wife, his children, and his money, and he left."

"Did he regret doing 'something foolish'?"

"Actually, no, believe it or not, he never regretted it. Quite the opposite, he was pleased. Because of the incident, he had been forced to quickly sell off everything. A few months later came the first round of nationalization, then the Suez crisis. My father's cousins and my mother's brothers and all foreigners—or those who were considered foreign—were forced to flee Egypt in a mad rush leaving everything behind. The Greeks, the Italians, the Jews, the Levantine Christians … Their factories were appropriated, their lands, their shops, their bank accounts. They lost everything. My father, by doing something foolish, had sold everything before 'the deluge,' and so he kept his fortune. That was how he was able to buy land when he moved here, and build several houses, including the one that I converted into a hotel.

"A thousand times, I heard Egyptian immigrants congratulate my father for his foresight and his shrewdness. So, because of what you call his 'sheer lunacy,' he acquired the reputation of a wise man, a reputation that stayed with him all his life."

"I'm guessing he never told these people why he had to leave Egypt so hurriedly?"

"Absolutely not! By the time we settled into this country, Nasser was considered a demi-god, his photo was plastered everywhere, he was worshipped more here than he was in Egypt. As you can imagine, my father was not going to boast about harbouring the man who had tried to assassinate the saviour of the Arab nation. He would have been torn to pieces. He only began to mention it in the 1980s, when Nasser was long dead and forgotten."

"Did your father ever go back to Egypt?"

"He never set foot in the country again. It was strange, actually. When he talked about Egypt, his face lit up; he never tired of saying it was the most beautiful country in the world. But he never went back, and he never wanted his children to go there."

"So you've never been?"

"I have, but only after he died. I wanted to see the house where I was born, the house I had heard so much about. I went to see it, but I didn't feel anything. I thought, given all the stories I had been told as a child, that I would feel moved. But nothing. No tears, no lump in my throat. The place where I did feel moved was in Upper Egypt, in Luxor, the Valley of the Kings, looking at the frescoes. That's where I was left speechless. I suddenly realized why so many men had dreamed of this country—conquerors, travellers, poets ... But my parents' nostalgia left me cold. In Egypt, they lived like outsiders, and they were treated like outsiders."

"Things are never that simple."

"Oh yes, they are that simple. When you look down on the local population, refuse to speak their language, sooner or later you're driven out. If my parents had wanted to carry on living in Egypt, they should have become Egyptians, rather than hanging out with the British and the French."

In her voice there was a tinge of a slow-burning anger

that had never guttered out. After a few seconds of pregnant silence, she continued:

"If I'm honest, I should lump my father and my mother together. He used to tell me exactly what I've just told you, that they should have integrated with the local people—and in fact he had friends, and probably lovers, from all walks of life. But he was one of the few people who took that attitude. In his family, and even more so in my mother's family, most people felt like outsiders, and behaved like colonists. When the colonial period ended, they had to pack up and leave. You might say they reaped what they sowed ..."

"I'm in no position to defend your family, but in every situation, there are faults on both sides. What you've just said could easily be reversed: if they behaved like outsiders it was because they were always treated as outsiders. When people refuse to integrate, it is often because the society they're living in doesn't allow them to integrate. Because of their name, their religion, their accent, their appearance ..."

The two friends were pensive for a moment. Then Adam said more cheerfully:

"But let's get back to you. You could have had a career wiggling your hips in the cabarets of Cairo."

"My father was adamant; it was pointless to even try and argue. But I don't hold it against him, he was a product of his time, and he thought he was acting in my best interests. Besides, I never really had the ambition to make it as a professional singer. I love singing for my friends, I'm flattered when they say I have a beautiful voice, but I wouldn't have left my parents to entrust my life to an impresario. When I was young, I had a very different ambition: I wanted to be a surgeon."

Adam remembers now. When he had first met her,

Sémiramis was in her first year studying medicine.

"I'd read somewhere that there were almost no female surgeons, and I wanted to be a pioneer. At university, the professors and the other students all tried to put me off, telling me that, when they place their lives in someone's hands, patients need a reassuring—meaning male—figure. In short, there were careers that were unworthy of me—singer; and careers that I was unworthy of—surgeon. But it didn't put me off, I studied furiously, relentlessly, I wanted to be the top of my class. And in the second semester, I was."

"Then you got bored with it ..."

"No. Then I met Bilal. Then we fell madly, hopelessly in love. Then he died. And then, for three years, I was devastated. By the time I crawled out of my black hole, the war was raging, and it was too late for me to go back to medicine. I felt like I'd forgotten everything I'd learned. I never went back to university, and now I've ended up as a hotel manager."

"Chatelaine," Adam corrected.

She smiled.

"Sorry, I'd forgotten your title for me."

"Chatelaine. My beloved chatelaine."

"It's done me good, you coming back here, even if only briefly. I should be grateful to Mourad for phoning you. I'll remember our champagne dinners for a long time."

Her voice was sad. Her friend turned and saw she had tears in her eyes.

"Don't you think it's a little early for us to be saying goodbye?" he said. "I'm not leaving anytime soon. I've still got my room here for a while ..."

She smiled. Paused. Seemed to hesitate before saying:

"I had a long conversation with Dolores this morning."

"You phoned her again?"

"No, this time, she phoned me. You'd only just left. It was like she could sense that we'd spent the night together. And ..."

She trailed off. There was a long silence. Adam had to prompt her:

"And?"

"And it's been decided that from now on you'll sleep in your room and I'll sleep in mine."

"It's been decided," Adam echoed with a smile as ambiguous as the feelings stirred in him.

"I wasn't supposed to say anything," Sémiramis apologized, "and you'll have to pretend we never had this conversation. But I need you to help me keep my promise."

When Adam said nothing, she insisted, her voice at once apologetic and exasperated:

"Forget your male pride for a minute and just say: *I'll help you.*"

He grumbled, then gave a heavy sigh and said:

"Alright, I'll help you."

In an instant, the driver's tone shifted to playful and coquettish:

"It goes without saying this does not exclude longing, desire, compliments, tenderness, and even courtship. In fact, everything except ..."

Her passenger apprehensively waited for the crude words that would follow, but she said no more. She had finished her sentence.

"Everything except everything except everything except," he said over and over, trying to make the word sound as preposterous as possible.

When he set down the conversation in his notebook, Adam observed:

During the conversation, I was careful not to tell Sémi that I had already reached the same conclusion after my emails with Dolores. Etiquette dictated that I was meant to pretend to be disappointed, and more importantly, not let it be seen that, in my cowardly way, I was relieved not to have to tell my lover that our idyll was at an end. Not for the first time, the complicity between these two women has spared me from rudeness and remorse.

I make myself a promise to respect this pledge of abstinence; but, if I'm honest, I'm not completely sure that it is one that I can keep in all times, all places, all situations.

I will let life be my guide.

The Tenth Day

1

When morning came, Adam was still fully dressed. The night before, he had collapsed on his bed without eating, without brushing his teeth, and without closing the shutters as he usually did to avoid being woken early by the harsh, raw sunlight.

He had not had the strength to write a detailed account of his meeting with Brother Basil. He had done so when he woke at 5:00 a.m. When it was done, he phoned down to order breakfast, then checked his email.

During the night, he had received a laconic message from Naïm stating that he would be flying out of São Paulo on Wednesday morning, and would arrive on Thursday evening after a brief layover in Milan. Adam was delighted. The reunion was beginning to take shape, and sooner than he had hoped. He hurriedly replied that he would be at the airport to welcome Naïm.

Then he called Sémiramis.

"I hope I just woke you!"

"No such luck!" she laughed. "I'm already halfway through breakfast. Next time, try phoning earlier?"

"I've got more good news."

"Let me guess—Albert or Naïm has written to say they're coming. Am I right?"

Adam was taken aback.

"You're right. But you spoiled my surprise."

She laughed.

"You seem particularly perky this morning."

"I'm out on the terrace, there's a gentle breeze, the birds are chirruping, and the coffee is strong. If I thought I could trust you, I'd invite you to join me."

Ten minutes later, he was sitting with her. Everything was as she had painted it—the breeze, the chirruping, the aroma of the coffee. Additionally, the table was laden with food, and Sémiramis's nightgown was slightly open. Adam felt a pang of regret when he remembered that the "parenthesis" of their affair was over.

"So, Naïm will arrive on Thursday night at about seven. And Albert won't be far behind; since he's already told the institute that his 'adoptive mother' is at death's door, he should be here soon. So, it looks like the reunion will be next week. I can hardly believe it. A couple of days ago I was talking in terms of months, and now I'm just waiting on flight times. I feel like I'm living in a dream. It's wonderful, but a little scary." Silence. "Maybe it's time to seriously think about the practicalities."

"I've already thought about them," Sémiramis said. "Everyone will stay here in the hotel."

This was also Adam's preferred solution, so it was only for form's sake that he asked:

"You don't think Tania will insist on us staying with her, in the old house? That was the original plan."

"So soon after Mourad's death? No, it's unthinkable! The family is in mourning, we'd have to whisper all the time and wander around with long faces. No laughing. No raised voices. The whole reunion would be grim. No, I've thought things through and decided everyone will stay here. Including Tania. It will do her good to get away from that house for a few days, otherwise mourners will constantly be traipsing through. Here at the hotel, we can talk and yell and laugh, we can even sing at the tops of our lungs, if we feel like it. Everyone will have their own room, and we can all eat in the big first-floor reception room. Leave the logistics to me, it's my job."

Adam raised his hands in a gesture that said "I surrender" or "Fine, have it your way."

"On the other hand, it's your job to send the invitations," she said.

"It's pretty much all done. I'll call Ramez and his wife this morning."

"And Dolores ..."

"And Dolores, of course; I'll phone her this afternoon."

"And Brother Basil ..."

"I doubt he'll agree to come. But I'll send him a formal invitation ..."

"Have you made up your mind about Nidal?"

"Yes, I'm going to call him."

"You see? You've still got lots to do. Have you got his number?"

"No, but I assume you'll give it to me in a minute."

Sémiramis heaved a loud sigh:

"What would you do without me?"

"Check the telephone directory!"

"Bastard!"

He took her hand and pressed it to his lips.

"If it weren't for you, I'd already be back in Paris, I'd have given up on the idea of a reunion, I'd be slogging away at my biography of Attila."

She withdrew her hand.

"Do you really find him so interesting, that maniac?"

"*Attila, c'est moi*, as Flaubert might have said."

"Really? I'll need you to explain a little, I fail to see the similarities."

"Attila is the archetypal immigrant. If someone had told him: 'You are a Roman citizen,' he would have wrapped himself in a toga, started speaking Latin, and become the armed wing of the Empire. Instead, they said: 'You're nothing but a barbarian and an infidel!' and after that he dreamed only of destroying their Empire."

"And that's you?"

"It could have been me, it's certainly true of a large number of immigrants. Europe is full of Attilas who dream of being citizens and will eventually turn into barbarian hordes. Welcome me with open arms and I'm prepared to die for you. Slam the door in my face, and all I want is to kick down the door and destroy your whole house."

"So you're saying I was wise to welcome you with open arms?"

He laughed.

"It wasn't the best choice of words, but you know what I mean."

He paused for a moment, then added.

"As for you, I already felt you'd welcomed me with open arms the moment I called you from the taxi and you shrieked my name. What happened between us later, I'll call an 'unexpected blessing' ..."

Their fingers entwined again and they shared an intimate silence.

It was Sémiramis who finally broke the silence.

"So, you wanted Nidal's mobile number," she said, withdrawing her hand and searching through the contacts on her phone.

When she found the number, she handed the phone to her friend to use, but he simply copied the number onto a page of his notebook. He obviously wanted to make the call later, when he was alone in his room.

2

I wasn't sure Bilal's brother would remember me, Adam would write in his notebook on Sunday, April 29. *I hadn't met him more than three times in my life, and the last time was more than a quarter century ago, at Bilal's funeral. Nidal had seemed even more distraught than his mother and his sisters that day. He was sobbing uncontrollably. He had not yet turned seventeen, and Bilal was his role model, his guide, his idol. To make matters worse, they looked very alike—the same crooked nose, the same close-cropped black hair, the same look in their eyes, like a hunted deer—so as I watched the sobbing brother, I had the eerie feeling that Bilal had risen from the grave to mourn himself.*

"Nidal, this is Adam, I don't know if you remember me ..."

"I only know one person by that name—apart from our common ancestor to all, peace be upon him! So you've come back to us?"

"Well, I'm passing through ..."

"Why only 'passing through'?"

"These days I live in France."

"I lived in France for many years, too, but I came back to live among my people."

This was clearly a reproach. I had to retaliate.

"You lived in France, and you never thought to call your brother's best friend? Shame on you!"

He gave a little laugh to signal that our usual teasing could stop.

"I'm so happy to hear your voice. What can I do for you?"

"I'm trying to organize a get-together. I wanted to let you know ..."

"A political meeting?"

His tone was ironic and incredulous. I quickly reassured him.

"No, a reunion of old friends. Bilal's friends ..."

No answer. A long silence. I could tell Nidal was choked up. In fact, when he finally did speak, his voice was different, he was no longer blasé.

"A reunion of old friends ..."

I didn't know whether by slowly repeating my words in a whisper, Nidal was expressing nostalgia or suspicion. To forestall a negative reaction, I needed to say something.

"It would be wonderful if we could meet up: us, you and me. To talk about my little plan, and obviously about what you've been up to all these years."

"Sure, why not? Where are you now?"

Before I called, I decided it was best not to mention Sémi; or at least, not right now, anyway.

"I'm in the mountains, but I can come and meet you in town whenever suits you."

"In that case, let's have lunch! Do you want me to send a car?"

I preferred to lie.

"No thanks, I've got one. Just give me the address."

The little local restaurant where he suggested we meet was one I wouldn't ordinarily have set foot in. Not that there was anything uninviting or unpleasant about it, it's just one of those places that seem reserved for regulars, where an outsider feels that everyone is looking at him; an "outsider" in this case doesn't have to be European or Asian, it means anyone not from the neighbourhood.

Nidal seemed to know everyone, but he simply nodded and smiled as we made our way through the restaurant.

The owner had reserved us a private room with a window overlooking a small courtyard. Preferential treatment. The table was already set with dishes of olives, cucumbers, pickled turnips, and bread rolls cut into quarters.

"I usually just order the plat du jour, and I'm never disappointed. But they have other things too."

"Let's go for the plat du jour then."

"You don't even know what it is yet!"

"It doesn't matter. I'll take it anyway."

"Sunday is always stuffed courgettes."

"Fine by me!"

"You're an easy-going man, your wives must be delighted."

"Wives, plural?"

"I meant sequential, not simultaneous."

"Do you have simultaneous wives?"

"No, just the one. She warned me from the start: if I marry anyone else, she'll gouge my eyes out."

"And you just gave in."

"I'm very attached to my eyes."

Nidal smiled, and it was Bilal's smile.

"You've got a point," I said. "For those of us who like reading, two eyes are more useful than two wives."

"That's one point we agree on. I'm not sure there will be many more."

The owner comes over with a pencil and pad. He jots down the two plats du jour and asks what we would like to drink. Nidal orders a lemonade, and I nod to indicate that I'll have the same, though, when the owner has disappeared, I add:

"I never drink wine at lunch, it gives me a headache."

Since I had been careful not to smile, my host felt it necessary to explain:

"This place doesn't serve alcohol."

"I worked that out. I was just joking ..."

I smile. Not to be outdone, Nidal gives a faint half-smile. Then, looking away, he says as though to some third person:

"Emigrant jokes!"

I don't ask what he means by this but simply say again:

"I was just joking ..."

Then, before giving him time to respond, I add:

"But it's true that I never drink at lunchtime. Only at night."

"So, if I'd invited you for dinner rather than lunch, what would you have done?"

"I'd have abstained. I like a glass of wine in the evening, but I can easily go without. On the other hand, if someone tried to forbid me ..."

"It's forbidden to forbid," Nidal says mockingly in French.

Up to this point, we have been speaking Arabic, and it is in Arabic that I reply:

"If a person decides to refrain from certain drinks or certain foods because of his beliefs, I respect that. What I don't accept is trying to impose those beliefs on others, especially when governments get involved."

"Because you believe each citizen should decide for himself, and governments have no business banning things, right? But don't they ban the consumption of cocaine or hash? But maybe you think they shouldn't ban drugs?"

Rather too quickly, the conversation is turning into a clichéd sparring match between the zealot and the libertine. But maybe this is something he needs to do before we can talk man to man. One way or another, I'm not about to give in just because I'm on his home ground. On the contrary. In the Levant, people are supposed to accede to their guest's wishes, not subject him to their own laws. Or at least this is how people behaved in better times.

"No one claims that nothing should ever be banned. But some of your fellow believers like to ban things left and right. It's like they comb through the sacred texts searching for something else to prohibit, and make a proclamation. As someone once said about the English Puritans: 'They're not really fanatics, they just want to make sure no one has any fun.'"

Nidal gives a forced smile and says nothing. I continue:

"But to answer your question directly, I'd say: yes, of course, some substances are toxic, and I understand why they're banned. But wine? The same wine that has been sung about by Arab, Persian, and Turkish poets alike? The same wine that is the drink of the mystic? It is a noble, innocent pleasure to meet up with friends of an evening; to laugh, to talk, and put the world to rights over a bottle of good wine. Am I supposed to allow myself to be deprived of this by some authority just because some people drink too much? Or because certain religious traditions forbid it?"

"You only see one side of things!" Nidal growls.

He takes a few mouthfuls to allow himself time to collect his thoughts, then says:

"What you refuse to see is that, in the West, everything that comes from here is treated with hostility. Everyone agrees that alcoholism is a scourge, but Islam has only to denounce alcohol for people to decide that it's a symbol of individual free will. Even people like you."

A waiter arrived with steaming plates, and bottles of lemonade. He asked if we would like him to pour the yoghurt over the stuffed courgettes, or leave it on the side. Then he sprinkled everything with dried mint and was about to pour the lemonade into our glasses when Nidal gestured that he would do it, and, when the man had disappeared, he carried on where he had left off.

"A lot of European men have a wife and a mistress, and children by both of them; but if Islam says you can marry both, the very idea of two wives is seen as scandalous, outrageous, immoral, and the illicit relationship becomes respectable."

"Maybe that's because, when it comes to the way we treat women, our country leaves a lot to be desired, don't you think? If women here were free to work, to travel, to dress as they pleased ..."

"You really think that's the reason? You really think that the West is worried about emancipating our women? You don't think that, for centuries, they've been systematically hostile to any idea that comes from us? Time was, they criticized Oriental countries like ours for their beautiful boys and their wanton women, and now we're criticized for being unduly modest. In their eyes, whatever we do, we're wrong."

I took a few bites of my food before saying, hesitantly:

"You're not completely wrong, there is a genuine hostility, and it sometimes seems systematic. But it's not one-sided. To put it bluntly, they hate us as much as we hate them."

Nidal instantly dropped his knife and fork and stared at me suspiciously, perhaps even angrily.

"When you say 'we,' who exactly are you talking about?"

The question was neither anodyne nor innocent. And to me, as his guest, it was deeply discourteous. What Nidal was saying, essentially, was that, as an emigrant, I had "gone over to the enemy." I felt all the more insulted, because the accusation was not completely unjustified. Whose side do I think I am on, as a Christian Arab who has lived for years in France? On the side of Islam, or the side of the West? And when I say "we," who am I talking about? The phrase I had just used—"They hate us as much as we hate them"—unwittingly revealed the ambiguity of my position. Truth be told, I don't know myself what I meant by the words "they" and "we." To me, both of these rival worlds are "they" and "we."

Nidal had hit home, he had found the chink in my armour. But there could be no question of agreeing with him, or tolerating his hurtful insinuations. Swathing myself in a dignified silence, I conspicuously turned away and looked out the window, or down at my plate, and once even at my watch.

From my actions, Nidal realized that he had gone too far. He mentally erased his insulting question, and began to talk about what I had said in a different tone. In doing so, he did not have to back down, but what he said, though polemical, contained an implicit apology.

"Maybe they hate us as much as we hate them, as you put it. But as a historian, you have to admit that the relationship between them and us today is profoundly unequal. In the past four hundred years, we have not invaded a Western country, it is they who invade us, they who impose their law, they who subjugate us, colonize us, humiliate us. All we have done is suffer, suffer, suffer … But here you are, a historian concerned with truth and objectivity, putting us on the same footing. 'They hate us as much as we hate …' There are faults on both sides, is that it?

"The French invade Algeria, annexe the country, massacre anyone who resists, ship in European colonists who act as though they own the land and as if the local populace exist merely to serve and to obey. Faults on both sides, right? They use every possible means to force the inhabitants to stop speaking Arabic and to turn away from Islam. Then, a hundred and thirty years later, they go home, leaving behind a country so devastated it might never recover. But according to you, there are faults on both sides, right?

"Jews emigrate en masse to Palestine, occupy the land and drive out people who, overnight, find themselves stateless and spend the next half century living in refugee camps. But according to you, there are faults on both sides."

He was attacking me again, but this time I couldn't react as I had before. What Nidal was attacking was not me, personally, but my views as a historian. In such circumstances, all arguments are legitimate. So rather than adopt the position of an offended guest, I decided to cross swords with my host.

"Are you going to let me answer?"

Nidal stops abruptly.

"Go on, I'm listening."

"For a start, I didn't say 'there are faults on both sides,' I simply said: 'They hate us as much as we hate them.' I did not mention 'faults.' You put words in my mouth and then used them to attack me. It's a questionable process."

"You may not have said it today, but it is something you say all the time!"

"I suppose you secretly record my conversations?" I said flippantly, to lighten the mood.

Nidal didn't smile.

"No, Adam, I don't record your conversations, but I have listened to you speak. I went to the university where you teach several times, I sat at the back of the lecture hall and I listened to you. I didn't just make up that phrase, you said it, you said it a hundred times. 'There are faults on both sides.' They invade our country, drive us from our homes, bomb us, appropriate what is ours—but, to you, there are always faults on both sides. A historian is supposed to be neutral, isn't he? Between the invader and invaded, between predator and prey, between murderer and victim, you remain neutral. Whatever happens, you mustn't seem to be defending your own people. Is that objective? Is that what you call intellectual honesty?"

For a long time, I sat in silence as though I had run out of arguments. I suddenly realized that this meeting with my friend's brother was not going to be a simple resumption of contact, but a settling of scores.

3

I had not seen Nidal in more than twenty-five years, while he, for his part, had never taken his eyes off me. Unbeknownst to me, he had been observing me, watching me, sizing me up.

I was still wondering whether to say this, when he preempted me.

"When I went to see you speak the first time, I intended to talk to you after the lecture. I knew how close you were to my brother, and I thought you'd welcome me with open arms."

"And I probably would have done that day," I said coldly, unwilling to respond to his digs with a gesture of friendship.

He went on:

"But as I listened to you, I thought: here is an Arab who doesn't want anyone to think he's an Arab. Why embarrass him?"

This was too much! My host had gone too far. I had to answer immediately or get up and walk out. What stopped me from making a scene was that Nidal looked deeply distressed. He seemed close to tears. Suddenly, what he was saying no longer sounded like cold sarcasm, but genuine reproach. Awkward, insulting, unjustified—but genuine.

I decided to treat my deceased friend's younger brother as though he were my younger brother. Strictly, but with an almost paternal strictness.

"If we believe in the hereafter, it's possible that Bilal is here at this table with us now, watching and listening to us. Some of the things you've said would have made him happy, others not. And when I reply, sometimes he might nod, and sometimes he might frown. I don't know what his views would be if he were still alive, this benign, invisible witness without whom we would not be together right now. But I do know one thing: he would not have wanted me to doubt your sincerity, or for you to doubt mine."

I pause for a moment to separate the emotional prologue from the argument itself. And to glance at Nidal to see whether he has softened, and is now prepared to listen. Then I go on:

"When I say there are faults on both sides, that doesn't necessarily mean they're shared out fifty-fifty. More than anything, it means: try to understand why others won, and why we lost. You say: they invaded our countries, occupied them, humiliated us. The first question that comes to my mind is: why could we not stop them? Are we, perhaps, staunch advocates of nonviolence? No, we are not. So why were they able to invade us, subjugate us, humiliate us? Because we're weak, you might say, because we're divided, poorly organized, and badly equipped. And why are we weak? Why have we been unable to produce weapons as powerful as those of the West? Why are our industries so inadequate? Why did the industrial revolution occur in Europe and not here? Why did we remain underdeveloped, vulnerable, dependent? You can go on saying: it's someone else's fault, it's someone else's fault. But sooner or later we have to face up to our own shortcomings, our own mistakes, our own weaknesses. Sooner or later we have to face up to our own defeat, to the vast, resounding historic collapse of the civilization that is ours."

Without realizing, I had raised my voice. Two young men immediately come into the room and lean against the wall behind Nidal, who does not notice their presence until he sees me looking at them; my host turns to them and nods to say: "It's alright, we're just talking, you can go." *They leave.*

I lower my voice and continue in French:

"Losers are always tempted to present themselves as innocent victims. But that doesn't square with reality. They're not entirely innocent. They're guilty of being defeated. In the eyes of their people, their civilization, they are culpable. And I don't just mean the leaders, I mean you, me, all of us. If we are on the losing side of history now, if we are humiliated in the eyes of the world and in our own eyes, it is not simply the fault of others, it is primarily our own fault."

"In a minute, you'll be telling me that Islam is to blame."

"No, Nidal, that's not what I was going to say. Religion is just one element. To me, it's not the problem, but it's not the solution either. But don't expect me to give you facile reassurances. I'm not comfortable with what's going on around us. You think it's a wonderful sight, these women covered from head to toe, these huge portraits of turbaned men, this forest of beards."

"What have our beards got to do with you?"

"What's in your heart is none of my business. How you present yourself is a public statement for the benefit of third parties, and therefore it is my business. I've got the right to approve or disapprove. I have the right to feel reassured, and the right to feel uncomfortable. But I don't plan to go on and on about your beard. I was just trying to say that I've got the right to talk about anything, without exception, encouraging you to do the same."

As he listens, Nidal instinctively brings his hand up to his beard, stroking it as though to renew his allegiance. It's not really much of a beard, it just looks as though he hasn't shaved for a couple of weeks.

"When I first met you, when you were sixteen, you already had a beard—well, more bum fluff ..."

He smiles at this image. I carry on:

"But you also wore a Che Guevara beret emblazoned with a red star."

"I wasn't the only one!"

"And now you're not the only one to have a bushy beard."

"You're saying I've been blindly following every passing fad."

"I don't blame you, we all do. It's what the Germans call Zeitgeist, 'the spirit of the times,' we all follow it in one way or another. It's nothing to be either ashamed or proud of, it's how human societies function."

"So says the professor ..." Nidal says with a trace of sarcasm.

"You're right, I am speaking as a professor of history. In every era, people have expressed opinions and taken up positions they think are the result of individual thought when in fact they're the spirit of the time. It's not inevitable, but it is a like a strong wind—it's difficult not to bend."

"So, I'm spinning in the wind like a weathervane, is that it?" I smile.

"You really want to make me sound like I'm insulting you, when actually I'm just trying to explain a common phenomenon. It was as normal for you to identify with Che Guevara in the early '70s as it is for you to be an Islamist today. There's a certainty continuity between the two positions."

"Which is?"

"You still think of yourself as a revolutionary."

"While you think I'm not ..."

"Let's just say that the revolution has taken a different path. For a long time, the concept of revolution was the prerogative of progressives, then one day it was taken over by reactionaries. I've got a colleague who's working on the subject. We have lunch sometimes and talk about it. He calls it the 'inversion.' He's writing a book on the subject he plans to call The Year of Inversion ..."

"Because it is linked to one particular year?"

"That's his thesis. He argues that things changed dramatically in the world between the summer of 1978 and the spring of '79. Iran underwent the socially conservative Islamic revolution. In the West, 1979 marked the start of a different 'conservative revolution,' spearheaded by Margaret Thatcher in Britain and Ronald Reagan in the United States. Deng Xiaoping instigated a new Chinese revolution that year, moving away from socialism and eventually leading to spectacular economic growth. In Rome, John Paul II became Pope, and he, too, would prove to be as revolutionary as he was reactionary ... My colleague has a long list of events from the same period, all tending to be indicative of a social upheaval that has permanently affected attitudes. The right has become all-conquering, while the left simply tried to preserve its achievements. This is what I was thinking when I said ..."

"... that I'd just swapped beards and carried on thinking of myself as a revolutionary. Is that it?"

"Yes. Kind of."

"While, as you see it, I've become a reactionary, right?"

"I wouldn't put it precisely that way, but it's more or less what I think, yes."

"At least you're honest," he said with a very slight smile of impatience; before adding, "This conversation could go on for a hundred years."

"It doesn't matter, we can carry on when we get to paradise."

"If we end up in the same one."

"You think there's more than one? Or that paradise is divided up between nations and religions?"

"I don't have the faintest idea. That's a problem you'll have to pose to the Sophists. That's what people used to call you, isn't it?"

"Yes, it was. The 'Circle of Sophists.' But why do you say 'you'? You used to come to our meetings."

"Not very often. Once or twice, with my brother."

"With your brother, yes. I often think about him."

Hardly had I said the words than I felt I had usurped a role that was not mine, having been a close friend of Bilal only at the end of his life. By way of apology, I added:

"You must have thought about him a thousand times more often."

As he did every time I mentioned his brother, Nidal was silent and thoughtful. He sipped the last of his lemonade, then let his eyes stray to the window, and beyond.

"He promised to take me with him when he went out on the

barricades. *Our mother started crying. She said I was too young, that I had to do my homework. Bilal tried to reason with her, told her he'd stay right beside me, that he'd never put me in danger, and that, when we got home, he'd help me with my homework. But she wouldn't listen. She said, 'Not both of you! Not both at once!' As though she sensed what was coming. Bilal whispered that he'd take me next time. He left. An hour later, there was a knock on our door to tell us that he was injured.*

"I've thought about that scene a thousand times, imagining the other ways it might have played out. My brother deciding not to go after all, or he and I going together, and me forcing him to shelter in a doorway. Or both of us being blown limb from limb by the same bomb. I've often dreamed that I was the martyr, wrapped in a shroud, my mother and my sisters standing over me, crying, and Bilal next to me, holding my hand to the very last moment, sobbing the way I sobbed at his funeral.

"And every time I wake up, I'm disappointed that it's just a dream, a fiction, that my brother is still in his grave, and I am on the outside, wretched, among the living ..."

As he was speaking, the two young men who had briefly stepped into the room earlier reappeared and posted themselves on either side of the curtain separating us from the main restaurant. But this time it was Nidal who was speaking, and in a low voice—nothing that was likely to upset militants.

I look up at them and once again my host follows my gaze. I see him get to his feet and, just then, a man in a black turban appears. Nidal greets him deferentially, introduces us to each other, and invites the man to sit. They clearly had something to discuss, so I quickly took my leave, making it seem, for form's sake, as though I had been about to leave anyway.

Which was obviously not true. I would happily have stayed for another hour; we still had things to say, Nidal and I.

As I left Bilal's brother, his restaurant, his neighbourhood, his friends, I felt a certain malaise; but I was not unhappy to have seen him again. So many things divide us, and the only thing that binds us is the memory of his deceased brother. A slender thread? Undeniably. It will never be enough to resolve our differences, but I will not be the one to break it.

Sémiramis was right, of course, Nidal has changed. And even if the change is not what I might have wished, as a human being and particularly as a historian, I understand him. I was careful not to remind him, for example, that when he was alive his brother did not believe in God or the Devil, and hence was a very singular "martyr." I sensed that the memory of Bilal was a sanctum where I should venture only with infinite verbal precautions. Anything that might be interpreted as sarcastic or mocking would be rude, insulting, and almost sacrilegious. So I thought it best to hold my tongue.

Since coming back to the country, I have been trying to pick up the thread, not settle scores. Besides, what scores do I have to settle? Can I really blame Nidal for not having the same convictions at forty as he did when he was sixteen? He has changed, I've changed, the country has changed, our world is not the same. Yesterday's avant-garde has been relegated to the scrap heap, discarded, and the rear guard is not on the front lines. It is something I can continue to deplore, but I can hardly pretend to be surprised. Nor can I criticize Bilal's brother. He is the one who is in step with his time, and I am the one from another era, one that has prematurely ended. But—however much people may mock my stubbornness—I am still convinced that I am right and it is humanity that has lost its way.

4

"But you still invited him to come?" Sémiramis said suspiciously after Adam had given her a detailed account of their lunch, and their animated discussions.

"I haven't sent him a formal invitation, but it went without saying. I didn't meet up with him to subject him to a final exam whose results would determine where or not he was included. The invitation was implicit when I phoned him this morning. I was hardly going to leave, shake his hand, and say, 'Thanks for lunch, but I'm sorry, you're not invited, you don't meet the criteria ...'"

"And you're planning to put him in a room with Albert, who works for the Pentagon? And with Naïm, who's Jewish and has been to Israel a dozen times?"

Adam shrugged.

"They're both grown up, they spend their time traveling the world, if they haven't met anyone who thinks like Nidal before now, this will be an opportunity. He's intelligent, he's rational, he seems sincere, and he knows how to express what he thinks."

"And we won't be drinking champagne?"

"Of course, we'll drink champagne. The bottles will be in the ice buckets, those who want can help themselves, those who don't, can abstain."

"What if he insisted we remove the bottles?"

"I'll tell him it's not for him to decide, I said as much over lunch, and I won't hesitate to say it again. If he stays, that's great. If he leaves, too bad. Any other questions, my beautiful chatelaine?"

"No, Professor, not one!" Sémiramis reassured him in a mock-fearful tone. "You seem to have all the answers, but I'm still sceptical. You've got this impression that you can reunite old friends after a quarter of a century as though nothing had happened. I hope you're right."

"Better to be wrong and hope than to be right and despair."

"Is that your motto?"

"That's not a rule to live by, just a basic requirement for honesty. It's too easy to say there'll never be peace, that people will never be able to live together, to wait for the cataclysm with arms folded and a mocking smile, so that when it comes, you can say, 'I told you so.' In this part of the world, a prophet of doom is almost certain to be proved right by the future. Predict that there'll be a war within a decade, and you won't be disappointed. Predict that two factions will kill each other and it's more than likely to happen. If you really want to take a risk, you have to predict the opposite. Today, my own minor ambition is to bring a group of old friends together again, so that we can have a polite and informative conversation. Is that too much to ask?"

His friend gazed at him with amused tenderness, stroked his forehead as though he were a boy of six and said, in a motherly tone:

"Yes, darling, it's too much to ask. But don't give up hope, I like you when you're indignant."

This completely unsettled Adam. He didn't know whether he should rage against this "motherly instinct" or attempt to restart a serious discussion.

He grabbed the hand caressing him, wanting to pull it away from his face. But rather than letting it go, he clasped it to his own. They both sat, motionless, and said nothing more.

From their twined hands rose the desire to make love. But still they avoided each other's eyes, each waiting for the other to utter the sensible words that would put an end to this temptation.

The knowledge that they would soon have to move apart made it possible for them to experience this moment of tenderness with a sense of innocence. Did they not know, he as well as she, that there was an invisible line they would not cross? What mattered was not to reach it too quickly; what mattered was to move with infinite slowness.

Sémiramis had come up to Adam's room in the late afternoon so he could tell her about his encounter with Bilal's brother. She had found him at his desk, feverishly jotting down notes. He had stopped writing, and gestured for her to sit, but she had decided to remain standing, leaning against the closed door.

Later, in the heat of the exchange, he had got to his feet, taken a few steps, and found himself close to her. This was how it had begun.

How long did they stand, pressed against each other in silence, eyes closed, hands twined? At some point their lips brushed, then parted. Which of them would take the initiative, tell the other they had to stop, that they had to keep their promise?

A second furtive kiss, then a third, not so fleeting, and a fourth that lingered. Their bodies clung together. Sémiramis stretched out her free hand to switch off the light.

Only when they had collapsed on the bed did the visitor whisper to her friend:

"You promised you'd help me."

And he, in his distraction, could find no answer.

When I opened my eyes, he would note some time later, *Sémi was no longer next to me. I turned on the bedside lamp and looked at my watch. It was not yet seven o'clock. I had only dozed off for a few minutes. I sat up in bed, bare-chested, my mind reeling.*

It was bound to happen!

Having eaten of the offered fruit, we longed for the forbidden fruit.

Having made love with permission, we made love without it.

Does this mean that my relationship with Sémi is not the digression whose end was scheduled the moment it began? Yes, it is, it cannot be anything else, in my mind, or in hers. But if an affair is to be, it must run its course. Not just its mature years, but its childhood and its adolescence, even if these are in the wrong order. It must find its own alchemy, its own alloy of reason and folly, passion and disinterest, emotion and humour, intimacy and distance, word and flesh.

What matters, for the lovers, is the ability to safeguard the memory of their affair as though it were a shared journey.

Journeys often offer the opportunity to build lasting friendships with strangers who were travelling companions. It should be possible to remember our amorous adventures in a similar frame of mind. I'm not suggesting the lovers meet up on the anniversary of their first encounter to celebrate and recall shared moments, but they should do what they can to overcome the bitterness of separation so that, for the rest of their lives, they can fondly remember this "journey."

It is a word that fits perfectly with my circumstances since I came back to my native land. I am on a romantic journey with Sémi as my companion. A journey through time rather than space. In theory, I came back to reconnect with the land of my youth, but I am not really looking at the country, I am searching for the traces of my youth. I'm oblivious to the things, the people I did not know in my former life. I am not seeking to learn anything, to relearn anything, to discover anything. I am simply trying to recover what was already familiar to me. I am looking for traces, vestiges, remnants. Everything new here is like an unwelcome intrusion in my dream, an insult to memory, an act of aggression.

This is not a boast, in fact I'm willing to acknowledge it as a weakness. But, from the very first day, this is how I perceived this journey. Those things I recognize, I see in technicolour; everything else is a dull grey.

As a result, for as long as I am on this journey, there can be no more desirable woman than Sémi. But I feel sure that, when I go back to Paris, she will suddenly seem very distant. And Dolores will once again fill my every thought, whereas while I'm here, I have to make an effort to think of her.

5

An hour after their impromptu lovemaking, Sémiramis called Adam and suggested they go back to see Mourad's widow. Her guest was all the more eager to agree since he wanted to talk to Tania about the swift progress of the planned reunion.

The two lovers made not the slightest allusion to what had just happened. Neither on the phone nor while they drove.

This time, the widow was alone. The only other person, a woman in mourning black, doubtless a neighbour or a relative, left the moment the two friends arrived.

Tania explained that the house had not been empty that day either, that she had to resort to subterfuge to persuade the last visitors to leave.

"It's taken me some time to realize, but condolence in our culture is designed to exhaust, to leave the bereaved so shattered they no longer have the energy to think about their grief."

"If it works, so much the better," Adam said.

"Oh, it works. I am emotionally numbed. I see everything, hear everything, but I feel nothing."

Although she may have been exhausted, and "numbed," she seemed wired, as though under the effect of a powerful stimulant. Her gestures were a little more brusque, her smiles appeared and faded more quickly than usual.

She was sitting in the small salon where, long ago, they had held the "farewell evening" with Naïm, before he emigrated with his family. Seeing her friends arrive, she made to get up, but they stopped her, and, as they had on their previous visit, they both bent and kissed her.

Adam sat down next to her and in a fraternal gesture put an arm around her shoulder. She tilted her head back, closed her eyes, and lay very still. Sémiramis had taken a chair at the far end of the room, as though to give them space to savour this moment of closeness and reconciliation.

"When you want to go to bed, just tell us," Adam whispered.

"Yes, just tell us, we're all family," Sémiramis said.

"I have no desire to sleep," the widow said, opening her eyes. "It feels good, being here with you. I'm so happy you came."

She raised her head and looked from one to the other.

"You're both looking well."

Sémiramis nodded and a blissful smile lit up her face.

Adam smiled too, and said:

"Yes, things are good. I've been rediscovering the country, the people ..."

"You didn't get to talk to your friend," said Tania, "but you don't regret coming, do you?"

"I should have come back years ago, but I kept putting it off. It was thanks to your call that I finally made the decision."

"And you don't regret it," she said again.

Adam and Sémiramis exchanged a furtive glance and then he said:

"No, I don't regret it. Absolutely not."

"I'm happy," said the widow.

Once more, she let her head rest on Adam's arm only to quickly sit up and look from one to the other, first him, then her, then him, then her again, before announcing:

"You're sleeping together, the two of you."

"What are you talking about?" Sémiramis protested with a forced laugh.

But Tania looked into her eyes.

"If you tell me I'm wrong, I'll believe you."

This was not a promise, but a challenge. The "chatelaine" did not quite know how to react. But her brief hesitation was tantamount to a confession. After a moment, she answered with a question:

"What if you're not wrong?"

"In that case I'd say: make the most of it. We never get them back, those moments we let slip through our fingers. We spent our whole lives telling each other that one day we would go to Venice, one day we'd go to Beijing and visit the Forbidden City. In the end, we never went anywhere. We spent our whole lives saying: Later, we'll do it later. When this issue has been sorted. When that invoice has been paid. When we've dealt with that. When we've got the house back ... Then he was struck down by that terrible disease, and from that moment we never knew a single second of joy.

"So, what I'm telling you is: Don't be like me. Make the most of every minute. Don't let some excuse make you turn away from happiness. Make the most of it. Take each other's hands and never let go."

"I don't want to disappoint you," Sémiramis said, "but Adam and I aren't planning to get married."

"Who said anything about marriage?"

Only to contradict herself:

"And anyway, why not? What's stopping you?"

"What's stopping us is that I don't want to get married, and neither does he. We just want to be together, to hold hands, and to remember our time at university."

"I admire you, Sémi. You're such a strong woman."

"There's not much to admire, Tania. If I were strong, I'd have walked away from my family, I'd have had the career I always dreamed of. I should have been breaking with traditions twenty years ago, not now."

"Don't be so hard on yourself. Twenty years ago, you were the bravest of us all. What we did in secret, you did in broad daylight."

"It didn't do me much good. Bilal is dead ..."

"There's nothing either you or I can do about that. We love them, they die. However much we try to hang on to them, they slip through our fingers, they leave, they die."

Some minutes later, the three friends went into the dining room.

"I only have the leftovers from lunch," their hostess said.

But still her guests suspected that there would be far too much to eat, and responded to her polite apology with polite protests.

When they had sat down, Adam told Tania, not without a tinge of pride, that the reunion she had wished for was actually going to take place, and much earlier than anticipated.

"Naïm and Albert are already on their way, and Ramez and his wife have promised to come as soon as we're all together. That should be at the end of next week at the latest."

Tania was visibly delighted, and thanked him profusely. In her voice, in her eyes, he saw, for the first time in years, the Tania of old, his friend, his "loving sister." But this fleeting moment of joy and gratitude quickly faded and the widow's eyes grew dark again.

"Do you think they will speak well of their friend?" she asked.

"Of course, Tania, don't worry. They know that you wanted this reunion, they know it is to mourn his death. They're coming because they are nostalgic for the gatherings we used to have. You have no reason to be worried."

But she clearly was. She could not help it.

"All I want is for people to be fair to him. If he is watching us, listening to us, I want him to feel that his friends still keep him in their hearts. He suffered so much these last years."

Was she talking about the mental anguish triggered by the disapproval of his friends—of Adam first and foremost? Or the physical pain of the cancer eating away at him? It was not clear from her words; it probably was not clear in her mind. The twin pains became one and each inflamed the other.

"You've got nothing to worry about, they're coming as friends," said Adam. "We all have things that we regret, no one is about to cast the first stone."

"Otherwise there would be stones flying in all directions," said Sémiramis.

She seemed more amused than troubled at the prospect.

On the way back, the two friends drove in silence for several minutes before Adam said, with a pent-up sigh:

"Don't you think Tania was a bit insistent tonight?"

Sémiramis nodded wordlessly. Adam said:

"You know more about the rules of mourning etiquette than I do. How long are we supposed to put up with these mood swings just because she's grieving?"

His friend made a helpless gesture. It was Adam who eventually answered his own question.

"As far as I'm concerned, she's used up my compassion. Next time she talks to us the way she did tonight, I'm not going to mince words, I'll tell her exactly what I think of her and her husband."

"God rest his soul."

"Yes, fine, God rest his soul. But it was like it was his voice I was hearing the other night, and again tonight. Tania used to be so tactful, so discreet, so sensitive. Her husband was the one who used to come out with offensive remarks."

"In the thirty years they were together, maybe it rubbed off on her."

"That said, Mourad had a certain way of saying even the most offensive things ... It was impossible to be too angry with him. With Tania, it's different. What she said about us was so inappropriate, so unsubtle. I wanted to slap her."

"Oh, let it go. So, she accused us of sleeping together— as long as she doesn't do it in public, I don't give a damn. At my age, after everything I've been through, it honestly doesn't bother me. I just laugh at such gossip as though it were about someone else. A friend once phoned to tell me what so-and-so had said about me, how I'd had plenty of lovers. I said: better a reputation for plenty then a reputation for penury."

"I'm sure you're right to look at it like that. Even so, the difference in Tania is one of the things that has disappointed me since I came back. I expected to find the friend I used to know, I thought we'd put the bitter legacy of the war behind us and go back to being like brother and sister. Especially since I only came because she asked!"

They drove for some minutes in companionable silence before Sémiramis said, by way of explanation:

"Mourad spent those years caught up in his political struggles, in his business, he probably didn't often think about his old friends. Whereas Tania had time to brood about your argument ..."

"And another thing ..." Adam went on, as though continuing the same thought, "Mourad knew perfectly well that he'd done something wrong, that I was right to reproach him. While Tania seems to be convinced that I was unfair to him. She must hate me even more than he did."

He paused a moment and then went on:

"I had a strange feeling the morning they called and asked me to come. It was vague and, at the time, I didn't really understand it. I got the impression that Mourad knew he had been at fault, and wanted to justify himself before he died—otherwise why waste his last breath talking to me? Whereas I felt as though Tania was trying to make me feel guilty."

"From what I know of both of them, I'm sure you're right. In our country, wives tend to take family quarrels to heart, much more so than their husbands."

"Or their sons. Mourad used to say that when he fell out with someone, he never told his mother, because she would immediately turn against that person, making any reconciliation impossible. I guess Tania is behaving towards me the way that her mother-in-law would have."

"Tante Aïda ..."

"Yes, Tante Aïda ... She was always nice to me. I suppose she's no longer of this world ..."

Sémiramis giggled. Her friend eyed her suspiciously, reproachfully. It took her more than a minute to regain her composure.

"I'm sorry, I couldn't help it! The story isn't even funny, it's horrible."

"Tell me anyway," Adam said, scowling.

He was burning with curiosity.

"Aunt Aïda died seven or eight years ago. She wasn't particularly old, but she had presenile dementia. In the last few months, she didn't recognize anyone, not even her family, it was very hard for them. I heard she spent her days rocking in her chair. Physically, she was still strong, but her mind was gone. At one point, she developed a particular mania. She'd say, 'I want to go to the house in the mountains,' and Mourad and Tania would take her there; the next day she'd say, 'I want to go to the house in the city,' and they'd take her back ... At first, they did so the way you would grant the last wish of someone who is dying. But this happened at least a dozen times—they were getting desperate—and then the doctor told them, 'In her condition, she's got no idea where she is, she can't tell one place from another. Next time she asks you to move her, spin the chair around two or three times and say: *We've arrived.*' And that's what they did. Whenever she asked to go somewhere, they spun her around and said, 'We're in the city,' or 'We're in the mountains.' And she believed them.

"A few months later, the poor thing died. I went to offer my condolences. I was sitting in the living room, next to Tania, and not knowing how to begin the conversation I whispered to her, 'Did your mother-in-law die in the city or in the mountains?' Tania burst out laughing. It was scandalous! Mourad was furious with her, and they were both furious with me. But I swear, I didn't know the story about the chair, I didn't even know what was wrong with Aïda. By that point, I rarely saw them, I had no contact with them, I'd read the funeral announcement in the paper and gone to offer my condolences. But, to his dying day, Mourad was convinced I'd made a tasteless joke at his mother's funeral. I don't think he ever forgave me."

She turned to her passenger, who was looking at her doubtfully.

"You don't believe me, do you? You think I did it on purpose. You really think I could be so rude? Do you want me to swear on my father's grave again?"

"No, that won't be necessary," Adam said enigmatically. "I'll give you the benefit of the doubt."

The Eleventh Day

1

I've decided to go and visit Brother Basil today, Adam wrote in his notebook the moment he opened his eyes on Monday, April 30. *Starting tomorrow, my other friends are gradually going to arrive, and I won't have time to spend a whole day and night in his company.*

Yesterday, Sémi offered to drive me, as she did last time. I flatly refused. I still feel bad for forcing her to make the four-hour round trip that day, especially since I made her wait on a patch of waste ground in the blazing sun for nearly two and a half hours. She didn't protest, but she is insistent I be driven there in her air-conditioned car by the hotel chauffeur who took me to Tania's house the night of the funeral, who is the brother of Francis, our champagne waiter.

Later in the day, Adam set down a detailed account of his second visit to the monastery at Les Grottes.

The aforementioned Kiwan was as courteous and friendly as he had been last time, and his driving isn't, in itself, bad. He carefully negotiates the hairpin bends, which is important since there are dozens of them. His one fault is that every time he speaks to me, he feels it is only polite to turn and look at me, and so takes his eyes off the road—only briefly, of course, but it's pretty nerve-racking.

I have brought nothing but a small overnight bag—of the kind that in Paris in the Roaring Twenties was called a "baise-en-ville," a rather inappropriate name when one is spending the night in a place of prayer and meditation. I managed to fit inside my laptop, my toiletry bag, two shirts, some underwear, a thick sweater, and—as a gift for my hosts—a bottle of Benedictine that I bought in the city yesterday.

I arrived in the early afternoon. The door was opened by the same colossus as last time. When I asked, I discovered that I had been right, he is indeed an Abyssinian. On my previous visit, his smile had been polite, though I sensed a suspiciousness beneath his greying beard. This time, he smiled broadly. Clearly, Brother Basil had since told him I was a close friend, and that I would be coming back to visit. In addition, the fact that I had shown up with an overnight bag made him see me in a very different light—perhaps as a potential recruit.

A few seconds later, my friend came to greet me. He insisted on taking my bag and, telling me to follow him, led me directly to the cell in which I am writing these lines. It goes without saying that it is small and spartan—a narrow bed, a table, a chair, a lamp, a shower, a closet. The floor is bare stone, and the only window is too high to be able to gaze out at the landscape.

"It's not exactly luxurious," Ramzi said by way of apology.

"Maybe not, but you can feel the tranquility, I'm sure I'll be perfectly comfortable."

I did not say this to please him. Asceticism appeals to me. I wouldn't go so far as to say I could spend the rest of my life here; eventually, I'd feel other needs, other desires, frustrations. But for a night, or even a week or two, I have no fear of hardship or solitude.

Truth be told, I could have been a monk. The fact that I never seriously considered the possibility is not so much because the lifestyle is different to mine—I could have adapted—the problem was religion itself. For as long as I can remember, I have always had an uncertain, ambivalent relationship with religion.

I feel no instinctive antipathy to signs of faith. In front of me, on the wall of my cell, hangs a small polished wooden cross of sober black. It is a gentle presence, not troubling, almost comforting. But it will not stop me from writing in this notebook, in large, round letters: I am not a follower of any religion, and feel no need to become one.

My position on this issue is all the more complicated by the fact that I don't consider myself an atheist either. I can't believe that Heaven is empty, that after death there is only nothing-ness. What lies beyond? I don't know. Is there something? I don't know. I hope so, but I don't know; I'm suspicious of peo-ple—whether religious or atheist—who claim they do.

I hover somewhere between belief and non-belief just as I hover somewhere between my two homelands, first toying with one, then the other, but belonging truly to neither. I never feel more like a non-believer than when listening to a man of God preach a sermon; with every exhortation, every quotation from the holy scripture, my mind rebels, my attention wan-ders, my lips mumble imprecations. But whenever I attend a secular funeral, I feel a chill in my soul, and I feel like humming Syriac or Byzantine hymns, or even the "Tantum ergo" people say was composed by Thomas Aquinas.

This is the winding path I walk when it comes to religion. Naturally, I walk it alone; I follow no one, and invite no one to follow me.

Brother Basil just came by and warily opened my cell door, which has neither latch nor lock.

"I'm sorry for not knocking, I didn't want to wake you if you were asleep."

I had not been sleeping. I was lying on my narrow bed, jot-ting down notes.

"We're going to the chapel for a service. If you like, I'll come and fetch you when we're done."

"No, I didn't come to the monastery to write or sleep, I came to spend time with you. I'll come with you, I'd genuinely like to."

As I walked behind my friend, I glanced around at the archi-tecture of the place. My cell opens onto a corridor with eight identical doors. It is a recently built wing, presumably designed by Ramzi. I imagine that in earlier times, the monks had smaller, less comfortable cells. With no showers, obviously. And no electricity.

At the end of this corridor, is another, darker corridor that leads to a door of unusual dimensions; it is low but broad, and the top and sides are rounded like a squat barrel. Only when we reach this second corridor do I realize that we are now deep in the cliff face. The walls have been carved into the rock, very crudely, as though it were created simply as a cavity with no thought to smoothing the walls. Only the floor is level, there are even flagstones, though these are obviously more recent.

The monks are seated on pews with no backs. I count eight, including my friend. I slip into the last pew. Brother Basil walks to a lectern at the front, takes a missal from his pocket, opens it and begins to read. Immediately, the other monks get to their feet and recite the prayers with him.

They are of all ages and sizes. All, apart from my friend, have beards, and all, without exception, are balding—some just at the crown of the head, others completely. Their voices are barely audible. I remain silent. I don't know the prayers; and when they sing, I don't recognize the hymns. But I get to my feet every time they do.

Though indifferent to religion, I've always had a weakness for places of worship. And in this old cave chapel, I feel a fraternal affection for these strangers at prayer. I cannot believe that a man would go to live in a monastery these days unless spurred by noble feelings.

This is certainly the case with Brother Basil. I watch affectionately as he leafs through the missal for his page. He moves with tremulous gestures, my friend the engineer who became a monk. So many men, as they grow up, move from innocence to cynicism; the reverse is rare. I have nothing but respect for the path he has taken, the life he has chosen. Even if I could, I would *not try to persuade him to return to his former life, to go back to building palaces, towers, prisons, or military bases.*

At the end of the service, I stand motionless as they file out, the monks greet me with a nod and a smile. My friend is the last to leave. He gestures for me to follow.

"I'm glad you stayed, but you shouldn't feel obliged to attend every service. I just wanted you to have an idea of how our days are regulated. Prayer is our clock, you might say, it tolls every three hours."

"Even in the middle of the night?"

"In theory, yes, even in the middle of the night. In the past, that was the rule: there were eight divine offices every twenty-four hours. These days, we observe only seven."

"You're getting slack," I say, heretic that I am.

My friend smiles.

"Our view, which is also that of the Church, is that a man should not inflict unnecessary torture on himself. 'Monasticism, yes; masochism, no,'" he said in French before slipping back into Arabic, our common language, and, laying a hand affectionately on my shoulder, says, "I suppose you've never taken much of an interest in the religious life."

I have to confess that, on this particular subject, I am ignorant. Well, no, not entirely. Having studied the Roman and Byzantine empires, I know when and in what circumstances the early monastic orders were founded. But it's true that I've never paid much attention to how they developed or to their daily routines.

"We've long since given up torturing ourselves," my friend explains. "It's possible to lead an ascetic life without freezing during winter, without depriving yourself of sleep. The canonical offices that punctuate our days, however, are irreplaceable. It's not about reciting rote prayers, as laymen often imagine. It is a way of reminding ourselves why we are here—here, in the

monastery, and here on earth. And it divides the twenty-four hours into different sections, each with its own mood.

"Time was, I spent my days going from one meeting to another, the weeks flashed past, the months, the years ... Today, there are seven time slots in my day. Every three hours, I pause, I meditate, and then I embark on a completely different activity—not only spiritual or intellectual, but agricultural, artistic, social, and even culinary or sporting."

I almost retort that it is precisely because he has worked all his life, because he built palaces and earned a lot of money, that he can now devote himself to this other way of life; that such a life is possible only for someone who does not have to support a family, to work for a living. But I have not come all this way to argue, I came to listen, to observe his daily life, to understand his transformation, and to repair the strained ties of our friendship.

When his partner, Ramez, visited last year, Ramzi had felt it necessary to remind him that he was not a prisoner, that he had come to the monastery of his own free will. It's true that, when someone withdraws from the world, we can be tempted to assume they are in distress, the victim of a jailer, a manipulator, or their own anxieties. Our friend deserves to be treated differently. His path must be respected. He is neither a visionary nor a gullible fool. He's a thoughtful, educated, honest, and hardworking man. If, at the age of fifty—having travelled the world, negotiated with sharks, generated fortunes, and built an empire—he has decided to leave everything and withdraw to a monastery, the least we can do is to ask, in all humility, why he did so. His motives are certainly not base. He deserves to have us listen to him, without condemnation, without cynicism.

2

At 7:00 a.m. precisely we go to the refectory. It is a room that could hold forty people, but there are only nine of us, eight monks and me, sitting at the bare wooden table. Two similar tables lie empty, and another, pushed against the wall, is laid with a large oval platter, a soup tureen, a carafe of wine, a sliced loaf of bread, and a jug of water.

"A woman from the village makes our food," Ramzi explains. "When we settle in a village, it's best not to try to seem self-sufficient, as though we need no one. Otherwise, we would quickly make enemies, and a bad reputation.

"People are naturally curious, and a little suspicious when they find out that strangers have moved in nearby. In a village, the rumour mill is always running. The fact that this good woman, Olga, has keys to the monastery, that she comes here from time to time with her husband or her daughter, her sister or her neighbour, makes all the difference. She also does the shopping for us. It's important that people who live around here—the farmers, the grocer, the baker, the butcher—see our presence here as a godsend for reasons other than the fact that we pray for them.

"It's a principle I adhered to back when I was a civil engineer. Sometimes, when we were working in a small town, project managers would argue that it was more practical and less expensive to bring everything we needed with us. I always said, 'No! You go to the market, you buy what you need, and you don't haggle over the price. It's important that people consider you a boon, and that they're sorry on the day you finally leave.'"

"Do the villagers attend Mass sometimes?"

"We don't celebrate Mass here, we are monks, not priests. We go to the village church on Sundays. But if someone wants to pray with us, they can come along, as you did, our door is always open."

In the first minutes of the meal, Brother Basil and I were the only ones speaking. I asked questions, he answered; the other seven people at our table were content to eat, to listen, and to nod from time to time in agreement. The cook had made white rice with stewed okra. All the monks filled their plates. Several had second helpings.

There was a long silence before I steeled myself to ask, to no one in particular:

"Did you all come to the monastery at the same time?"

The question was only an excuse to get them to talk. At first glance, it was obvious that these men weren't from the same country or the same background, and had not ended up here for the same reasons. I knew one of their stories—and even that one incompletely. Of the others, I knew nothing.

At a nod from my friend, they began to speak, one after another, according to where they were sitting. Four of their first names were clearly borrowed, like masks used by Greek tragedies—Chrysostom, Hormisdas, Ignatius, Nicephorus. The others had more ordinary names—Emile, Thomas, Habib, Basil; however, since I knew Basil as Ramzi, I assumed that these, too, were adopted names. For these men, making the break with their former lives must have been like a second baptism, so it was hardly surprising that they would want to don a new name.

But although they wanted to change their names, it is far from certain they wanted to changed their identities. Quite the contrary. In fact, I'd say that by merging their individual identities, they were trying to emphasize their collective identity—that of Oriental Christians. I was struck by that fact that my friend had given up a neutral name in order to take on one with strong religious connotations, of a Doctor of the Church.

Curiously, during my previous visit, when Brother Basil had explained why he withdrew from civilian life, he was silent—consciously or otherwise—about the specific issues he had had to face as part of a minority community.

I'm not surprised by his silence; it's one that I, too, have used. A member of a minority longs to pass over his difference in silence, rather than highlighting it or carrying it like a banner. He reveals his difference only when backed into a corner—something that inevitably happens. Sometimes, it takes only a word, a look, and suddenly he feels like a stranger in a land where his people have been living for centuries, for millennia, long before the majority communities of today. Faced with such circumstances, everyone reacts according to their temperament—meekly, bitterly, deferentially, or with flair. "Our ancestors were Christians when all of Europe was still pagan, and they spoke Arabic long before the advent of Islam," I remember saying to a coreligionist one day, somewhat smugly. "A beautiful turn of phrase," he said sadly, "Remember it. It will make a fine epitaph for our gravestones."

Needless to say, although they never spoke about it, the monks were constantly aware of their status as a minority. It would gradually become obvious as they spoke.

At Brother Basil's invitation, they introduced themselves, one after another, giving their religious names; the places they had been born—from Tyre to Mosul, from Haifa to Aleppo, and even Gondar; their ages—which ranged from twenty-eight to sixty-four years; and their former professions—aside from my friend, there was a second civil engineer, a geometrics engineer, a doctor, an agronomist, a builder, a landscape gardener, even a former soldier. None of them directly explained the path they had taken and how they had come to be there, but each of their stories hinted at the tragedy that led him to withdraw from the world in order to pray.

Their tragedies were most apparent when they told me where they hailed from. This prompted me to ask, when the introductions were concluded:

"Do you think the communities you were born into have a future?"

My question was not directly related to anything any one of them had just said, but none of them seemed surprised by it.

"I pray it might have, but I have little hope."

It was Chrysostom who said this, and there was a rebelliousness in his words. Against men, but also against Heaven. The others turned to him, more sad than outraged. They all harboured the same feelings towards their Creator, first formulated by the man they followed, by He whom they follow, the Son of God, the Christ, who, in his final agony, asked his God, "Why hast thou forsaken me?"

For some reason I cannot explain, I felt as though I had backed Ramzi's fellow monks into a corner, and I heard myself repeat the words of the abandoned Christ:

"Eli Eli Lama Sabachthani?"

I had deliberately phrased it in an inquiring tone, as though genuinely asking the question, if not of the Creator, then of his monks. They, too, seemed helpless; hearing these words from the lips of a stranger had once again plunged them into the bleak atmosphere of Good Friday. They all set down their forks and sat, wordless, overwhelmed, mute.

Looking at them, I felt a little ashamed. It was hardly my role as a secular visitor, a monk for a night, to provoke such a reaction. But this was no game. I had always found these words of Jesus shocking. There are a number of elements in the Gospels that, to a sceptical historian like me, seem too commonplace to be true. In keeping with the spirit of the age, there had to be twelve apostles—just as there are twelve months of the year, twelve tribes of Israel, twelve gods on Olympus; and Jesus had to die at the age of thirty-three—the iconic age at which Alexander died. It was important that he have no siblings, no wife, no child, and that he be born of a virgin. Many episodes in the Gospels are clearly embellished, and perhaps borrowed from earlier folk tales so that the myth corresponds with the expectations of the faithful ... Then suddenly, this howl of pain— "Eli, Eli, Lama Sabachthani." The word made flesh suddenly becomes a man again, a weak, frightened, tremulous man. A man with doubts. These words ring true. We do not need to believe, only to listen to know that these words were not made up, or borrowed, or adapted, or even embellished.

To me, miracles are of no importance and parables are overrated. The greatness of Christianity is that it worships a man who was weak, ridiculed, persecuted, tortured, who refused to stone an adulterous woman, who praised the heretic Samaritan, one who was not entirely sure of God's mercy.

In the end, it is Brother Basil who breaks the silence and answers my question.

"If all men are mortal, then we, as Christians in the Orient, are twice mortal. Once as individuals—this is as Heaven dictates; and once as a community, a civilization, and, in this, Heaven is not to blame, it is the fault of man."

I think he intended to say more. But he didn't. Abruptly, he fell silent. I even felt that he already regretted the few words that had escaped him. He got up to get himself some fruit; the other monks followed suit, and so did I.

Should I bring up the subject again tonight? No. These men usually eat in silence; my presence in their world is unsettling enough. Tomorrow morning, if the opportunity presents itself, I'll bring it up with Ramzi, one on one, when we go to wander through his maze.

I did not say another word. I slowly peeled, sliced, and ate a large, cold apple. When they rose from the table to offer a short *prayer of thanks, I rose with them. Then I came back to my cell to write these few lines before going to sleep.*

The Twelfth Day

1

In the morning, when Brother Basil came by to fetch me and we walked up the steep path to the labyrinth, the sun was still hidden behind the mountains, but its light was everywhere.

"This is the time of day when it's easiest to tell the black flagstones from the white," my friend explained as we approached, speaking in a soft whisper as though we were in church.

He took up a position on the edge of the maze, then stepped forward as though crossing a threshold, as if there were a tangible doorway.

I watched him. He walked with slow tread. His head, bowed at first, gradually straightened so that he could gaze into the distance.

He had said nothing about what I should do, had given me no sign. Eventually I realized that I should follow his route, through the invisible "door" rather than stepping over the invisible "walls."

The maze sketched out on the ground was not too tortuous, the path formed by the white flagstones was not narrow, but nonetheless I had to focus some of my attention on my feet in order to stay "within the lines," which I managed to do, without much effort. The human mind—or mine, at least—seems to adapt to this ritual as easily as it does in the theatre, when it is asked to believe that a young actor sitting on a wicker chair is an ageing king upon his throne.

Soon, I no longer thought about the labyrinth through which I was walking, no longer looked at Brother Basil, no longer felt the chill air. I took wing from the landscape, as though under the effects of a potion prepared by St. Marie-Jeanne. My thoughts became dissociated from place and time, and focused entirely on a question that suddenly seemed of vital importance, "What is my real reason for returning to this beloved country whose name I fear writing down just as Tania fears saying aloud the name of the man whose widow she now is?"

And a strange answer came to me, one whose formulation is as limpid as its meaning is opaque: I have only come back to gather flowers. And it occurred to me that this action of picking a flower and adding it to the spray already in one's hand, perhaps even pressed against one's heart, is at once beautiful and cruel, because it pays homage to the flower only in killing it.

Why this image? In that moment I couldn't say, and even now as I write this, seven or eight hours later, I'm still not sure. Does it relate to some anxiety, some feeling of guilt connected to the discovery of so many intimate things about my friends, my country, and myself? The man who writes a memoir is a traitor to his own people, or at the very least a gravedigger. All the fond words that flow from my pen are kisses of death.

But as I wandered through the labyrinth, I also experienced a serenity; a feeling of invincibility that was, curiously, accompanied by humility rather than arrogance; and above all a longing for silence.

I had come up to this place intending to continue my conversation with Brother Basil about the Christians of the Orient, about his beliefs, his vision of the world, his former life, his "sea change," about Ramez; but when I emerged from the labyrinth I was in a different frame of mind. If the maze facilitates contemplation, it is to the detriment of any conversation. I did not want to speak, let alone to listen. My friend knew this, of course, and was careful not to interfere with my contemplation.

It was only much later, when I realized the time that I had arranged for the hotel chauffeur to drive me back was fast approaching, that I felt the need to talk to Ramzi about the *reunion I am planning, to ask whether he would be willing to join us. I was careful to explain that it would be a moment of reflection on what our lives have been, what the world has become, and I invited him to open the reunion with a brief ecumenical prayer for the repose of Mourad's soul. He nodded enigmatically, and did not ask any questions. I went on speaking, listing the names of those who were coming, and explaining that the reunion would probably take place next Saturday, at about noon. Until that moment, I had not thought in such precise terms, but as I was talking to the Brother Basil it seemed clear to me that I couldn't leave without giving him a date and a time. In answer, he said that it was a wonderful initiative on my part, and that he was not ruling out the possibility that he might join us. Vague though it was, I was happy with his reaction, and I felt it best to stop there, without pressing him for a commitment.*

On the drive back, I sat in silence, with only a minimal conversation with Kiwan, dictated by politeness. And when I arrived back at the hotel, I did not call Sémi. I holed up in my room to set down these notes.

Sémiramis had hoped that Adam would tell her the details of his visit to the monastery, as he had last time. Obviously, he did not feel the need. And she did not want to press him. To avoid disrupting him, she did not phone, as she usually did, to ask whether he wanted to join her for lunch, for fear it might seem like an oblique attempt at seduction.

As a result, he did not have lunch that day. After writing a few paragraphs and snacking on the fruit in his room, he dozed off. He did not wake up until Sémiramis knocked on his door at about four o'clock to tell him it was time to leave for the airport.

2

To his shame, Adam did not recognize Naïm.

Though he stared at the stream of travellers as they came through customs, scanning the men one by one, both those travelling alone and those who were accompanied, he was unable to recognize his friend.

Naïm had to come and stand in front of him, and say "Adam!" before he threw his arms around him.

The voice was the same. But the long curly hair was more white than grey, and the features of his face thirty years ago were now hidden beneath plump cheeks, a bronzed complexion, and a South American moustache.

"You haven't changed a bit!" the newcomer said.

"Oh, I have. I'm myopic," Adam said.

This was his way of apologizing.

"It has to be said that the man who's just arrived doesn't look much like the one you used to know," said Naïm.

This was his way of returning his apologies.

The traveller was carrying a green canvas bag, striped with yellow and blue. Adam took it, leaving his friend behind to wheel the large suitcase emblazoned with the same Brazilian colours.

"Sémi drove me in her car, but she couldn't find a parking space. She'll probably be just outside."

And there she was. Cheery and garrulous. Trying to justify herself to a uniformed officer who clearly wanted to be stern but had just as clearly fallen under her spell. She'd only be a minute, she said, only a minute, not a second more.

"Actually, here they are right now!" her friends heard her shout.

As soon as they were in the car, Naïm opened fire:

"Adam was so convinced that I was going to be arrested he didn't even see me come out."

Sémiramis added, in the same tone:

"You, you've piled on the weight; he's piled on the neuroses."

Sitting in the back seat, Adam laughed. These quips reminded him of the conversations in the Circle of Sophists back at University. That same tender hostility that kept their minds alert, and avoided lapsing into conformity.

In keeping with this habitual mockery, Adam had to respond in the same vein.

"You show up forty kilos heavier and expect to be recognized from five hundred metres!"

At the hotel, Naïm was checked into room seven, next to that of his friend. He was scarcely given time to unpack. By now it was ten o'clock, and Sémiramis had planned to celebrate his arrival with a candlelight dinner.

"You're not going to be much help losing my extra kilos," the newcomer said to his hostess, gesturing to the groaning table.

"Here, every night is mezze and champagne," Adam said, nodding to the open bottle cradled by the irreplaceable Francis.

"Champagne? Mezze with champagne? That's madness! With your permission, I'll have mine with *arak*."

Naïm seemed genuinely outraged. And when the waiter returned with a dimpled bottle of the local liquor in a bucket of ice, Naïm called on Francis for support.

"Mezze with champagne! It's heresy, tell them, monsieur! Tell them!"

Francis clearly agreed, but he wouldn't have dared

criticize his employer, even in jest, for the world. Leaving the purist to pour his own arak, he ceremoniously poured the heretical bubbles.

Having duly clinked glasses with his friends to toast their reunion, Naïm said:

"So what have you been up to, the two of you, since I left?"

He said it in the casual tone of someone asking what they had done that afternoon before coming to the airport. But the protocol of the Circle of Sophists dictated that one should never be caught off guard; or, at least, never let it be seen. Adam's first response, therefore, hewed to that rule:

"Two years after you left, I left, Sémi stayed behind to keep our seats warm ..."

"And because she was too lazy to emigrate ..." chimed in Sémi.

But this was merely a prelude. Naïm's question deserved a genuine answer. The three friends had not seen each other for a quarter of a century; beyond a few scant episodes, none of them knew what paths the others' lives had taken. If they wanted this reunion to be meaningful, they had to recount their past.

It was Sémiramis who began, in a tone simultaneously cheerful and jaded, where it was impossible to tell which emotion was feigned.

"There's not much to tell where I'm concerned. I can sum up my last twenty years in less than twenty seconds. My friends left, war broke out, I holed up waiting for it to end. After my parents died, I opened this hotel. In winter, it's empty, in summer it's full, and this April two old friends came to pay me a visit, rooms seven and eight.

"Right, that's that done. Over to you two!"

She fell silent. And, to emphasize that she had finished, she folded her arms.

"It is a little brisk, this story of yours," said Adam. "Too brief to be honest."

"I could embellish it, obviously, but I've told you the essentials."

She raised her glass, her friends did likewise. Everyone took a long, thoughtful sip. Then Naïm, in a slightly suspicious tone, said:

"So, you never married."

"No."

"Why?"

"I have my reasons."

"Your reasons, you mean Bilal?"

"I'd rather not talk about that."

"Naïm, don't wind her up!" Adam said softly.

"I'm not trying to wind her up, but I'm not going to give up, either. If she'd said, 'Every morning, I wake up to the birds singing, I breathe fresh air, this hotel is my kingdom, an oasis of tranquillity that makes me forget the tumult of the world!' I'd have said, 'Sémi, I envy you, you can't imagine what life is like in our monstrous cities, carve out a little space for me in your paradise, and if I can't come and seek refuge here, at least I can dream.' But that's not what she said. She said, 'My friends left, my parents died, and I've buried myself alive while waiting to grow old.'"

"That's not what I said."

"Well, that's what I heard. 'I couldn't even find twenty seconds' worth to say about my past twenty years.' Tell me if I'm wrong, Sémi."

"Maybe I didn't express myself very well. I wasn't complaining. I just meant to say I have done nothing remarkable, nothing memorable, in my opinion. But I live as I please, there is nobody to give me orders, every morning my breakfast appears on my veranda, I can hear the birds singing; and every night I drink champagne. I haven't taken a vow of poverty, or—just to reassure you—of chastity."

"That does reassure me."

"But I didn't want a husband always on my back."

"There are other positions, you know."

"Very funny!"

"Sorry, that wasn't very subtle. I just meant to say that a man doesn't have to be a burden or a nuisance. He can be an ally, a support, a partner ..."

"That's where you're wrong. At least as far as I'm concerned. I didn't need a man in my life."

"Let's be clear: I wasn't offering my services."

"Shut up, you idiot!"

She took Naïm's hand in hers; then, for the sake of fairness, she took Adam's too.

"I'm so happy to have both of you here. Even if you tease me a little, I know you do it in the right spirit, and it reminds me of the most wonderful period of my life."

For as long as the three friends stood this way, Francis, a tactful sommelier, kept his distance. He possessed the skill and wisdom to see all while looking at nothing. Only when Adam and Sémiramis unclasped their hands did he refill their champagne flutes and offer Naïm another arak in a clean glass.

"And what did you do during the war?" asked the Brazilian.

"I spent my winters in Rio, and summers in the Alps," his hostess said as though she had already prepared her response.

Before her friends had time to recover from this two-pronged attack, she once again laid her hands on theirs, soothing and affectionate, and said, as though talking to two schoolboys:

"Those who lived here through those years never use the word 'war.' They say 'the events.' And this is not a matter of trying to avoid using the dreadful word. Try asking anyone here about the war. They'll bluntly ask: *which war?* Because, when it comes to war, we've had several. The forces were not always the same, nor were the alliances, the leaders, or the battlefields. Sometimes foreign armies were involved, sometimes it was only local forces; sometimes the conflicts were between two different communities, sometimes within a single community; sometimes war followed war, and sometimes they were waged simultaneously.

"As for me, there were times when I had to lie low; when shells were falling all around me, and I didn't know whether I would be alive by morning; meanwhile barely ten kilometres away, everything was quiet, my friends were tanning themselves on the beach. Two months later, the situation would be reversed; my friends would be in hiding while I was on the beach. People only worried about what was happening nearby, in their village, in their neighbourhood, on their street. The only people who conflate all of these separate events, the only ones to group them together, the only ones to talk about 'war' are those who were living far away."

"Winter in Rio, and summer in the Alps," Adam mumbled. "Message received. That said, I'm not convinced that one sees things better from up close than from a distance. Obviously, those who are there suffer more, for sure, but they do not necessarily see things calmly and clearly. On the phone one day, Mourad said, 'You're not here, you haven't been through what we've been through, you can't understand!' And I said, 'You're right, I'm far away, I can't. So explain it. I'm listening.' And of course, he couldn't explain anything. He just wanted me to admit he was the victim, and, as the victim, he had the right to behave however he saw fit. Even kill, if he thought it necessary. I had no right to lecture him, since I was elsewhere and I was not suffering."

"I didn't kill anyone," Sémiramis said, as though anyone might think to accuse her.

Adam brought her hand to his lips.

"Of course you didn't kill anybody. I wasn't talking to you, I was talking to him, to our absent friend. Sometimes I talk to him in my head."

"I didn't kill anyone," Sémiramis repeated slowly, pulling her hand away. "But it's not as though I didn't want to. If I could, I'd have killed all the leaders, and disarmed all the kids. A widow's fantasies."

A silence ensured that her friends dared not break it. Then, looking down at her plate, she added:

"I was probably the first war widow. Not that there's any glory in that. Have you ever seen a monument to war widows?"

Another silence. The maître d'hôtel took this opportunity to refresh their drinks. Sémiramis looked up again.

"If you really want to know what I did during the 'war,' then I'll tell you, it won't take long.

"In the early stages, I was still in the depths of depression. Bilal's death had already been buried beneath thousands more, but I still hadn't got over it. I was pumped full of drugs; I was wretched. I didn't do anything, I didn't leave the house, I barely left my bedroom. Sometimes, I'd sit with a book on my lap, but I could go for half a day without turning a page.

"When the bombings began in our neighbourhood, I had to be physically carried to the shelter. My parents treated me like I was a four-year-old. They were wonderful, they never uttered a word of reproach, they were nothing but kindness. They seemed almost happy that their daughter had regressed to childhood and was constantly by their side. I was treated by an old psychiatrist of eighty-five, also a family friend, who had also emigrated from Egypt. He visited me every other day, and reassured my parents. 'She'll get through this, you just need to give her some time and lots of affection. I'll deal with the rest.'

"The therapy he gave helped me, I suppose, and the affection. But the true therapy was the bombing of our neighbourhood. In fact, it was one specific shell that changed me. Up until that day, I still had to be dragged to the shelter; after that explosion, I was the one leading my parents to the shelter. It was as if, until that moment, my mind, my senses were seeing through a glass darkly, and in a split second the glass had been shattered by that shell. Suddenly, I was engaged with what was going on around me. I rediscovered my voice, my appetite; and in my eyes, it seems, there was a distant glow. I began to listen to the radio every day to find out where the battles were raging. I started reading again. I started living again.

"Then my parents died, six months apart. My mother went first, of cancer, then my father, of a broken heart. Both my brothers were living in Canada, in Vancouver, and they asked me to go join them. But I didn't have the will or the strength to start over, so I decided to take on this property, which was derelict at the time, and I turned it into a hotel.

"Now you know everything. I told you about my war. Now it's your turn. I'm listening ... One of you can start ..."

As though he hadn't heard, Naïm glanced around and said sceptically:

"And you make enough to live from the hotel?"

"Let's say in the last five or six years I haven't made a loss. But I don't live off the profits."

"What do you live off?"

Sémiramis turned to Adam.

"Has your friend always been so pushy?"

"Yes," Adam sighed. "I'd almost forgotten, but I think he's always been this way, even when he was forty kilos lighter. You can always refuse to answer if you've got something to hide."

"You're as infuriating as each other! I've got nothing to hide. I live off the money my father left me. He left Egypt with a small fortune."

"Really?" Naïm said, incredulous. "He must have been the only one! The Jews who fled Egypt in the '50s and '60s had only the clothes on their backs."

"That was true of everyone, not just the Jews," Sémiramis nodded. "But my father was lucky. Adam already knows the story so I won't bore him with it again."

"You can if you want, I don't mind."

She explained the "something foolish" that had forced her father to sell off everything and flee Egypt before the nationalizations and the sequestration. Naïm was spellbound. When she finished, he said:

"Would you allow me to write up this story for my newspaper?"

"As long as you don't use real names, I don't have a problem."

"I don't have to remind you that this happened half a century ago and Nasser's been dead for more than thirty years. But, if it makes you more comfortable, I can change the names …"

"The only time my father ever told the story to strangers, he pretended it had happened, not to him, but to one of his brothers. That's why I assume he wouldn't have wanted his name associated with it. Maybe if he were still alive, he would have changed his mind, but it's too late to ask him now."

"It's not a problem, I'll change the names ..."

"From what you've just said, I take it you're a journalist," Sémiramis retorted, glad to be the one posing the questions.

"Didn't you know?"

"OK, if I'm honest, I did know that much. But that's about all I know. Start from the beginning. So you and your parents caught a plane to São Paulo. And then ...?"

The Brazilian raised his glass, toasted his friends, then moistened his throat with a long draught of his milky liquor.

"After two days travelling and two shots of arak, I don't really feel capable of telling my whole life story. But I'll give you the broad outline. When I got there, I went back to university, I studied journalism, and I got a job with a business weekly. That was the same year I got married. I was twenty-three. I'm still a journalist and I'm still married."

"To the same person?" Sémiramis asked.

"To the same person."

"Brazilian?"

"Yes, Brazilian."

"And Jewish?"

"That's what my mother thought. She asked me straight out, 'Is she Jewish?' and I just said, 'Maman, her name is Rachel.' And her name really *is* Rachel, or rather 'Raquel,' the Brazilian equivalent, but she's a devout Catholic. My mother never questioned it. I kept up the ambiguity until the night before the wedding."

"You should have brought her with you so we could meet her," Adam said.

"Raquel's not like me, she can't take off whenever she likes. She owns a restaurant in São Paulo, *Chez Raquel*, one of the best in the city. She spends her days and nights there, and she's convinced that if she went away for a week, all her customers would desert her. She thinks she's indispensable; personally, I think that's a bit of an exaggeration ..."

"Do you ever help her out?" Sémiramis asked.

"At the restaurant, you mean? Yes, sure, in my own way. Whenever she comes up with a new dish, I'm the first to taste it. If I say 'It's delicious!' she adds it the menu; if I say 'It's okay,' she ditches it."

"So you're the one who is actually irreplaceable," Adam said mockingly.

"I hope you get paid for your efforts," his hostess added.

"Of course, she pays him," Adam said. "She pays him in kilos. Just look at him!"

"It's true I've put on weight, but that's not because of Raquel. When we're together, I am a model of restraint. It's when I'm travelling that I eat too much. When I'm on an assignment somewhere, my greatest pleasure is to reserve a table at a fancy restaurant, order a big meal, a huge mug of beer, and write my article while I'm eating. Three sentences, one bite, three more sentences, one sip. The ideas flow freely and I feel as though I'm in a state of rapture."

"Just listen to how he talks!" Adam whispered.

"I'm an incurable glutton, and I'm not ashamed of it," Naïm confessed. "Loving to eat is a heaven-sent blessing. Every morning you wake up to the aroma of roasted coffee. It's the smell of Brazil, the most delicious anywhere on earth. Already you're in a good mood, then you remind yourself that you've got three more feasts before the day is over. Three delicious daily feasts. Eleven hundred a year! Who said gluttony was a vice? It's a godsend, a blessing, an art! You don't believe me?"

"Of course I do," Adam grumbled. "It's the perfect marriage between sophistication and animality."

"I'm going to make a confession," Naïm said, shamelessly. "I know you two will use my honesty against me, but I'll tell you anyway: I've never known when to stop eating. I never feel full. I only stop when all the plates are empty, or when I have to leave the table."

"Hang on, Naïm, that sounds worrying," Adam frowned. "What you're describing is a pathology. If you've never experienced the sensation of being full ..."

"Don't worry," said Naïm. "I know the diagnosis. It's a relatively benign condition called 'Jewish mother syndrome.' When I was a boy, she force-fed me, *literally*. I didn't eat when I was hungry, I ate when she told me to open my mouth. And I didn't stop when I was full, only when she stopped reloading the spoon. As far as my mother was concerned, there were two kinds of children, the scrawny and the healthy. The former were a disgrace to their mothers, the latter were their pride and joy.

"It could have put me off food for life. But it didn't. I loved every bite, and I never wanted it to end. As I grew up, things carried on like that. My mother was forever telling me I looked sallow, that I didn't eat enough. I didn't want to argue, so I helped myself to seconds and thirds until every plate was empty. So I never learned when to stop. I could carry on eating forever. Provided the food is good, obviously."

"Obviously," Adam laughed. Then, raising his glass, he added, "What I think you're saying is that the forty kilos you've put on isn't down to your gluttony, it's the fault of your mother."

"Mock all you like, but that's the truth. I've had my fair share of problems because of her. Don't get me wrong, I've always loved my mother, I'll always love her, but I am clear-sighted. What I just told you about food also applies to other areas of life."

"Sex …" Sémiramis hissed.

"No, not sex! Something much more serious." Naïm said.

"What could be more serious than sex?" Adam asked in a booming voice that made diners at nearby tables turn to stare.

Sémiramis flashed an apologetic smile.

Our friend did not explain what other problems he suffered by having a Jewish mother, Adam would write in his notebook at the end of the day. We were hanging on his every word, but Naïm closed his eyes and fell asleep at the table, like a dormouse.

When the Brazilian began to slump in his chair, Sémiramis gently patted the back of his hand, twice, three times. He opened his eyes.

"Do you feel alright?"

"I feel fine. I didn't miss a word of what you were saying."

"What we were saying? We haven't said a word," Adam laughed. "You were the last person to speak."

"What was I saying?"

"You were saying you wanted to go back to your room," their hostess suggested kindly.

Naïm nodded.

"I didn't get much sleep last night," he apologized.

"Me neither," Adam said. Then he added casually, "In a monastery, they wake you at dawn."

At this, Naïm stared at me, complete bewildered. Sémi glowered, believing—quite fairly—that I was taking advantage of our friend's exhaustion to sow confusion. I didn't say another word. Naïm closed his eyes. Our chatelaine patted his hand again.

"My bed, my bed, my kingdom for whoever carries me to my bed," *Naïm pleaded with his last Shakespearean breath.*

But as soon as he got to his feet he was able to go downstairs to his room without our help.

The Thirteenth Day

1

When Adam opened his eyes, he discovered a note had been slipped under his door by Sémiramis inviting him to come up to the veranda for breakfast as soon as he woke. She had sent the same invitation to Naïm, who was already there, eating fig bread.

"When I closed my eyes last night, he was eating; I open them this morning, and he's still eating!" Adam quipped.

Naïm was about to answer, but his hostess preempted him.

"Leave the cockfighting until later. Naïm and I were working out a morning schedule. He wants to visit the house his parents used to rent for the summer. It's only a half-hour drive. I'll go with you."

"I'm not planning to hang around," Naïm said. "I just want to see whether my memory of the place corresponds to reality or whether I've embellished."

"If that's what you were hoping, you might as well give up now," Sémiramis said. "Even if your memory tallied with what it looked like then, it certainly won't tally with what it looks like today."

"Don't worry, Sémi, I know what to expect. Revisiting one's childhood is a masochistic pastime. We set off expecting to be disappointed and—surprise, surprise—we are."

The house indeed proved to be disappointing. The external walls and the shutters looked as though they had never been painted. The roof was low and flat. The front door was barely two metres from a busy road with trucks roaring past. The air was pervaded by smell of petrol and burnt oil.

As soon as Naïm recognized the building, Sémiramis pulled in and parked outside. There followed a few minutes of indecision. The "pilgrim" stared out the window, unable to make up his mind whether to get out of the car. His friends waited in compassionate silence, watching him out of the corners of their eyes. It was Naïm who finally broke the silence, doing his best to sound more amused than upset:

"It doesn't look like anything anymore."

It was difficult to contradict him.

"The war made its mark here," Adam sighed, by way of consolation.

"It wasn't the war that did this, it was this road," Naïm said. "Back when we used to come, there was only a narrow dirt track. There was a small courtyard in front of the house with railings and a wrought-iron gate, and a driveway leading to this door you see here. But now the road has taken over the driveway, the courtyard, the railings, and the gate.

"Every year when we arrived in early July, the ritual was the same. The owner, Halim, would be waiting to greet us. We politely addressed him as *ustaz* Halim. He was a customs officer, and always showed up in a suit and tie. We would give him the keys so that he could open the gate; he would formally welcome us and hand back the keys, then my father would give him an envelope that contained the annual rent. The man would say 'There's no hurry ...,' then, 'Time enough another day!' and only when my father insisted for the third time would he take the money and slip it, uncounted, into the pocket of his jacket.

"After the owner left, my mother would go out into the garden and every year she would say, 'This place is a jungle!' and every year my father would say, 'So much the better! Naïm can tidy it up. It'll put muscles on him.' But this was only a joke. I never did much work in that garden."

"Where is the garden?"

"Round the other side. Come on ..."

The garden of the summer house was indistinguishable from the surrounding pine forest. The low concrete wall was more of a seat than a barrier and here the three friends sat, shaded from the sun by a tree with dense foliage. Instantly, they forgot their first impressions. Sitting hip to hip, their feet dangling, intoxicated by the heady scent of the pines, they savoured the tranquil wilderness that had been Naïm's childhood place.

"Two or three times over the summer, ustaz Halim would come round to see my father. They would have coffee together, leaf through old books. Halim used to say, 'In this village, no one knows who's Muslim, who's Jewish, and who's Christian. Am I right?' My father would nod in agreement. Of course, he was wrong, as both of them knew only too well. When you encountered someone in the street you always knew, as if by instinct, which community they belonged to. But it felt good to hear him say the words. Because his intentions were good."

"It was a civilized white lie," Sémiramis nodded. "Today, you constantly hear people saying, 'as a Christian, I believe this,' or 'as a Muslim I believe that.' I keep wanting to shout at them: 'You should be ashamed! Even if your every thought is dictated by your community, you could at least pretend to think for yourselves!' They could at least have the decency to lie ..."

"The lies of yesterday were much more civilized than today's 'straight talking,'" Adam said. 'People still thought in terms of their religious affiliation, they couldn't help but do so, but they knew that was wrong, that they should be ashamed. So they lied. And by their transparent lies, they showed that they could tell the difference between how people actually behaved and how people should behave. People these days spew out whatever is in their hearts, and it's not exactly pretty. Not in this country, not anywhere in the world."

"The least they could do is apologize, but that doesn't even occur to them," Sémiramis said. "People around them do the same thing, so they think it's normal. They're proud of it, rather than ashamed."

"My dear friends," Naïm interrupted, "I hate to be the bearer of bad news, but at your age you need you to know: the era of propriety is passed. Or, to put it bluntly: decency is dead."

Adam greeted his friend's stentorian words with the requisite smile, then asked:

"When did it die, in your opinion?"

"In 1914," Naïm said confidently, as though this was an acknowledged fact. "Decency died in 1914. Obviously, in the span of human history, there's never been an era when people were perfect, and it's also true that decency is not the defining trait of our species. That said, as far as I'm concerned, everything that happened before 1914 falls into the category of youthful indiscretion.

"Before that date, humanity was powerless. Natural disasters were man's chief enemy; his medicine killed more than it cured, and his technology was in its infancy. It was in 1914 that we saw the first great man-made disasters: the First World War, mustard gas, the October Revolution ..."

"That's not how you used to talk about communism!" Sémiramis said.

"No, you're right; when I was young I said something

very different. But looking back I'm convinced it was a catastrophe of the first order. A great dream of equality between men, hijacked by a cynical and totalitarian state. We still haven't finished paying the price. In just five years, between the slaughter of the trenches and the Treaty of Versailles—the insidious precursor to every war that would follow—the scene was set. It is a scenario from which we have never escaped. All the horrors that have since befallen us have their roots here, whether in the Levant, in Central Europe, in the Far East, or elsewhere. But perhaps our esteemed historian does not share my opinion?"

"Yes and no," Adam said, causing his two friends to exchange a complicit wink and giggle. But they allowed him to marshal his thoughts. "I think that the previous century was marked by two destructive ideologies: communism and anti-communism. The former unquestionably distorted the idea of equality, the idea of progress, of revolution, and a thousand other ideas that should still be respectable. But the death toll of the latter was still worse. People were so busy chanting 'Better Mussolini than Lenin,' 'Better Hitler than Stalin,' 'Better Nazism than the Popular Front,' that they allowed the world to founder into wickedness and barbarism."

"I don't disagree," Naïm said. "Anti-communism was never my creed, but I did believe in the ideals of communism, we all did. We championed communism for honourable reasons, and we found ourselves betrayed."

Adam had a similar comparison in mind.

"It's our destiny to be betrayed," he observed, "by our beliefs, by our friends, by our bodies, by life, by history ..."

His two companions marked a moment of silence, then Naïm jumped down on the ground and, with somewhat forced cheerfulness, said:

"Right, let's go! I've had my fifteen minutes of melancholy. I came, I saw, I was disappointed. Now let's hit the road. All things considered, I prefer my cabin in Brazil."

"Wait, not so fast!" Adam said, "I seem to remember that this house once served as a hub of lascivious activities, that's what I wanted you to tell us about. That's the only reason I came with you. Are you with me, Sémi?"

Naïm's face lit up with a childlike smile, as though images of the past were flooding back to him, and his friends assumed that given his proverbial loquaciousness he would launch into a long story. But this was not his intention.

"I'm more than happy to reveal my secrets, Adam. But there's something that's been bothering me since last night."

He turned to Sémiramis:

"Don't you think it's strange that our friend here is happy to make you and me tell him our life stories, our most personal, most intimate secrets, while he hasn't told us anything?"

"We've only just met up again," Adam said defensively, "We've got all the time in the world."

"Sémi and I have already had our time, but not you. I've told you about my intemperance, about my problems with my wife and my mother. Sémi has talked about her depression and how she came through it. And you haven't told us anything. Not a single secret. All I know about you is that you teach history and that you're supposed to be writing a biography of Attila. But I know nothing about your personal life, not a thing! I'm not about to make a big deal of it, but this is a flaw of yours I noticed a long time ago. You might want to think about dealing with it before the three of us are old and senile."

As though they had planned this together, Sémiramis added:

"He's right, Adam. Confidences have to be reciprocal. Naïm has showed us his old country house, now you should show us yours. We know it exists, we're bound to see it one day. It's now or never, don't you think?"

I don't know whether my friends had planned this in advance, or whether it simply occurred to them at the time, but their demand would brook no argument, and I sensed that I couldn't get out of it.

Their criticisms were not entirely unfounded. It's true that, since childhood, I've been in the habit of getting others to tell their stories without confiding much in return. It's a flaw I'm all the more ready to acknowledge since it stems from a virtue. I enjoy listening to others, drifting away on the sea of their stories, navigating their dilemmas. But listening, while it is a generous trait, can become predatory if you feed on the experiences of others yet share nothing with them.

Faced with my old friends' mutiny, what could I do but give in? Besides, the only feelings underlying my behaviour were shyness and modesty. I still can't imagine that my stories would be of interest to anyone. When someone tells me otherwise and insists that I relate them, I'm happy to comply. I have nothing to hide. Well, obviously, I have things to hide, but more from myself than from others.

In this particular case, I had always avoided talking about my childhood home simply because I did my best never to think about it.

But today, I had to force myself. I told Sémi how to get to the village, and after a little trial and error, I finally spotted the outline of "my" house.

When my friends saw it, their eyes grew wide. As though to mock me, it looked magnificent. Sémi kept saying, "This place is a palace!" Naïm said, "This is what you've been ashamed of? This is the house you've been hiding for thirty years?" And they were right; it does look like a palace, I should feel proud, yet instead I feel ashamed, because I lost it.

Everything changed when I was twelve and a half. Until then, this house had been the centre of my world. All my childhood friends knew it, I loved inviting them to come. In doing so, I felt I was showing them the best of myself. It was a kind of vanity, an arrogance, and can only be called class pride. But until adolescence such sins are venial; we need to feel we have a place in this world, that we're not interlopers.

It's so comforting to grow up feeling you have a country of your own, one you can proudly stake a claim to. When I was in this house, I had that feeling, and afterwards, I never had it again. If this house had still belonged to me at the outbreak of the war, I don't know what I would have done in order to keep it. But the question didn't arise; I was spared that dilemma. Given everything that happened, I should be happy about this, but it has always been like a curse. I envied Mourad, who managed to hold on to his ancestors' house; now I feel I should pity him. In the end, I was the one cosseted by fate. But it has taken me a long time to realize.

My parents adored this house. You could say they had two children: me, and this house.

My father did not simply inherit it from his father. For a long time it was jointly owned by twenty cousins, all of whom were prepared to give it up but none of whom were prepared to take care of it. So my father bought them out, just as long-pious souls used to buy back the freedom of their fellows enslaved by infidels. My father got himself into debt to buy out his cousins' shares, then got into more debt in order to pay for the repairs. Which were never-ending. He was an architect, and wanted to make his home not only the magnum opus of his career but also, somehow, his calling card. He felt that anyone who saw it would want the same.

His conceived it as two almost identical buildings, some fifteen metres apart: the old, restored house, and another based on the same design, both swathed in vines. The two wings were connected in three ways: on the first floor by a suspended living room with a picture window overlooking the mountain slopes on one side and the valley on the other; on the ground floor by a path lined with flowers; and in the basement via a tunnel. To my parents and to me, it was more than a house, it was a kingdom, and certainly a source of pride.

Earlier, I mentioned class pride. That was unwarranted self-flagellation, and almost an insult to the memory of my parents. What distinguished the house was not the size or the gilded mouldings; it was the style. It was not a vulgar display of wealth; it was an artistic manifesto. Both my mother and father had a confident, understated taste. Their house was the product of their love of beauty, and of their love for each other.

Their life together was a joy, to which I was not only a witness, but chief admirer and sole beneficiary. This made the fall, when it came, all the harder.

Everything was played out in a few short minutes over the Gulf of Oman. The plane on which my parents were travelling plunged into the sea, and my life was destroyed in the wake.

This was in August '66. An airline company had decided to commence direct flights to Karachi and, to promote the event, had invited a number of prominent personalities on the maiden flight. My parents were hugely proud to have been selected, it was recognition of their status in the country. I can still see them packing their bags, happy, excited, wonderstruck in advance by all the things they would see, without the slightest feeling of nervousness or foreboding.

It was a night flight, scheduled to take off in early evening and land as dawn was breaking. My maternal grandfather drove my parents to the airport, and I went with him. The two of us stayed there until the plane had taken off and disappeared over the horizon. I felt not the slightest foreboding either. I was simply disappointed that I had not been invited to go with them.

Back at home, I read late into the night, as I always did in the summer months, perhaps a little later than usual, since my parents were not there to babysit.

When I woke, sometime in the late morning, I heard unfamiliar sounds. It seemed as though the house had been invaded by a murmuring crowd. I emerged from my bedroom to see who was there, and from the way the men looked at me and, especially, the way the village women took me in their arms, I immediately realized there had been a tragedy.

As if this catastrophe were not enough, it was quickly followed by another: I was penniless. This I discovered a month later. As my parents' sole beneficiary, I had inherited a house that was worth "a fortune," but also a bank debt estimated at twice that fortune. My father had never been prudent. Why should he have been? His order book was full, he earned a lot of money, he was in the prime of life. At his usual rate of work, he would have repaid his debts in two or three years. But the moment he died, everything collapsed. There was almost no money coming into the accounts, no life insurance ...

In my youth I railed against the bankers; at that time I was driven by a furious rage. In fact, this is undoubtedly the reason why, at fourteen, I started calling myself a Marxist. Later, I would come up with intellectual justifications for my position, but at the time, it was blind fury. The family lawyer explained that my only option was to cede ownership of the house to the bank in settlement of the debt. At the time, I harboured a black hatred for him and every other lawyer on earth. Now I realize that he brokered the best deal I could possibly have got. Apart from the house, I owned absolutely nothing. With my father dead, "our" architectural practice wasn't worth a penny; he had not owned the office premises, and before long I wouldn't be able to pay the rent. My lawyer persuaded the bank to write off a debt of 1.2 million in exchange for a house worth half of that. And even to leave me a small sum so that I was not completely destitute.

But at the time, I didn't see things that way. I railed against the lawyers and the banks, against architects, airlines, against Heaven itself ... Out of spite, when I moved out of the house, I decided not to take anything with me, not even my books. I went to live with my maternal grandparents. I don't know how long I wept for my parents, my home, my dreams of the future. I must have been unbearable, and it required all the patience, the forbearance, and the love of my grandparents to bring me through.

I never wanted to talk about any of this. And I never once tried to visit "our" house, or even to drive past. Many times, I would drive miles out of my way in order to avoid catching a glimpse of it. It took the coercion of Sémi and Naïm for me to agree to visit the place again, it took war and exile, it took the passing of a third of a century, and with it the taming of the furious adolescent that raged inside.

And so I returned to the lost domain on an enforced pilgrimage. As soon as I saw the facade, I felt a lump in my throat. I said nothing, but simply pointed to it. "That one?" I nodded. "This is what you've been ashamed of? This is the house you've been hiding ...?" I started to sob like a child. Now it was my friends who felt ashamed. They apologized for having pressured me. So I told them the whole story, or almost: my former life, the plane crash, the bank, the day I moved out of this house, which had been my first exile ...

"We didn't know," Sémi said.

She ran her fingers through my hair, then leaned over and kissed me on the forehead. We had not even got out of the car. I *was in the passenger seat. Naïm was sitting in the back. He said:*

"How could you have managed to keep this all inside for all these years?"

I said laconically:

"I managed."

Then, for no reason, I started laughing. My friends laughed too. It was something we all needed. We were at the edge of a quagmire of sentimentality and had no desire to fall in. Laughing had the advantage of making our eyes well up without us having to distinguish between the tears of sadness, joy, nostalgia, empathy, or simple friendship.

There followed several tumultuous minutes before I said, by way of conclusion:

"Until now, the only people who knew my story were my grandparents, my old governess, the lawyer, and the banker, and they're all dead. I have never told anyone before today. This was the first time, and it will be the last."

"I'm not so sure about 'the last,'" Sémi said with implacable gentleness. "Now that the dam has burst, you won't be able to stop the water flowing."

At these words, this image, I foolishly started to sob once more. Sémiramis didn't know what to do, how to comfort me. She pressed my head against her chest, stroking my hair and my neck.

"If I'd know that was the reward, I'd have found some excuse to cry, too," Naïm mumbled, as though to himself.

And, once again, we went from tears to laughter. Then I continued:

"I'm not going to tell you stories of some lost paradise, though that's exactly how I remember it. An Eden from which I was banished, like our common ancestor, my namesake. But not because of a sin, because of an accident.

"My parents were a joy to behold. They were happy to be

alive, and they loved me intelligently, for want of a better word. My father talked about painting and architecture, my mother about fabrics, about flowers, about music; she often bought LP records, and would call me down to listen to them with her."

"And you were their only child," said Sémi, who had doubtless suffered from growing up as the middle child between two beloved brothers.

"I never felt having no brothers or sisters was a privilege. I didn't have anyone to play with, and I missed it. I played by myself. At twelve, I was still lining up toy soldiers. I only abandoned them when I left this house."

"If I were you, Adam, I wouldn't say that out loud," Naïm commented.

"Why?" Sémi said. "Some men spend their whole lives playing with toy soldiers."

I'm not quite sure that she said this in my defence. I would probably have been wiser to say nothing.

"So, when you hit puberty, you bought yourself a regiment wearing kilts ...?"

This brutal attack from Naïm earned me another hug from Sémi.

Throughout the whole conversation, we sat in the car outside the gates of my old house. It looked uninhabited, perhaps even abandoned and derelict. Of what we could see from the road, a few shutters on the first floor of the new wing were nailed shut and the paint was peeling.

"Should we try to sneak in?"

This was Sémi's suggestion.

"No!"

I screamed the word so loudly she felt she had to apologize. Then I apologized to her for having shouted. I pressed her hand to my lips. She smiled, and said softly:

"I don't suppose you know who owns it?"

"No. No idea. I never wanted to know."

I had answered instinctively. A rather different idea had just occurred to me.

"Can you move the car about twenty metres? That's it, just past the house. Park under this tree. If memory serves, there used to be a path there."

It was still there, exactly as I remembered it. A path paved with irregular flagstones, like a homemade version of the ancient Roman roads.

The moment I saw it I climbed out of the car, gesturing for my friends to follow.

3

The path dipped steeply. In rainy weather, it would have been slippery, but on this day it was hot and dry.

The three friends found themselves between two hills, as though in the hollow of a small valley. The undergrowth was thick. From here, no road was visible, no houses, no tilled fields. Nothing but leafy trees and brushwood; on both sides brambles had overgrown the paved path, without completely blocking it.

They walked in single file. Adam went first, now and then pushing aside a branch or stepping over a thorny spur. From time to time, he turned to check for his friends. They were still following, Sémiramis hard on his heels and Naïm just behind her; even so, he called back, "Follow me!"

At some point he paused and glanced around before confidently declaring:

"Nearly there!"

"Thank goodness!" Naïm panted, mopping his face and neck.

They had only been walking for five minutes, but what had at first been a gentle downhill slope was now a steep climb. A few minutes later, Adam, now also breathless, stopped and turned to his companions.

"There it is. Look!"

His voice was muted, almost a whisper, as much out of respect for the tranquility of the place as for his own memories.

Sémiramis and Naïm looked around. There was not much to see. Just a wall with an old wooden door.

But Adam wouldn't have led them this far had he not had a story to tell them in this very place.

He began with a prologue.

"What struck me the first time I came here is the fact that the path suddenly stops. You assume it leads all the way down to the valley, then suddenly you're walking back uphill, until you come to a high wall built from the same stones as the path, arranged in the same manner, except that, obviously, one is horizontal, the other vertical."

"So, what's on the other side?" Sémiramis asked.

"That's exactly what I used to wonder when I was a boy. But the wall was so high and I was so short that I couldn't see over it.

"I used to imagine all sorts of things, from Sleeping Beauty to Bluebeard, by way of Doctor Moreau. Then one day I decided to take a look.

"I needed a ladder, ideally a folding stepladder. We had a number of them at home. I snuck one out. Just getting it this far was quite a trek."

"Why don't we all sit down?" Naïm suggested, leaning against a tree. "I feel like this is going to take some time." He mopped his forehead again.

A few steps away there was a fallen trunk, and there the three of them sat, their faces in shadow. Adam picked up the thread of his story, pointing to a spot on the wall.

"I placed the ladder right there, made sure it was stable, and climbed up. It wasn't quite high enough. Even on the top rung, the wall still came up to my chin. I had to stand on tiptoe to see over.

"The first thing I saw was a head wrapped in a pink towel. Then I saw the silhouette of a woman in a pink bathrobe. She was sitting on her windowsill, half turned towards the outside, and therefore to me. She was holding a piece of paper, seemingly a letter, and studying it in the sunlight. Time passed. She sat, motionless, and I stood, motionless, holding my breath. Then she put down her letter, took off her towel, and shook her head, her hair whipped by the breeze. She was movie-star blonde.

"At some point, she was about to take off her bathrobe, but then, as if she sensed something, she looked out the window and upwards. And she saw me. Our eyes met, and I couldn't tear myself away. I'm sure you know the story of the birds on a branch held spellbound by a snake staring up from the foot of the tree? To escape, they have only to fly away, but their wings refuse to obey them, and they fall into the jaws of the predator."

That morning, I was just like those birds, Adam later wrote in his notebook, in terms that were very similar to what his friends had heard him tell. *Rooted to the spot, spellbound, unable to turn away, to move a muscle. And the "predator" swooped. In a flash, she had opened the door in the wall and stepped outside. Still in her pink dressing gown, her hair still wet, the towel now draped around her shoulders.*

She ordered me to get down immediately. And I obeyed. Not because I was afraid that I might be thrown into a dungeon, all I felt was shame, but that, too, is a kind of fear.

She ushered me through the door, gesturing for me to bring the stepladder, so I folded it, put it under my arm and brought it with me. She followed, closing and locking the door behind her.

I find myself standing there in front of her, like a soldier standing to attention, the stepladder under my arm like a makeshift rifle, while this lady looks me up and down. She takes her time, probably because she doesn't know what to do with me. I stare at the ground. On her bare feet, she is wearing pink open-toed slippers made of the same fabric as her dressing gown.

"Are you proud of yourself?" she says when she has finished sizing me up. I shake my head. "Do you want me to talk to your parents?" I shake my head again. "Are you planning to do this every morning?" I shake my head again, still unable to say a word, my eyes still moving restlessly over the ground between the lawn, the pink slippers, and the nail polish on her toes, also pink. "Cat got your tongue?" Again, I shake my head. "So, why haven't you said a single word?" I take my courage in both hands and say, "Out of politeness." She laughs, and repeats my words in a mocking tone as though to an invisible audience. Then she asks, "So I assume it's out of politeness that you're staring at the ground?" I nod vigorously, as though finally we understand each other. "You're right to bow you head in the presence of a lady. It's a sign of good manners." I'm just starting to feel reassured when she adds, "In the same way that it's good manners for a young man to climb a stepladder so he can peer at ladies over the wall, isn't it?"

At this point, I don't dare venture an answer. I simply look up at her as though waiting for a judge to pronounce sentence. The lady smiles, I smile. She knits her brows, still smiling, and asks, "So if you're not spying on me out of politeness, then why?" Feeling somewhat comforted by her smile, I say, "Out of curiosity." This, of course, was the simple truth.

She falls silent, never taking her eyes off me, studying me from head to toe, as though deciding on my punishment. "If I wanted, I could keep this ladder here and tell your parents to come and collect it themselves." She pauses for a few seconds before reassuring me. "But I won't do that. I'm sure you're going to apologize, and promise never to spy on me again."

I hurriedly promised as much. But she was only half listening as she mulled over an appropriate punishment. "In order to be forgiven," she said at length, "I want you to leave your step-ladder here, against the wall, and go into the kitchen, where you will find an elderly woman in a blue apron. Her name is

Oum Maher. Tell her I want my morning coffee. You'll need to raise your voice, because she's very hard of hearing. She makes the best Turkish coffee in the country, but she has trouble walking. You've got a good pair of legs, you can help her ..."

The house was a long, low building, measuring at least thirty metres from the kitchen to where we were standing. The lady tells me to wait in the kitchen while the coffee is prepared then bring it to her on a tray without spilling it. "Would you like a cup, too? How old are you?" "I'm ten and a half!" "... and a half?" she says, frowning as though this half makes a significant difference. "In that case, you're a big boy, you can have some. Do you like it with sugar?" I nod. "Very well, your punishment is to take it like I do, without sugar." I nodded again. "I see you've swallowed your tongue again. You can't even manage to say yes or no."

In the presence of this woman, I feel like I'm four years old and simultaneously like an adult. Eventually I manage a timorous "Yes." Immediately she corrects me: "Yes, Hanum! You will address me as 'Hanum.'" Until that moment, I'd never heard of this old-fashioned honorific. During the Ottoman period, it was the polite way to address a lady, apparently, but in my day, and even in my parents' day, no one used it anymore, except for a handful of very conservative old men.

Our neighbour asks me what I am called. "Adam." I pronounce my name the way I used to before I moved to France, emphasizing the initial A and lingering on the final m. She repeats it after me, as though practising. "Adamm. That's what I'll call you. Adamm, just Adamm, because you're young. But you must refer to me politely as Hanum, as though I have no first name, because I am old enough to be your mother."

"Yes, Hanum," I say, meekly and politely, then I head off to the kitchen, where Oum Maher menacingly looks me up and down as though I were a fig stealer. When I loudly tell her that Hanum would like two Turkish coffees without sugar, she screams in my face that she's not deaf. Then, as though she, too, wants to punish me, she makes me carry a huge tray with two glasses filled to the brim with cold water, two cups of coffee, a plate of thyme in oil, another of goat's cheese, and a basket of bread from the village. Although the tray was not particularly heavy, it was so large that when I carried it in front of me, I couldn't see where I was going. I had to move very slowly so as not to trip.

But then, since every transgression deserves both punishment and reward, my jailer bids me come inside. By now, she is in her living room, already dressed and made up, her hair held in place by a silver headband that looks like a tiara. She points to the table where I should set down the tray and the seat where I am to sit. I didn't feel remotely comfortable, but it was clear that my status had changed. I was no longer the pilfering kid about to be punished, I was almost a guest.

Having picked up her cup, she gestures to mine. I sip the bitter coffee, forcing myself not to wince. She watches my every movement, her eyebrows once more furrowed, which makes me clumsy. It takes an effort for me not to spill my coffee.

Then she says: "So, what does Adam do when he's not climbing walls?"

I say, "I read."

People often talk about the magic of books. But they rarely say that it is a two-fold magic. There is the enchantment of reading books, and that of talking about them. All the charm of a writer like Borges is that, even as we are reading his stories, we are imagining other books of fictions, dreams, phantasmagorias. In the space of a few pages, we experience two enchantments at once.

It is a magic I have experienced many times. But this was the day I first discovered it. You are with a stranger, she asks what you are reading, or perhaps you ask her, and if you both belong to the universe of those who read, you are about to step, hand in hand, into a shared paradise. As one book conjures another, together you will discover feats, emotions, myths, ideas, styles, and expectations.

In response to my declaration "I read!" the lady keeping me prisoner in her house did not, as she might have done, vaguely ask what sort of books I read—a trivial question—she asked what I was reading right now. I remember it was an adventure novel called "The Prisoner of Zenda." She was reading a book by a German archaeologist named Schliemann, the man who rediscovered the ancient city of Troy. We did not quite favour the same reading matter, but she took the time to ask me about my book and talked at length about hers, and we discovered similarities between the two. Then she suggested that, when we had finished, we swap.

After that, whenever I chose a book, my first thought was of her. Her passions were history, archaeology, and biography. At the time, I mostly read comic books and spy novels, I gorged on them thirstily the way I gulped down fizzy drinks. Thanks to Hanum, who would not have appreciated me turning up at her house with episode thirty in the adventures of some secret agent, I was forced to expand my horizons. I wanted to impress her, or at least earn her respect. To do this, I had to introduce her to books she didn't know. I don't think I taught her anything much; I do know that I learned a lot from her. About ancient Egypt, classical Greece, Byzantium, and especially Mesopotamia.

All through that summer, and the next, and even the next, I visited her regularly, sometimes three or four days in a row. We would talk endlessly about this and that, but sometimes we would simply sit in our corner and read our books in silence.

I wasn't surprised when one day she told me that she had been married to an archaeologist. She was from Iraq, as I had guessed from her accent, and her husband had worked at the Museum of Baghdad. When the monarchy was overthrown in the July 14 Revolution, 1958, they had been on holiday abroad, something that may have saved their lives. She was the niece of a former prime minister of the old regime, and they had often been invited to the Royal Palace. In the days following the coup d'état, many of their relatives had been slaughtered. It would have been foolish, even suicidal for them to go back to Iraq. So they built this house and shortly afterwards her husband had died. I assumed he was much older than she was.

One day she showed me his collection of ancient coins, explaining where each of them came from. Some were emblazoned with the heads of Roman emperors, others with Ottoman mottoes: "Khan of Khans of the Two Lands and the Two Seas." I was impressed, and promised myself when I was older, I'd have a collection of ancient coins. Of course, I never did. I'm not a collector by temperament, it requires more dedication than I am capable of. But I am convinced it was thanks to 'la Hanum' that I first became interested in history.

Up to that point, under my parents' influence, I wanted to be an architect. Not that they ever talked about it, I was much too young, but as far as I was concerned it went without saying. The plane crash, the closure of my father's practice bureau, and the loss of our house turned me from the appointed path. I wanted to take a very different direction, and that was history. In a sense, the career I chose had its roots in this chance meeting with our blonde neighbour.

But to get back to the coin collection, since it resulted in an incident that I would never forget. I was so fascinated by what Hanum had shown me that from that day, I stared at the ground wherever I went, as though it was enough to be vigilant to stumble upon ancient coins. This was not as ridiculous as it sounds, since there were vestiges of the Roman and Byzantine empires in our village; buried statues had been found there, carved columns, and probably old coins.

Then, one day, I see what I think is an ancient coin lying

between two stones. Having picked it up and rubbed it a little, I see the outline of a head and an inscription that is partially worn away. I race to Hanum's house at full speed as though it is a matter of life and death. It is three, maybe four o'clock in the afternoon and I know most people take a siesta at this time, especially in summer; but in my excitement, this doesn't occur to me.

The garden door is unlocked, I slip inside and wander through the garden, then the living room. No one. I come to the wide veranda overlooking the valley where she and I sometimes sit with our books. No one.

At the far end of the veranda is a glass door. As I race towards it, I come face to face with Hanum. Pale, undressed, almost naked. Though I did not know it, having never been there, this is the door to her bedroom. She has, visibly, just woken from her siesta and taken a shower, and is getting dressed.

When she sees me appear she gives a surprised cry, throws her arm across her chest, and takes a step back. I am even more startled than she is—in fact, I'm terrified—I stammer something, turn to run away, stumble, and end up sprawled on the floor.

I feel so embarrassed, so helpless, that I don't move. I play dead. When she bends over me, I don't react. She says my name; I don't respond. She pats my cheeks worriedly saying, "Adam! Adam?" I slowly open my eyes as though waking from a long sleep, oblivious to where I am. Then she says, "Shut your eyes, I'm not dressed!" I do as she says, though she has already clapped her hand over my eyes. "Will you give me your word as a gentleman that you'll keep them closed for three minutes?" I say, "Yes." She disappears and then reappears wearing a dressing gown. "That's fine, you can open them now." Which I do. Then I sit up. "Are you hurt?" I shake my head. "That's good! Now, go wait in the living room! I'll just get dressed and then I'll join you."

While I wait, and I prepare my apology, I realize that I'm no longer holding the coin that prompted me to race here in the first place. I must have dropped it on the veranda. When the lady joins me in the living room, now dressed, perfumed, and made up, I ask permission to go and look for my lost treasure. I can't find it. Did it slip between the railings? Did it roll into a gutter? I have no way of knowing. I had it in my hand and must have dropped it when I tripped. In that moment, I felt devastated. Not simply because I was proud of my discovery, but more especially because this was the "piece of evidence" that excused my rude behaviour.

That said, Hanum wasn't angry with me, and she never mentioned the incident again. Looking back, it seems to me that, in introducing to our relationship a secret that no one in the world could know about, my blunder brought us closer together.

Sometimes teenagers have a torrid rite-of-passage experience. Mine was nothing like that. But I was marked by its gentleness, its subtlety. When I think back on it sometimes, the word that comes to mind is "clemency." I made my childish blunders and there beside me was a beautiful stranger who responded to my unruliness with kindness, who patiently, delicately, tenderly, taught me to be a man.

4

"Do you know what happened to her?" Sémiramis said when Adam had finished telling the story of the lost coin.

He said that he had no idea. He had last seen her in August '66, the day after his parents died.

"When news of the accident got around, the whole neighbourhood showed up at our house. Hanum was among the women in black, and she hugged me as they did, to console me. Shortly afterwards, I moved away from the village and never set foot in it again."

"Do you think she might still live here?" Naïm said.

"No, definitely not!" Adam replied, without explaining how he could be so definite given what he had just said.

"If you give me a leg up, I can look over the wall," Sémiramis suggested.

"No. And I'm not going to fetch a stepladder like last time. Come on, that's enough, I've told you everything, let's go."

Had he been alone, Adam would almost certainly have knocked on the door. And had he not just told the preceding story, he might have done so, even with his friends in tow. But having recounted how he had come face to face with Hanum naked, he no longer felt he could introduce them to her without betraying her kindness, proving himself unworthy of her trust.

"God bless your days, Hanum," he murmured to himself, "in youth as in old age, in this life, and in the hereafter!"

Then, loudly to his friends:

"Come on, that's enough, let's go!"

But the happenstance of doors and paths had decided otherwise.

As the three friends walked away, there came a sound from behind them. Turning first, Sémiramis saw the door open and a lady emerge wearing a broad-brimmed straw hat with a pink ribbon.

It was her! There was no point weighing the evidence, it could only be her. Adam retraced his steps, as though compelled by some greater force.

"Hanum?" he said, his voice quavering with emotion as much as politeness.

"Do I know you?"

"My name is Adam. I used to live ..."

"My little boy!"

Ashamed, she clapped her hand over her mouth. Adam took the hand and pressed it to his lips, then let it go and said:

"I was a little boy when you saw me last, Hanum. My parents had just died."

"Yes, yes, I remember, my poor boy!" she said, this time without embarrassment.

"Then the house was repossessed by debtors, and I never came back."

"I know," she said, as though she had been watching over him all these years. "How big you've grown!"

"I'm forty-seven now."

"I didn't ask your age for fear you might ask me mine."

She laughed, and it was a youthful laugh. Sémiramis and Naïm who, until now, had been discreetly watching this reunion, joined in the laughter. Adam took the opportunity to introduce them.

"Sémiramis," Hanum echoed melodiously. "To me, it's always been the most beautiful name, and you wear it well."

Adam's friend blushed.

"Your names are also very interesting, gentlemen. 'Naïm' is another name for Paradise, and 'Adam' was chosen by the Creator Himself. But you'll forgive me if I still prefer Sémiramis. As you can tell from my accent, I'm from Mesopotamia."

As she uttered the ancient name, a sad smile played on her lips.

"My husband said that, to him, the most beautiful melody on earth was to hear the names Mesopotamia, Euphrates, Sumer, Akkad, Assyria, Babylon, Gilgamesh, Sémiramis. He was an archaeologist."

"Yes," said Naïm, "Adam told us."

"And what else did he tell you about me?"

The three friends were more than a little embarrassed. But there were several elegant escape routes. It was Sémiramis who first found one.

"He told us about the books you made him read."

"I was impressed by him as a child. Every other day, he would show up with some huge tomes he'd just read."

"The truth is, I read quickly so I could come back and see you, Hanum," the former child mumbled.

"But come on! Come inside! I should be ashamed, chatting away like this and not inviting you into my home."

"It looked to me as though you were heading out, Hanum," Adam feebly protested.

"I was about to take my daily walk, but I can do that later. It's not often I receive important visitors."

As she was speaking, she had gone back to the door which she now held open so that the three friends could enter.

Adam was still staring at her, incredulous, as though by some miracle he had just been readmitted to Eden before the Fall.

How graceful she still was! Her favourite colour, pink, was still evident in subtle touches—the ribbon of her hat, the piping on her dress.

How old would she be? Adam had a point of reference, since he knew the lady was from the same generation as his parents. Had they still been alive, his father would have been seventy-six, his mother seventy-two. Hanum must be about the same age.

Curiously, the house was even more beautiful than it had been in his childhood memory. Although the building itself had not changed, a long wall of russet stone now ran from the kitchen door to the living room, the garden was better maintained, the lawn was neatly mown and the flower beds looked as though they had been carved out with a set square. He would quickly discover the reason for this improvement. The irascible Oum Maher had been expediently replaced by a woman from Hanum's native land, a cheerful refugee who hailed from outside Mosul.

It was she who brought the coffee and the various pastries into the living room, then returned a few minutes later with three large glasses of blackberry syrup for the guests, and, for her mistress, a glass of water and a small plate with three colourful pills.

"Later!" Hanum murmured, embarrassed at having to perform this ritual of old age in front of her guests.

"No. Not later. Now!" the other woman said firmly, without moving an inch, yet retaining the same broad smile.

The lady had no choice but to swallow her tablets with sips of water. Then she explained:

"Sabah tends to my garden as though it were her own, and to me as though I were a sickly rosebush. Which I am ..."

When the woman had disappeared, she added:

"In our countries, we make revolutions in the name of the people, and the people are driven out of their homes, thrown out onto the streets. I'm talking about Sabah, but I could just as easily be talking about myself. I have not been back to my homeland since our glorious revolution."

Adam glanced around him and said:

"Everyone in this room is an exile, Hanum. I ended up in France, Naïm in Brazil, and Sémiramis was forced to flee Egypt with her parents when she was only a year old."

"Because of the revolution?" Hanum asked.

Sémiramis nodded, without explaining the circumstances of their premature departure.

"Revolutions are a catastrophe!" their hostess sighed, waving her hand with the same gesture she might have shooed away a fly.

"They certainly have been in our region," said Adam, who was reluctant to contradict her, but, as a historian, could not countenance such a generalization.

But the lady would brook no compromise.

"Not just in our region, Adam! Look at Russia! Before the Bolsheviks, the country was in full bloom. In a few decades, they had had Chekhov, Dostoevsky, Tolstoy, Turgenev ... Then revolution descended on the country like a long winter night, and the buds withered and died."

"But if people rose up, it is because they had reasons, Hanum. You're forgetting that Dostoevsky was a member of a revolutionary group; he narrowly avoided being executed and spent years in a gulag in Siberia."

"Have you read the story he wrote after his release?"

To his embarrassment, Adam had not. He dodged the question with a joke.

"If you'd given it to me, Hanum, I'd have read it."

"Back then, I hadn't read it either. As a result, I had a high opinion of the Russian revolution, which compared favourably to the ones that have racked our country. I used to think that Soviet leaders had succeeded in building a great power respected all over the world, and that they had emerged from the Second World War as victors, while the Arab leaders had simply racked up a series of defeats and failures. When it comes to our revolutionaries, our self-proclaimed 'progressives,' I haven't changed my mind, but when it comes to the Soviets, I have. When I read *One Day in the Life of Ivan Denisovich*, a book Solzhenitsyn wrote after his time in the Gulag, I remembered that I had a copy of *The House of the Dead*, Dostoevsky's memoir of his experiences of prison, on my bookshelves. So, somewhat belatedly, I read it. And I sincerely recommend that you and your friends do the same. Read them, as I did, in reverse order. First the twentieth-century account, then the nineteenth. They are separated by exactly one hundred years. You will discover that, compared to the gulags of the Stalinist era, the prison camps in Tsarist times were like a holiday camp. And you can't help but wonder: was this the unspeakable Tsarist regime that had to be toppled at all costs?"

Smiling all the while, she knitted her brows, just as she had done the day she caught Adam spying.

"You're probably thinking I'm a bitter old émigrée."

As one, the three friends protested.

"And maybe that's what I've become, with age. I've spent my whole life desperate to see the region we live in evolve, develop, progress. But all I've had are disappointments. In the name of progress, of justice, of freedom, of nationalism, of religion, we keep embarking on adventures that end in disaster. People who call for revolution should first have to prove that the society they intend to establish will be more free, more just, and less corrupt than what already exists. Don't you think?"

Her guests nodded politely, glancing at each other to see whether perhaps they should take their leave. Adam discreetly signalled for them to wait a little. He did not want their hostess to think that, by leaving, they were passing judgment on what she had just said.

At present, she seemed engrossed in anxious meditation. It was Naïm who lightened the mood.

"There's a question I've been wanting to ask you since we got here, Hanum."

She smiles. Because Naïm has a mischievous grin. But also because he has just joined the ranks of those who call her Hanum.

"I wanted to know whether, as a boy, Adam was a little angel or a little devil."

The lady's smile grew broader still. She seemed to marshal her thoughts before answering:

"When he was a little devil, it was because he was thoughtless. And when he was a little angel, it was because he was shy."

The three friends greeted this with a polite laugh before getting up to leave. For the sake of form, their hostess invited them to stay and lunch with her; they made their excuses, claiming that they were expected elsewhere, and promising that they would come back to visit.

As she was opening the garden gate to let them out, Hanum seemed to remember something and asked them to wait. They watched as she walked away, then reappeared two minutes later clutching a handkerchief. She unfolded it for Adam, whose friends watched him suddenly blush.

"You dropped this coin one day, it rolled under a bed and got stuck in a groove," the lady said in a tremulous voice. "By the time I found it, you had left so I couldn't give it back to you. Keep it safe, it's a genuine Byzantine coin dating from the reign of the emperor Justinian."

Adam cupped his hands as though receiving alms. He could no longer fight back his tears. His friends looked away, then hurriedly stepped through the door and set off along the flagstone path.

MAY 2 (CONTINUED)

The coin Hanum "returned" is not the one I discovered between the stones and later lost. Mine wasn't Byzantine or Roman or Ottoman, at best it was a timeworn local coin. Of course, I didn't say anything, I played along so as not to betray my co-conspirator, my benefactor, who wanted to give me this touching gift.

Unexpectedly, I now realize that the memory left by our time together was no less intense for her than it was for me; that if, to me, she had been a dazzling sun, perhaps I, to her, had been a sunbeam. Curiously, it is something I never thought about. Caught up in my own nostalgia, I rarely notice nostalgia in those I have known. It seems natural to me that they should have made their mark on my memory; the idea that I might have made my mark on theirs, I find surprising. Whether this is a sign of modesty or tactlessness on my part remains to be seen.

The Fourteenth Day

1

Today, Albert arrived. Our little gathering of friends is beginning to take shape.

When I called him yesterday evening, he was already in Atlanta, Georgia, about to board a flight to London, where he planned to spend the night. He was so insistent that I not pick him up from the airport that, in the end, I promised not to.

Then, at the last minute, I regretted my promise and went anyway. After all, it is only because I asked that he's coming back to the country. Besides, my own arrival two weeks ago when no one was waiting for me, has left a bitter aftertaste. Like Albert, I hadn't wanted to put anyone out, but I wouldn't have been unhappy to come to customs and be greeted by a few familiar faces.

Sémi did not come with me. She simply lent me her car, and Kiwan, the hotel chauffeur.

Once I arrived in the cavernous arrivals hall, I stood at the back so I could see the people arriving without my face being the first that Albert saw. He had made his own arrangements, he had told me, there would be people waiting to accompany him to his old apartment where he planned to spend the night. Given that he had sworn never to set foot in the country again, I assumed he had long since sold the apartment, but it seemed he had kept it. In fact, I could only assume he had someone who took care of it; otherwise, why would he think of spending the night there?

When he appeared, I recognized him instantly. Unlike Naïm, he has changed very little. He has even less grey hair than I do. Besides, his aquiline nose and triangular face meant that his profile is recognisable at a distance.

There was a couple waiting for him. The man was stocky, his wrinkled face surmounted by a shock of frizzy white hair; the woman was wearing a grey dress and matching head scarf. No sooner did the wanderer appear than two people rushed forward, each seizing an arm, and, in a flash, I knew who they were. Something about their gestures reminded me of the account Mourad had given of his visit to the garage where Albert had been held hostage.

I wouldn't have made the connection had I not written the story down last week. But I am completely convinced. Something about their appearance, their gestures, betrays the fact that these people come from a different world to the one in which Albert and I grew up. Remembering Mourad's account of the couple's farewell to their former hostage, it occurred to me that the "adoptive mother" Albert had mentioned in his coded message could only be her.

I smiled, and took a step back. This was why he did not want other people to come and meet him. If I hadn't phoned him last night, he would have waited until he was safely in the country before he called me.

I retreated two more steps and melted into the crowd of strangers. Had he spotted me? Maybe. Maybe not. His attention seemed to be monopolized by these unlikely parents, chatting to him, listening to him, stroking his hair, his arms, his shoulders.

The man had already commandeered his suitcase and his travel bag and was hurrying on ahead, presumably to his car. Albert was fighting to keep hold of one of the pieces of luggage, while the woman was trotting behind.

Should I try to catch them up? No. I slipped away and went back to the waiting car. When Kiwan asked if my friend had arrived safely, I told him all was well and we could head back to the hotel.

On the drive back, I waited for twenty minutes and then dialled Albert's US cell phone. A recorded female voice informed me that the person I was calling could not be reached. I didn't leave a message, preferring to wait until he calls me.

This he did an hour later, by which time I was back in my hotel room. It was obvious that he had no idea I'd gone to the airport. So much the better.

His flight was fine, he tells me, he's back at his old apartment, he thinks he might go straight to bed, since he feels horribly jet-lagged and didn't sleep a wink in London. He suggests that I call by his place tomorrow morning and asks whether I will be able to find the old apartment. Remembering how, when we were young, I used to make fun of his terrible sense of direction, I say that if he's been able to find it, then I definitely can. He does not rise to the bait, but simply gives a little laugh, then we both say, "See you tomorrow."

When his other friends called asking for news of the traveller, at about seven o'clock that evening, Adam did not mention the scene he had witnessed at the airport.

He simply told them that Albert had just called, that he had arrived safely and in good spirits, but was exhausted and planned to go straight to bed.

That evening Sémi and Naïm were planning to visit Tania, to whom Naïm had not yet offered his condolences, and asked if Adam wanted to join them, but he demurred, explaining that he was tired and had a migraine, probably from the hours spent driving at rush hour through clouds of exhaust fumes.

This was probably just an excuse. Was it because he had already seen enough of the widow, and because, where Tania was concerned, he felt a certain weariness? Perhaps. Another plausible explanation was that he did not want to see anyone before he had a long face-to-face conversation with Albert.

He decided not to leave his room that evening. He ordered a light supper, just a plate of cheese and some fruit, and set about organizing the notes he had been taking, and writing some general observations.

On the drive back, while we were stuck in traffic, the hotel chauffeur confessed—apologizing profusely as though he was about to commit the greatest faux pas—that he'd never met anyone called Adam before. I reassured him, saying that I wasn't in the least offended by his remark, that in this country my name was very rare, and that I found it flattering rather than embarrassing. Surely, bearing the name of the first man was a privilege?

He nodded politely, though he did not seem convinced by the argument. If I was right in deciphering his expression, he seemed to think I was making the best of a bad job. But he was clearly grateful that I had not taken offence at his comment.

When Kiwan fell silent, I carried on the conversation in my head. Responding to the assurances I had just made in a way that he could not have done. It is true that my name encompasses all of nascent humanity, yet I belong to a humanity that is dying. I've always been struck by the fact that the last Roman emperor was named after Romulus, the founder of the city; and the last emperor in Constantinople was named Constantine— again, after its founder. As a result, Adam, as a name, has always filled me more with fear than with pride.

I have never known why my parents chose to give me this name [...] I remember asking my father one day, and he merely answered: "He is our common ancestor!" as though this was something I might not know. I was ten years old and I made do with this explanation. Perhaps I should have asked him, while he was still alive, whether, behind the choice, there was some goal, some dream.

I believe there was. In his mind I was destined to belong to the cohort of founders. Today, at the age of forty-seven, I am forced to admit that my mission will not be accomplished. I will not be the first of a line, I will be the last, the very last of my family, the repository of their collected sorrows, their disappointments, and their shame. To me falls the hateful task of recognizing the faces of those I have loved, to nod my head and watch as the sheet is drawn over them. [...]

The Fifteenth Day

1

I spent the whole morning with Albert, in the apartment where he had once planned to commit suicide. He spoke as though we had never confided in each other before, and as though we would never meet again.

I had taken the precaution of arriving in his neighbourhood early, and I had marshalled my memories in order to find his building, which was still recognizable. The lobby, decorated with blue tiles, seemed to have survived the war unscathed. The only change was that a thick metal grille with a keypad, as ugly as a prison gate, had been fitted outside the lift; a futile precaution, since the keypad had been ripped apart and there was no lock on the gate.

When I reached the sixth floor, I pressed my ear to the door to make sure my friend was awake. It was not yet eight o'clock, but already there were noises from within. The doorbell worked; he opened the door, already dressed, and we threw our arms around each other.

I wanted to suggest that we go out for breakfast, as we had that day in Paris, after he had been released by his captors and was about to fly to the United States. But he had already set the table.

"Anyone would think you've been living here all this time."

"Somebody's been looking after the apartment in my absence."

"Your adoptive parents?"

I smiled and he responded with the same knowing smile.

"Okay, let's call them my 'adoptive parents,' since you find the term amusing."

"I'm just using the words you used in your email ..."

"To get a permit to come here, I had to claim a family

emergency. And I could hardly explain who they really were."

"'I've been missing my kidnappers, Sir, and I'd like to go and visit them.'"

He laughed.

"Not only would I not have been given a permit to travel, I'd probably have been subjected to enhanced interrogation techniques. Not to mention a psych evaluation ..."

"So, you've kept in touch with them?"

"Yes, from the day I left. When they released me, they made me promise to come back and visit. And I wanted to. I asked Mourad and Tania to take me to see them before I went to the airport."

"They told me all about it on the phone as soon as you were on the plane. I won't repeat what Mourad—God rest his soul— said about you."

"God rest his soul. Whatever he said that day, he was probably right. I was pigheaded, heedless to danger. I was suicidal."

He said this last word as though savouring a familiar bitterness. And this reminded me that, at that moment, Albert and I were in the very place where the tragedy had almost happened twenty years earlier.

Each probably recalling similar memories, Albert and I fell silent for several moments and stared down at our cups of café au lait. Then he went on:

"When I started working in the US, I decided to send them part of my salary every month. Why? Because I had suddenly discovered how fascinating and wonderful life could be, how it was worth living, and I was horrified, in hindsight, at the thought of what I might have lost. I was—I still am—enormously grateful to those people, who, on two separate occasions, were agents of Providence. Blind agents initially, when they kidnapped me and, in doing so, prevented me from doing something irreversible. But later, conscious agents, who, when they found out that their son was dead, were magnanimous and selfless and, despite their grief and their rage, did not take it out on me, their prisoner.

"So I decided to transfer ten percent of my salary to them. 'Tithing,' it used to be called ... It has not made them rich, but it has meant they have been free of financial worries, and have even been able to renovate their house. When I arrived yesterday, they took me to see the renovations they had done with that money. They also looked after this apartment. Look around! It's a lot tidier than it was when I lived here. They are fundamentally good, fundamentally honest people; the fact that they were forced to resort to kidnapping says a lot about the twisted nature of the war."

"In short, you've played the role of their lost son, and they've assumed the role ..."

"... of the parents I lost. Yes, that's about it, I don't need to explain it to you. Of all the friends I've kept in touch with, you're the only one who knows my past."

I smiled.

"In that case, the others must be completely in the dark, because I don't know much!"

"You know my father was murdered in Liberia."

"I knew it was somewhere in West Africa, but I didn't know which country. We never talked about it. All I remember are the rumours that went around in school."

"I know they said horrible things. That he was a trafficker, a spy, and God knows what else. Actually, he had an import-export business in Monrovia, and one day some thugs showed up and murdered him in his office near the port. Either thieves planning to rob him or hired killers in the pay of one of his rivals. If there was a police investigation, no one ever told me the conclusions. Now you know as much as I do."

"And he used to come to visit you sometimes?"

"He came twice, I think. But if I hadn't seen photographs, I wouldn't even remember what he looked like. He never wrote to me either. My only relationship with him was a monthly bank transfer."

"Like your adoptive parents' relationship with you ..."

He smiled.

"I'd never thought of that ... Maybe that's how I came up with the idea. But the similarities end there."

"And your mother was in a sanatorium in Switzerland, wasn't she? Or was it a rumour?"

"It was just a rumour, though in that case I'm the one who started it. My parents split up when I was four. My father left for Liberia, where two of his brothers were already working. And my mother married a man who didn't want anything to do with another man's child."

He trailed off. I was about to ask a question when I saw that he was close to tears. So I stared down at my coffee until he continued.

At length, he said in a quavering voice:

"She accepted this arrangement. She dismissed me as though I were a bad memory, as though even caring about me might compromise her new life. I got nothing from her, no letters, no bank transfers. When she dropped me off at boarding school, I told my friends that she was seriously ill and was going to a sanatorium for treatment. I couldn't think of anything else to explain her abandoning me, and it sounded plausible. Actually, she was living in Nice, with her new husband and her new children."

"You have half brothers and sisters?"

"I don't know their names or how many of them there are."

"Did you ever see your mother again?"

"Not once! One day, when I was nineteen, she wrote to tell me she was ill and wanted me to visit her. I didn't go. I abandoned her on her death bed the same way she had abandoned me.

"I'm not proud, it's something I've regretted my whole life. But, at the time, that's what I wanted. She'd never written to me before, no birthday cards, not even a letter when my father died. And even in the letter informing me she was ill, she couldn't find the right words. 'Every Sunday I pray that you will be happy.' I was tempted to write back and say I didn't need her prayers because, as far as prayers were concerned, I had more than enough at boarding school; and that, when I was growing up, what I needed was a mother who would hug me to her breast, not one who prayed for me in a church on the French Riviera. She explained to me that her second husband had wanted to start a new life with her, one that was not 'tainted' by memories of the past. I almost wrote back to say that, since she hadn't wanted me to taint her life, maybe I shouldn't taint her death.

"In the end, I didn't write anything, didn't reply. Two weeks later, I received a card with a sombre grey border informing me of her death; there was no note. The way I'd treated her was no more than she probably deserved. Even so I felt devastated. When I think back to my suicide attempt, to that macabre card I had printed, I tell myself that maybe this was guilt making me pay for my spiteful act of revenge."

A silence. I sat and waited. He continued:

"I've never been much interested by religion. Any religion. I'd had my fill with all the morning Masses I had to attend at the Christian Brothers school. But there's a saying attributed to the Prophet, one that has haunted me ever since I first heard it. It says: What we do in this world will be rewarded in the next, except for the way we treat our parents, which will be punished or rewarded in this world."

"Do you think the precept applies to your 'adoptive parents'?"

"They certainly think so. They tell me that when I'm old, my children will look after me just as I've looked after them. I say: 'yes, Uncle,' 'yes, Auntie.' They would be upset if I told them I'll never have children."

Albert fell silent. I asked no questions. We stared at each

other. We exchanged mute words. Then he said:

"You've always known, haven't you?"

The truthful answer was "no," since I found out only a few days ago when Ramez confided in me. But, given how he had phrased the question, I felt saying "no" would sound like a clumsy way of saying "yes." In the end, I said:

"We never talked about it."

"It was difficult to talk about it here. Despite how close we were. We grew up together, our friendship developed at an age when every secret could be seen as an invitation. It was safer to trust to what was unsaid ..."

"I assume it's different In America ..."

"There are bigots everywhere, but as long as you follow the 'instruction manual,' they don't make your life a living hell. You quickly learn to hang out with these people rather than those people, to phrase things in a certain way in order to defuse the situation. Anyway, I've never been in favour of forced 'outing.' Everyone has the right to choose whether or not to come out, to whom, and how. The people who pressurize you into making rash statements aren't your friends. Decent people don't pressure you. Whether or not they're gay, they're simply happy to be your friends, your colleagues, your students, your neighbours. And I don't disturb them either. Either because of their way of life, or because of the way of mine.

"I tell people what they're willing to hear. Not what they want to hear but what they're able to hear. I'll never tell my 'adoptive parents' the truth. Why upset them? Every time they write, they say they want me to find a nice girl and settle down. I make no promises, but I allow them to hope for what they believe they should hope for. What good would it do to tell them that my 'fiancée' is called James?"

A silence. A tinkle of coffee cups.

"So, what about you? I assume you're not still with the adorable girl I met in Paris twenty years ago. Since you never mentioned her in your emails, I'd assumed she was out of the picture. She was a psychologist, wasn't she?"

"Yes. Patricia."

"You're not with her anymore?"

"It's ancient history."

"Were you together long?"

"Seven years."

"So, what about more recent history, what's her name?"

"Dolores. She's a magazine editor."

"And you've been together ..."

"Six years now. Maybe a little more."

"Am I to understand that you're thinking about moving on?"

"Absolutely not. That's not how it works. When I'm with a woman, I always want it to last forever, and I always believe it's possible."

"But, one after another, they let you down ..."

"The problem isn't them, it's me. As soon as my happiness is complete, I become convinced that it can't last. So I do whatever it takes to make sure it doesn't. It's pathological, and I know I'm doing it. I know I'm destroying the relationship, but I can't stop until the destruction is complete."

What I didn't say to Albert, because it didn't occur to me at the time, is that the image that has always haunted me is of my parents, laughing, a few short hours before their plane crashed. How many times has this image resurfaced, at moments of great happiness in my life, as if to remind me that happiness is temporary, that the laughter I hear is the herald of some imminent tragedy.

When happiness becomes the enemy of happiness ...

Our conversation ended when his "adoptive father" came to pick him up. Apparently, there was a party being thrown in his honour. The mechanic duly invited me, but only because I happened to be there, so I politely declined the invitation, claiming I had a prior engagement.

I was saddened by this interruption. Albert and I still had a million things to say to each other—about his job, about his research and mine, about the collection of music boxes I'd seen on the shelves.

I also regretted having been so cavalier when talking about my lovers. While talking about love is a noble thing, talking about lovers is vulgar. I still remember a conversation I had with Bilal just before he died in which he tried to persuade me otherwise. I had been impressed by the daring, the audacity of what he said, but thinking back, a quarter century later, I feel more than ever wedded to my position. And today's conversation was not likely to change my mind.

Since Albert had confided in me, I felt I had to do likewise. This, it seems, is the nature of polite conversation ... But the way I talked about the women in my life was an insult to my love for them. Naming one after another, in a single sentence, was callous, perhaps even hateful. While we were together, Patricia had been my whole life, and the thought that she is now merely an episode, an incident, is repulsive to me. And Dolores is not my most recent girlfriend, she is the person I love most in the world; I would shed bitter tears if I were to lose her.

What about Sémi? Is she simply a parenthesis, as I've described her in this book? Thinking back, I was wrong to speak about her in such terms. A parenthesis that opens the doors to paradise is not a commonplace parenthesis, and I do not want it to end. In a few days we will go our separate ways, but the love I pledge her now will never be forgotten or betrayed.

As he took his leave of Albert outside the building, Adam was planning to go to a local café to record snatches of their conversation in his notebook before he forgot them; then he would wander through the city at random, as once upon a time he loved to do, but has not done since his return.

But by the time he had finished making his notes, it was 1:00 p.m., the streets were hot and sweltering, there were roadworks everywhere. He no longer had the energy to walk. He closed his notebook and hailed the first passing taxi.

When he arrived back at the Auberge Sémiramis, he made no attempt to contact the chatelaine or Naïm. Tired and dripping with sweat, he went straight up to his room, undressed as soon as he walked through the door, took a long shower, and fell asleep in his dressing gown.

Two hours later, he was woken by a hand stroking his forehead. He smiled, without opening his eyes, without stirring, without saying a word. Fortunately in this case, since, if he had said a name, it would have been "Sémiramis."

But it wasn't her.

2

Dolores had given Adam little hope that she would join them.

When Adam first tried to persuade her to come to the reunion, his partner had been less than enthusiastic. The old friends he longed to bring together were strangers to her, she did not share their memories, had no place there, and she told him as much; besides, she did not speak a word of Arabic, so her presence would stop them speaking freely in their native tongue. "You'll spend the whole time explaining things to me, and end up regretting inviting me."

But all this was merely an excuse so that she could make up her mind at the last minute, and so that she could be sure that he genuinely wanted her to come. In fact, she longed to spend time with him in the country where he had been born, to meet the friends he had known, to finally feel a connection—if only through a "catch-up session"—to one of the happiest periods of his life. Most importantly, she was determined that he not experience this important moment with only Sémiramis for company.

Dolores was doing her best not to succumb to jealousy, she even felt a certain pride that she did not feel resentful towards the woman who had "borrowed" her partner. She had met the woman only twice, but felt an instinctive sympathy for Sémiramis, she trusted her, despite what had happened, perhaps because of what had happened. In fact, it was thanks to the complicity of her "rival" that she had been discreetly able to organize her journey. As a result, she felt no bitterness towards the hotel manager ... But Dolores knew it was high time that she reclaimed this man who was hers. And definitively closed this "parenthesis."

It was Sémiramis who greeted her at the airport and drove her to the hotel, where the receptionist informed them that Adam was in his room. Dolores expected to surprise him working at his laptop. Slowly, she opened the door. The room was in darkness. Leaving her suitcases outside, she tiptoed in and found her partner asleep.

And so, stroking his forehead, she woke him. Even before he opened his eyes, he recognized her perfume. He wrapped his arms about her, whispering "*Querida*" as though he had been expecting her. She slipped between the sheets next to him.

The lovers' tender siesta was interrupted by a phone call from Albert, apologizing for abruptly abandoning his friend that morning, and suggesting that they meet up in the city that evening.

"Are you sure your kidnappers are prepared to release you?" Adam joked.

"No," his friend said, "but they've given me a furlough for the evening. You remember the restaurant Le Code Civil?"

"Next to the University? How could I forget? It was our local ..."

"I just walked past and was astonished to discover that it still exists. Or, to be exact, that it exists again. It closed at the outbreak of the war, then someone decided to reopen it. I'm also inviting Sémi and Naïm. I think it'll be an excellent preface to our reunion."

Adam was delighted.

"I'll sit in my usual seat, and order exactly what I used to order."

Dolores didn't know what he was talking about, but her

partner's delight was infectious; she mimicked his smile and laid her head on his bare shoulder.

"Beneath that rebellious pose of yours, you're a dyed-in-the-wool conservative," his friend said at the other end of the line.

Adam made no attempt to deny it.

"If I had countless lives, I'd spend one of them going to the same restaurant every day, sitting at the same table, in the same chair, ordering the same thing."

"With the same partner," Dolores whispered in his ear.

"Yes ... with you," he said, holding the receiver away from his face so he could kiss her.

"I also thought of inviting Tania," Albert went on, "but maybe that's not such a good idea, since I haven't gone to pay my condolences yet."

"You're right, it would be a very bad idea. She's not going to want to be seen in public so soon after the death of her husband, and she'd only criticize you for becoming an American ignoramus who knows nothing about the proprieties of your native land. She's changed a lot, you know. The conversations I've had with her in the past few days have left a bitter taste in my mouth."

"In forty-eight hours, I'll let you know whether I share your diagnosis. As for tonight, I won't invite her."

"But I should mention that there will five of us," Adam said.

Without warning, he pressed the phone to his partner's ear; somewhat taken aback, all she could think to say was:

"My name is Dolores."

She seemed intimidated, which was very unlike her. In their relationship, she was usually the more talkative, the more brazen, the one more likely to command and be obeyed. But she clearly still felt nervous, like a conqueror on the border of an unknown country.

It was an attitude she would maintain for a little while that evening; saying little, smiling politely at other people's jokes, observing the tics of some and the quirks of others.

Arriving at their former university canteen triggered a flood of incidental memories, of waiters who sold marijuana, of lustful old women in search of strapping, muscular students, of memorable brawls involving kitchen knives.

Dolores waited. She meekly allowed the regulars to choose her dishes; raised her glass to toast to their reunion; then, making the most of a brief silence while the four friends were tasting the wine they had chosen, she said, in the gentle, no-nonsense tone she used when talking to junior editors:

"So, tell me everything! How you met, what brought you all together, and what's kept you apart for so long. I know practically nothing, and I want to know everything. I'm going to need a crash course to follow your conversations over the next few days. So come on, all four of you; I'm all ears."

To soften the blow of this peremptory order, she adopted her most luminous, most disarming smile. Then raised the glass to her lips.

The four old friends exchanged furtive looks, each hoping the others would speak first. Eventually, it was Albert who took the plunge.

"Adam and I met when we were at school. There was a horde of us, and he was one of the less barbaric."

"Coming from Albert, that's a huge compliment," Adam whispered to his partner. She pressed a finger to his lips so he would allow his friend to carry on.

"We applied to university together, and that's where we met the others. More or less all at the same time. At least that's how I remember it."

"What was it that brought you all together?" the outsider asked.

Albert took a moment to think.

"There are a couple of possible answers. The first one that comes to mind is that none of us quite fitted into the communities we came from."

"So, the fact that you were all atypical was what drew you to each other ..."

"That's not quite what I meant. Let me try a different tack."

It took some time for Albert to marshal his thoughts.

"My closest friend among the Muslims was Ramez; my best Jewish friend was Naïm; and my best friend from the Christian community was Adam. Now, obviously, not all Christians were like Adam, all Muslims like Ramez, or all Jews like Naïm. But they were my friends. They were my blinkers, the reason I couldn't see the wood for the trees, if you like."

"And you think that was a good thing?"

"Oh yes, it was a great thing. It's important not to see the wood. And for that, you need blinkers."

"So that's what friends are for?"

"Yes, I think so. Friends help you to preserve your youthful illusions for as long as possible."

"But you still lose them in the end."

"Of course, over time, you end up losing your illusions. But it is better not to lose them too soon. Otherwise, you also lose the will to live."

He felt a lump in his throat, as though the simple fact of seeing his native city and his friends again had brought all his old fears to the surface. An awkward silence settled over the table, and the friends stared down at their plates or their glasses of red wine. Eventually, between mouthfuls, Naïm said:

"And you get kidnapped ..."

For a second, everyone was speechless, then Albert retorted:

"Yeah, you get kidnapped. And that turns out to be the best thing that could have happened to you."

Suddenly, as though to relieve the tension, there came a gale of laughter from the four old friends; even Dolores, who had long ago heard the story of Albert's abduction told to her by Adam, belatedly joined in. She also stopped before they did, and carried on with her "interrogation":

"Since Albert mentioned everyone's religion, I have to ask you all a question that's been niggling at me for a long time, a question Adam has never really taken the time to answer: why is faith so important in this part of the world?"

The friends looked at each other questioningly, and it was Naïm who finally spoke.

"That's what people in the West say, but don't believe a word! It's just a myth. The truth is exactly the opposite ..."

"Really?"

"It's the West that has clung to faith, even in its secularism, and it's the West that is religious, even about its atheism. Here, in the Levant, no one cares about your beliefs, it's about belonging. The religions here are like tribes, and our religious fervour is a kind of nationalism ..."

"And a kind of internationalism, too," Adam said. "It's both at once. The community of the faithful replaces the nation; and inasmuch as religion cheerfully spans the frontiers of country and of race, it becomes a substitute for the workers of the world, who, apparently, are supposed to unite."

"A notion that's been formally refuted these days," said Naïm, twisting the knife in his own wound and those of his friends.

"The twentieth century was one of secular monstrosities, the twenty-first will be the backlash," announced the historian.

"Personally, I liked the twentieth century," Dolores ventured, at the risk of sounding naïve.

"Because you only experienced the latter part," said Adam, who was ten years older than his partner. "The first half was particularly monstrous. After that, things settled down a little, but by then it was too late, the damage was done."

"Why do you say 'too late'?" Sémiramis asked, her tone genuinely worried.

Adam was just about to answer when Albert laid a hand on his arm and interrupted:

"It's important to remember that for our friend here, being more French than the French themselves, secularism is the supreme virtue. As he sees it, if the world moves away from secularism and towards religion, that means it's in decline."

"And you don't see it that way?" said Adam.

"I think things aren't so clear-cut. In a world ruled by Mammon, I'm not sure our top priority should be getting rid of God. It's the golden calf we need to defeat, that's the greatest threat to democracy and to all other human values. In the name of equality, communism reduced people to slavery, capitalism is trying to do the same thing in the name of economic freedom. Both then and now, God has been the last refuge of the oppressed, the last resort. Why would you want to deprive them of that? And what would you replace it with?"

His comments, also phrased as a question, were spoken like a judge passing sentence. There ensued a long silence, which was finally broken by Sémiramis attempting, unsuccessfully, to steer the debate onto a different track.

"The other day, Adam was saying that the two major catastrophes of the twentieth century were communism and anti-communism."

"And the two major catastrophes of the twenty-first century will be Islamic fundamentalism and anti-Islamic fundamentalism," the historian predicted. "Which, with all due respect to our esteemed futurologist, promises a century of decline."

"Don't listen to them, Dolores!" Sémiramis whispered loudly enough for everyone to hear. "They're depressing, our three companions. They left the country when they heard the first gunshot, and now they're predicting the apocalypse to justify the fact that they left."

"The apocalypse I'm predicting doesn't just involve this country, it's involved the whole planet!" Adam protested.

His partner shot him a bewildered look.

"Oh, well that's reassuring," she said, "I was starting to get worried."

Once more, all five burst out laughing; it went on for a long time. Nobody wanted to talk any more. Then followed a silence. Then Naïm, who never joked when it came to the epicurean arts, said in a solemn tone:

"Do you think the bartender here knows how to make a *caipirinha*?"

The Sixteenth Day

1

That day in May was supposed to be the day of the reunion. It was to be the day of the final separation, the final dispersal.

Adam had planned a precise schedule, and set it down on paper, presumably to clarify his thoughts.

We'll meet in Sémi's little house at twelve, twelve thirty at the latest. If Ramzi joins us, I'll let him say an ecumenical prayer, then I'll give a welcome speech. It might sound inappropriate for a reunion of friends, but I'd rather do it to set the tone, so everyone knows this is no ordinary occasion.

Ramez has promised to bring some kind of collage he's had his daughter make at the office, a collection of forty photographs, most of them from the old days, of everyone who will be there, he tells me, and the two who will be absent, Bilal and Mourad. He'll give a copy to everyone, inscribed: The Sophists' Symposium. May 5–6, 2001, Auberge Sémiramis. *This rather pretentious name will give the gathering a certain solemnity. But why not? I rather like the idea.*

In a thoughtful touch, Ramez wanted Dolores to be part of the collage. I had no photos of her with me, but Sémi found one that she had taken the evening she had come to dinner with us in Paris. It showed the three of us, arm in arm, our cheeks pressed together, a physical closeness that takes on a very different significance in the light of our recent intimate "adventures."

Dunia and Ramez will set off on their private jet at dawn. I trust them, they'll be the first to arrive even though they're coming from farther away than anyone else.

Albert has promised that his "adoptive father" will drop him off at noon precisely; I trust him, too.

Nidal has confirmed that he's coming, said he wouldn't be

late. I've got no reason to doubt him, militants are always punctual. Sémi still thinks it was a mistake to invite him ... But even so, she bought a six-pack of non-alcoholic beer for him.

Tania, on the other hand, is never on time, I'm told. Given her behaviour in the past few days, I should probably be happy, but I can't see myself giving the welcome speech before she arrives. After all, she's the one who came up with the idea for the reunion. We'll see ...

The person I'd be most upset not to see there would be Brother Basil. More than anyone else, he would lift this reunion to new heights. Not just by the words he chooses to say, which are unlikely to stray into hackneyed cliché, but by the simple fact of his coming, and how that will affect everyone, especially Ramez and his wife. There will probably be a few reproaches, a few regrets, maybe a few tears; but I'm convinced that they will have made up by the time they leave.

The monk's presence would add both intellectual stimulation and emotional intensity. Whether or not he comes is another matter ... Unlike the others, he didn't formally commit himself. He said "maybe" and "it's a wonderful initiative on your part," but I can't see him just turning up unannounced. And I don't think it would be a good idea to phone him. I'm pretty sure that if I were to call, he'd find some excuse not to come.

The only thing to do would be to head off with the inimitable Kiwan to go and fetch him; without warning him, relying simply on the last conversation we had, on the edge of the labyrinth. If he sees I've come all the way to fetch him, he'll feel too ashamed to let me go away alone, he'll stifle his qualms, he'll come.

In order to do this, we'll need to set off very early, arrive at the monastery by nine thirty, and head back before ten o'clock so we arrive back at the hotel shortly before noon. This means leaving here at about 7:00 a.m.

Dolores said she'll come with me.

But Dolores would change her mind. They had arrived back from the restaurant late the night before, at about two o'clock in the morning. When the alarm rang at 6:30 a.m. she had not stirred. Adam got up, tapped her very gently on the shoulder two or three times. Without opening her eyes, she asked what time it was. He told her. She grunted, then fell asleep again.

Adam had shaved, taken a shower, dressed, and then come back and bent down to plant a gentle kiss on her lips. Instinctively, she reached her arms out to hug him. Then she let him go. He left.

2

By the time Adam arrived at the monastery, Brother Basil was already prepared. The night before, he had told the monks that he was going away and would be back on Sunday night.

His friend offered to take his rucksack, but he insisted on carrying it himself. Besides, it was only a battered leather bag and visibly not very heavy.

Of what happened in the hour that followed we know very little, no witnesses have come forward, so we can only speculate.

The bare facts are these: Sémiramis's car was involved in an accident, the driver and one of the passengers were killed outright, the third occupant was seriously injured and, at the time of writing, has still not regained consciousness.

The theory is that the car suddenly swerved off the road, and rolled once or twice before somehow plummeting into the void. It smashed onto the rocks below. Then it exploded, and the fire spread to the undergrowth.

Two charred bodies were found in the wreckage. "Kiwan Y., chauffeur, 41" and "Ramzi H., engineer, 50," according to the police report. There is no mention of Brother Basil. "Adam W., professor, 47" was found lying some fifteen metres away, having been thrown from the vehicle; he had probably opened the door in an attempt to get out.

Nobody saw the accident happen, no one heard the explosion, and the fire burned itself out. It has to be said that that particular stretch of mountain road, about ten kilometres from the Monastery at Les Grottes, is arid, rocky, winding, and sees little traffic.

We cannot exclude the possibility that someone witnessed the accident and has chosen to remain silent. If the car swerved, it may have been to avoid an oncoming vehicle. In that case, the other driver would bear some responsibility for the tragedy, and might decide not to come forward. But this is not the only possible scenario. Kiwan may have swerved to avoid an animal—a fox or a jackal, or maybe a dog.

Adam has already mentioned the hotel chauffeur's polite but inappropriate habit of turning towards the person he was speaking to and taking his eyes off the road. The possibility that this is what caused the tragedy cannot be ruled out. But all of this is pure speculation, and it is possible that no one will ever know what actually happened. "... veered off the road for some unknown reason, at a point known as Al-Sanassel." This may be the extent of the police investigation.

Initially, Adam's friends had not been worried.

All of them had arrived on time, even a little early. Sémiramis had greeted them in her private residence, which was painted in warm tones: terracotta, ochre, and burnt sienna; it was relatively spacious, even if its owner called it the "little house" to distinguish it from the building that had been converted into a hotel.

In the vast square living room, the walls were lined with books, and the floor was piled with two or three layers of Persian rugs. The chairs and sofas were old and mismatched, but the colour matched the warm décor and the cushions were soft and comfortable.

It had been planned that the friends would gather here for a brief welcome drink before heading up to the top floor of the hotel, where Sémiramis had prepared a sumptuous meal.

Shortly before 12:30 p.m., Dolores phoned Adam to see how far away he was. There was no answer. She called several times and, after about fifteen minutes, asked Sémiramis for the chauffeur's number. His phone did not answer either. Ramez reassured them, explaining that the car was probably in an area with no cell-phone signal. This was plausible, and it succeeded in reassuring some of the friends. But not Dolores. By now, it was 1:35 p.m., and Dolores knew her partner well enough to know how much he hated being late. Especially for an event like this, a reunion that he had organized.

It is true that, initially, Adam had not had much faith that his plan would succeed. He had written the first invitations more to console Mourad's widow and to ease his own guilt. He was surprised by his friends' enthusiasm and the speed at which the plan had come together.

That these people, who had been scattered across the globe by war and the vagaries of life, who now lived on four different continents, working in very different professional, political, or spiritual fields, that these people who had not seen each other for a quarter of a century were willing to come to this remote mountain hotel, at a word from him, might seem understandable in hindsight, but when Adam first wrote the letters, he was not expecting it.

Each of them must have felt a powerful urge to reconnect with the friends they had known; and, of course, through these friends with the life they had known before the war, before the diaspora, before the breakdown of their Levantine society, before the deaths of people they had loved. Perhaps Albert was right when he suggested in one of his emails that, if they had not met up again since university, it was because of Mourad. "A reunion with him had become unthinkable, a reunion without him made no sense. [...] his death is the perfect pretext for us all to meet up again."

Whatever the reason, the dream was now coming true ... but it was also about to come crashing down. Figuratively and literally. Of the ten people who were expected, eight had arrived early, impatient for the "chairperson" to arrive and the "symposium" to begin. Aside from Sémiramis, Dolores, and Naïm, who were staying at the hotel, the first to arrive was Albert, followed by Ramez and Dunia; Nidal arrived at precisely 12:30 p.m., taciturn, aloof, still obviously wondering what he was doing with this bunch of heathens; Tania showed up at about one o'clock, cheerful and chatty in her widow's weeds. The only people missing were Adam and Brother Basil.

It was at about 2:30 p.m. that worry turned to panic. Ramez jumped to his feet. "We have to go and find out where they are!" A minute later, two cars set off. Dunia and Dolores went in Ramez's car while Nidal took Albert and Francis, the maître d'hôtel, who was worried for his brother and who knew the stretch of road. Since Sémiramis had to stay behind, Tania and Naïm decided to stay with her.

It took an hour for the two cars to reach the accursed spot. By now, a crowd had gathered—cars parked on the hard shoulder, people waving and pointing down into the ravine from which rose a thin cloud of smoke. There were other people down on the valley floor, some in khaki uniforms.

"I have come to meet the ghost of a friend, and already I am a

ghost myself," Adam wrote on the day he arrived. He did not know how right he was. Those who saw him as he lay in a hospital bed, faceless, his eyes vacant, stiff, and white in his bandages, felt as though they were looking at a ghost.

In his last notebook, which was found on him, he had written several pages dated Friday, May 4, and even some dated Saturday, May 5—which had probably been written when he got back from dinner at Le Code Civil.

I'll wait until the last person has arrived and we've gone upstairs to the restaurant before calling for silence and formally standing up to take the floor, with my speech in front of me. Since there will only be about a dozen of us gathered around the groaning table, I feel I should say, by way of introduction, that I'm not about to make a big speech. Though this is exactly what I plan to do. Having written to some and met up with others so I could persuade them to come, it seems appropriate for me to remind them, with a certain solemnity, why it was important that we meet up again after so many years of estrangement, and what we should talk about.

I'll speak in French so that Dolores doesn't feel left out. And also because it's the language in which I find it easiest to express myself after so many years teaching in Paris.

My first words must, necessarily, be the most conciliatory. Later—over dinner or at some point on Sunday—I'll touch on more sensitive subjects, since I feel that this is important.

"What brings us together, first and foremost," I'll say, "is the memory of those who are no longer with us. Mourad's untimely death has reminded us how we should have remained closer, and how we became scattered. No one did more than Mourad to bring us together, back when we were twenty years old, and today, it is thanks to him that we are gathered together again.

Thanks to him, and to Tania, who urged me to invite you all to this reunion. Which, I have to confess, I first thought of as an impossible idea, especially at such short notice. I would especially like to thank her for setting aside her grief to come here and share, not just our nostalgic tears, but our inevitable laughter. I would like to dedicate those tears and that laughter to those who are no longer with us.

"Firstly, to Bilal. Those of us who knew him will never forget him. I often think about him, about our long walks, our arguments, his eyes, his voice. Even now, after all the years that have passed, there are stories I still long to tell him, books I want to make him read, subjects I want to discuss with him, that I could only discuss with him, and I curse the circumstances that took him from us too soon. I know that Nidal feels the same. He agreed to be here with us because I mentioned his brother's name. There are many things that separate us, but we will always be connected by the memory of a budding writer cut down by a shell in the early days of the war.

"I sometimes wonder what sort of literature he would have written if he had had time to get down to it. Did he have the talent of the poets and novelists we read together? I'd like to think so. But one thing I know for certain is that he had a writer's temperament, and also the harebrained ideas.

"One of these harebrained ideas had to do with me. When he first heard my name, he didn't say How's Eve?—most people can't resist. But he clearly decided from then on to address me as though I was that other Adam, our common ancestor, as though I carried within me all of human history.

"I could have found it tiresome, especially since he insisted on bringing it up every time we met. But I didn't. I was flattered by this special attention. More than that, it was his insistence that caused me to reflect on the meaning of names, and the fate attached to them. We get accustomed to our name so quickly that we barely stop to think about its meaning, or the reason that we bear it."

Then, over several paragraphs, Adam mused about the names of those who were to be gathered around the table, with a mixture of erudition and imagination, and the occasional witticism. He brought up what Hanum had said: "Naïm is another name for Paradise." He explained that Bilal was a freed slave from Abyssinia, whose beautiful voice was so beloved by the Prophet that he made him the first *muezzin*; adding that, in Java, "even today, every muezzin is called Bilal." He touched on the name Sémiramis, "legendary queen of Mesopotamia, who was—even then—worshipped as a goddess," and, at the words "even then," we can imagine him discreetly winking at his chatelaine; then he moved on to Mourad, "the Desired, the Coveted, a name coined by mystics to refer to the Most High, and one that medieval Europeans pronounced *Amurath*"; before going on to explain the Marian origins of the name Dolores, and the German etymology of Albert—noble and illustrious. Not to mention Basil, which means "king" or "emperor"—"hardly the most humble name for a monk to adopt."

When he came to his own name, Adam initially referred the would-be orator to what he had written two days earlier.

See entry dated May 3, passage beginning with "My name encompasses all of nascent humanity, yet I belong to a humanity that is dying ..."; it seems appropriate for the occasion.

But, immediately, he changed his mind.

Having reread the entry, I am not so sure that I want to read it to my friends. Not on the first day, anyway. It is not a text of opening and welcome, but one of closure and farewell. What purpose would be served by saying to them: "To me falls the hateful task of recognizing the faces of those I have loved, to nod my head and watch as the sheet is drawn over them. I am the attendant to the dead ..."

The end is a little less sinister: "My great joy has been to find amid the floodwaters a few small islands of Levantine delicacy, or tranquil tenderness. And this, at least for the moment, has given me a new thirst for life, new reasons to struggle, perhaps even a quiver of hope. And in the long term? In the long term, all the sons and daughters of Adam and Eve are lost children."

I could stop at the word "hope" and keep the rest to myself.

No. Thinking about it, I need an epilogue that is more moving, more powerful, something more likely to spark debate. I need some time to think about it, but I'll come up with something ...

Adam never wrote this other epilogue. Perhaps he was writing it in his head as the car went off the road. This is something we will only find out on the day he regains consciousness.

Will that happen? The doctors are reluctant to give an opinion. They say he will hover between life and death for some time, before tipping one way or the other.

Dolores, who had him transported to a Paris hospital by air ambulance, and is constantly at his bedside, prefers to say he is on borrowed time. "Like his country, like this planet," she adds. "On borrowed time, like all of us."

FRANK WYNNE is a literary translator and writer. Born in Ireland, he moved to France in 1984 where he discovered a passion for language. He began translating literature in the late 1990s, and in 2001 decided to devote himself to this full time. He has translated works by Michel Houellebecq, Frédéric Beigbeder, Ahmadou Kourouma, Boualem Sansal, Claude Lanzmann, Tómas Eloy Martínez, and Almudena Grandes. His work has earned him a number of awards, including the Scott Moncrieff Prize and the Premio Valle Inclán. Most recently, his translation of *Vernon Subutex* by Virginie Despentes was shortlisted for the Man Booker International 2018.

On the Design

As book design is an integral part of the reading experience, we would like to acknowledge the work of those who shaped the form in which the story is housed.

Tessa van der Waals (Netherlands) is responsible for the cover design, cover typography, and art direction of all World Editions books. She works in the internationally renowned tradition of Dutch Design. Her bright and powerful visual aesthetic maintains a harmony between image and typography and captures the unique atmosphere of each book. She works closely with internationally celebrated photographers, artists, and letter designers. Her work has frequently been awarded prizes for Best Dutch Book Design.

The photograph on the cover was taken by Italian photographer Andrea Jemolo, who specializes in photographing architecture and art for magazines and publishing houses. This particular image, "Ceiling of the artrium," shows detail from the Mosque of the Imam (formerly the Royal Mosque or Shah Mosque), which stands in Naghsh-e Jahan Square in Isfahan, Iran.

The cover has been edited by lithographer Bert van der Horst of BFC Graphics (Netherlands).

Suzan Beijer (Netherlands) is responsible for the typography and careful interior book design of all World Editions titles.

The text on the inside covers and the press quotes are set in Circular, designed by Laurenz Brunner (Switzerland) and published by Swiss type foundry Lineto.

All World Editions books are set in the typeface Dolly, specifically designed for book typography. Dolly creates a warm page image perfect for an enjoyable reading experience. This typeface is designed by Underware, a European collective formed by Bas Jacobs (Netherlands), Akiem Helmling (Germany), and Sami Kortemäki (Finland). Underware are also the creators of the World Editions logo, which meets the design requirement that "a strong shape can always be drawn with a toe in the sand."